OBLIVION

OBLI

PETER ABRAHAMS

VION

WILLIAM MORROW
An Imprint of HarperCollins*Publishers*

G 3

This book is a work of fiction. The characters, incidents, and dialogue are drawn from the author's imagination and are not to be construed as real. Any resemblance to actual events or persons, living or dead, is entirely coincidental.

Designed by Renato Stanisic

ISBN 0-06-072657-1

Printed in the U.S.A.

To Niki and her children, Josh, Jan and Caitlin

*But it must be said from the outset that
a disease is never a mere loss or excess——that there
is always a reaction, on the part of the
affected organism or individual, to restore, to replace,
to compensate for and to preserve its identity,
however strange the means may be.*
—OLIVER SACKS,
The Man Who Mistook His Wife for a Hat

1

LOST WEEKEND

Nick Petrov, in the witness box, waited for the next question. The lawyer for the accused looked up from his yellow pad and fastened his skeptical gaze—familiar to millions of cable talk show viewers—on Petrov's face. The lawyer had eyebrows like Einstein's, resembled him in general, Petrov thought, but with a better haircut. Perfume from the previous witness still hung in the air.

"Been quite the career," said the lawyer, "hasn't it, Mr. Petrov? So far."

A better haircut and a meaner disposition. "That's not for me to say," Petrov said. He'd been on the stand for twenty-eight minutes, long enough to have formed the opinion that there was only one juror to worry about—the middle-aged woman in the back row, a lapis butterfly brooch on her lapel. The eleven other faces said guilty in the first degree, at least to him; but her face, soft, pretty, unadorned, had mercy written all over it. The defendant, Ty Canning, polishing his glasses on the end of his tie, had shown none.

"But it's what you think," said the lawyer. "That you're the sharpest tool in the shed."

"Is that a question?" Petrov said.

"Most definitely," said the lawyer.

"Do I have to answer it, Your Honor?"

"The witness will answer the question," said the judge.

"I'm more like a leaf blower," Petrov said.

Some people laughed; but not the butterfly woman.

"You think this is funny?" said the lawyer. Petrov remained silent, and the lawyer, perhaps slightly off-stride, didn't demand an answer. He flipped through the yellow pad in an irritated way. Petrov, habitual noticer of little things, saw that his eyes weren't moving, meaning he wasn't actually reading. Was this a dramatic pause or had he lost the thread? "Your Honor," the lawyer said, "I'd like the jury to hear that last question and answer again." He'd lost the thread; the self-confident but inferior younger brother who'd never arrived to disturb the Einstein family dynamic. Petrov waited for an opening.

"Question," said the court reporter. "What did the defendant say on the ride back from Mexico? Answer: He said, 'You got me.' "

" 'You got me,' " said the lawyer, facing the jury. "Sounds definitive. Practically an admission of guilt." He spun around to Petrov. "But in your deposition of June eleven, you stated the defendant's words were 'What makes you think it was me?' Not an admission of guilt, more like the aggrieved response of an innocent man." He paused. "Now, remembering that you are under oath, which one of your answers should the jury believe?"

Petrov felt the butterfly woman's gaze on his face, knew that phrase—the aggrieved response of an innocent man—touched something deep inside her. The jurors, wide awake now, leaned forward in anticipation. "Both," Petrov said.

"Both?" Those eyebrows, lively and articulate, rose in disbelief. "Are you aware of what would happen to your license if you put yourself in the position of giving false testimony?"

"I am aware," Petrov said. He met the lawyer's gaze. "In the deposition, I was asked only what the defendant's first words were—'What makes you think it was me?' It was after I explained the leads I'd followed that he made the second remark—'You got me.' There was also a third remark, just before I turned him over."

Silence. The lawyer understood, the judge understood, everyone with the slightest knowledge of cross-examination tactics understood that you never asked a question without knowing the answer. But a trial had dramatic form, and that form now demanded the question be asked.

The lawyer licked his lips. "Third remark?"

"The defendant also said, 'I enjoyed every minute of it.' "

Before the lawyer could respond, Ty Canning, a rich young man whose manner had been impeccable throughout the trial, shouted, "The fuck I did," and pounded his fist on the table. A vein throbbed in his neck and his face swelled and reddened, the effect phallic, out of control, dangerous: one of those electric courtroom moments that happened mostly in stories. The butterfly woman recoiled. The judge banged her gavel. The marshals moved in.

There were no further questions. Petrov stepped down. One of the marshals gave him a discreet pat on the back on the way out.

The Santa Ana was blowing, hot and dry. Petrov loved the heat, possibly some reaction to his birthplace, even though he'd left Russia at the age of two and had no memories of it. But crossing the parking lot outside the county courthouse, Petrov found himself thinking of a cooling swim. Friday afternoon, a few minutes after three. He'd been planning to spend the weekend at the lake—why not leave now, arrive in daylight, maybe do a little fishing too? He had the car door open when a woman called, "Mr. Petrov?"

She was hurrying across the lot: midthirties, judging by her face, although her body looked ten years younger and her clothes—halter top and midthigh skirt—belonged on a teenager. Her eyes were the anxious eyes of a prospective client.

"My name's Liza," she said. She came to a stop, rocking back slightly on her high heels. "Lisa, really, but Liza professionally. Liza Rummel. It's about Amanda."

"Who's she?"

Liza Rummel shook her head, a quick side-to-side, erasing and starting over. "I saw on Court TV you'd be testifying today. That's why I came down here."

"From where?"

"From where? Van Nuys. We've been living in Encino but now we're in Van Nuys. Amanda liked the old place much better, come to think of it—I wonder if that's a factor."

"In what?"

"Amanda's disappearance, Mr. Petrov, the reason I'm here. That's your specialty, right? Missing children?"

"Missing persons in general," Petrov said. "Is Amanda your daughter?"

"She's a good kid, despite everything."

Petrov took that for a yes. "What kind of everything?" he said.

"Normal teenage rebellion, I guess you'd say. She'll be sixteen in November. The twenty-third." Her eyes teared up a little "She was born on Thanksgiving."

"How long has she been missing?"

"Three days and two nights."

"When did you last see her?"

"Actually see her? Tuesday morning. She'd gone to sleep by the time I got home."

"When was that?"

"About four, four-thirty."

"Wednesday morning?"

She looked him in the eye. "Correct."

"Did you check her room?"

"No. But her breakfast dishes were on the table when I got up."

"Did you call the police?"

"Wednesday night, when she didn't come home. But you know the cops. They think she's just another runaway. Turn up again when she gets hungry."

"Has she disappeared before?"

"Sort of. But this time I'm really worried."

"What's different?"

"I've got a bad feeling."

A bad feeling. Petrov searched for signs of it on her face. Years ago, just starting out, he'd sketched and labeled ninety-three facial expressions. Anxiety, number sixty-one, was what he saw now. Dread, absent from her face, was sixty-eight. "Why?" he said.

"The other times were after we had a fight or something. This is for no good reason."

"What kind of fights?" Petrov said.

"The usual—homework, curfew, smoking."

"Physical fights?"

"Oh, no." Liza Rummel put her hand to her breast, the gesture innocent, the breast heavy; both somewhat artificial.

"What have you done to find her?"

"Besides calling the police? Everything I could think of—driving around, checking with the school."

In Petrov's experience, most people could think of more. He watched her. Was there something familiar about her, around the mouth, perhaps? She had full, shapely lips, mobile and expressive. "Have we met somewhere?" he said.

"No. I'd of remembered meeting you." He knew what was coming next. "From the movie," she said.

The movie: ten years old now, and not a real movie in Petrov's eyes, just a TV movie-of-the-week, *The Reasoner Case*, Armand Assante starring as Nick Petrov; here, riding a tiny wave of hype, and gone. Was there another town in the whole country where anyone would remember? But this was L.A.

"Have you got a picture of Amanda?"

Liza Rummel flipped open her wallet. "This was at the Empty Box concert in July."

Petrov took the photo of Amanda. Face, mouth, eyes: a little lost already, the runaway look. Finding them, returning them, hardly ever changed it. Hardly ever, but not never. "Empty Box is a band?"

"She thinks they're God."

"What kind of music?"

"You know. Hard to describe."

Petrov liked the name of the band; he was also drawn to that age discrepancy between Liza Rummel's face and body, one of those human fault lines he had trouble staying away from. But the truth was he'd never turned down a case that involved a child. "I'll need to see her room," he said.

"Meaning you'll help?" Excitement lit her eyes, got washed over almost at once by worry. "I don't have a lot of money." Liza fumbled in her bag. "Here's fifty bucks. Is that okay to start?" She placed it on his palm, folded his hand around the money, squeezed it in both of hers. Her hands were hot and wet; the money hot and wet too. A big motorcycle cop watched from the other side of the parking lot, sunlight glinting on his blond mustache.

"My retainer is five hundred dollars," Petrov said. "After that, it's three hundred a day plus any special expenses like air travel, which I always clear with the client first."

"Oh," she said, letting go of his hand.

"Maybe you should try the police again," Petrov said. "I'll give you the name of someone good."

"Do you take checks?" Liza Rummel said.

Petrov took a check for four hundred and fifty dollars. He walked Liza to her car, an old baby blue Mustang convertible, dented on the outside, littered within, the ashtray full of red-tipped cigarette butts. Climbing in, she looked up and said, "Did you ever actually get to meet Armand Assante?"

"Once or twice."

"What's he like?"

Liza Rummel drove the baby blue Mustang in a way that said the car—in its ideal, brand-new form—was her. Petrov followed—110 to the 101—listening to a Jussi Bjoerling recital. A man in the audience—probably long dead, this was Paris, 1956—called out a request: *"Nessun Dorma."* Laughter followed. Petrov had often listened to the recording, but now for the first time picked out one woman quite clearly, her amusement and excitement, sexuality even, captured in digital form forever. He could almost see the pearls around her neck.

Liza Rummel lived in a small clapboard house with a single palm tree on the lawn, its leaves dusty and gray. She held the door for him. "Don't mind the mess."

Petrov went inside. He didn't see any mess, didn't see much at all. The only light came through a single round hole in one of the drawn shades, dust motes drifting through the narrow beam. Shadowy furniture shapes stood here and there. He smelled bacon.

"I work nights," Liza said, explaining what, he didn't know: mess? darkness? Amanda?

"Doing what?" said Petrov, although he had a notion.

Pause. "Is everything we discuss between just us, or does there have to be some paperwork first?"

"I'm obligated to report crimes, paperwork or not," Petrov said. "On the other hand, there's discretion in everything."

"How about an escort service?"

"Working for one," said Petrov, "or owning it?"

"Owning it? In my dreams."

"Then it's between you and me." Petrov switched on a lamp.

On the rug at its base—a blue rug, same shade as the Mustang—lay a stuffed animal. Elephant with a gold crown: Babar.

"Amanda has a little brother or sister?" Petrov said.

"She's an only child," said Liza.

Petrov picked up Babar: spats, green suit, the face of a steady king. He had a sudden memory: the feel of the thick page of a Babar book as his mother read to him, and the crisp sound it made when she turned to the next one. He could also picture the ruby ring on her hand, like a wonderful candy. Another amazing memory came to him: he'd licked the ruby once—no taste at all, like licking a windowpane. And had his mother, thinking he'd been licking her hand, actually smacked him? Petrov was astonished. He'd been three years old when his mother died, had no memories of her or of that time at all. Yet here were two, coming out of nowhere.

He looked up. Liza was watching him. "I know what you're thinking," she said. "Amanda's too old to be playing with stuffed animals."

"Is that your opinion?"

"She doesn't actually play with him, not make believe or anything like that. They just sort of cuddle when she watches TV."

A big flat-screen, probably worth more than the Mustang, hung on the opposite wall. "What does she watch?"

"The Weather Channel mostly, I'd say. But I don't see what that has to do with anything. Didn't you want to see her room?"

Amanda's room: unmade bed, desk with two drawers half open, closet door open too, clothes and gum wrappers on the floor; disorder everywhere, except for the Empty Box poster taped perfectly straight on the wall. "I'll need to look around," Petrov said. He noticed a ticket stub stapled to the poster: Empty Box at the Beacon Theater in Inglewood, August 23.

"Do whatever you have to," Liza said.

Petrov took out his notebook, tore out a sheet, handed it to her. "I'd like a list of her friends—addresses and phone numbers if possible."

"Amanda hasn't really made new friends here yet, not since the move."

"What about her old friends?"

"From Encino? They've kind of fallen away."

"Why is that?"

She shrugged. "Not in the same school anymore, you know kids." An idea came to her: he could see its movements behind her eyes. "Have you got any yourself?"

Unusual: clients seldom had questions about him. First, they weren't interested to begin with. Second, they were consumed by their problem, whatever it was. Therefore: Was this woman interested in him in some way? Was she not consumed by her problem? Or was she an exception to the rule, and if so, why? "I have a son."

"How old?"

"About Amanda's age."

"What's his name?"

"Dmitri."

"That's kind of different. What's your wife's name?"

"We're divorced." He tapped the notebook page in her hand. "Do your best with this." Liza went out.

Petrov searched Amanda's room. Not from top to bottom, but from bottom to top. Long ago he'd learned that the best discoveries were made low down. He knelt, took out his pencil flash, shone it under Amanda's bed; and made a discovery right away—a Hallmark card, torn in three pieces. As he rose to examine it, a tiny, penny-size headache popped up above his left eye, centered perhaps three centimeters behind his brow.

two

P etrov found Liza Rummel sitting at her kitchen table,
chewing on a pencil, the notebook page and a phone
book before her. "This is all I could come up with," she
said, handing him the sheet.

At the top was a crossed-out name, Mindy or Mandy. Below
that, Petrov read:

> Sarah Mathis? Mathews? still at Encino HS
> Abby somebody from volleyball
> Maybe Beth Franklin?

Below that, she'd doodled a tulip with a bee hovering over
the petals. A good drawing, the bee not cute or anthropomor-
phized in any way.

"Amanda plays volleyball?" Petrov said.

"Until last year. She kind of gave it up. The coach even called
a few times, trying to change her mind."

"What's the coach's name?"

"Ms. . . . Oh, it's on the tip of my tongue," said Liza. "It'll
come to me." But it didn't. "Beth Franklin might be better. I'm
not saying they were friends, but she does live down the street.
Twelve ninety-six. Her mother's our landlord."

"Was Amanda good at volleyball?"

"I think so. She's five-ten, you know."

Liza was about five-three. "How tall is her father?" Petrov said.

"Her father?"

"To account for Amanda's height."

"Oh." Liza bit her lip. "I'm not sure exactly."

"Approximately."

"A little taller than you."

"I'd like to talk to him."

"He's not around."

"You're divorced?"

"More like never married in the first place."

"Does Amanda use your surname?"

"Correct."

"What's her father's name?"

She shook her head. "He's got nothing to do with this."

Petrov glanced at the bee again, noticed she'd even included the stinger. The penny-size headache over his left eye sharpened slightly. Petrov did not get headaches, had trouble recalling even a single one since college morning-afters.

"How long have you been separated?" he said.

"Ages. Amanda doesn't know him at all, if that's where you're going with this."

"What's her attitude toward him?"

"None. I told you. She doesn't know him and doesn't want to know him."

"What about you and Amanda?"

"Huh?"

"Describe your relationship."

"Great. We're more like sisters."

The phone rang. Liza grabbed it, answered. He read her mind: *Amanda.* But it wasn't. She twisted around, took a napkin from the counter, wrote on it. Petrov read upside down: Airport Marriott—9:30—#219. She clicked off.

Petrov said: "Was Amanda's father a client?"

Pause: she absorbed it. He sensed something tough and hard inside her, like scar tissue. "That's an ugly thing to say."

"But what's the answer?"

She pushed herself away from the table, got to her feet. "You were much nicer in the movie."

Petrov got ready to return her check and the fifty dollars, something he realized at that moment he didn't want to do. The case had pulled him in quickly, although he couldn't see why: there was nothing atypical about it so far.

Liza turned her back, stared out the kitchen window. Had he mishandled the questioning? If a kid disappears you had to account for both parents, and right away: that was basic. He heard her take a deep breath. "I was still in school when Amanda was born," she said.

Her voice caught, so slightly he almost missed it. A year or two more of the life she was leading and it might not, the past fully scarred over. "Where was this?" Petrov said.

"UC-Irvine."

"What was your major?"

"Communications, it would have been."

"But?"

"I didn't graduate."

"Because of Amanda?"

Liza faced him. "Amanda?"

An obvious question. Why did it puzzle her? "The burden of single motherhood and being a student at the same time," Petrov said.

"Amanda had nothing to do with my dropping out. And you know something else? I don't know how you ever find anybody, sitting here asking a lot of irrelevant questions while time ticks away."

The answer was almost always luck and persistence. He kept it to himself. "I'd like to see Amanda's birth certificate."

"Why?"

"I always do that in a missing persons case."

"It's lost."

"When did that happen?"

"Search me."

From his pocket, Petrov took the Hallmark card he'd found under Amanda's bed, fitted the pieces together on the table. On the front was a picture of two little kids walking through a field of flowers, a wicker basket between them. Inside, in big girlish script: *Hey, Rui—we'll help each other, ok? xo Amanda.*

"Is that Amanda's writing?"

"Yes."

"Any idea what it means?"

"No."

"Who is Rui?"

"Couldn't tell you."

"She never mentioned him?"

"Not to me."

"Possibly a boyfriend you didn't approve of?"

"No."

Their eyes met. Liza had no trouble holding his gaze, but there was something about the cast of light in her irises, a tiny fluctuation, as though she were being sucked down some well of thought. That, and the fact that she didn't ask any questions about the card, where found, why not sent, why torn in pieces: Petrov decided he couldn't trust her.

"Has Amanda seemed worried about anything lately?"

"Not that I know of."

"Some problem with you maybe?" Petrov said. "Unrelated to a boyfriend."

"I told you—we get along great. What are you driving at?"

"Does she know what you do for a living?" Petrov said.

Liza blinked, a long, slow blink, as though she couldn't bear to see him anymore. When her eyelids opened, she could no longer meet his gaze. "Are you trying to upset me deliberately?" she said.

"I'm trying to find out why your daughter's gone." More than once, in his experience, the shortest route to getting them back.

Liza's eyes filled with tears, color and form vanishing, as though they'd liquefied. The blood drained from her face, except for the lips, which went very red. "There's no justice—that's why she's gone." Liza started crying.

"What do you mean?"

She might not have heard him. The crying took over, unrestrained, croaking, mucousy. Petrov opened the back door and went outside.

Liza had a little swimming pool in her backyard. A white ball—a volleyball—floated on the scummy surface, out of arm's reach. The skimmer lay by the fence dividing the property from the neighbor's. Petrov knelt by the edge of the water, extended the aluminum pole, fished for the ball. He had it about halfway in when something rippled just under the surface. He had a wild thought: Amanda, bloated with the gases of decomposition, floating up. But it wasn't Amanda. Instead a snake—thick and black—came gliding out of the water and up the pole. Petrov let go. The skimmer sank out of sight, taking the snake with it.

All at once he felt strange, very hot and breathless. Sweat started pouring off his face. He loosened his tie. A third memory from prememory time came to him: opening the door of his father's study to find his father at the desk and Pauline, the babysitter, on the floor between his legs. He even remembered—where was this coming from?—his father saying to him: "Pauline has dropped my pen." And only now, at this very moment, here by Liza Rummel's swimming pool, did he understand the scene. Easy to fix his age by Pauline's presence—he knew from family history that Pauline had gone back east after his mother's death. Therefore his mother had still been dying of breast cancer at the time, and he'd been not yet three.

The back door opened. Liza came out, no longer crying, wearing jeans and a loose T-shirt, makeup removed, hair in a ponytail. The volleyball had drifted within reach. Petrov picked it up, rose. "What did you mean," he said, " 'there's no justice'?"

She shrugged. "How could there be, with Amanda gone?"

He handed her the ball. *Great season, Amanda* was written on it in red ink, and some teammates had signed—Tiffany Mattes, Jen Dupuis, Abby Cohen, BJ Tillison, Angie Garcia; plus Coach Betsy Matsu.

"Betsy Matsu," said Liza. "I knew it would come to me. Sorry if I lost it in there. You'll still try your hardest, won't you?"

"I'll need the ball."

She gave it back. "Amanda thinks I work for a caterer," she said.

"I won't tell her anything different," Petrov said, immediately regretting the words, which implied he would find her, giving hope he had no right to give.

P etrov drove half a mile down the block. The houses got nicer. He parked in front of 1296, knocked on the front door. The welcome mat read: *Home Sweet Home.*

The door opened and a woman in an exercise outfit looked out. She had a wiry body, leathery skin, impatient face.

"Ms. Franklin?"

"I'm not buying anything."

"Nick Petrov," he said, showing her his license. "One of your neighbors is missing and I'm hoping you can help me find her."

"I don't know any of the neighbors."

"Amanda Rummel," he said. "I believe she's a friend of your daughter Beth."

Over her shoulder, he could see down a hallway and into the kitchen; an exercise show played on the countertop TV.

"Who told you that?"

"Liza Rummel. I understand you're her landlord."

"Not for much longer."

"Why is that?"

"The lease is up, end of the month."

"And they're not renewing?"

"Correct."

"Any idea why?"

"Yeah, I've got an idea why. But I don't see how it's any concern of yours."

"Everything about the Rummels is my concern. I want to get the girl home safe."

A car full of teenagers squealed up to the curb and one got out, a chubby girl with a butterfly tattoo—big and red—on her bare midriff. Petrov thought at once of the juror with the butterfly brooch. A coincidence, meaningless: but suddenly his heart started beating very fast, as though he'd done something wrong and fate was stepping in. His headache disappeared. Or not quite: instead it had grown almost undetectably faint and changed its position, moving outside his head and hovering just a little above. Not possible, of course: but he could feel it there, poised.

The girl came up the path, backpack dangling from her hand. Ms. Franklin checked her watch. "Where have you been?" she said.

"Pizza," said the girl, glancing up at Petrov.

"Go on in the house."

Petrov stepped aside. The girl went in, dropping her backpack, kicking off her shoes, heading for the kitchen.

"Pizza, my ass," said her mother. "They've been smoking weed."

Petrov nodded; he'd caught the smell too. "But she's home safe," he said.

The woman gave him a long look, let out a resigned sort of breath. "They're not renewing because I raised the rent." Her eyes narrowed. "As I have every right to do. I checked around. They're way below market. I could be getting eighteen hundred a month for that place. And you know what she's been paying?"

"Fifteen fifty."

"She told you?"

"Just a guess," Petrov said. "Does she want to stay there?"

"What do you think? Two bedrooms, one and a half baths, swimming pool, brand-name appliances, good neighborhood—who wouldn't?"

Did it mean anything that Liza could cover his retainer and fee, but not this rent increase? Petrov didn't know. He took out his wallet, counted two hundred and fifty dollars from what he thought of as his bribe roll. "Tell her you're granting an extension at the old rate. Make up some reason." He held out the money.

"I don't get it," she said. "Are you some kind of do-gooder?"

"No," Petrov said. But added instability in Liza's life wouldn't help him solve the case.

"Any strings attached?"

"Just one," Petrov said. "Have the pool cleaned."

"That's easy enough," the woman said, taking the money. "I'll do it myself."

Like I've got no idea where she'd go," Beth said. "We don't really hang out or anything." They sat in the family room, Beth and her mother at opposite ends of a white leather couch, Petrov in a matching chair.

"But you go to the same school."

"Van Nuys West. We're not in the same classes. Amanda's kind of a brain."

Petrov thought of the photograph: had he seen signs of braininess? "What makes you say that?"

"Just the way she talks."

"How does she talk?"

"Like you."

"Can you remember anything brainy she said?"

Beth adjusted her face for thinking, surprised herself by

coming up with something. "She was standing next to me at the pep rally. This was for the Agoura game, a couple weeks ago. The captain of the team made this speech about how not enough kids are coming to the games, real pissed off. Amanda said, 'Do you think he likes football for its own sake, or is it just the attention?' That's brainy, right?"

"What was your answer?"

" 'He does it to get laid.' "

"Beth!" said her mother.

"Mom—I'm fifteen."

"That's no excuse for—"

Petrov interrupted. "What was her reaction to that?"

"She laughed."

He took out the photograph. "Is this a good picture of her?"

"Not really. She looks kind of drunk or something."

He examined it himself. Braininess? He wasn't sure. There was something blurry about the girl, even though the shot was in focus. "Does Amanda drink?"

"Not that I know of."

"What about drugs?"

"I wouldn't know about that either."

Petrov could still smell pot, probably trapped in her hair. "I'm talking about serious drugs."

Beth stared at her feet, short, wide feet with scarlet toenails. They matched the butterfly and her bloodshot eyes.

"Amanda may be in danger," Petrov said.

Beth's gaze stayed on her feet. Was she just waiting for this to be over?

"Has she ever said anything about running away?" Petrov said.

"No."

"Does she have any enemies?"

"She only came the middle of last year. Making enemies takes longer at our school."

"What about enemies outside the school?"

Beth shrugged.

"How does she get along with her mother?"

"Okay, I guess."

"Are they like sisters?"

Beth's eyes went to him quickly, then away. "Like sisters?" she said.

Her mother said, "Some mothers and daughters get along like sisters, believe it or not."

"What's so good about that?" said Beth.

"What's so good about enjoying each other's company?" her mother said. "Speaking respectfully to one another? Having the common—"

Petrov held up his hand. A little to his surprise, she stopped talking. Mother and daughter watched him. In the silence, his mind went back to the look in Beth's eyes when he'd asked about Amanda's and Liza's relationship. Of course, he'd meant *Do they get along like sisters?* but he'd said, *Are they like sisters?* and it had triggered something inside her. He took a wild guess, based on almost nothing, just that shift in Beth's eyes and the missing birth certificate. "Are you suggesting that Amanda and Liza Rummel are actually sisters?"

Beth shook her head, a little too vigorously.

"But you're suggesting something."

A pause. Petrov let it get longer. Finally Beth spoke: "I promised Amanda I wouldn't tell."

He waited. Her mother, silent now, waited too.

"Promise you won't tell," Beth said.

"I can't," Petrov said.

"Then promise not to tell where you heard it."

"I'll try to avoid that. But I can't promise."

Beth looked up at him, understood, nodded. "Amanda's mom's not her real mom. She's adopted."

"When did she tell you this?"

"After that pep rally. We missed the bus, on account of it went on so long, and ended up walking home together."

"Who's her real mom?" Petrov said.

"Like, the name?"

"The name."

"She didn't say. Anyway, her real mom's dead."

"When did that happen?"

"A long time ago. She got killed."

"Killed?"

"Murdered, Amanda said."

Petrov heard Beth's mother suck in her breath. "By whom?" he said.

"It's a secret."

"I don't understand," Petrov said.

"That's what she told me," said Beth.

"Did she mean it's an unsolved case?"

"I guess."

three

P etrov drove back to Liza Rummel's house. The blue Mustang was no longer in the driveway. He got out, knocked on the front door. No one came; nothing stirred inside. Walking around to the back, he heard something rummaging in the trash barrel.

Shadows were falling, turning the sky a bruised color. A small plane with flashing wing lights cut across it and banked toward Van Nuys Airport. Petrov felt his headache, still faint and hovering above. He tried rubbing his forehead. The headache disappeared, like a reverse genie. Was that all it took?

Petrov tested the back door. Locked. He tried a window—locked—and then another. Locked too, but cheaply made. Had he ever broken into a client's house before? Several times, in different circumstances but always with clients of the lying kind. He wanted to see that birth certificate.

The window gave to his pressure. He opened it, had one leg inside the downstairs bathroom when his cell phone vibrated soundlessly in his pocket. It gave him a little scare, as though God were watching. Petrov climbed all the way in, closed the window, answered his phone.

"Nick? Elaine Kostelnik. Congratulations."

"For what?"

"You haven't heard? The Canning verdict came in half an

hour ago. Guilty on all charges, and Eddie says your testimony was dynamite."

Eddie Flores was the D.A. Petrov opened the medicine cabinet. Bottom shelf: face cream, body lotion, exfoliant, curling iron, curlers. Middle shelf: pink razor, Advil, nail clippers, nail polish. Top shelf: Old Spice Extra-Dry deodorant, black razor.

"I should be congratulating you," Petrov said, "if it isn't too late."

"Not tired of hearing it yet," Elaine said. She'd been chief of police—the first female chief of the LAPD—for about four months; close to God, at least in terms of law enforcement. "Guess who sent the most incredible flowers."

Petrov picked up the deodorant, examined the label. *For the active man,* it read. "Who?"

"Kim Delaney."

Should have known: Kim Delaney had played Elaine in *The Reasoner Case,* a year or two before she hit it big. Better looking than Elaine, of course, and she'd pretty much stolen the picture, turning Elaine into an irresistibly appealing character, despite, or because of, taking the edge off her intelligence and drive. "What kind of flowers?" Petrov said.

Elaine laughed. "How the fuck would I know? What a question! You haven't changed at all."

Petrov closed the medicine cabinet, moved through the house, came to Liza's bedroom at the end of the hall. Birth certificates might be in a safe deposit box, but if not: he opened the top right-hand drawer of Liza's desk.

"Tell me something," Elaine said. "Did the guy really say that—'I enjoyed every minute of it'?"

"That's a strange question," Petrov said.

Elaine laughed again. "Especially from the chief of police, right?" she said. "I haven't seen you in ages, Nick. What are you up to these days?"

"The usual," Petrov said. He searched his client's drawer,

found a checkbook, address book, lease agreement, and at the bottom, one birth certificate, state of California.

"Working on anything interesting?" Elaine said.

"Not really." He unfolded the birth certificate: Liza's, not Amanda's.

"We should get together sometime," Elaine said.

"That'd be nice." Lisa Anne Rummel was Liza's birth name, born in Barstow, thirty-six years ago. Father: George Bennet Rummel. Mother: Cynthia Louise Connerly Rummel. Residence: 4922 Quartzsite Road, Barstow. Birthplace of both parents: Barstow.

"How about tonight?" Elaine said.

"Tonight?"

"Why not? I'm in the car right now. Where are you? We could swing by and pick you up. We being me and the driver—I'll send the motorcycle guys home." Another laugh: the sound brought her back to him, her appetites, that weekend in Cabo. Maybe she was remembering too, because she said, "There's that new place on San Vicente. Still like Mexican?"

"Yes."

"Remember Casa Felix?"

"Yes."

"Those were the days. Where are you?"

Those were the days? What did that mean? Elaine was the one who'd put an end to them. At that moment, his headache reappeared, now back inside his skull. Petrov tried rubbing his forehead again; this time it didn't work. He glimpsed his face in the closet door mirror: completely white.

"Nick? You still there?"

He found himself back in the bathroom, gazing into the medicine cabinet. Petrov took no pills, not even vitamins. He reached for Liza Rummel's Advil.

"Nick?"

"Tonight's not possible," he said.

"Hot date waiting?" she said.

"No." He laid the phone on the counter, opened the Advil bottle.

Her voice, now tiny, came through the phone. "You're on the job right now?"

Petrov put two pills in his mouth, turned on the tap, drank them down.

"Nick?"

He picked up the phone. "I'm on the job."

He felt her questioning mind, inaudible, yet somehow translating itself into digital form.

"If I can ever help," Elaine said, "let me know."

"Sure."

"Meaning you'd die first."

He laughed, saw his white-faced self laughing in the medicine cabinet mirror.

"Take care of yourself, Nick."

Petrov searched the house for Amanda's birth certificate, didn't find it. He examined Liza's check register and the terms of her lease, copied a few names from her address book, took two more Advil, repaired the catch on the window he'd come through and left by the back door. Dark now: he sat in his car outside Liza's house, listening to Jussi Bjoerling. No one sang like that anymore; even worse, he was pretty sure that no one wanted to. What was the secret of staying optimistic as the years went by? Petrov didn't know. The Advil did its job. At 9:05, he drove to the Airport Marriott—101, 405—and went inside.

Juwan Barnes was the head of security. They'd been with the sheriff's department together, working vice out of Huntington Park, two or three years before the Reasoner case. Juwan Barnes shook his hand. "Hell of a job today," he said. "Flying somewhere?"

"No."

"Then I'll buy you a drink."

"Some other time, thanks."

"You're working?"

"Yes."

"Here?"

"Yes."

"What on?"

"Ever heard of Liza Rummel?"

"Who's she?"

Petrov took out his notebook. "Works for Candyland Escorts."

"Never heard of them, either," Barnes said. "So goddamned many, can't keep track. How can I help?"

"Room 219," Petrov said.

Barnes turned to his computer, started tapping at the keys. "Why do they all have to fuck at my place?"

"Beds, privacy, the illusion of anonymity."

"I wasn't really asking."

Room 219 was booked to James McMurray, vice president, marketing, for the Chemcom Company in Saint Paul. He was upgrading to a suite the next day, wife and kids coming in for the weekend. Petrov knocked on his door at 9:45.

It opened right away. The man on the other side, wearing briefs and holding a minibar bottle of Jack Daniel's, started to say, "You're late," but cut himself off. By that time Petrov was in the room, closing the door with his heel, looking around. No sign of Liza.

"What the hell's going on?" said James McMurray.

Bed turned down, soft-core porn on pay-per-view. Petrov glanced in the bathroom, saw a bottle of Viagra by the sink. Bed, porn, Viagra: transparency. "I'm looking for Liza Rummel," he said over his shoulder.

"Never heard of her." James McMurray, big and heavy, followed him. "You're in the wrong room, buddy."

Petrov turned to him. "James, Jimmy, Jimbo, whatever you call yourself—we're not buddies. That's one. Two: Liza had a nine-thirty appointment here."

"The fuck she did. Whoever she is. Get out or I'll call the cops."

Petrov stepped past him, picked up a wallet lying on the night table, shook a bunch of business cards onto the bed. *Candyland Escorts* landed on top. Petrov pocketed the card. "Call them."

Jimbo came up behind him, snatched at the wallet, gave Petrov a push. Petrov let himself be pushed, just enough to complete a half-turn and get his shoulder in position; and pushed back, harder than he'd intended. Was it the headache—all of a sudden back in place, the Advil in retreat around its edges— making him mean? Jimbo cracked his own head against the opposite wall, subsided into a sitting position on the floor. His eyelids fluttered shut, then fluttered back open; he stopped trying to hold in his stomach. Petrov thought of Jimbo's kids, at that very moment probably all excited about the trip, and didn't feel sorry for him.

"Mind if I check the minibar?" he said. No answer. Petrov opened it, found Johnnie Walker Black. He sat in the only easy chair, shut off the TV, poured himself a glass. One sip and his headache vanished. He took another, felt really good, realized how hungry he was. When had he last eaten? Breakfast: slices of green apple with extra-sharp cheddar and a banana. No— he'd been out of bananas. At that moment, he understood what this headache thing was all about: nerve spasms in the forehead, caused by lack of potassium and fatigue. He remembered reading about it on the science page. The cure was a banana and a good night's sleep. Petrov reopened the minibar. No bananas. He examined a bag of cashews: 150 mg. of potassium per ounce, 4 percent of daily requirement, plus lots of iron, magnesium and copper, all good. He took the cashews and sat back down.

"Put some clothes on, Jimbo. Then we'll talk."

Jimbo looked over at him. "I get it," he said. "You're a cop yourself."

"Even a T-shirt will be okay."

"You can't come in here without a warrant."

Petrov opened the cashews. "When's your family arriving?"

Jimbo made an odd face, perhaps just the Viagra activating at an inconvenient moment. The clothes he'd worn that day lay on the bureau. He put them on—dress shirt, suit pants, jacket, even the tie, leaving off only socks and shoes—then sat on the edge of the bed, hands folded in his lap. His fingernails were nicely manicured, all pink; but his toenails were thick, yellow, scaly.

"Has Liza ever been late before?" Petrov said.

"No."

"How many times have you been with her?"

"I don't know. Three or four maybe."

"How did you find her in the first place?"

"Through the service."

"What does it cost?"

"Three hundred an hour. A grand for the night."

"You sprang for a whole night?"

"Once."

"Can I ask you a personal question?"

"What else have you been doing?"

"Those were all professional."

"Then what's personal?"

"How much did you make last year?" Petrov said.

"A hundred and ten grand, give or take."

"So you spent about one percent of it on Liza?"

"If you want to put it that way."

"Tell me about her."

"How do you mean?"

"There must be something special."

"Special?"

How to reach him? "In order to justify that level of expenditure in the context of your budget."

Jimbo understood immediately, the vocabulary and syntax familiar from countless meetings. "She's easy to be with, good conversationalist, that kind of thing," he said. "And she doesn't get all hung up on condoms."

Petrov checked his watch: 10:05. She wasn't coming. He took another sip, ate a few cashews, kept feeling better and better. "So you talk when you're together," he said.

"Some."

"What subjects?"

"Football mostly, I guess."

"Football?"

"I'm a big Vikings fan."

"Is Liza a fan too?"

"Not really. But her old man played for the Bears. Follow football?"

"Not anymore."

"But you probably heard of Dick Butkus. George Rummel played with him, offensive tackle. Went up against Dick Butkus in practice, day after day."

"Are Liza and her father close?" Petrov said.

Jimbo screwed up his eyes. "Something about that, one way or the other, I can't recall."

"Did she ever mention her daughter?"

"She's got a daughter?"

"Why is that a surprise?"

Jimbo shrugged. "She doesn't seem like the type."

Petrov swallowed the rest of his scotch, stood up. "No condoms, Jimbo. You know that for a fact. Making her the type that has daughters."

He took the cashews on his way out.

Petrov deposited Liza's check at an ATM in the lobby. Juwan Barnes came over.

"Everything okay?"

Petrov nodded. "These cashews are really good."

"Kiss them good-bye."

"How come?"

"Peanuts as of next quarter," Barnes said. "Cutting costs. Find the girl?"

"Not yet," Petrov said. Barnes had been referring to Liza, but at that moment Petrov knew they were both gone, mother and daughter—adopted daughter, the real mother murdered; he could feel the case expanding in the night.

Barnes walked him to the door. "Your movie was on channel three ninety-two the other night."

Petrov hadn't known it was still out there; had Liza seen it too? "It's not my movie," he said.

"Ever meet Kim Delaney?"

"No."

"Armand Assante?"

"Briefly."

"He doesn't look like you."

"I know that."

"He's kind of rough-edged too, but in a prettier way."

"I'm not as pretty as Armand Assante?"

"Not close."

Barnes held the door open for him. "Reasoner still on death row?"

"Yes."

"What's happening?"

"Another appeal," Petrov said. "I don't follow it anymore."

Barnes lowered his voice. "He should've got shot while resisting arrest."

Their eyes met. Barnes looked away.

four

Nick Petrov ate the last cashew. Did human lives have turning points? In stories, almost always; in real life, almost never, unless you counted as turning points those that preceded birth. Real life was mostly more of the same. But in his own life—Petrov was back in his car outside Liza Rummel's dark house, parked in the shadow between two streetlights, waiting for the blue Mustang to come down the street and swing into the driveway even though he knew it wouldn't—in his own life, he could spot turning points, two, to be exact. The first, leaving Russia—more accurately, defecting, most accurately, fleeing—he didn't remember, not yet two at the time. The second was the Reasoner case. Take away the Reasoner case and there'd have been no going out on his own, no movie money to pay for the cabin on Big Bear Lake. He thought of driving up there now, instead took out his pencil flash, opened his notebook, began writing his notes on the Rummel case.

Petrov wrote in a code, mostly of his own devising, but based on an idea of his father's, and therefore probably related to KGB procedures of the Beria period. It had taken him years to approach fluidity: now it came almost as easily as English. Why had he bothered? In the beginning, he'd told himself it was about safeguarding information, protecting clients, protecting

himself, but deep down Petrov knew these were rationaliza-
tions after the emotional fact. It—meaning secrecy—just felt
right.

Known
Liza
1. Hid Amanda's birth certificate. Possible motives:
   (a) to keep me from finding out she's not Amanda's
   real mother; (b) to keep the real mother's name
   secret.

Amanda
1. Brainy.
2. Drug problem.

Questions
1. Why didn't Liza show up at Jimbo's room?
2. Why does her face seem familiar?
3. Old Spice deodorant in Liza's downstairs
   bathroom—whose?
4. Who is Rui?
5. Who was Amanda's mother? Father?
6. Why did Liza send me to Beth Franklin first?

Suspicions
1. Liza knows who Rui is.
2. Liza and Amanda quarreled. Why?
   (a) Liza's job? (b) Rui? (c) Amanda's father?
3. If c—is Amanda looking for him?
4. Liza and her father, George Rummel—bad
   relationship.
5. Liza planted the Hallmark card under Amanda's bed.

REMOTE POSSIBILITIES

1. Amanda's disappearance—connected to the
    unsolved murder of her mother (assuming Beth's
    story is true).
2. Liza—setting me up.

Why would she do that? Petrov had no idea. But her failure
to ask questions about the Hallmark card had cost her his trust.
Not trusting her meant not trusting anything she said; and she'd
said Amanda was missing. Any chance Amanda wasn't missing,
that it was all some scheme of Liza's to use him? Petrov couldn't
imagine why.

TO DO

1. Candyland
2. Volleyball coach—Betsy Matsu
3. George Rummel—Barstow

The night grew quiet around him, the city still humming,
but at a lower pitch now, an engine on idle. Petrov closed
his eyes, let his mind wander. It wandered back to the Reasoner
case, specifically the seven postcards of Rembrandt's *Anatomy Lesson of Dr. Tulp.* The painting came back vividly: the fascinated expressions on the faces of Dr. Tulp's students; the intelligence in
Dr. Tulp's eyes, questing, almost manic; the definition of the
muscles and tendons in the flayed forearm of the corpse. Seven
postcards, seven victims: Janet Cody, Elizabeth Chang, Cindy
Motton, Flora Gutierrez, Tiffany LeVasseur, Nicolette Levy, Lara
Deems.

Petrov had first noticed the Dr. Tulp postcard in the house of
the third victim, Cindy Motton. Cindy Motton: hairdresser, living alone—they'd all lived alone except Lara Deems—in the
back of a carriage house in North Hollywood. Half an hour or so

after the crime scene people had left, finding nothing useful—
Gerald Reasoner, as they learned later, had worn surgical gloves,
cap and scrubs—Petrov had looked through a drawer in her
kitchen, a drawer full of recipes, copied out in Cindy Motton's
careful handwriting. She'd noted the source of each one: *Aunt
Ida, J at Xmas, Mom's macadamia snaps—these are great!* Down at the
bottom, he'd come upon the Dr. Tulp postcard, blank on the
back, and thought no more about it.

But six months later, leafing through a photo album belong-
ing to the sixth victim, Nicolette Levy (sound tech, Culver City),
he'd found the Dr. Tulp postcard again, again blank on the back.
Petrov then revisited all the killings, the postcard showing up
somewhere in the effects of every victim. He'd worked feverishly
after that, but not feverishly enough. Although all the other
murders had been months apart, Reasoner hadn't waited
twenty-four hours before killing Lara Deems, taping the seventh
postcard to her fridge. Why had he broken the pattern? No one
knew. Reasoner had invoked his Miranda rights, had not taken
the stand, had admitted nothing.

Three oh five. Petrov got out of the car and slid a note under
Liza's door: *Call me immediately.* Then he started driving home—
101, 405, 10.

After his divorce, Petrov had bought a little place that backed
onto one of the canals in Venice. Kitchen, living room, two bath-
rooms, two bedrooms, rooftop deck. The upstairs bedroom had
been for Dmitri on those every second weekends and alternating
Christmases. But Dmitri had stopped coming, and technological
progress—voice mail, e-mail, call forwarding—had eliminated
the need for a secretary. Petrov had ended up closing his downtown office, now worked out of Dmitri's bedroom.

To make room for office furniture, he'd cleared out Dmitri's
bed, bureau, miniature basketball hoop, all the toys. One cold
winter night, finding the wood box empty, he'd used the building blocks for firewood. A rational act: they took up a surprising

amount of space, and had burned beautifully. On the other hand, he often thought of them; and once, he'd even gone into a toy shop and almost bought more.

The walls he'd left decorated with Dmitri's finger paintings. Petrov's favorite: a neckless little boy holding a ball out to a furry dog, its red tongue bigger than anything else in the picture. He'd moved it to the downstairs hall, visible the moment he came in. Petrov parked and walked up the path, looking forward to seeing it now. Only at the front door, smelling the mountain air, did he realize he wasn't home, but had somehow driven up to the cabin instead.

The cabin, meaning he'd gone 101, 134, 210, 10, 91 and up the canyon; must have, but he remembered none of it. What was happening to him? Had to be fatigue, but he didn't feel the least bit tired. If not fatigue, then what?

Petrov unlocked the cabin, felt the thin Indian rug under his feet, sat in the wicker rocking chair, facing the lake. The moon hung low in the sky, its glow reflected in multiples on the water, like fish scales. A dark shadow flew by, an owl almost certainly, seeing keenly in the night, in search of prey that could not Petrov heard the slow beat of its heavy wings, realized he was rocking at the same rhythm. He felt fine, was just in the wrong place.

Or maybe the right place after all. Big Bear was halfway to Barstow. *George Rummel—Barstow.* Ranked number three on his to-do list, but what if some unconscious part of his brain was chipping in with some guidance, putting him on the right track? He always started with birth certificates for a reason.

Barstow in the morning. Nick Petrov went to bed feeling tip-top. Something splashed in the lake just before he fell asleep.

G. Rummel had a listing in Barstow, 2928 Calico Way. Calico Way was a dirt road running northwest out of town, the Soda Mountains pink in the distance. Two-nine-two-eight stood by itself at the very end, a sun-bleached double-wide that would never move again. A shady-side thermometer read 110, but Petrov didn't seem to be feeling the heat today. He knocked on the door, smelled whiskey. A man opened up.

"Mr. Rummel?" Petrov said. But he knew he had the right man, just from the look of him: an old guy with a big frame—shoulders, chest, wrists—that had once carried a lot more weight, and huge, powerful, mangled hands. One held a paper cup half full of golden liquid, the other a cigarette. The old man squinted into the sun, his eyes watery and blue.

"Who's askin'?" he said.

Petrov held up his license. "I'm working for your daughter, Liza. Her daughter Amanda—your granddaughter—is missing."

"I don't like cops," said the man.

"Who does?"

"Suck-ups," said the man. "Ass-lickers."

"I meant with obvious exceptions," Petrov said. "But I'm a private investigator, not a cop."

"Investigatin' what?"

"Amanda's disappearance. Can we discuss it inside?"

"Cooler out here," said the man. "Know what it costs to air-condition this dump?"

"One fifty a month?" Petrov said.

The man gazed down at him, turned, disappeared in the shadows inside, came back with an electric bill: $148.97.

"You been checking up on me?" the man said.

Petrov handed back the bill, but not before noticing that it was in the name of George Rummel. "Amanda's missing, Mr. Rummel," he said. "And your daughter may be too."

"I got no daughter."

"I have information that you do."

"Your information's wrong."

"My information is that you were born here in Barstow,

have a daughter also born here, named Lisa Anne at birth, and that you played pro football for the Chicago Bears."

"Don't like being checked up on," Rummel said, his cigarette burning down between his thick fingers, the fiery part about to touch his skin, unnoticed. His face came up a little, lips curling down at the same time: contempt, number forty-one on Petrov's old chart of facial expressions. "And you can't hardly call it professional," Rummel said, "the chicken feed they paid us."

Petrov peered past him into the gloom, smelled masculine smells exclusively; almost impossible that a woman lived here. "Are you still married to Cynthia?"

"Don't go speaking her name."

"I'd like to talk to her."

Rummel blinked. "She passed."

"When?"

"That's not what you're supposed to say, city guy. Supposed to say 'Condolences' or some shit like that." Rummel had a prominent jaw to begin with; now it came jutting out. "I don't like the looks of you," he said.

"Why is that?"

Rummel glanced down at his cigarette, its red tip now singeing his fingers. He flicked the cigarette outside. " 'Cause you're a coldhearted bastard," he said. "Written all over you."

"Your family is in trouble," Petrov said. "I need your help."

Rummel drained the paper cup. "Coldhearted bastard," he said, his voice a little slurred. "Worry about your own family."

"None of mine's gone missing," Petrov said.

Red splotches appeared on Rummel's face. "Know what I'da done to you, even ten years ago?"

"What?"

"This." Rummel took a sloppy roundhouse swing. Petrov leaned back. The big fist missed by an inch or two and Rummel lurched forward, lost his balance, sprawled on the hard bare ground, minerals glittering around him. Petrov went inside.

"Amanda?" he called. He had a feeling, just from the way Rummel didn't want him in there. Dark and hot: Petrov hurried down an unlit corridor, past a galley kitchen, bedroom with a bare mattress, back room with a TV, the screen cracked, and a little fan, spinning fast but accomplishing nothing. Bottles and paper cups everywhere; smells of whiskey and an unflushed toilet; no Amanda. Petrov ripped open a shade, let in some light. It shone on a CD case, lying on the floor. Petrov picked it up: *Empty Box: Retards Picnic.*

"Rummel," he called. "Where is she?" No answer. He looked around for more signs of her—lip gloss, schoolbook, hair band—saw none. "Rummel?"

Petrov walked back along the narrow corridor. A framed black-and-white photograph hung on the wall, yellow, dusty, crooked: a football team picture. He paused to examine it, mostly to confirm that Rummel had indeed played with Dick Butkus. But these weren't the Bears, the faces of the players much too young to be professionals, or even college kids.

Desert H.S. Eastern Regional Champions. Three rows of boys in their uniforms, sitting in aluminum stands, the year 1950 marked in the lower left corner. Petrov scanned their faces, couldn't spot the Rummel of long ago. He checked the names at the bottom—Georgie Rummel, middle of the first row—ran his finger along it. Georgie wore number 55 and held the trophy: a big, unsmiling kid with wavy blond hair. Was there anything left of the boy in Rummel's face? Only the unsmiling part.

The names in the bottom row drew him back: Donny Deems, Dickie Conn, Bobby Weathers, Bobby Morris, C.J. Hilton, Buddy Hilton, Georgie Rummel, Mel Lippett, Mike Waters, Herm LeBeau, Donny Stone, W. Moore (trainer), F. Kostelnik (coach).

Kostelnik? Not a common name.

Petrov took the picture off the wall, moved back toward the good light in the end room, gazed at F. Kostelnik. F. Kostelnik didn't appear much older than the boys on the team. He was watching something off-camera, and whatever it was annoyed him. Petrov remembered that look, almost identical, on Elaine's face.

"Rummel?"

He glanced down the corridor, through the bedroom and kitchen, to the front door. Rummel was on his feet, coming back inside, framed in golden light. Photograph in one hand, CD in the other, Petrov started toward him, questions rising in his mind. He almost didn't hear a door opening behind him. A door off the corridor: What would that be? The bathroom? He wheeled around—thinking, How did I forget the bathroom, especially with that smell?—glimpsed a tall, bony man emerging from the shadows, tattoos all over his forearms, prison-style, and an empty whiskey bottle raised high.

"Rui?" he said; at the same time leaning sideways like a boxer slipping a punch. The case was coming together and flying apart at the same time, like some theoretical anomaly in physics. Petrov had boxed in college, was very quick, so quick that despite the suddenness of the attack and his unreadiness, the bottle hardly touched him, barely glancing off the side of his head.

ſive

Petrov opened his eyes. He saw a three-toed foot, much
like a chicken foot, but bigger and red. Soon he spotted
a second one, a few inches behind the first. Rough-
skinned feet, with bumps and yellow markings, plus pointy black
nails, or claws, or talons—yes, call them talons: but he couldn't
make all those high-definition details add up to anything.

The big red toes seemed to tense, curving up slightly. Petrov
felt a stab in the flesh of his upper arm. The feet tensed some
more and the pain grew sharper. Then the feet relaxed and the
pain got duller. Cause and effect or coincidence? To infer causa-
tion from correlation: a dangerous fallacy. A red drop fell in the
dust, made the tiniest possible splash, red, dusty, beautiful.
Petrov glanced up, trying to see where it came from. The two
black-taloned feet rose off the ground. Petrov rolled over. A vulture lifted itself heavily into the air, a scrap of his navy-blue suit
jacket dangling from its beak.

He got to his feet, waved his arms, made angry noises. The
vulture rose higher, but in no particular hurry. Blood seeped
through a ragged tear in Petrov's jacket. He picked up a stone,
threw it with all his strength, not high enough. The bird reduced itself in the sky, to a blob, a point, nothing. Petrov bent
over and vomited.

Alone, and in the middle of a desert wasteland; the sun

lower in the sky now, furnace-red, blasting. Nearby stood a faded wooden sign, the painted words almost worn away—SILVER CITY GHOST TOWN—the arrow snapped off, pointing nowhere. Petrov's tongue felt thick. How long could a man last in this heat without water? He went over the basics. The sun rose in the east, set in the west. At the same time, the earth circled the sun. Time was very strict, no matter how it happened to feel while you were living it. People fooled themselves. All people fooled themselves some of the time; some people fooled themselves all of the time; no people fooled themselves none of the time. His head light but somehow pounding at the same time, Petrov sat on a rock. A glancing blow, barely touching him—how could that have caused a concussion? Impossible.

A dog barked, not far away.

Petrov rose, followed the sound over a rise, found himself in the middle of a desert wasteland perhaps, but it was also George Rummel's backyard, downtown Barstow glinting in the middle distance. His head cleared. He felt sharp again, sharp and angry.

Petrov hammered on the shell of the double-wide, got no response. A collarless dog came panting up, white with splotchy rust-colored markings, ugly.

"Go home," Petrov said, hammering again.

The dog looked up at him, tongue hanging out.

"Thirsty?"

The dog wagged its tail.

Petrov walked around to the front, the dog trotting beside him. His car was gone. He banged on the front door, heard nothing inside. The Empty Box CD and the Desert High School team picture lay in some scrub by the door. Petrov picked them up and started down Calico Way, toward town.

The dog followed.

"Stay," Petrov said.

It didn't want to stay. Petrov said, "Stay," again, louder this time. The dog cringed, but kept coming.

Their shadows—Petrov's and the dog's—grew longer; the Soda Mountains went from pink to red. They came to pavement, and soon after, a 7-Eleven. Petrov went inside, bought a jug of water and a plastic bowl. They drank in the parking lot.

"Now go home," Petrov said.

The dog wagged its tail.

Petrov bent, gave it a little scratch between the ears. He was about to go back inside, ask if the clerk recognized the dog, when he noticed a bar called .45 on the other side of the street, thirty or forty yards farther on. A car that looked like his sat outside.

"Stay," he said. But the dog followed.

His car: dusty but undamaged, the Jussi Bjoerling live performance CD lying on the floor. That annoyed him.

"Go home," he said, and went inside.

Early on a Saturday night, but the place was already crowded, bar on the right, stage and dance floor up front. Musicians in fringed shirts and cowboy hats were setting up. Petrov spotted the tall bony man with the tattooed arms halfway down the bar, sitting between two plump, pretty young women. They had a couple of pitchers of beer in front of them and were laughing about something. Only then did Petrov think to feel in his pocket. His bribe roll was gone.

Petrov took an empty stool next to one of the plump women. She smelled of tobacco and perfume, lots of both. Her bare arm rested on the bar. From the shape and angle of it he read availability.

The bartender came over. "Johnnie Walker Black," Petrov said.

The bartender poured. "Run you a tab?" he said.

"It's on that gentleman," said Petrov.

The plump woman, the man, the second plump woman, all turned to him. Petrov raised his glass. Their mouths opened, the women's expectantly, the man's in surprise, the bad kind.

"Hey, Rui," said the second plump woman, "introduce us to your friend."

Rui's mouth closed, opened again. His right hand slipped inside his jacket.

"Name's Nick," Petrov said.

"I'm Ellyn, with a *y*," said one.

"D. J., but everybody calls me Deej," said the other. "Looks like you've had too much sun."

"I've been careless," Petrov said. "How do you know Rui?"

"We just met," said Ellyn.

"Are you a private eye too?" said Deej. "Like Rui, I mean?"

"Just a beginner," Petrov said. "Rui's showing me the ropes."

"So it's true?" said Ellyn. "Rui's a private eye?"

"Has he filled you in on Amanda yet?" Petrov said.

"Amanda?" said Ellyn. "Who's she?"

"Hiding a girlfriend on us, Rui?" said Deej.

Rui stared straight ahead. "Never heard of no Amanda."

The women looked confused. Petrov drank up. "Hiding a girlfriend is one possibility," he said. "Mind if I borrow Rui for a minute? I need to bring him up to speed."

"Bring him up to speed?" said Deej. "What's that mean?"

"Rui'll explain when he gets back." Petrov stood behind him, smelled his unwashed hair. In the mirror, Rui too looked confused. "Got the petty cash on you, Rui?"

"Petty cash?"

"From my pocket."

Rui didn't answer.

"Leave something," Petrov said. "In case your friends need to order while you're out."

Deej wriggled on her stool.

Rui took out the bribe roll, fumbled through, hands unsteady.

"Let me help," Petrov said, taking the money. He laid fifty dollars on the bar. "All set?"

The social situation was too complicated for Rui. He rose.

"You coming back too, Nick?" said Deej.

I n the parking lot, Petrov said, "Got the keys?"

Rui nodded. Petrov held out his hand. Rui reached inside his jacket. Who kept car keys in there? Rui adopted a nonchalant, harmless expression. Gun or knife?

Knife. A switchblade, horn handle with a seven-inch blade, that came snapping out as Rui's hand emerged from inside the jacket. Petrov was already chopping down on Rui's wrist, at the same time driving the toe of his shoe hard into Rui's kneecap. The knife clattered on the pavement. Rui went down too. The dog came out of nowhere and bit him on the thigh. Rui cried out.

"Sit," Petrov said. The dog sat at once. Petrov picked up the knife, knelt by Rui. "Got the keys?"

"You broke my fuckin' knee."

"Which one?" Petrov said.

"Left."

"Then you can still drive. It's an automatic."

"And your fuckin' dog bit me. What if I get rabies?"

Petrov gave the dog a little pat. "He's the picture of health."

The dog pressed against his hand.

R ui drove. Petrov took the passenger seat. The dog sat in back, nose out the open window.

"Drool like that's a sign of rabies," Rui said.

"It's just from the wind," said Petrov. "Let's see your ID."

"Don't have it on me."

"Give me your wallet."

"Don't have that neither."

The dog growled. Rui handed over the wallet. "What do you want from me?" he said.

"Turn right."

Rui turned right, onto a dark road heading south. Petrov switched on the interior light, examined the contents of Rui's wallet. Eleven dollars—two fives and a one; one Powerball ticket for that night, estimated prize $78,000,000; a ticket stub from the Empty Box concert at the Beacon Theater in Inglewood, August 23, same night Amanda had gone; a California driver's license in the name of Rui Estrella, age twenty-eight, residence 1491 Rosetta Street, Glendale.

"What do you think I want from you?" Petrov said.

"Fuck if I know."

"Amanda."

"You don't listen good—I never heard of no Amanda." The lights of a passing car shone on Rui's face. The lower part, around the mouth especially, looked young, younger than twenty-eight; the upper part could have passed for forty-five. "And my knee's fuckin' throbbing."

"Just a sprain," Petrov said. "Speed up a little."

"Where are we going?"

Petrov didn't answer.

"Gonna kill me?" Rui said. "Dump my body in some remote place?"

"Where would I get an idea like that?"

"Look," said Rui. "The allowing you to come to harm thing. I didn't mean it. You just surprised me is all. I'm looking out for her myself."

"Who?"

"You know."

"Amanda."

Rui nodded.

"Then take me to her."

"Don't know where she is, man."

"Pull over," Petrov said.

Rui pulled off the road, stopped by some creosote bushes, a black clump in the night.

"Shut off the car."

Rui shut it off. Metal made popping sounds for a moment or two. Then there was just the wind.

"Are you a three-strike candidate, Rui?"

Rui didn't answer.

"Meaning your assault on me, attempted murder, whatever the D.A. wants to call it, will put you away for good." Rui shook his head, said nothing. "But if you help me find Amanda, I'll keep you out of jail."

Rui snorted. "You talk all smart," he said, "but you don't know a goddamn thing."

"Such as?"

Rui waved the question away with the back of his hand.

"What are you on, Rui?"

"Nothin'."

"You're buzzing inside."

"Just from the crank."

"Do you understand what's going on? Amanda's mother hired me to find her. She's worried."

"Her mother?" Rui pounded the steering wheel, so hard the car shook. Petrov felt that shaking in his skull; his headache spread, reaching every corner of his brain.

"I don't fucking believe that," Rui said.

"Why not?"

"Why not? How stupid are you? Never heard that parents are the ones supposed to be looking out for their kids . . ." Rui paused. The moon was up now, and in its light Rui's eyes had gone all watery. Rui went on: ". . . not setting them up for murder?"

"What are you saying? That Liza wants Amanda killed?" That made no sense at all.

"I'm not sayin' nothin'."

"What are you and Amanda helping each other with?" Petrov said.

Rui's tears spilled over, made silvery tracks on his face. He didn't answer the question.

Petrov tried another. "What's scaring you?"

"Fuck," said Rui, "if you don't know, who does?"

"Explain that," Petrov said.

Instead, Rui made a little noise, snarl and sob mixed together, accompanied by that waving-away-the-question motion with his right hand, but more violently this time. More violently, but not by that much. His hand, just the backs of the fingers really, struck Petrov's forehead about an inch above the left eye. Not hard.

Petrov's kindergarten teacher, Miss Michaels, had written about his "insatiable curiosity" on the report card. She'd also told his father this story on parents' day: one morning she had led the class on an imaginary walk, up a mountain, over a narrow bridge, through a low tunnel, et cetera. At one point she'd said, "Watch out for the puddle, kids." And everyone but Nikolai had walked around. He'd marched right through.

"What about the puddle, Nicky?"

"I've got boots on."

He remembered that day: his earliest memory, until the penny-size headache came along.

SIX

No one liked whining. It went on and on until Nick Petrov opened his eyes and found himself in the passenger seat of his car, slumped against the door. And Rui gone. The backs of his fingers? How was that possible?

Front paws on the headrest, the dog gazed down at him, making a sound like whining, but with added desperation. Petrov got out of the car. The dog sprang past him, darted to a creosote bush, lifted its leg.

The eastern sky was the milky color of predawn, the west still dark. Petrov felt good, no aches and pains, no sign of a headache, if anything the opposite, a head full of warm, pleasant sensations, almost pulsing with them. Nothing wrong with him, and he still had the car. Petrov knew who to thank for that.

"Good boy."

The dog, still pissing, wagged its tail awkwardly.

Petrov found an energy bar in the glove box, ate half, held out the rest. The dog snapped it up. Petrov got out his notebook. Under *Known,* he added Rui's address, 1491 Rosetta Street, Glendale.

QUESTIONS
7. Amanda and Rui—on the run? From what?

SUSPICIONS
6. Rui—abused as a child.

He thought about moving *Liza and Amanda quarreled,* number two under *Suspicions,* up to *Known,* left it for now. Running off to her grandfather's: it was possible Amanda had been hiding somewhere in the trailer, but his only evidence was the Empty Box CD, not enough for certainty. Anything else? Just one thing, unconnected to this case, or any case; but he was curious.

TO DO
4. F. Kostelnik.

Dawn was breaking as Petrov drove into the parking lot of Desert High School, *Home of the Rattlers.* Wild colors got scattered across the sky; then the sun rose a little higher and everything settled down. On one side of the parking lot stood the school, a low desert-colored building; on the other side lay the football field, the only green in sight, a bright, healthy green, the green of football fields in Olympia or Eugene. In-ground sprinklers were making rainbows of the aquifer. The pulse in Petrov's brain changed its rhythm, speeding up.

The sprinklers shut off, the last plumes of spray losing their shape and subsiding. The doors of an equipment shed behind the nearer end zone flapped open and an old man, slightly bent, came out, pushing a chalk duster. Petrov got out of the car, the photograph of George Rummel's team under his arm.

"Stay in the car."

But the dog was already out.

Petrov felt the heat right away, already rising fast, making him a little dizzy. Had heat ever affected him like this? No. Maybe he was starting to age. The heat, nerve spasms, getting knocked out twice by a hundred-and-fifty-pound speed freak: what else could it be? You had to laugh.

The old man started chalking the goal line. He looked up as Petrov crossed the ten, the grass drying fast under his feet.

"He'p you?" he said. The sun had burned red marks on his head, visible through his soft white hair. He noticed the dog. "He gonna piss on my field?"

"Absolutely not," Petrov said, although it was probably an even bet. "How's the team?"

"Bunch of pussies."

"But they've been pretty good in the past."

"Depends when."

"Go back a long way with them?"

"Fifty-eight seasons."

Petrov showed him the picture. "How was this one?"

The old man reached into his shirt pocket for glasses, huge and black-rimmed, put them on the end of his nose. He scanned the faces, lips moving a little. "That one was good," he said. "Where'd you get this?"

"I'm looking into coaching philosophy, then and now."

"You could write a book on that."

"I was going to start with an article."

The old man nodded. "So's if no one wants it you haven't wasted too much time."

Petrov smiled. He was liking everything today—the green, the rainbows, the old man. The pulse throbbed happily in his head. "Did you know this coach?"

"Frank Kostelnik? Sure."

"I'd like to interview him."

"You'll have to go through one of them psychics."

Petrov laughed. "Got time for coffee? Or breakfast? I'm buying."

The old man shook his head. "Practice at nine," he said.

"Is his wife around?"

"Long gone. Atomic tests got her."

"What about kids?"

"He had just the one. Name of Elaine. But she ain't here. Elaine's down in L.A., making it big."

"Yeah?"

"The new chief of police, if you can believe that. What's just as bad, we got a girl kicking point-afters on the freshmen this year."

"She any good?"

"That's not the issue. The issue is what the hell is going on."

Petrov watched his face, was struck by a possibility. He bent toward the photograph, studied the picture of the trainer, W. Moore, standing next to Frank Kostelnik. "That you?"

"Yup."

"Looks like you might have played some football yourself, Mr. Moore."

"Surely did. Baseball and basketball too. Played 'em all. How it was back then. Not now. Bunch of pussies." He smiled. Possibly as a result of playing them all he was down to a handful of teeth, widely spaced. "And you can call me Wally."

"What kind of coach was Frank Kostelnik, Wally?"

"Hard."

"How so?"

"No mercy," said Wally. "Coach K was one of those people that does what has to be done. Saw every weakness on every team. And when it was time to go in for the kill?" Wally made a quick stabbing motion with an imaginary knife, grunting at the same time.

Been in some knife fights, Wally? Petrov almost asked; but the answer was clear from the smooth underhand technique, and instead he said: "He doesn't look much older than the players."

"He weren't. But he'd been to the war, was the difference."

A dusty pickup turned into the parking lot, stopped close to the shed. Two big men in sweatsuits got out and went inside.

"Tell me about the kid with the trophy."

"Georgie Rummel? Still the best player ever come out of Desert High. He played for the Bears, with Dick Butkus, which should mean something even to a young fella like yourself. Course, Dick Butkus was one in a million. Georgie Rummel was more like one in a hunnert thousand." Wally thought for a moment. "Maybe one in ten thousand."

"What became of him?"

"Became of him?"

"After football."

Wally shrugged. "He come back here, started a construction business, mostly contract work at Fort Irwin and up at China Lake, then managed the ghost town for a spell."

"Ghost town?" Petrov remembered the sign.

"Silver City Ghost Town, seven, eight miles north. Owned by the Deems family going way back. Kind of an important feature in these parts—our roots and such—but it went bust and Georgie's retired now."

"Did his daughter know Elaine Kostelnik?"

Wally blinked, a little confused. "How'd you know Georgie Rummel had a daughter?"

"She lent me this picture."

He blinked again, slower this time, gave Petrov a quick sideways look. "Was this a long time ago?"

"Yesterday."

"Then you're talkin' about the other daughter, the younger one."

"There are two daughters?"

"Was. There was two daughters, Liza and Lara. Lara was the older one. She passed. Georgie took it hard."

"Passed how?"

"Huh?"

A long time ago. Amanda's friend Beth Franklin had used the same phrase, speaking of the death, the murder, of Amanda's real mother. At first, he'd thought that Beth was trying to tell him that Liza and Amanda were sisters. Now Petrov started to get it, felt the buildup of inner tension that precedes some mechanism snapping into place. "Come on, Wally, you know what I'm asking. How did she die?"

Had his voice risen a little too high? Was there too much aggression in his tone? The shed doors opened again and the two men came out, clipboards under their arms. The expression on Wally's face had changed completely, from friend to foe.

"Whoa," he said. "What's goin' on?"

But if too loud, too aggressive, it was because of the pulse inside Petrov's head, which suddenly turned bad, the last pleasurable one still falling like a soft tide as the next rolled in with a sting. He flinched, couldn't help himself; *flinch* maybe not the right word, more of a tiny lurch or microspasm.

Wally backed away, eyes narrowing. "Cause I happen to know Georgie has nothin' to do with the younger daughter, on account of her . . . on account of how she's turned out. So if you saw her yesterday, what's this all about?"

The old man, now cranky, suspicious, slipping away, had information he needed. Petrov thought fast, trying to come up with the magic words. How about the simple truth? He was working on a missing persons case and Wally might have valuable information. Petrov said: "You might be able to help me, Wally." He felt a funny hitch inside his head, a moment of zero gravity. "I'm worried that Babar is dead."

What had he said? Petrov tried to rehear whatever it was, what he feared it was, to somehow reel the words back out of the air. But they were gone. And Wally's eyes were slits.

The two men came over, one with *Coach Costa* knitted on his sleeve, the other with *Coach Girn*. "Hey, Wally," Coach Costa said. "Is that the Brennermans' dog?"

Wally gazed at the dog. "Kinda looks like him, now that I think. Buster, right? This guy brung'm."

They all turned to Petrov. He stayed silent, for the first time in his life not trusting what might come out of his mouth.

"Buster," said Coach Girn, "c'mere."

Buster sidled the other way.

"That's him all right," said Coach Costa. He took out a cell phone, punched in some numbers. "Mrs. Brennerman?" he said.

"Coach Costa. Buster still missing?" He listened for a moment. "We got him down at the field." Happy sounds leaked out of the phone. "How about Mikey brings him home after practice?" A pickup drove into the parking lot and some boys got out. "He just come in now, Mrs. Brennerman." Pause. "Don't even mention it."

No words of any kind came to Petrov. The heat beat down on him. Buster saw Mikey Brennerman and went bounding off.

seven

Fifteen, 10, 210, 134. Petrov headed toward Glendale: Rui Estrella, 1491 Rosetta Street. The freeways were blue on the map, like rivers, their courses locked in his head, navigation automatic after so many years. In traffic backups—and there were always lots on Sunday—he checked his notes. Buster's smell lingered in the car.

KNOWN
LIZA

1. Hid Amanda's birth certificate. Possible motives: (a) to keep me from finding out she's not Amanda's real mother; (b) to keep the real mother's name secret.

Now he added:

2. Had an older sister Lara who died long ago.

Under *Suspicions,* he added:

7. Lara—Amanda's mother.

On what evidence? None; nothing that rose to the standard of real evidence. Lack of evidence didn't always bother him.

Petrov preferred to work the scientific way, assembling evidence until it formed a theory. But sometimes he could work the other way, beginning with understanding—as on that last wild day of the Reasoner case.

Once he'd realized the importance of the Dr. Tulp postcard, Petrov had begun scientifically, tracking down places that sold it, learning there might be hundreds in Southern California alone. But when the body of Lara Deems turned up less than twenty-four hours after Nicolette Levy's, he'd abandoned science, jumped in his car, and raced to the Getty. Why the Getty? Because there was something grandiose about the place and something grandiose about the crimes, as though the murderer were making an important statement. That was the nonscientific way; call it religious.

The postcard was for sale in the gift shop. Petrov asked if anyone remembered selling more than one copy to the same customer.

Didn't Jerry buy a couple just the other day?

Jerry?

Jerry Reasoner. He's a security guard upstairs.

Reasoner was alone in a marble alcove, standing before a sculpture of two Greek wrestlers, when Petrov tapped him on the shoulder and said, "Dr. Tulp?" Reasoner's shoulder had sagged, as though under a heavy weight. Shooting him while resisting arrest, Juwan Barnes's suggestion and that of a few others? Impossible. Petrov would have required at least a little resistance, and Reasoner, despite pleading not guilty and confessing to nothing, had offered none.

The pulses in Petrov's head faded, leaving empty space, empty but somehow pregnant, like an unused echo chamber. Past the San Dimas exit, traffic thinned a little and Petrov closed his notebook. He hadn't dealt with the question, if it was a question, of Frank Kostelnik. Elaine's father had coached Liza's—and Lara's—father in football, meaning that the three girls had grown up in the same town. Had Elaine ever mentioned Barstow or her father? Not that he recalled. Had the girls known each other? If so, did it mean anything? Did it fit into any of the categories—Known, Questions, Suspicions, Remote Possibilities? Not that he could see, using either method, scientific or religious. One hand on the wheel, he opened the notebook to a blank page and jotted down *Elaine, L&L, Barstow,* uncoded. Then he stuck *Retards Picnic* in the CD player.

First came a pretty little guitar melody that reminded him of "Teddy Bears' Picnic." Then more guitars joined in, buzzing and droning, and a keyboard made scary movie music, like the soundtrack for the shower scene in *Psycho.* A woman sang, screamed really, some lyrics he couldn't degarble, until the lines:

And you don't even know
What's buried in your yard
Retard.

"Retard, retard," sang a male voice in the background, sweet and light like a choirboy, "in your yard, in your yard."

After that, more garble, a buzzing solo, a droning one, another verse, a conclusion, ragged and thundering, during which he realized the pretty little guitar was still playing underneath all that, might have been playing the whole time. Petrov listened to the song again, decided he liked it. And once more, now liking even the droning and the buzzing. He hit the repeat button and locked it in.

By then he was about half an hour from Glendale if the traffic stayed like this, almost in Pasadena. Kathleen lived in Pasadena, Kathleen and Dmitri. Had to put it that way, with the upstairs bedroom in Venice now his office—Dmitri lived in Pasadena, full-time. They had a nice house halfway up a hillside, with a red-tile roof and redbrick stairs winding up to the front

door. You took the Altadena exit. Petrov had always liked those
stairs.

> And you don't even know
> What's buried in your yard
> Retard.

Now he found he could hear without straining that acoustic
guitar running softly through the Teddy Bear changes. Indeed,
it was obvious. How could he have missed it? This was a great
song. Petrov was actually singing along when he found he'd
taken the Altadena exit.

Not only that, but he was driving up Kathleen's street, slow-
ing down, in fact, in front of her house. Petrov stopped the car.
He sat there, at first asking himself *What am I doing here?* then just
taking it all in: the two little orange trees on the close-cut, sloping lawn; that long redbrick staircase; flower pots—those were
new—overflowing with yellow flowers, flanking the front door.
It was lovely, smaller but much nicer—and much better cared
for—than the house he and Kathleen had shared in Santa Monica, the one where Kathleen, coming home sick from work one
day, a day in June between the Tiffany LeVasseur and Nicolette
Levy murders in the Reasoner case, had walked in on Elaine and
him; the kind of situation European films always played for
laughs.

The front door opened. Out came his son, MP3 earbuds in
place. Dmitri—in shorts, T-shirt, baseball cap, sneakers—
hopped on a skateboard and flew down the winding redbrick
staircase. The danger of it, the recklessness: Dmitri went airborne for the last three steps, landed with a clatter on the side-
walk, skidded to a stop.

Petrov got out of the car. "Dmitri."

Dmitri turned. "What are you doing here?" he said, lowering
the volume but leaving the earbuds in place.

"Thought I'd drop by," Petrov said.

Dmitri stared back at him.

Petrov smiled. "The truth is I just dropped by, no thinking involved."

"I'm kind of busy today."

"Skateboarding?" Petrov said, meaning it as a kind of joke; but funny in what way? Had it had come out wrong, sarcastic, demeaning?

He was still thinking how to make it right when Dmitri said: "Yeah. Skateboarding."

Petrov knew he should have said, *No problem, I didn't let you know I was coming,* or something like that. So nice just to see him, how fine he looked, his face changing, nose and jaw strengthening, someone the world would take seriously one day. Petrov tried to think of a way to put all that in words, negate his stupid remark. He said: "How's soccer?"

"I quit."

"You quit the team?"

"I told you I was going to."

Petrov thought back to their last conversation, two weeks before, or possibly a little longer, their times together less scheduled now. Petrov had taken Dmitri to the gym, thinking, wrongly, he might enjoy working out together. "That's not what you said, Dmitri. You asked what I thought about the idea of quitting soccer, and I told you to give it more time."

"Whatever," Dmitri said.

"You always liked soccer."

"Where'd you get that idea?"

"And quitting's never the way to go," Petrov said. Here they were, right into an argument, not his intention at all. But there was something Dmitri had to understand: "Don't close doors on yourself."

"Thanks for the tip," Dmitri said. "Got to go."

"Tip? It's not a goddamn tip, I just want—"

"Bye." Dmitri pushed off, glided quickly away.

"Dmitri!"

Around the corner and out of sight, leaning low, perfectly balanced; not looking back.

Get in the car. Go. Petrov's first thought, but driven off by one more powerful. Instead he climbed the stairs, plucking a flower out of one of the pots on the landing. He knocked on the door, not hard. Wind chimes sounded close by.

T he door opened, and there was Kathleen. She had her hair back, wore a white silk robe, looked great. "Nick?" she said. "What are you doing here?"

"Hello," he said.

"But it's not your day."

Petrov held out the flower. She looked at it without comprehension; he didn't exactly understand what he was doing with it either. "I know, Kat," he said; hadn't called her Kat in twelve years. Plus two months. "May I come in?"

"Dmitri's gone to a friend's."

"I saw him," Petrov said. "He quit soccer."

"His decision."

"But couldn't you have——" He stopped himself. "I won't stay long."

"I don't understand."

"We should talk."

"About what?"

"The future." He pushed past her, not pushed, more like walked around respectfully.

"Do you need the bathroom or something?" she said. "What's going on?"

"No, thanks," Petrov said. "I'm fine."

He went into the kitchen. Had it always been so white? White everywhere, except for the two glasses of orange juice on the table.

She followed him. "Are you all right?"

"Oh, yes," Petrov said. "Don't worry about me. The fact is, Kat, I've been thinking." The fact was he hadn't, was just starting to think now. "Sit down."

"I'm sorry?"

"Please. Or stand, it doesn't matter. The point is—" He felt a flood rising in his brain, warm, blissful. "The point is I'm starting to understand a few things."

At that moment, the sliding door to the patio opened and a man, also in a white silk robe, but covered with an apron, came in, bearing grilled salmon on a tray, seared to perfection, as Petrov could tell from the parallel grill markings on the pink flesh. *A man* was the wrong way to put it, of course: this was the software guy, Randy, Kathleen's husband. Somehow Petrov had forgotten all about him, his memory, always reliable, suddenly playing a very big trick. The software guy, Randy, Kathleen's husband, stopped where he was, lemon wedges lined up neatly around the salmon, his eyes on Petrov.

"Kathleen?" he said.

Petrov realized he'd never liked Randy's voice. There was something fishwifey about that voice.

"Hi, Randy," he said. "The salmon looks good."

"Uh, thanks."

"You're probably wondering what the hell I'm doing here."

"Well, it did—"

"I just barged in," Petrov said, "hoping for a quick word with Kathleen."

Randy looked at Kathleen; she looked at Randy. Petrov saw nothing pass between them, nothing but confusion, maybe the beginnings of alarm. He took this for a sign of weakness in their marriage.

Kathleen turned to him, her forehead creasing in two planes, horizontal and vertical; that vertical component—two parallel grooves between her eyebrows, about a centimeter in length—was new. "Have you been drinking?" she said.

"No."

"You're acting so weird," she said.

"He's stoned on something," said Randy.

So much wrong with that: wrong on the facts, fishwifey in tone, rushing to negative judgment, speaking of a collocutor in the third person. Petrov gazed at him, understood him to the core; and at that core, the foundation of Randy's being, lay the fear of violence, of coming to harm. He raised the tray slightly higher, like a shield.

"I'm totally unstoned, Randy," Petrov said. "If you'll just give me a minute with Kathleen, Kat as I used to call her and——" Here he almost added, *hope to again,* censoring himself for tactical reasons.

Randy licked his lips. An unattractive tongue: where on Kathleen had it touched down? "Is this about Dmitri?" he said.

"Indirectly."

Kathleen and Randy exchanged another look. Some sort of understanding did pass between them this time. Randy set the tray down on the counter. "I'll just warm the croissants," he said, drawing a folded square of tinfoil from his apron pocket. He went out through the sliders, closed them to approximately four inches from totally shut.

Kathleen said: "What is it?"

Petrov's gaze was drawn to her neck, specifically that finely rounded little hollow at its base, flanked by two fragile-looking tendons. "You're having brunch?" he said.

"Of course," said Kathleen. "What does it look like?"

He hadn't realized.

"Can we sit down? Talk for a moment?" Petrov moved to the table, took a chair at one of the place settings.

"About what?" she said, coming closer to the table, slowly sitting opposite him. The whites of her eyes, the silk robe, the whole room: everything so white, except for the orange juice. All at once very thirsty, Petrov picked up a glass and drank it down. Kathleen's eyes narrowed as she watched him; possibly just squinting against the brassy sunlight they had out here. Yes, there were more lines on her face now, not just the new vertical pair between her eyes, but he could warm to them, perhaps had warmed to them already.

"How to begin?" he said.

"Begin what?"

Over her shoulder, he saw Randy in front of the barbecue, glancing back, tongs in hand. Petrov leaned forward.

"Making changes," he said.

Kathleen's voice, almost harsh up till now, not like her at all, softened. "What's wrong with you, Nick?"

"That's what I want to talk to you about. I have a religious side you were never aware of. Neither was I." Her face started closing up; he thought he knew where her mind was going, toward some thought like *Christ, he's gone born again or some other California thing*. Petrov held up his hand. "Not religious in an alarming way," he said. "Simply that this weekend I've begun to understand a few things."

"You mentioned that," Kathleen said. "Like what?"

Petrov felt an odd little hitch inside his head, like shifting gears. A voice spoke, reminding him of his own. It said: "The importance of Babar."

She reddened. "Is this a joke?"

"Oh, no, never." Babar: had he really done it again? "Forget I mentioned him. I don't know what I'm saying." He felt his face reddening too, bright red hot. "I'm talking about the importance of . . ." In the nick of time, Petrov realized what he was in fact talking about—how was it that some parts of his mind were all of a sudden working so fast and others so slow, even going backward?—and he said: "love."

"You realized the importance of love?" said Kathleen.

He nodded.

"This is earthshaking?"

Something about the way she said that—the Yiddish inflection, maybe, coming from Kathleen née O'Reilly—seemed very funny. Petrov started laughing, stopped abruptly when he remembered that Randy was Jewish. He reached across the table, laid his hand on hers, felt a circuit complete itself, and everything was all right. "I've made a huge mistake, Kat. A whopper. A Hiroshima and Nagasaki of a mistake."

"What are you talking about?"

"Our divorce," he said.

"The divorce," said Kathleen, withdrawing her hand, "was my decision, not your mistake. Your mistake was Elaine Kostelnik."

"That couldn't be helped." He had to make an effort not to reach for her hand, pull it back.

"Couldn't be helped?" Her voice rose; all softness gone. Was she still angry, after all these years?

"Not given the way I was then. That case—" Petrov cut himself off before he started making excuses. "Mistakes can be fixed," he said. "You can even do something about the worst ones."

Confusion: number twenty-seven on Petrov's old list of facial expressions. It took over Kathleen's face.

"Kat: I want you back."

The slider opened and Randy came in, basket of croissants in hand. "A crime to let these babies get cold," he said. "Croissant, anybody?"

"Reparations," Petrov said. "I'll make reparations."

Kathleen got up. "You're way out of line," she said.

"It just means repairs," Petrov said. "I'll make any repair you want. Name it."

Facial expression fifty-three: disgust.

"What's broken?" Randy said.

Kathleen crossed the room and stood beside him, her wedding ring glowing like a Hollywood special effect. "Nothing," she said.

Petrov, watching Randy grow aware of the emotions in the room, said, "Nothing he'd understand."

Kathleen's face: expression two—anger. Was she angry at him for treating Randy that way? Petrov started getting angry too.

"Keep your mouth shut, Randy." He stood up, but for some reason other things were falling down—the glasses of orange juice, the table, knives, forks, spoons, too much to quantify at the moment. "You're interrupting." Petrov waded toward them through the wreckage.

Kathleen's face: number one—fear. What was she afraid of?

Petrov halted. Afraid of him? What was he doing? The pulses in his head were back, heating up now, surely audible to everyone.

He backed away, went out. Last sight: Kathleen, her hand over her mouth, Randy opening the broom closet.

eight

And you don't even know
What's buried in your yard
Retard.

Petrov, back in the flow of the blue river, sang along, but quietly now, under his breath. The powerful pulses in his head were gone. All he felt was the original penny-size headache just above his left eye, centered perhaps three centimeters behind his brow. He squirmed away from what had just happened with Kathleen, although he knew it had to be the result of two concussions. But: two concussions dealt out by someone like Rui? Was it possible? Had he ever been knocked out before?

Once: his junior year in college. Boxing had been a club sport, a Golden Gloves trainer coming for practice Monday, Wednesday and Friday and to the bouts on Saturday; Tuesday and Thursday they'd been on their own. On one of those Tuesdays or Thursdays, fooling around without headgear, Petrov, then a light-heavy, had sparred with the club heavyweight, Tommy Gugliotta. All he remembered was Tommy bending over him. "Geez, Nick, did I do that?"

Had that concussion created a susceptibility, hidden all these years? It sounded medically plausible. Old concussion, leading to new concussions—aggravated by possible potassium deficiency and the heat—leading to acts of unplanned behavior, the visit to Kathleen, for example. How to undo that one? Petrov didn't know. Somehow he'd make it up to her next time.

Regrets. One: losing Kathleen. Two: everything that happened with Elaine Kostelnik. Three: including, most of all, that she had ended it.

Whoa, as Wally Moore had said. *What's going on?* How could regrets one, two and three coexist, occupy space in the same head? Petrov didn't know that either.

He glanced around, saw he'd left the blue river for a little tributary. The air was thick and brown, the few faces he saw defeated by the heat. Petrov topped a rise with hazy mountains in the distance: the Verdugos, and therefore he was in Glendale. He took the Thomas Guide from the glove box, hunted for Rosetta Street, couldn't find it. In fact, he couldn't find anything, couldn't read the maps at all. Could a concussion do that, temporarily scramble map-reading skills? Medically plausible. He rubbed his forehead furiously, hard enough to hurt—hurt on the outside—trying to make things right. They wouldn't go right. Only a good sleep and maybe a day or two of rest would do that. But not now. Amanda was out there. He stopped at a gas station for directions.

Rosetta Street ran northwest, paralleling the boulevard toward Burbank. Little houses went by, numbers in the three thousands, one after the other, so many. Petrov had the strange sensation he'd been here before, but knew he hadn't, knew no one in Glendale, had never had a client or worked a case here. Déjà vu, then, possibly another effect of the concussions. There must be research on that: he made a mental note to look it up. Rosetta Street topped a rise, curved to the right, due north, and there was 1491 on the opposite side of the street, a small and grimy stucco box.

Could Rui be inside? If so, would he recognize the car? Fourteen ninety-one had a picture window and three smaller ones in front, yellowed blinds fully drawn behind them all. Petrov played it safe, continuing to the end of the block, intending to park around the corner, out of sight. But making the turn, he glanced up at the street sign and caught the name of the crossing street: Glenholme Way.

Glenholme Way? Why was that familiar? He remembered: there was a Glenholme Way in Burbank, a Glenholme Way that crossed Coursin Street, Gerald Reasoner's last address in the outside world. At that moment, Petrov realized he was probably in the westernmost part of Glendale, perhaps—was it possible?— close to the Burbank line. He kept driving west on Glenholme Way, came to the next street, read the sign, its green paint bleached and peeling from the sun: Coursin.

Petrov turned left and saw at once that he was on Reasoner's block. The trees, a few eucalyptus yellowed with dead leaves and some dusty palms, should have been bigger now, almost twelve years later, but were not. If anything they'd shrunk. The houses looked unchanged, as if no one had had the money or energy for a single renovation—all except for number 313, Gerald Reasoner's old house, once yellow with red trim, now white and aquamarine. Petrov got out of his car. The heat made a direct connection to the penny-sized headache, setting off a little bomb in his head.

Petrov walked across the lawn that had once been Gerald Reasoner's, along the side of his old house and into the backyard; a small backyard with two lawn chairs and a wading pool where a plastic frog floated on the surface. The grass was yellow and stunted, perhaps because of water restrictions; or else the county had stinted on the resodding. Petrov remembered what forensics had found underneath.

The tall wooden fence at the end of the backyard had been replaced with chain-link, not high. Petrov should have climbed it with ease. For some reason, he almost couldn't get over at all.

Petrov picked himself up on the other side, crossed the backyard of the house behind Reasoner's, a yard with no grass at all, just big weeds with glossy, spatulate leaves gripping the earth. He smelled tea, weak and sugary, and had another memory from prememory time: the samovar on the side table, glowing silver, and his mother's ruby ring clicking on the ornate lid.

The tea smell followed him as he approached the back of the house, a stucco house with a long diagonal earthquake crack in the wall and a door with a plywood-filled window. He walked around it, saw that the house stood on Rosetta Street; and checked the number on the doorpost just to be sure: 1491. So 1491 Rosetta Street and 313 Coursin Street—Rui Estrella's house, at least as recorded on his driver's license, and Gerald Reasoner's old house—stood back to back.

What did that mean? Petrov had no idea. He listened for any sound from 1491, heard nothing, not even the hum of air-conditioning or a fridge. The unblinded basement half-windows were opaque with dust. He recrossed the backyard, reclimbed the fence with no difficulty this time—reinvigorated somehow by all that tea in the air—circled 313 and knocked on the front door.

It opened. The tea smell vanished, just like that, so fast it scared him; and if not that, he was scared for some other reason. A little girl, maybe four or five years old, looked out. She was dressed in underpants and one sock, had a sparkly conical party hat hanging from the back of her neck.

"I got a booboo," she said, and held out her right hand. There was a Band-Aid around the first knuckle of her index finger.

"Who's that on the Band-Aid?" Petrov said.

She giggled. "Goofy, you dumdum."

Petrov found himself gazing at Goofy. A voice that sounded like his said, "Did you ever wonder why Goofy can talk and Pluto can't?" Had to be his own remark, but it baffled him until he realized they were dogs in the same cartoons.

The little girl gazed down at her bare foot—toenails painted green—and pawed at the floor. "Uh-uh," she said.

He rubbed his forehead, began again. "My name's Nick. What's yours?"

"Cassie. My mommy's favorite name in the whole world."

"Is she here?"

The little girl shook her head. "It's short for Cassandra."

"What about your daddy?"

"Daddy lives far away."

"Where is your mommy?"

"At work. She works at Nordstrom."

"Who's taking care of you?"

"In accounting. Mommy got her CPA."

"But who's home with you right now?"

Cassie pawed at the floor again. "When Mommy's not home I don't ever ever open the door or ever ever answer the phone." She glanced at the door.

"How long have you been living here, Cassie?"

"Long."

"Were you born in this house?"

"In the hospital, dumdum."

"What hospital?"

"Massachusetts General Hospital."

"In Boston?"

"I'm a Boston bean."

"Do you know who lived in this house before you?"

"Armenians."

"Have you ever heard of Gerald Reasoner?"

She shook her head.

"What about Rui Estrella?"

Cassie put her thumb in her mouth.

"You know Rui?"

She talked around her thumb, something unintelligible.

"I can't hear you."

Cassie stopped talking, just sucked her thumb, belly sticking out, feet pigeon-toed. The idea of her and Gerald Reasoner in the same house, even in different time periods, sickened him.

"Do you know how to call your mommy at work?" Petrov said.

Cassie took her thumb out of her mouth. "Instadial one," she said.

"Show me," said Petrov. He entered the house, closed the door behind him. Cassie led him down a hall and into the kitchen at the back: no dishes in the sink, floor spotless, everything neat and tidy. Through the window he could see the wading pool, the chain-link fence, the back of 1491 Rosetta Street, with the big crack in the stucco wall.

The phone sat on the kitchen table. Cassie climbed onto a chair. "Press this button," she said. "That number says one. I can count to ten billion."

"What's your last name, Cassie?"

"DiPardo. What's yours?"

"Petrov."

"I never heard that name."

"I never heard DiPardo." He picked up the phone, pressed one on the speed dial.

A woman answered on the first ring. "Stephanie DiPardo," she said.

"This is Nick Petrov. I'm a private investigator looking for a neighbor of yours, Rui Estrella."

"I don't really know anything about him," said Stephanie Di-Pardo. "And I can't talk to you now—I'm at work."

"You'd better come home."

"Excuse me?"

"I'm in your kitchen right now with Cassie." He heard a little gasp. "She's fine, but too young to be left alone, as you don't need me to tell you. I'll wait till you get here." He hung up. "Your mommy's coming home," he said.

"But I'm hungry now," said Cassie.

"What would you like?"

"Grilled cheese sandwich."

Petrov made a grilled cheese sandwich, set it on the table.

"That's not the way Mommy does it," said Cassie.

"This is Goofy's secret recipe," said Petrov. "Milk or juice?"

"Juice."

"When was the last time you had milk?"

"Yesterday."

"Then it's milk."

Petrov poured her a glass of milk, opened a few drawers, found a bottle of Advil, took four. He sat at the table, facing the window. Cassie bit into her sandwich. She finished it in silence, eating every crumb, draining her glass. Petrov thought he could hear the milk running down her throat. Time came to a stop on a peaceful note.

"Now read me a story," Cassie said.

"Okay."

"How about *Babar and Celeste*?"

"Something else."

"*Goodnight Moon*?"

"Sure."

The moment Cassie left the kitchen, another little bomb went off inside his skull. Petrov rubbed his forehead savagely, trying to straighten out everything inside. His vision went red all around the edges and kind of blurry in between. He almost didn't see the cigarette come spinning out the back door of 1491 Rosetta Street; but was on his feet before the door closed.

Petrov rattled the knob. A whimper came from the other side. He kicked the plywood out of the window frame, reached through, unlocked the door. An old woman stood in a dark room on the other side, dressed all in black like a European peasant.

"Where's Rui?" Petrov said.

She wrung her hands. He went inside. Still wringing her

hands, she moved to block his way. Petrov pushed past her, walked through the dark room and then another. No air-conditioning: it was like a foundry that gave off no light. From somewhere below, a man yelled, "Ma?"

Petrov followed the sound, down some stairs, along a corridor—the floor sticky in places—and into a room slightly cooler than the rest of the house, lit only by a TV tuned to the Weather Channel. A tall teenage girl lay on the couch. Rui knelt beside her, patting her forehead with a damp towel.

"What have you done to her?" Petrov said.

"Nothin'," said Rui, rising. "She had a little too much, is all."

"Too much what?"

"A speedball kind of thing mostly."

Petrov took one step forward and hit Rui in the mouth. Rui went down and stayed down. Petrov bent over the girl: Amanda. Amanda, thinner and dirtier than in the photograph, but Amanda, beyond doubt. He placed his finger on her neck, felt her pulse, slow and steady; put his face close to hers, felt the breath from her nostrils on his cheek. She was alive. He'd found her and she was alive.

"Amanda. Wake up."

She didn't.

A bowl of water lay on the floor. Petrov splattered some on her face. Her eyelids fluttered open. "Don't," she said.

"Sit up," Petrov said. "I'm taking you home."

Her eyes closed. "Tha's a good one," she said, so softly he could hardly hear.

"Why?"

There was a long pause, so long he thought she'd drifted off. Then, almost just mouthing the words now, Amanda said, "I am home."

What did she mean? Had Amanda been here the whole time, a rather obvious place for Liza to look, depending on whether and how much she knew about Rui? Or had she been in Barstow at her grandfather's, forced by his own arrival to flee?

Petrov heard a faint sucking sound from the corridor: the old woman moving on the sticky floor. "Don't come in," he said. The noises stopped. He lowered his cupped hand into the bowl, splashed more water on Amanda's face. Her eyelids rose again, quivering.

"Don't."

"I'm taking you home."

She gazed at him. "Who are you?"

"Nick Petrov. Your mother hired me to find you."

"The detective from the movie?"

"Yes."

"This is so fucked up."

"What do you mean?"

Amanda turned her head aside and vomited, retching and retching. Rui stirred on the floor. Petrov cleaned Amanda's face with the damp towel and picked her up.

"You're safe," he said.

But she was panting and her face was white. Where was the nearest hospital? Petrov waited for the map to pop up in his mind, the map with all the rivers and tributaries, but it refused. Something else popped up in its place, a red pounding thing of superhuman strength. Petrov staggered. Rui got up on his hands and knees. Petrov took a deep breath, the air hot and dusty, found his balance and his strength, lifted Amanda in his arms and walked out of the room. The old woman leaned into the shadows as he went by.

He carried Amanda on his shoulder, back over the chain-link fence and around Gerald Reasoner's old house, the red pounding thing fighting him every step. Her head bobbed upside down against his chest, hair greasy and matted. The sun was red and pounding too. Petrov sat Amanda in the passenger seat of his car, strapped her in, closed the door, got in the other side. He was driving off when another car pulled in behind him. A woman jumped out, ran toward 313.

The pain in his head vanished the moment he turned the

key, the red monster washed away by an optimistic blue tide. From now on his whole life, present, future, even past, if that made sense, would be good. His mind expanded like a star in its last stages. The missing map zipped by—the nearest hospital was St. Joe's. But other things, far more important, kept coming. Example: He was wrong about Kathleen. Not only did he have no right to reenter her life, but way down deep he didn't really want her, and would therefore hurt her again. But he wanted changes, oh yes; having realized the importance of love. And Dmitri: he suddenly knew the answer there too, exactly how to square things with Dmitri, a step-by-step approach, so obvious. He almost laughed out loud from happiness.

"What's funny?"

The question startled him. He'd forgotten all about Amanda. He whipped around toward her. Her eyes were open, watching him.

"Everything's going to be all right," Petrov said.

"After you kill me?" said Amanda.

The poor kid. Where were they? Outside the emergency entrance at St. Joe's. Petrov stopped the car. "Rui's a big mistake," he said. "Too many things buried in his yard." Amanda's eyes opened wide. "And I would never hurt you."

Her voice got small, like Cassie's. "Then what about my mother?"

"Your real mother?" said Petrov. "I didn't even know her."

"So?" said Amanda. "That still leaves the cover-up."

"Cover-up?"

She started shaking. Petrov got quickly out of the car, opened her door. Amanda bent over, hugging herself. He took her hand, a cold hand that sent a freeze wave up his arm, although the Santa Ana was blowing hot off the desert. Maybe he'd guessed wrong, and somehow they were talking about different things. "Isn't Liza your aunt?" he said. "Wasn't your mother Lara Rummel?"

"That was before she got married," Amanda said.

"What was her married name?"

Amanda's teeth chattered. He helped her up. She wobbled and he steadied her. The ground wobbled too, possibly a temblor, and he tried to steady it as well with the power of his expanding mind.

"What was her married name?" he said again.

"Deems," said Amanda.

Deems? "Your mother's name was Lara Deems?"

"You didn't know?"

Lara Deems? Amanda's mother was Lara Deems, Gerald Reasoner's last victim? Things smashed together in Petrov's brain, like subatomic particles in a cyclotron, throwing off more thoughts than he could cope with. But two stood out: *Remote Possibility* number two—*Liza*—*setting me up*—was dead-on. His second thought, more urgent, he voiced aloud.

"Why did you tell Beth Franklin your mother's case was unsolved? Everyone knows the killer was Gerald Reasoner."

Amanda's face changed. For a second or two, Petrov could see how she was going to look as an old woman. "You're either stupid or horrible," she said.

"Why?" Was she telling him she didn't believe Reasoner was the murderer, in which case . . . *in which case someone else killed Lara Deems?* But that was impossible. Petrov's voice rose. "What are you saying?"

She turned toward him, her mouth close to his ear. "We're all ghosts from the ghost town," she said; a whisper that set off another freeze wave, right through his body this time.

"What do you mean?"

Amanda didn't answer. Her eyes turned up and she sagged against him. He held her, walked her toward the entrance. It took some time—how much he didn't know, time bending sharply in a universe expanding so fast—before he realized he wasn't actually walking, but more accurately was lying on the pavement, with Amanda high above, peering down. And that foot, sort of spasming out there, whose was that? It looked just like his.

Amanda's eyes registered some kind of shock. Hugging herself again, she started backing away.

"Amanda!" Petrov called in what he thought was a booming voice, although he seemed to have temporarily lost the ability to make any external sound. Amanda kept backing away. He reached out, grabbed her, took her in, made sure she was all right, had her vital signs checked and rechecked, brought her home safe to Liza with all the necessary prescriptions and instructions for her care, wrapped up the case. Only none of that happened. The only movement was Amanda, backing, backing, and that spasming foot, just on the periphery of his sight.

Then he couldn't see her, could see nothing but the foot, useless.

"Amanda!"

He smelled tar. Had he somehow fallen into the Tar Pits with all the old bones? Medical people came running up.

"The girl," he told them. "Get the girl first."

"Did he say something?" said a medical person.

"Not that I heard," said another.

The photograph of Amanda slid from his chest pocket and blew away.

2

BRAIN WORK

The lights were much too bright, like interrogation lights in a B movie. Petrov couldn't see his interrogators but sensed their presence in the shadows. He knew what they were going after—his testimony at the trial, specifically that climactic revelation of the killer's confession: *I enjoyed every minute of it.*

A woman spoke: "He has nice hair."

"I'm supposed to shave it off," said a man.

Good cop, bad cop: did they think that would work on him? A second man spoke: "How're we doing?"

"IV in," said the other man. "Here's what we're running."

Paper rustled, a note being passed. Were they filling him up with sodium pentathol or some other truth serum? Petrov had no experience with drugs like that. They worked by inducing euphoria. Could he resist? Petrov was worried, but just knowing they were using it would help. He had to guard against euphoria.

"What's his name?" said the second man. His face came into view.

"Nick Petrov," said the first man.

The second man gazed down at him. A surgical mask covered most of his face, which was just as well: Petrov didn't like the look of him at all.

"Hey, Nick," he said. "How're you doing?"

An innocent-seeming question, but Petrov was being careful. He gazed back, noncommittal.

"Can you hear me okay?"

Perfectly, but I have the right to remain silent.

"If you can hear me, raise your right hand."

Petrov refused to play games like that. "Just get the girl," he said. "She's in trouble."

"Did he say something?" said the man.

The woman leaned into the picture. She too wore a surgical mask. "I couldn't make it out."

"Amanda," Petrov said.

"What was that?" said the man.

"*Canada*, maybe?" said the woman.

"Is he Canadian?"

"Don't think so," said the other man, stepping into visual range, also masked, hair clippers in hand. "Ever see the movie about that serial killer in the Valley some years back? The scalpel guy?"

"Wasn't Kim Delaney in that?" said the woman.

"And Armand Assante. I think this is the Armand Assante guy. The one who solved the case."

"No shit."

They all peered down at him. Their names, possibly fake, were stitched in red letters on their white jackets: *Anne Samuels, M.D., Neuroradiology; Mike Vasquez, R.N.; Phil Tulp, M.D., Chief of Neurosurgery.*

"You're probably a little scared right now," said Dr. Samuels.

"Fuck you," Petrov said.

"Did he say something?" said Mike Vasquez.

"I don't think so," said Phil Tulp, M.D., chief of neurosurgery.

Dr. Tulp? His name was Dr. Tulp? The red-stitched letters kept hiding in the folds of the white jacket, refusing to link together. Petrov hadn't been scared before. Now he was: the name did it.

"You're probably wondering what's going on," said Dr. Tulp.

But Petrov knew. It was a vast conspiracy. They were going to flay him alive.

"These pictures show you've had what we call a cerebral hemorrhage," said Dr. Tulp. "Just a lot of fancy talk for bleeding in the brain."

Petrov gazed at the pictures, saw fogs within fogs.

"We've got a little pressure building up right now," said Dr. Tulp, "not unusual in stroke cases. The plan is to go in there and relieve it, just as soon as we're set up in the OR."

"Never," Petrov said.

"Anyone catch that?"

"Nope."

Petrov tried to get up, couldn't move an inch. "Let me go," he said. "I made it all up."

"Did he say something?"

"Canning's confession," Petrov said. "What this is all about, what you're digging for—'I enjoyed every minute.' He never said that. I made it up. But he was guilty as sin and that butterfly woman—she's the type that feels sad when she should feel angry and she was going to hang the jury. How could I let that happen?"

"I can't make out a word."

"All set," called someone out of sight.

"Wheel him in."

"Wheel me in?" said Petrov. "That's not fair. I confessed."

Then he was on the move, the ceiling gliding overhead. A sign went by: ALARM WILL SOUND. Doors opened with a hydraulic hiss and it got very cold. He realized why Liza Rummel's face had seemed familiar to him: the mouth, with those full lips, was identical to Lara's. Why did he remember Lara's lips so well, as though they were lips he'd kissed?

Truth serum flowed into him. "Count to ten," someone said. Instead he spilled his guts on every conceivable subject and still had time left over to fall into a dream. A very nice dream at first, with Dmitri, Buster and a Frisbee. Then they went away. Gerald Reasoner showed up and started rooting around in his brain.

e just opened his eyes."

"How are his vitals?"

"Real good."

A face loomed up. "How do you feel?"

"Uh-huh."

"Feel okay? You did great."

"Uh-huh."

"Not in any pain?"

"Don'."

"Don't what?"

"Don' feel . . ."

"Don't feel any pain?"

"Uh-huh."

"Good. Can you wiggle your toes for me? What about the other foot? Awesome. How about your fingers? Other hand? Okay, but the other one, your right. Awesome. Feel this?"

"Uh-huh."

"And this?"

"Uh-huh."

"Nice. I'm Dr. Tully. What's your name?"

"You don' know?"

"I know. I just want to make sure you do."

"Uh-huh."

"So what is it? Your name?"

"Looks like he's drifting off. Here's the chart."

"You're right about his vitals."

"Like an athlete or something."

"He must've been strong. I'll be back tonight."

e felt no pain, hunger or thirst, just breathed. Filled his lungs with air and let it out, his function to pump air. It was peaceful, like being a . . . he didn't know what. A clam, maybe, a clam at the bottom of the sea. He was happy with that image until he realized he didn't know what a clam was. He just knew the word *clam.*

"His eyes are open."

A face. Woman. Black. Soft. Midthirties. Little white hat. Bright eyes. "Hey, Nick. How are you doing?"

Another voice. "It says not to use his name until Dr. Tully gives the okay."

"Oops."

"He's out in the hall. I'll get him."

He breathed, in and out.

A man's face came in view. "I'm Dr. Tully. Remember me?"

"Uh-huh."

"What's your name?"

"Nick."

"Awesome. What's your last name, Nick?"

He breathed. The black woman in the little white hat was gazing off in the distance.

"What about that last name, Nick?" said Dr. Tully.

"Mud."

"Mud?" said Dr. Tully.

"Uh-huh."

"Maybe it's a joke," said the black woman. "Like his name is mud."

"Uh-huh."

"Is it a joke, Nick?" said Dr. Tully.

"Uh-huh."

"That's pretty funny. But what's your last name really?"

"Looks like he's drifting off," said the black woman.

"But that's not a bad sign, remembering his first name," said Dr. Tully. "Considering the potential deficits. I'll be back in the morning."

He breathed. Someone squeezed his hand. It felt good. He tried to squeeze back, but wasn't sure he was doing it.

"You get some rest now, honey."

Honey. That was nice. It carried him away.

He woke up in darkness. What was honey? He tried to picture it and could not. Somewhere nearby a machine went *ping ping ping.*

"Help."

No one came.

He pumped more air, in and out.

"Some help here." No one came. Maybe that was better. He didn't want to be heard talking like that.

Nick drifted off.

Morning, Nick. Remember me?"

"Dr. T—T—T . . ." Nick tried to read the name stitched in red on his white jacket. The letters of the last name ran around on him for a few moments before settling down: T-U-L . . . L-Y. Phil Tully, M.D. "Dr. Tully," Nick said. Not a bad name. He'd expected something else, some name he didn't like, couldn't think why.

"No fair cheating," said Dr. Tully. "They got you sitting up a little, huh?"

"Yeah. Yes."

"Ate some solid food, it says here. What did you have?"

"Meal."

"What was in it?"

Nick remembered, could picture it clearly, a brown plastic tray with different foods, but none of their names would come.

"Was there toast?"

"Yeah."

"Cream of Wheat?"

"Uh-huh."

"Fruit cup?"

"Fruit cup."

"What's your last name, Nick?"

"He's drifting off."

"Nick. Try to stay awake. Open your eyes."

Nick opened his eyes. Dr. Tully pulled up a chair. "You must be wondering what's happened to you."

"Bleeding. Bleeding in the head. I'm going home later."

"Where do you live?"

He breathed.

"You're right about the brain hemorrhage, Nick. A little artery burst in there. We got it stopped and relieved the pressure."

"Thanks."

"Lucky it happened where it did. We got you in here pretty quick."

"Yeah. Yes."

"Remember where it happened, Nick?"

"In my head."

"I meant where you were when it happened."

"At the beach."

"What beach?"

"Where the surfers go."

"What's a surfer, Nick?"

"Um. Later."

"You're at St. Joe's, Nick. In Glendale. Remember how you got here?"

"Ambulance."

Dr. Tully made a note on his clipboard. "The problem now has to do with what we found to be the cause of the hemorrhage, what made that artery wall give."

"Don'—don't worry, Doc. Never happen again."

"We can always hope," said Dr. Tully. He put his hand on Nick's shoulder. His hand felt strong even though Dr. Tully was a little guy, not nearly as powerful as he was. "What made that artery wall give, Nick, was pressure from the outside. You had a tumor growing in there. It pushed against the artery until it tore the wall. We removed the tumor—as much as we could without impairing function. And the way you've got movement in all extremities and can converse so well are real good signs."

"Tumor?"

"About the size of a walnut."

Nick knew the word *walnut* but couldn't picture the thing itself. "Not very big," he said.

"It's all relative," said Dr. Tully. "This tumor was growing for some time. The location makes me wonder if any of your recent behavior has been uncharacteristic at all, not like you."

"Uh-uh."

"Any headaches?"

"No, sir."

"Nausea? Vomiting?"

"Uh-uh."

"Any changes in your sense of smell?"

"Tea."

"You smell tea?"

"Not now."

"What about your speech? Any confusion, saying strange things?"

"Uh-uh."

"Memory been acting up? Playing tricks on you? An example would be offering up images from long-forgotten times in your life, possibly when you were very young."

"Uh-uh."

"Or maybe mixing things up, being unreliable."

"My memory is . . ."

"Is what?"

"Um. Reliable."

"What's the last thing you remember?"

"Saying *reliable*."

"I meant the last thing before you ended up in here."

"Sitting down."

"Where?"

"In a box."

"A box?"

He breathed.

"Can you open your eyes, Nick?"

He opened them and said: "Witness box."

"Where was this?"

"Um. Later."

Dr. Tully made another note. "What do you do for a living?"

"Work hard."

"In what field?"

Nick knew *field*—green and spacious, like a meadow. "Out-doors," he said.

Dr. Tully leaned forward. Nick smelled coffee on his breath. "You understand what a cancerous tumor is, don't you, Nick?"

"All gone."

"Mostly gone," said Dr. Tully. "Some we couldn't touch be-cause of the risk. You were under for eleven hours."

"Be leaving after lunch." Nick tried to sit up higher so he could look around. "I've got boots on."

"Easy there."

Kept trying until he did. "Better pack my things."

"We'll come up with a treatment plan to go after what we couldn't cut out, immunotherapy or radiation, maybe a combi-nation. You may also be a candidate for monoclonal antibodies."

"Nice." Nick lay back, closed his eyes. "I want coffee too."

ten

Nick awoke in the night. The door was open; an oblong of light slanted across the floor, got reflected in a mirror in the far corner. Someone laughed in the corridor—the black soft-skinned nurse who'd held his hand. He recognized the sound of her voice. Had to be a good sign, recognizing her voice like that. He wiggled his toes, peered down at the end of the bed, saw them wiggling in the shadows, although not as energetically as they should have from the effort he was putting in. He wiggled them harder—instructed them to wiggle harder, at least—but they didn't cooperate. The toes on his right foot were especially disobedient.

Nick moved his hands around. He put them together, squeezed as hard as he could, tried to estimate his strength: not too bad. Be going home soon, maybe in the morning, hit the gym in a couple of days. He reached up and felt his head. Some kind of cloth all around, maybe a turban. The mirror glowed in the far corner.

He sat up. It took some time. His stomach muscles wouldn't do it on their own; he had to use his elbows, then his hands, levering himself up inch by inch, which was when he remembered the tubes in him, now all twisted. And then, finally sitting up, he couldn't see himself in the mirror. Why? The angle was right. It was as though he wasn't there.

A sheet covered his legs. He pulled it off. His right hand, despite its strength not being too bad, didn't feel like helping at the moment, so he used his left. He checked his bare legs: maybe not as powerful-looking as normal—possibly due to the bad light—but still plenty strong enough to support him. Nick swung them over the side of the bed. Not swung, exactly, more like he ended up inching them around.

There. He sat on the edge of the bed, feet hanging about six inches off the floor. Next would be to lower them and walk over to that mirror, see if he could figure out why it wasn't working.

Lowering his feet to the floor: how did that go? They didn't seem to be doing it. He was stuck there, on the edge of the bed. And starting to tip, for some reason, tipping toward the right. Had to stop that tipping, but before he could he'd fallen sideways on the bed, rolling onto his front. And voilà—his toes touched the floor. It was icy cold. He pushed himself to a standing position, his left arm a good and loyal friend, the right picking a bad time to screw up.

But he was on his feet. Mission accomplished. He felt much taller than before, his head now way up there, as though he were seven feet tall, instead of . . . Instead of what? Crazily, enough, for a moment, that statistic—his height—was missing.

Nick took a step toward the mirror. Something tugged him back. The tubes. He examined them, two tubes, one in the back of his left hand, the other coming out from under the front of this short gown they had him in, both of them attached to plastic bags—a clear one up high and a yellow one down low—on a nearby pole. A pole on wheels: this was going to work. But first, he had to raise the front of his gown and see where that second tube was coming from. Uh-oh. Pretty grim. Should have hurt like hell, shoved up his penis that way, but it didn't. In fact, he was pain-free, felt good. He let the front of the gown drop down, drew the pole up beside him, took a step toward the mirror—left foot first, his right preferring to drag behind for the present.

"Nick! What are you doing?"

The nurse was at the door.

"Going for a walk," Nick said.

"Don't be crazy." She hurried into the room. "We don't even know if you can—" She stopped herself.

"I'm up."

"You get right back in that bed."

"Not tired."

She put her hands on his shoulders as though to ease him back down. Nick liked her, liked those bright eyes and little white hat, but had no intention of getting eased back down.

She eased him back down; hands soft but amazingly strong. "Let me help get your legs up."

"No help," Nick said. Getting his legs up: a snap. He could do a hundred leg-lifting sit-ups anytime he wanted. Plus the stupid little gown: he didn't want her to see him like that. Nick raised his legs onto the bed by himself, maybe with the smallest bit of help from her. He lay down. She covered him with the sheet, laid a hand, so soft, on his forehead.

"How do you feel?" she said.

"Great."

"Changed your mind about visitors?"

"Changed my mind?"

"There've been people wanting to visit. You said no."

"I'll see them tomorrow," Nick said.

She patted his shoulder. "Good."

"At home," Nick said. "I'm checking out in the A.M. Better take the tubes out."

"Where do you live, Nick?"

"I've got a place."

"In L.A.?"

"Uh-huh."

"What part?"

He closed his eyes, felt her hand still on his shoulder.

"What's your name?" he said.

"Billie."

"Like Billie Holiday?"

"Yes."

"I love her," said Nick.

"Me too," said Billie. "What's your favorite song?"

"Of hers?" Nick couldn't think of a single one. He tried to open his eyes, but the lids were too heavy. "No visitors in the hospital, Billie," he said. "Do I have your word?"

He missed her answer, falling asleep so fast. His mind had a lot to do, needed him out of the way; he could feel it closing him down. Changing his mind was getting it backward. His mind was changing him.

Nick awoke. Dark; oblong of light falling through the doorway; silence in the hall. He sat up, pulled off the sheet, got his legs over the edge of the bed, tipped sideways—on purpose this time—felt the floor with his feet, pushed himself up. Nothing to it. He pulled the pole up close, untangled the tubes, walked across the room. Step-drag, step-drag, step-drag, and as he entered the oblong of light, someone appeared in the mirror, a man with bandages around his head. As Nick moved closer, out of the light, the man disappeared, but then, within touching distance of the mirror, he reemerged.

It was him, of course. He'd known it all along, had just been fooled by some superficial differences. Nick gazed at his face. Thinner than he'd expected, almost stripped down, and different from before in other ways he couldn't define at the moment, but that was him all right, the very essence, take it or leave it. He raised his hands, mostly just the left one, and unwound the bandages. Nick leaned toward the mirror.

No hair: they'd shaved him bald, a cool look on some guys. A horseshoe row of stitches curved across the left side of his head and over the top, some of them crusty with dried blood. Nick tried counting but there were too many and the light was bad. He ran his finger along the row, felt no pain at all. What was that on his finger? Sticky blood, but only a little, like a shaving cut. No cause for alarm. Then Nick did a funny thing: he gave himself a left-handed thumbs-up sign in the mirror. Mirror Nick did what real Nick could not: gave him a right-handed thumbs-up sign back. They grinned at each other, sharing the secret that the worst was over.

Nick looked around for his clothes, didn't see them. He opened a closet. His navy-blue suit hung inside. He touched it, felt the fabric. His eyes filled with tears, which was crazy. No reason for that. Here he was, up and walking. Nick wiped his eyes with the back of his arm—left arm—the tubes getting in the way a little, and took his suit jacket off the hanger. His finger snagged on the right sleeve. What was that? A hole, not round, more of a jagged rip, about an inch and a half long and a quarter of an inch wide. How had that happened? He felt his right arm, up by the side of the biceps, came across a hard bumpy patch, about the size of a quarter. Lifting his right arm up with his left, he gazed down, saw a scab. They must have been giving him shots. But through his suit jacket? That seemed pretty careless. He step-dragged toward the door, suit jacket in hand, thinking of sending it out for repairs. He didn't want to make a fuss, but the navy-blue happened to be his favorite suit. Nick knew that, although for the time being he couldn't picture any of the others.

A flat box hung on the wall by the door, papers inside. Nick paused. He got his right arm in the sleeve, pulled the jacket on—half on, the tubes getting in the way. He felt better, more properly dressed. A vague memory rose in his mind and vanished almost at once, so fast he didn't see a mental image, just knew the memory existed in there somewhere—a barefoot man wearing a suit and tie.

Nick took the papers out of the box. He read the name at the top of the first page: *Nick Petrov*.

Petrov. Nick Petrov. He said it aloud. "Nick Petrov." The sound was good. Address: *221 Cooper St., Venice, CA*. At that moment, the other suits came back to him: black, charcoal gray, medium gray, light gray. They hung in his bedroom closet at 221 Cooper Street. He could picture the bedroom, the kitchen, the stairs: the whole layout bloomed in his mind like a flower in time-lapse photography. A good sign. His recovery was going gangbusters; Nick didn't need a doctor to tell him that.

Diagnosis: Glioblastoma Multiforme, Grade IV. No mention of cancer or tumors, meaning they'd made a correction or he'd dreamed the little scene with Dr. Tully. What was worse than cancer? Nothing. Therefore this glioblastoma multiforme wasn't as bad, most likely referred to bleeding in the brain, *multiforme* no doubt meaning different parts of the brain, and grade IV was probably a good sign, the way a third-rate burglary wasn't much to worry about and grade A eggs were the biggest.

> *Treatment:* postcraniotomy—interstitial chemo,
> radiation, possible MAbs—to be discussed.

This had to be some lag in the paperwork, all that treatment unnecessary now the diagnosis had been fixed.

> *Prognosis:* The subject is a 42-year-old white male
> in heretofore excellent physical condition, but—

"Nick!"

He looked up. The nurse was back in the doorway. She'd changed her earrings—red before and now blue: a funny thing to do in the middle of the night. Billie—her name came to him just like that, his memory working beautifully—snatched the papers from his hand.

"What are you doing?" she said.

"Going home. I've got a place in Venice. The door is black with a brass handle."

"You're going right back to bed," Billie said, taking his arm and leading him there. "And not getting up again until Dr. Tully says so. You haven't even started physio yet."

"Don't need it," Nick said.

She tried that easing him down trick again. Nick was going to resist, give her a demonstration of his physical strength, but suddenly he felt very tired, as though his tank had gone from full to empty in an instant. He lay down, got his legs up and in position by himself, or mostly. Billie started tugging at the loose sleeve of his suit jacket.

"Stop that," he said.

"I'll hang it in the closet for you," Billie said.

"I'm wearing it," Nick said, closing his eyes. "Checking out at first light."

She left his jacket alone. Nick felt her watching him for a while. "It looks good on you," she said, her voice quiet. Her footsteps moved toward the door and out.

Nick opened his eyes. All clear. He sat up, using his proven method—elbows to hands, levering inch by inch. Then legs over the edge, controlled tip, feet on the floor, push up, and he was on his feet again. He disentangled the tubes, drew the pole up beside him, step-dragged to the box on the wall, took out the papers.

> *Prognosis:* The subject is a 42-year-old white male in heretofore excellent physical condition, but given the pathology (see attached) and advanced metastasis, life expectancy will probably conform to median survival times in like cases (17 weeks).

Metastasis was a word Nick had known most of his life, a word going way back in his family history to early explanations of what had happened to his mother. He put the papers neatly in the box and returned to bed, got back in, legs up without the slightest help from anybody. Nick lay in his bed. The liquid volumes in the two plastic bags changed slowly, growing in the lower one, diminishing above. He breathed.

i, Nick. Remember me?"

"Dr. Phil Tully, M.D., chief of neurosurgery."

Dr. Tully smiled. "How're you feeling?"

"Hundred percent better."

"So I hear. Word is you've been up and about."

"Just waiting for the tubes to come out and I'll be on my way," Nick said. "No sense taking up space someone else could use."

"We'll have to run some tests first," said Dr. Tully, "measure the extent of your deficits."

"What deficits?"

"Neurological."

"Don't have any," Nick said. "I'm just a little sluggish from lying around too much."

Dr. Tully went to the box on the wall, took out the papers, paged through them on his way back. "Know what day it is, Nick?"

"I'd have to think." But no thoughts came.

"What day did you come here?"

"Friday," Nick said. "The twelfth."

"How do you know that?"

"I just do."

"What can you tell me about that day?"

Nick closed his eyes. "I took out the trash. Then I worked at my desk until it was time to go to court."

"What court?"

"The county courthouse. I was testifying in a murder trial."

"What is it you do, Nick?"

Nick smiled. "Last name's Petrov, by the way," he said. "I'm an investigator, specializing in missing persons cases. I can also identify toast, Cream of Wheat and fruit cup by name, and know what a clam is."

"Clam?"

"Meaning I'm ready to go home."

Dr. Tully laughed. "You're doing great," he said. "How did you feel that day, Friday the twelfth?"

"Fine."

"Any headaches, nausea, dizziness?"

"No."

"Did you do anything unusual? Lose your temper for no reason, say? Act on an impulse you'd normally suppress?"

"No."

"Say any strange things?"

"No."

"What do you remember of your testimony?"

"I—" Nothing came to him, a blank void.

"Do you remember being in court?"

"Yes."

"What do you remember about being in court?"

"Swearing to tell the truth." Nick could picture the judge clearly and the flag hanging beside her.

Dr. Tully made a note. "Anything after that?"

"Smelling perfume from the previous witness."

"And then?"

Blank. Void. Oblivion.

"What's the next thing you remember after the swearing in?"

Nick thought for a long time before saying, "You." *Can you wiggle your toes for me?*

He watched Dr. Tully. Dr. Tully met his gaze. He had rare eyes, experienced and kind at the same time. At that moment, something very strange happened: Nick read his prognosis in those eyes. This had nothing to do with all those charts Nick had drawn early in his career, those facial expressions numbered from one to ninety-three. It bypassed rational analysis completely, was more like a new way of seeing, a brand-new sense. He closed his eyes.

"Tired?" said Dr. Tully. "Want me to come back a little later?"

Nick shook his head. Oblivion, how long had it lasted? How many hours had elapsed between the swearing in at the courthouse and entering the hospital? "What time was I admitted?" he said.

He heard Dr. Tully turning pages. "Four fifty-eight P.M.," he said. His voice got gentler. "Sunday the fourteenth."

Not hours, but two days, a whole weekend: gone. What had happened between swearing to tell the truth and wiggling his toes? Nick had no idea. For some reason that scared him more than anything. He opened his eyes.

Dr. Tully rose. "The good news is we'll be getting those tubes out today."

Nick didn't ask for the bad news. "And then I can go home?"

"Soon, probably Thursday. We have to discuss the treatment options first."

"What's today?" Nick said.

"Tuesday," which was about what Nick had expected, until Dr. Tully added, "the twenty-third."

eleven

Glioblastoma multiforme," said Dr. Tully, taking a chair by the bed. "You understand what that is?"

Nick sat up straight, demonstrating how much stronger he was getting in case Dr. Tully doubted his progress, and extended his right hand for shaking. Extended was maybe a slight exaggeration, but his hand was out there and up a little off the sheet. Dr. Tully gripped it. Nick gripped back, giving it all he had. "A form of brain cancer," he said.

Still holding Nick's hand, Dr. Tully nodded. "I've learned it's important to deal openly with the facts," he said. "We have a grading system for determining malignancy in primary brain tumors like GBM, based on microscopic analysis of cell shape, diffusion and—"

"How come grade four's the worst?" Nick said, his mood changing fast. "Why not grade one? It's misleading." He withdrew his hand. It flopped down on the sheet.

The expression in Dr. Tully's eyes changed; very slightly, but Nick's new sense kicked in again and he read it easily: *patient anger, predictable, appropriate.* "I hear you've been peeking at your chart," Dr. Tully said.

"It's got my name on it," Nick said.

"But all that information, out of context, can be pretty unsettling."

"Then give me context," Nick said.

Dr. Tully put his fingertips together; a gesture Nick first took to be thoughtful, then suddenly realized might be one of prayer.

"Start with the seventeen weeks," Nick said.

"That's the median," said Dr. Tully. "Every case—every person—is different. You're in good physical shape, comparatively young, a promising candidate for some of the weapons we've got nowadays."

"What weapons?"

"There's chemo," said Dr. Tully, "traditionally not much help because of the blood-brain barrier, but we've made a lot of progress in the past few years. In your case, we've started interstitial chemotherapy. That's just a term for disc-shaped wafers treated with a cancer-fighting drug called carmustine and implanted in the surgical cavity."

"I'm already on chemo?"

"Since the surgery," said Dr. Tully.

"I've got wafers in my brain?"

Dr. Tully reached into his pocket, handed him a thin, dime-size disc that felt like hard candy.

"How many?" Nick said.

"Seven or eight," said Dr. Tully.

"Which?" said Nick.

"I'd have to check the report," said Dr. Tully. "Any nausea, bleeding, pain?"

"No."

"And hair loss is moot, since we had to shave you for the surgery."

They shared a laugh about that. Dr. Tully had a full head of wavy brown hair, swept back at the sides.

"As for other potential side effects," he said, "the risks are no greater than the surgery itself."

Nick, still laughing a little, stopped. He tried to make sense of that last bit of news and could not.

Dr. Tully rubbed his hands together. "What I'd like to do now is hit those tumor remnants with some stereotactic radiation. It gives us the kind of precision we never had before, minimizing damage to good tissue."

"Good brain tissue?"

"Exactly. That's always been a big drawback to radiation, impairment of mental function."

"What sort of mental function?"

"It varies—speech, thought, memory, you name it."

"And this stereo thing"—all these new words were drifting away—"keeps that from happening?"

"Nothing's a hundred percent."

"And after?"

"After?"

"How many more weeks will I get?"

"No one can say," said Dr. Tully. "There's a whole range of survival times."

"What's the longest?"

"I've seen some amazing things," said Dr. Tully. "Years, even."

"And the shortest?"

"You've already exceeded it." Dr. Tully's beeper went off. He checked it, rose. "No rush," he said, "but that's my recommendation—stereotaxy on top of the interstitial chemo, with monoclonal antibodies in reserve, just in case."

"In case what?"

"In case the results are disappointing."

Nick looked down at his hands, so pale. The IV tube was gone but they'd left the capped needle in place, also "just in case." Pale hands, and a little different from his own, as though they belonged to a brother or cousin. Nick felt Dr. Tully's gaze on him and raised his head to meet it. He knew what he wanted from Dr. Tully. "Give me something to hope for," Nick said.

"That's easy," said Dr. Tully. "We'll hope that the treatment goes well."

With the back of his right hand, Nick brushed that answer aside. An incomplete gesture, the movement just a few inches from end to end, but it almost reminded him of something; he could feel a memory stirring, out of reach. "I need a target," he said.

"A target?"

Nick tried to find the right question, one Dr. Tully would understand the same way he did. "Of all the people who've come in here just like me," he said, "what's the longest anyone lived?"

"That's a tough one," said Dr. Tully.

"Six months? A year? Five years? Ten?" He heard his voice: like an irritated old man.

"More toward the lower end," said Dr. Tully. "But every patient—every person—is different, as I said." His beeper went off again.

"When do I have to decide?"

"How about rounds tomorrow?"

Nick nodded. Dr. Tully smiled before he went out the door, an encouraging smile but almost unregistered by Nick's new sense, which was looking for other things. No need to wait until tomorrow: he made his decision there and then on the basis of what it told him. "I'll just stick with the chemical wafers," he called, but Dr. Tully was already out of range.

Under the sheet lay a rubber ball Billie had found for him. Nick got his right hand around it and started squeezing; although squeezing might have been a slight exaggeration. He tried to remember how tall he was, and when he couldn't, stopped trying, hoping the figure would just pop into his mind. It did not. He squeezed the rubber ball. With his left hand he held on to Dr. Tully's wafer.

Commotion in the hall. Nick opened his eyes. Daytime. Light streamed in through the half-open venetian blinds, buttery bands of horizontal sunshine. Nick gazed at them: the world he lived in now had a different light, fuzzy, flat, feeble.

Out in the hall, Billie said, "No exceptions."

Another woman said, "I'll just be a minute. He won't mind."

"He will," said Billie. "You can't—"

A woman came through the doorway, Billie right behind. The woman had light hair and wore a gold star on her jacket; her skin glowed as though feeding off that sunlight force. He knew her, would come up with name and details if given a little time.

Her eyes took him in and almost concealed their reaction. "Hi, Nick," she said.

"Elaine," he said. The voice did it. A whole Elaine Kostelnik module sparked to life in his mind: how they'd worked together on the Reasoner case—that module too lighting up—their affair, Cabo, all of it. He remembered everything about her. "Your hair's different," he said.

Elaine laughed. "It keeps getting blonder. I don't know what's happening."

"I told her no visitors," Billie said.

"It's all right," said Nick.

Billie went out the door, narrowed eyes on the back of Elaine's head. Nick turned to her.

"Congratulations," he said.

"For what?"

Nick glanced at the gold star. Was he getting mixed up? Hadn't she made chief, the first female chief of the LAPD? "On being chief," he said.

"Hey," she said. "Enough's enough."

"What do you mean?"

"It's not like you to lay it on thick," she said, and laughed. "Not like you to lay it on at all."

She'd lost him. Maybe she saw it on his face, because she came to the side of the bed and said, "You already congratulated me, Nick."

"Um." Nick sat up straighter, tried with all his might to do it without that whole levering thing and almost did.

"When I called about the Canning verdict," Elaine said.

Ty Canning. Nick remembered: son of an office-park developer; trolled for girls on the Internet; had ended up killing one in what he called rough sex initiated by her; and hid out in Mexico until Nick found him and brought him back.

"What was it?" said Nick.

Elaine's eyebrows went up. "What was the *verdict?*" she said.

"Uh-huh."

"But I told you."

"Memory's still coming back," Nick said.

"What exactly happened to you?" she said. "There've been all these rumors."

"A little artery sprang a leak, but all fixed now," Nick said. "What was the verdict?"

"Guilty," Elaine said. "And your testimony was key, according to Eddie Flores. You don't remember me telling you that?"

Eddie Flores: the D.A. "Maybe the Eddie Flores part," Nick said, but it wasn't true. She was watching him closely. Elaine had tiny gold flecks in her irises; there seemed to be more of them than he remembered.

"I called from the car," Elaine said. "Just after six. Where were you?"

"Not sure," Nick said. They were in the lost time, between swearing in and wriggling toes.

Elaine's gaze rose to the bandages around his head. "I heard a lot of crashing-around noises, like you were opening and shutting drawers." Her eyes came back down to his. "Maybe conducting a search."

Nick could imagine himself opening and shutting drawers; other than that, nothing came to him. Someone knocked on the door. It opened and a big man in the uniform of a motorcycle cop—high boots, leather jacket—leaned in with an armful of flowers.

"Thanks, Tommy," Elaine said, taking them. Tommy had a

thick blond mustache; for some reason, Nick couldn't take his eyes off it. Tommy backed out, closing the door. Elaine brought the flowers to the bed, handed them to Nick. "For you."

"Thanks." The smell amazed him, like the atmosphere on some planet where beauty was all. He laid them on his lap.

Elaine sat on the edge of the bed. He could feel her hip against the side of his leg, round, supple, strong; so long ago, but he remembered the pressure of that hip. "Were you working on something?" she said.

"Uh-uh." He'd been free for the weekend, was sure of it.

"What did you do after the courthouse?"

"Went up to the lake," Nick said, and thought about it. "Must have."

"But you don't remember?"

His voice rose. "What difference does it make?" He'd let her hear the irritated old man. "Sorry," he said in a voice he hoped was more like his own.

"Nothing to be sorry about," Elaine said. "The main thing is the artery's fixed, right? You're okay."

"Hundred percent better," Nick said. "Looks a lot worse than it is. I'll be leaving any time, back on the job before you know it."

Elaine touched his hand. Hers was warmer, almost hot. "I wish I could jog your memory on that call."

"Why?"

"Wouldn't it speed your recovery?"

"It's already speedy," Nick said. "Stronger every day."

Elaine leaned forward, teeth shining, skin glowing, eyes bright, as though she had her own little sun inside her. Had she always been this vital? If so, why would he be noticing it now? The answer seemed obvious. He felt the force of what was happening to him: he was fading out, dematerializing, and despite his intelligence and physical strength, there was nothing he could do about it. That was the way it worked, of course, intelligence and strength eroding too, hobbling you in this last struggle.

Elaine lowered her voice. "Do you still hate me?" she said. He felt her breath vibrating in the air.

"I never hated you. Why would I?"

"Because of what happened between us." Her eyes went again to the bandages around his head, and this new sense of his gave him an idea of what was coming next. "You haven't forgotten those days too, have you?"

"Uh-uh," he said.

"I've been thinking about them lately," Elaine said.

"Thinking what?"

She leaned a little closer. "How intense it was."

"Oh, yeah." Their heads were close, the air thick with flower smells.

"What can I do to help you?" she said.

"I don't need any help."

She squeezed his hand, not hard, but it was the left one, and the squeezing dug the capped-off needle into his flesh a little; easy to overlook, the plastic cap translucent. "There's nothing wrong with leaning on someone when you need it," she said. Another knock on the door. Elaine let go. The door opened and the motorcycle cop appeared.

"The mayor," he said.

Elaine rose. "Nick, this is Tommy. Tommy, Nick." The men nodded at each other. "Nick taught me everything I know about investigations," she said.

"I remember the movie," said Tommy.

Elaine bent down, kissed Nick's forehead; her lips were as hot as her hand, maybe hotter. One of Tommy's jaw muscles jumped. "Get well," Elaine said. Then they were gone.

"Nice of you to visit." Nick felt tired right away. He lay back, the flowers scattering, but he didn't have the strength to do anything about them. Nice of her to visit: was it possible she still felt something? Why had she mentioned the intensity of those days? And what about them? He'd told her he remembered, but was it true? He thought back. The flower smell, heavenly, put him to sleep.

Petrov was alone in Cindy Motton's bedroom when Elaine Kostelnik walked in. "Hi," she said. "I'm the new guy."

They shook hands. Petrov's old partner had resigned, taking over the department in some little town in Idaho. His boss at the time, later indicted in an evidence theft scandal, had sent him Elaine.

She glanced around Cindy Motton's bedroom. Not much to see: the crime scene people had taken away almost everything— bedding, curtains, clothes, rug, phone. "Number three in a series?" she said.

"Unless he's got a clone."

"A he?" Elaine said. "Sure about that?"

"Women don't do this."

Elaine gave him a look; conflict from the get-go. With his old partner it had taken years. But then she surprised him. "I'll go along with that," she said. Her eyes went to Cindy Motton's bare mattress, blue with silver decorations.

"Want to see something?" he said. He pointed to where the pillows would have been. "Lift that button, third from the left."

Elaine pulled out a mattress button. "Feel around," Petrov said. She felt under the ticking, removed a little Baggie with something green inside.

"What's this?" she said.

"A shamrock," said Petrov.

"Crime scene missed it?"

"It's not important," Petrov said. "But the button was loose and I started fiddling around."

Elaine held the shamrock up close, actually went a little cross-eyed looking at it. "What's it doing in the mattress?"

"Cindy must have had Irish blood," Petrov said.

"What do you mean?"

"She put it there for luck."

"How do you know?" Elaine said.

"Just a guess," Petrov told her, although he knew. His own wife, Kathleen, had done the same thing in their own bed; but that was a private detail and he didn't share it.

"People are weird," Elaine said.

twelve

M ind if I try a little experiment?" said Dr. Tully.

Nick opened his eyes. He'd been swimming in his dreams, up at the lake, although there'd been oceanic kelp fronds right below the surface. "Don't see how we can squeeze it in," Nick said. Was that drool at the right side of his mouth? He wiped it away quickly. "I'm out of here today."

"Not for a few hours," said Dr. Tully. "In the meantime, how about watching this?" He held up a videotape. "I got it from Court TV—your testimony in that murder trial. This is an unusual opportunity."

"For what?"

"For a subject with memory deficit to actually reexperience one of the lost periods, albeit as a spectator."

"Will it bring my memory back?"

"I don't see why," said Dr. Tully. "But what we don't know about the human brain would fill a library."

"Today's still the day."

"Yes."

"Thursday."

"Friday, actually."

"But I'm getting out."

"Correct."

"For sure?"

"For sure."

"Then let's get started," Nick said.

A small room, cold and white. Nick lay in the tube.

"Functional MRI," said Dr. Tully. "Functional because it's monitoring neuronal firing, four images per second. While you watch—the TV's over there but the picture's reflected in this mirror right above your head—we'll be scanning your brain's reactions. It makes some noise so we'll have to turn up the TV volume. Any questions?"

"Are you writing a paper?"

"Depends on the results."

Billie stuck the Court TV tape into a VCR on the far wall, pressed a button. A voice said, "Do you swear to tell the truth, the whole truth, and nothing but the truth?"

The screen flickered to life. In the mirror, Nick saw his old self, wearing the navy-blue suit, right hand raised, holding it up strong and easy. "I do," Petrov said, and sat down in the witness box. He had thick dark hair, a light tan, muscles that moved under his jacket. There was no hole in the sleeve.

A man with a white mane of well-cut hair stepped into the picture. The defense lawyer: Nick remembered seeing him on TV from time to time, although his name wouldn't come. He had unruly eyebrows that reminded Nick of someone, but that wouldn't come either. The lawyer started asking questions. Petrov gave careful answers, offering nothing extra, in the manner of cops or anyone familiar with interrogations. But watching from under the MRI machine, Nick hardly listened to what was being said, absorbed by Petrov's movements, the sound of his voice, his confidence. As for his memory of this scene, he had none. It was all new.

New and mesmerizing. For one thing, it became clear that the two men despised each other on sight. Nick's new sense, this

feeling for tone, made it transparent. It was clear from the way
the lawyer looked up from his yellow pad, and the way Petrov's
gaze fastened slowly on his face.

"Been quite the career," said the lawyer, "hasn't it, Mr.
Petrov? So far."

"That's not for me to say," Petrov said. How strong his voice
was! And there was contempt too, well hidden.

"But it's what you think," said the lawyer. The lawyer felt
that contempt—Nick could see it from the way his lower jaw
came slightly forward—and let it get to him. "That you're the
sharpest tool in the shed."

"Is that a question?" Petrov said.

"Most definitely," said the lawyer.

"Do I have to answer it, Your Honor?" said Petrov.

"The witness will answer the question," said the judge, off
camera.

"I'm more like a leaf blower," Petrov said.

Lots of laughter. Nick laughed too: so daring, so unexpected,
yet not a bad metaphor for his work.

"You think this is funny?" said the lawyer, his fury plain in
the way he flipped through the yellow pad. Perhaps to recover
his poise, he asked for a reread from the transcript.

"Question," said the court reporter. "What did the defendant say on the ride back from Mexico? Answer: He said, 'You got
me.'"

"'You got me.' Sounds definitive. Practically an admission of
guilt." The lawyer turned dramatically to Petrov. "But in your
deposition of June eleven, you stated the defendant's words were
'What makes you think it was me?' Not an admission of guilt,
more like the aggrieved response of an innocent man. Now, remembering that you are under oath, which one of your answers
should the jury believe?"

Oh-oh. A trap. Nick hadn't seen it coming at all, started getting nervous; but Petrov did not. Nick could sense that confidence of his actually growing under pressure. "Both," he said.

"Both?" said the lawyer. "Are you aware of what would happen to your license if you put yourself in the position of giving false testimony?"

Petrov seemed completely at ease. "I am aware. In the deposition, I was asked only what the defendant's first words were— 'What makes you think it was me?' It was after I explained the leads I'd followed that he made the second remark—'You got me.' There was also a third remark, just before I turned him over."

Nick's memory awoke: not his memory of this testimony, still totally new to him, like watching a movie for the first time, but of the ride back from Mexico with Ty Canning handcuffed beside him in the front seat, the prisoner making those two remarks in that order, just as Petrov had said.

The lawyer looked wary. "Third remark?"

Watching from inside the MRI tube, Nick had the same question: what third remark?

Petrov answered it. "The defendant also said, 'I enjoyed every minute of it.' "

Ty Canning, seen from behind, rose and pounded his fist on the table. "The fuck I did," he shouted. Pandemonium. The camera closed in on him. Nick heard the sound of the judge's gavel banging away. An Autozone commercial came on. The MRI machine went silent. Billie switched off the TV.

Dr. Tully came in from the control room. "All done," he said. "What did you think?"

"Don't you already know?"

Dr. Tully laughed. "No test will ever tell us that."

"Touch wood," said Billie, taking the tape from the machine. Nick turned to her. Their eyes met for the first time in a way that wasn't about sickness.

"But I meant did it uncover any memories?" said Dr. Tully.

Nick shook his head. And there was one memory he really wanted to find, not from the testimony itself, but from that car ride: the memory of Ty Canning saying, "I enjoyed every minute of it." Something—this new feeling-tone sense—told him he never would. The feeling-tone sense was a kind of scanner, taking emotional MRIs, and it had read Petrov's face. Nick didn't want Petrov to have perjured himself, no matter what the reason. Maybe the scanner malfunctioned sometimes, and Ty Canning *had* made the third remark, meaning this was part of the memory problem. Strange, to be hoping that the memory problem was even worse than it was. But if not, if this wasn't part of the memory problem and Petrov had perjured himself, the next question was already waiting: what else about Petrov didn't he know?

"What was that, Nick?" said Dr. Tully.

"I didn't say anything."

Billie gave him a funny look.

Nick shaved with his left hand, did a pretty good job. The hair on his head was growing back, a fuzz that didn't seem quite as dark as his old hair but promised to be especially thick along both sides of his stitches, which he took for a good sign. He stripped off that horrible johnnie and dressed in real clothes—boxers, socks, shirt, his navy-blue suit, black shoes. Only the shoes and socks fit the way they had before, everything else too big. Nick's left hand did most of the work, but needed some shoelace help from the right hand, help the right wasn't quite able to give. Nick pulled the laces as tight as he could and tucked the untied ends inside the shoes.

"All set?" Billie called from outside the door.

Nick picked up his cane. "All set."

Billie came in, pushing a wheelchair.

"No way," Nick said.

"Liability," said Billie. "Sit."

Nick sat. Billie placed a shopping bag on his lap. "Postop care instructions, medications, prescriptions for when you run out, list of scheduled appointments." She wheeled him out the door.

An operating room gurney was parked just outside, a gray-faced kid lying on it, eyes shut, head bandaged, tube up his nose. An orderly with huge arms guided it into Nick's old room.

Down the hall, past the nurses' station, into an elevator. The people in it made room. The way they all towered over him sent a funny feeling down the back of his head and shoulders, a pre-cringing sensation. He sat up straight. A sign on the wall read RE-SPECT PATIENT CONFIDENTIALITY. Under it, someone had scratched *Or die!* Nick smiled.

Ding. The doors opened. Billie pushed him across the lobby. "I notice you don't wear a wedding ring," Nick said.

"That makes us two peas in a pod," said Billie. She halted near the doors. "Last stop."

Nick rose. He managed to bend his right elbow, slide the shopping bag up his forearm. "I don't know how to thank you," he said.

"That'll do," said Billie. She patted his arm. "Take care of yourself, Nick."

"You too," said Nick. He got the cane in his left hand and moved toward the doors, cane paralleling the motion of his right leg, too slow to be called a limp. But this was going to work: he was walking out. Nick felt a crazy surge of triumph.

The doors slid open for him, the first time in his life he'd ever been grateful for that. A young man stood on the other side: Dmitri. He saw Nick but looked right past him.

"Dmitri," Nick said.

Dmitri's eyes came back to him. They widened. He was shocked—Nick didn't need his new scanner to see that—and too young and inexperienced to hide it. "Dad?"

"Thought I'd try the shaved-head look," Nick said. He put his left arm around Dmitri, the cane dangling from his hand. Dmitri leaned into him, very slightly and with hesitation, but it happened. "Good to see you," Nick said. A simple little sentence: he'd never spoken one truer.

"I wanted to visit," Dmitri said.

"This is better." Nick let go. "You look great," he said, and Dmitri did—taller and stronger than he remembered, his adult face taking shape. "How's soccer?"

"What?"

"I said, 'How's soccer?'"

Dmitri's eyes shifted, as though he were connecting with an internal bit of information, some fact he'd been told. "The truth is I quit," he said.

"I'm surprised," said Nick. Dmitri played center half, had some nifty moves. "Do you miss it?"

"No," said Dmitri.

"Then you made the right decision."

"You think so?"

"That's a sign, not missing it."

"Yeah," said Dmitri. He gave Nick a long look.

They crossed the parking lot. The sun, finally shining on Nick's face, ended up being too strong. "Want me to take that bag?" Dmitri said.

"I've got it," said Nick. He saw his car, shrouded in a thin coat of dust. Dmitri took a set of keys from his pocket, Nick's keys. When had he last had them? He realized that arrangements had been going on around him, a good thing because he'd forgotten to think about them himself. "You're driving me home?"

"Didn't they tell you?"

"Yeah. Sure." They must have.

Dmitri unlocked the passenger door, opened it. Nick saw things on the backseat. Some were familiar: his leather notebook, the Thomas street guide, the Jussi Bjoerling live concert CD. Some were not: a volleyball, a black-and-white football team photo, another CD with a picture of a burning picnic hamper on the cover—*Empty Box: Retards Picnic*. He got himself inside the car, facing the right way, shopping bag between his feet. Beads of sweat had popped up on his upper lip. Nick felt them with unusual intensity for some reason, as though they were much wetter and heavier than normal sweat beads, but he was a little too tired at that moment to wipe them off.

Dmitri slid in behind the wheel. Nick thought of something. "When did you get your license?"

"Last June," Dmitri said.

"My memory's still coming back," Nick said.

Dmitri gave him a quick glance, turned away.

"What was that look?" Nick said.

"You never knew I had my license."

"How come?"

There was a little silence. Then Dmitri said, "I guess it never came up."

How was that possible? A kid getting his license was a big deal. Either it was a memory problem and Dmitri was protecting him from embarrassment, or there was something wrong with their relationship. All at once, details in support of number two came flooding into his mind. "How's your driving?" Nick said.

"Buckle your seat belt," said Dmitri.

Nick laughed; but had some trouble with the belt. Dmitri started the car. He turned out to be not bad, a little too cautious and a little too aggressive, both at the wrong times, but in control of the car. They got on a freeway, Nick wasn't sure which one. What was the route home? He wasn't sure of that either. The map refused to take shape in his mind, an image of the ocean welling up in its place instead. "Do you know the way?" Nick said.

"One-oh-one, four-oh-five, ten," said Dmitri.

The young Petrov, just the way he would have said it. Nick wanted to cry. He mastered himself, of course, but any tears wouldn't have been wholly sad. This was bigger: maybe only seventeen weeks to go, but some little part of him would continue, as the clichés promised. Even a stupid old sentiment like *passing the torch* had some truth in it.

"They're kind of like rivers," Nick said.

"Rivers?" said Dmitri. "I don't get it."

Some truth, maybe a very little. And seventeen weeks was the median. He had the wafers going for him, secreting a powerful chemical—the name gone at the moment—from the heart of ground zero, wiping out any cancer cell that dared raise its deformed head. Nick sat up straight, got a grip.

A car passed them. The driver waved and Dmitri waved back.

"You know that guy?" said Nick.

"Randy," said Dmitri. "That's how I got to the hospital. He'll take me home."

Randy: software guy, Kathleen's husband. He looked different, almost cool in some Hollywood way, with wraparound shades and slicked-back hair; long and full enough to be slicked back. A wretched question stirred in Nick's mind, a putrid little whine he didn't even want to recognize. Two words: why me? He hated that question, but an answer would still be nice. One answer—a god with mysterious ways—begged the question and thus provided no comfort, at least to Nick. Another answer: it wasn't just him. Nick gazed out the window, saw heavy streams of traffic flowing both ways. Urgent, purposeful, healthy-looking traffic, but how many of the people in those cars had cancer too, or other bad things? What was the median survival time out there? Chaos and order coexisted, as though the heavenly bodies circling in their timeless orbits were made of dice: sun, moon, earth, each a colossal die. Nick's reasoning might have been a mess, but that image of a dicey solar system calmed him.

Dmitri merged smoothly onto the 405. "Let's see your license," Nick said.

Dmitri's brow furrowed. "Am I that bad?"

"You're actually pretty good," Nick said. "I just want to check out the picture."

"It's terrible."

"They always are."

Nick looked at the DMV photo of his son. Dmitri had turned a very serious face to the camera. "Can I make a copy of this?"

"A copy of my license?"

"I've got a copier at home."

"But why?"

Nick didn't really know why. "I'd like it."

"Guess so."

Dmitri turned into Nick's driveway and parked. Nick opened the door by himself, with his left hand, got out all on his own, shopping bag and cane under control. Randy sat in his car on the street. Nick went over to him, leaning more and more on the cane. Randy's window slid down.

"Thanks for helping out," Nick said.

"Oh, hey," said Randy. "Kathleen couldn't be here—a meeting in Phoenix. And Nick? We're both sorry about how things went that last time."

"What things?"

"Everybody could have behaved a little better, yours truly included."

"When was this?"

Randy blinked. Dmitri, suddenly beside him, said, "His memory's still coming back." Dmitri gave Randy an impatient look, a look that told Nick they both knew the diagnosis. *Respect patient confidentiality. Or die!*

"Sorry," Randy said.

"No need to be sorry," Nick said, at the beginning of a complicated thought about some things—like whatever incident Randy had in mind—being better forgotten. "It sounds like . . ." He broke off, unable to make the sentence happen; heavy, supersaturated sweat beaded on his upper lip.

"Want to go inside?" Dmitri said.

Nick nodded. They walked toward the door. Two little steps led up to the flagstone path, steps that had always been there, of course, and he remembered them. Only their significance had changed. He got himself over them, reached the front door. Dmitri unlocked it. The first thing Nick saw was Dmitri's finger painting of a neckless boy and a furry dog with a huge red tongue. From out of nowhere came a name for that dog: Buster. It was good to be home.

Nick awoke in the night, in his own bed, hearing the sounds of his own house, feeling its feel. For a moment, probably some fraction of a second, he forgot what had happened to him, and this could have been any wakeful moment in the past decade. Living in the moment: a nice idea, especially if you could choose your moment and stay there. His stitches scratched against the pillow. Must have happened in the hospital too, but he hadn't noticed. Here at home it was very loud.

Nick got up, turned on the light. The sample wafer Dr. Tully had given him lay in the pocket of his suit pants. Nick drew back the bedsheet, pulled out a mattress button beneath the spot where his sleeping head would lie, and stuck the wafer inside. Carmustine: the name of the chemical came back. He liked the name. Carmustine, whole cavalries of carmustine, attacking in a pincer movement from under his mattress and inside his head, doubly blasting that glioblastoma, giving it a taste of, yes, its own medicine.

Nick picked up his cane, went out to the kitchen. He opened the fridge. Someone had filled it with food, but he wasn't hungry. He drank water at the sink. From there, he could see his car, parked in the driveway.

Nick emptied the hospital shopping bag, took it outside. He opened the car, filled the bag with things from the backseat—his notebook, the volleyball, the Empty Box CD, the football team picture—went inside and dumped them on his bed. A little out of breath, he cleared a space for himself and lay down, just for a minute, two at the most. He breathed.

Nick awoke, passed through that partial second of forget-fulness. The bedside light was on. Something hard pressed against his neck. Nick reached up, found it was his note-book. He opened it to the first page, and saw lines and lines in his own handwriting:

> i45ew dht5j2k fdk421 ejefrn e4jk 594 aqw5dd
> 2krfdf089 eoif[oi r3-034-409i porf o09er)
> d89wwhj!dk 4^fjri34 3euie45 ewujs9 r5h23jhd

Code. He remembered that he wrote all his notes in a code devised by himself but inspired by a suggestion from his father, thus probably related to practices of the KGB or even the NKVD. But the code itself, the key and how to translate it into English, the ability to decipher his own notes, was gone; as though some connection had failed. He'd lost more than a weekend. Nick ran his hand over the top of his head. Any more bad connections in there? Would he even know?

thirteen

ick woke up, this time not passing through that blissful partial second of oblivion, but rising instantly into full knowledge, *brain cancer* the first words in his consciousness. But he was in his own bed, and that was good. No complaints.

Not actually in bed, but on it, surrounded by the collection of objects from the backseat of his car: notebook, volleyball, photo, CD. With his left hand, he rolled the volleyball closer. There was writing on it in red ink: *Great season, Amanda,* and some signatures: *Tiffany Mattes, Jen Dupuis, Abby Cohen, BJ Tillison, Angie Garcia, Coach Betsy Matsu.* None of the names meant anything to him. Did he play volleyball himself or know anyone who did? Not that he remembered. The homely little phrase made him smile. Amandas? He knew none. Perhaps she was a friend of Dmitri's, and Dmitri had put the ball in his car for some reason. He made a mental note to ask him.

Nick sat up, elbows, hands—there. Daylight flowed into his room. He was naked. He gazed down at his body; so much wasting, so fast. And the hospital bracelet still hung on his right wrist. The sight angered him. He got up, grabbed his cane, went to the kitchen, cut off the bracelet. Then he opened the back door and threw it over the narrow strip of lawn and into the canal. The bracelet drifted away.

He went back to the bedroom, picked up the volleyball, read the names again. Another list of female names arose in his head. Janet Cody, Elizabeth Chang, Cindy Motton, Flora Gutierrez, Tiffany LeVasseur, Nicolette Levy, Lara Deems: the victims of Gerald Reasoner. Funny how the mind worked, hooking up those two lists of female names even though there couldn't possibly be any connection. Would Dr. Tully or someone else have it all mapped out one day at four images per second, a Thomas street guide to the brain? And then what?

Unless . . . was it possible that while some connections in his mind had failed, others were now better than before? Nick took his pills, drank a little water, tried to ponder that. But his mind wasn't in a pondering mood. It made another strange connection instead: he was going to share the first sentence of his own obituary with Gerald Reasoner. Made sense: if there turned out to be a God after all, the kind of God who added up the score, then one thing Nick had in the plus column for sure was solving the Reasoner case, the best thing he'd ever done. His only regret was not moving quickly enough to save Lara Deems. Nick blamed himself for that, even though there'd been so little time, Lara's murder following Nicolette Levy's by a single day while all the others had been at least two months apart.

It suddenly struck him that he was on a kind of death row too. Gerald Reasoner might even outlive him. A horrible and bitter thought. He imagined Reasoner hearing the news in his cell, and that hideous smirk of his. An ending like that was unacceptable. *I need a target,* he'd told Dr. Tully. Here was a target: to outlive Gerald Reasoner.

Nick wasn't hungry, but made himself eat half a yogurt and a banana. He had to stop the wasting, start building himself back up. Nick chewed the banana slowly, his whole eating system reluctant, even his jaw muscles weak. The taste and smell of the banana were strangely powerful. Some banana memory almost took shape in his mind. Nick sat motionless at the table and waited, but it didn't come. What he did remember was that he'd made a mental note about something. That wouldn't come either. A wave of frustration roared through him. Nick pounded the table as hard as he could, knocking the yogurt to the floor. A moment or two passed before he realized that his right hand had done the pounding. Now it lay motionless in his lap. He raised it, using his left hand a little to help, made a fist, tried again. What happened couldn't be called pounding, but it was more than a dead drop.

Nick went to the freezer. Whoever had stocked it had included Ben and Jerry's chocolate chip fudge ice cream. Nick never ate ice cream. Now he forced down half the carton, carried the rest back into the bedroom.

He picked up the football photo: *Desert H.S. Eastern Regional Champions.* High school boys—shot in black and white that had faded almost to sepia with time—sat in three rows, wearing full uniform except for helmets. Overhead, an inch or two from leaving the frame, a bird had been captured in flight. Nick gazed at the faces of the boys, now old men or dead, and at that bird, tail feathers angled up toward the sky. He decided it was a great photograph, a work of art, making a statement through the bird about the fleetingness of youth, a statement that would only grow stronger as the picture itself kept fading. Nick couldn't remember buying it, but understood why it must have appealed to him. He hung it on a vacant wall hook in the kitchen. The names of the players, down at the bottom, didn't interest him.

Nick sat at the table, started a list.

1. Stop the wasting.
2. Build back up.

Eating wasn't going to be enough. Building back up meant exercise. Swimming sounded right. Nick lived three blocks from the beach. He put on a bathing suit, T-shirt, sandals, picked up his cane. Plan: walk to the beach, swim parallel to shore for fifty yards—adding, say, twenty-five a day—walk home, eat. A good plan. But right now, a short rest. Nick lay down on the bed, a little worn out from opening and closing dresser drawers, getting clothes on right. The volleyball rolled off and bounced on the floor.

Nick swam for miles, his stroke powerful and effortless, the water bubbling by beside him, kelp fronds brushing his chest. He'd always loved swimming. Only the ring of the telephone stopped him.

He came up from sleep, groggy and confused. "Hello?"

"Dad? Did I wake you?"

"Uh-uh." He struggled up to a sitting position, saw he was wearing his bathing suit, a T-shirt, one sandal. "Just doing some exercises."

"Yeah?"

"Nothing too strenuous," Nick said. He heard laughter in the background. "Is that a party going on?"

"I'm at school," Dmitri said.

"It's a school day?"

"Monday," said Dmitri.

"It feels like Sunday," Nick said.

Silence. "You doing all right?"

"Doing great," Nick said. "How's—" He caught himself just before the word *soccer* came out, remembering he already knew.

"Better get going," Dmitri said. "I'm on my way to class."

"What subject?"

"Chemistry."

"That was my favorite," Nick said.

"I hate it," Dmitri said.

"So did I," Nick said, "till we got to octane."

"Like at the gas station? That's chemistry?"

"Get the teacher to explain it—you won't buy premium again."

"Hey," said Dmitri. "That's pretty cool. Bye, Dad."

At that moment, Nick remembered the mental note, the question he'd meant to ask Dmitri. "Don't hang up!"

"What's wrong?"

"The volleyball." Nick realized he was shouting, quieted his voice. "Did you leave a volleyball in the car?"

"No."

"What about Amanda?"

"Amanda?"

"Do you know any Amandas?"

"No." Pause. "Sure you're all right?"

"Don't worry about me," Nick said.

Nick walked to the beach, making good time at first, leaning heavily on the cane and step-dragging by the end. But he made it, and next time would be easier. There were lots of people on the boardwalk and a few on the sand, but Nick hardly noticed them, the sea drawing him on. He laid down his T-shirt, sandals and cane, step-dragged into the water, the waves breaking at his knees, waist and soon taking all his weight, lifting him free. His initial idea, swimming fifty yards parallel to shore as the first of his strength-building workouts, faded away. Instead, he started swimming straight out to sea, his left side doing most of the work, his right doing what it could.

Nick swam. The sea felt good around him, supportive and soothing, and the swell, like a giant pulse, raised and lowered him in an easy rhythm, almost hypnotic. Down below, kelp waved in the watery breeze. Would he ever feel this good again? Nick made a clumsy duck dive and swam down toward the kelp, his skin hospital white in the darkening sea.

He reached the tops of the kelp, kicked down into colder water. The fronds wrapped around him. Seventeen weeks: what was the point? On one side stood glioblastoma multiforme, the name itself terrifying, like Darth Vader or Attila the Hun; on the other side—wafers. To take control here and now would be perfect in its way, a nicely rounded amniotic conclusion. Nick looked up toward the surface, saw golden sparkles, their distance surprisingly remote. A beautiful sight, and life was full of beauty. But what made Nick change his mind, or snap out of it, wasn't life's beauty, or the idea of Gerald Reasoner outliving him, or, even worse, of Reasoner being the last thought in his head: it was the simple but overpowering desire to draw one more breath, an animal force that wouldn't let go. Nick kicked up toward the surface.

Or tried to. But he was shrouded in kelp and weak, even his left leg not much help. He thrashed and struggled, his body an uncoordinated windmill, losing control instead of taking it, dying without dignity.

The kelp let him go. Nick shot up into the golden glitter, broke through the surface, gasping, coughing, swallowing water and coughing some more. The swell rocked his body, quieted him. His heartbeat returned to normal. He breathed.

Nick swam in. It took a long time. Once or twice he slipped under, thrashed around some more, choked on seawater. Then the incoming tide took over and set him on the beach.

Nick lay there, too weak to get up, too weak to move. Two joggers went by on springy legs, their foot beats like drums in the sand. They didn't even glance at him, maybe thinking he was working on his tan. He spotted his things—T-shirt, sandals, cane—about ten feet away. The tide lapped around them, lifted the cane. Nick got up on his hands and knees, crawled across the sand, grasped it. With the tip in the sand and both hands around the stem, he tried to rise.

"Need some help there, buddy?" said a man passing by, trash bag over his sun-blackened shoulder.

"No," said Nick. He stood up.

He started back home. His five-limbed shadow led the way, growing longer and longer, its jerky rhythm fading slowly with the light. Bed was his only thought. He arrived and fell on it, his skin sandy and crusted with salt.

Nick breathed. Lying on his bed, he began to feel good—not stronger or less diseased, but good the way a drug might make you feel. The twilit room turned blue around him, and a blue tide rose in his mind. An optimistic sort of tide he half remembered; it had the power to drown unpleasant facts, like the second round of pills he should have taken, or possibly the third. Where were they? In the kitchen, but it hardly mattered, not when he was feeling this good. A sandaled foot down at the other end of the bed began a little dance, or spasm. Nick watched it for a while, then turned his attention to the far wall, where Elaine appeared, blown up and in soft blue focus, like a movie star.

It was hot from the start—from that first greeting, *I'm the new guy*—but Petrov didn't realize it right away. At first he thought it was the hunt for Reasoner intensifying everything, forcing them into artificial closeness, like soldiers in battle. He stopped thinking that the night after the discovery of Tiffany LeVasseur's corpse; understructure of the face carefully exposed. He and Elaine drove down to a medical supplies warehouse in San Pedro, following a lead that turned out to be useless. By then they'd been on the job for twenty-four hours straight. In the car on the way back, Petrov could smell himself, could smell Elaine too. He felt her physical presence with an intensity that began to separate from the Reasoner case. It pressed against him tangibly, even though she was in the passenger seat, two feet away; a pressure that would stay with him long after she was gone. Petrov glanced over, saw her nostrils were flared, as though she was doing some smelling too. She met his gaze. Passing headlights glittered on those gold flecks in her eyes.

"Tired?" she said.

"Not really."

"How about a shot of something strong?"

Nick awoke, his bedsheets scratchy with sand. The clock read 2:27, its glowing digits spreading a green pool of light in the darkness. He was cold. He felt around for the blanket, couldn't find it, rolled himself in a ball. Was his head properly positioned, above the wafer in his mattress? He shifted it slightly and was about to close his eyes when a beam of light shone down the hall, through the open door, and vanished.

A beam of light? Had he imagined it? Nick knew brain cancer could affect vision; the chemo probably could as well. He gazed down the hall. It remained dark. He closed his eyes. Sleep came for him quickly. Was he starting to live for sleep? Not good. He had to guard against all—

Something squeaked. Nick knew that sound, a sneaker sole on tile. Someone was in the kitchen. He sat up, got his feet over the side. Where was the cane? He didn't see it. Nick stood up, found he was still wearing his sandals, slipped them silently off.

He moved through the unlit house; not step-dragging—this was better, more like a limp. Through the archway that led to the kitchen, he made out a large dark form he couldn't make sense of at first, then realized it was a man bent over the counter. He heard a drawer open. A light flashed on, shone in the drawer, illuminating the man's hand, covered in wiry blond hairs, rooting through matchboxes, tape, paper clips.

Nick remembered his gun, locked in the safe upstairs. "What the hell do you think you're doing?" he said.

The man spun around, aimed the light in Nick's eyes, took off toward the back door. With one big spring from his good leg,

Nick half-dove, half-fell across the floor. His left shoulder caught the man behind the knee. He went down. Nick crawled on top of him, got in a good left hand that crunched something bony, like nose. The man grunted in pain, swung the flashlight. Nick raised his right arm to block it, but so slowly. The flashlight struck him on the side of the head. Not hard enough to knock him out, or even hurt much, but it disconnected him from this sudden surge of strength. He toppled over. The man scrambled away, bolted out the back door. Nick heard his running footsteps on the grass by the canal, and not long after, the cough of a motorcycle engine coming to life. It droned away, out of hearing.

Nick got up. He switched on lights. One pane of glass in the back door, closest to the lock, was broken. He searched the room. Nothing was missing except the old Desert High School football team photograph. Was it valuable? Nick had no idea. But to be robbed in his own house: intolerable. He wasn't dead yet. Some vulture had come a little early.

Vulture: he stopped right there.

fourteen

Nick wasn't dead yet. He told himself that as he lay on his bed for hours, too wiped out to move. "Not dead yet." But he needed sleep, and every time his eyes closed a red three-toed foot with black talons came into view, accompanied by a dull pain in his right biceps, even though his right arm hadn't been feeling much of anything lately. And he'd open his eyes right back up.

After a while, he noticed that night was over. Daylight filled his room, heavy and yellow, almost a solid, as though you could weigh it. Nick had seen that kind of light once before, in the funeral home where his mother lay. How could he have a memory from so far back? Agitation—an invalid's agitation that he despised but couldn't quell—overcame fatigue; vultures, his mother, breast cancer, brain cancer, all spun through his thoughts.

Where was his navy-blue suit jacket? Hanging in the closet. Nick levered himself up to a sitting position—his strength not quite there, the recovery backsliding a little, but only because he was so tired—found his cane at the end of the bed, got to the edge, pushed up.

Minor dizziness; could have happened to anyone. Nick fell, but backward, safely onto the bed, totally in control. Dehydration caused dizziness: that was pure science. He formed a sensible, well-thought-out plan, all about going to the kitchen, getting a glass from the shelf, filling it with delicious spring water from the cooler. He could almost taste it. But first, a little sleep.

Nick awoke. Still daytime, but the light was back to normal, that suffocating living-dead heaviness all gone. He felt tip-top, got right out of bed with no trouble, or hardly any. The navy-blue suit hung in the closet. He examined the hole in the right sleeve, a jagged rip that a steel-tipped fingernail might make. In the mirror, his right biceps bore a faint but matching discoloration. A memory fragment of a furnace-red sun pulsating over empty desert came to him, but maybe it was a memory from movies instead of life, because his only desert experience had been driving to Las Vegas; to his knowledge. And to his knowledge, he'd never been bitten by a vulture.

He went into the kitchen, leaned his cane against the cooler, drank three glasses of water. Water equaled life: Nick could feel it on his tongue. He called the hospital and got Billie on the phone.

"Nick?" She sounded a little breathless, as though she'd come running. "Are you all right?"

"Doing great," Nick said. "Did you give me any shots while I was there?"

"I don't think so—you were on an IV."

"What about in the emergency room?" Nick said. "Like maybe right through my sleeve."

"Through the sleeve?" Billie said. "That wouldn't happen. What's wrong?"

"This hole in my navy-blue jacket," he said.

There was a long pause. "How about if I drop by after work?" Billie said.

"That would be good."

Nick shaved, showered, put on clean clothes, tightened his belt to the last notch, still needing one or two more. But from certain angles, he looked the same as always, or pretty close. And his hair, growing in thicker now: not as black as before, but you couldn't call it gray. He was standing in front of the mirror, cataloging all the healthy angles, when he thought she might arrive hungry. How about pretzels? He set a bag on the table.

But maybe actually making a snack would be better. Nick didn't do much cooking, had only one cookbook, *The Cheap and Speedy Gourmet,* which he finally found under the Cuisinart attachments, never used. He leafed through, found a recipe that looked good.

"What's this?" said Billie when she saw it. He'd been showing her around the house, came to the kitchen last.

"Bulgarian guacamole," Nick said. He had it in a bowl on the table, a yellowish paste with olive lumps poking through here and there.

"Looks . . . homemade," Billie said.

"You put it on these corn chips," said Nick.

Billie dipped her finger in the bowl, licked it off. "Hey," she said, "not bad."

Nick felt a kind of crazy pride. "Something to drink?" he said.

"What have you got?"

Drinks. He kept them . . . where? Cupboard over the sink. Nick opened it, found a half-full bottle of Johnnie Walker Black up front, various dusty bottles in back. "Scotch all right?"

"Never tasted it," said Billie. "But I've never tasted Bulgarian guacamole either, and that turns out to be pretty good."

Nick poured two small glasses. "Here's to you," he said.

Billie took a sip. "Very nice," she said. "Course bourbon's a different story—I down a fifth every night."

Nick laughed. They sat at the table, dipped corn chips in Bulgarian guacamole, drank scotch. With a little sigh, Billie stretched her legs, strong, well-shaped legs, and not as heavy as he would have thought. The nurse's uniform was misleading.

Billie still wore it, minus the white cap. He hadn't seen her hair like this, tied in about a dozen braids with little white balls at the ends. The clicking sound they made in time to her movements was lively and soothing at the same time. Their eyes met.

"How are you feeling?" Billie said.

"Better and better." Nick dipped another corn chip in the bowl, ate it with a show of appetite.

"Dr. Tully wants you to have radiation."

Nick emptied his glass, poured more. "No point," he said, "with how well I'm doing. Besides, I've been reading. Radiation messes with your faculties."

"That's where the stereotaxy comes in," Billie said. "Dr. Tully's an expert. People come from all over—"

At that moment, Nick did something bold, taking a huge chance; but if not now, when? To silence her and all this talk of further maneuvers inside his brain, he put his index finger lightly to her lips. Way too soon for a gesture like that, plus she might easily take it as sexist or racist, but this new sense of his gave the green light. Billie's eyes narrowed, the skin around them going a little gray, a look he thought of as pure Africa. And a definite red light; maybe this new sense didn't work across the racial gap. But then her eyes softened. Yellow light. And grew amused. Green.

"Next you're going to tell me this reading of yours happens on the Web," she said.

"What if it does?"

"I'll send you some proper information," Billie said.

"Won't change my mind," Nick said. "What's left of it."

Billie burst out laughing, spraying scotch across the table. She had one of those laughs that was easily caught; Nick started laughing too. Tears ran down their faces.

"That's the paradox with brain cancer," said Nick. "Just when you've got all these life-and-death decisions to make, your mind gets screwed up."

"I've seen it a thousand times," Billie said, a remark that

should have frozen him; but she was still laughing and so was he, and now they just laughed harder, almost doubling over.

They sat back in their chairs, gasping. "Whew," said Billie, dabbing her eyes. "I needed that."

"Me too," said Nick. They glanced at each other, like adventurers who'd just come through something big together; at least that was how Nick took it. He poured a little more, caught her looking at him again. "What do you like to do?" he said.

"For fun? Nothing special. Going to the movies, dancing, the usual."

"You're not married or anything like that?"

"Wouldn't be visiting in a man's home if I was."

"Kids?"

"Someday."

"How about a movie?" Nick said. He hadn't been to one in years, but dancing was out.

"Now?"

"Why not?"

They went to the movies. The nearest theater was only two blocks away; Nick hardly had to use his cane. The picture was a comedy about a frat boy who wins a Rhodes scholarship by mistake and ends up as an advisor to the queen. For some reason, it wasn't funny, but Nick had a good time anyway until the Prince Charles character entered the hospital for a hemorrhoid operation.

"I hate hospital scenes," Billie whispered. Their forearms were just touching on the padded armrest.

The prince ran screaming around the operating room, chased by doctors, his kilt flapping high. Nick heard other people laughing, but the prince's terror seemed real to him. After that, he wasn't sure how to take the movie and couldn't wait for it to be over.

They walked back, Billie's uniform glowing in the night. "Do you hate detective movies?" she said.

"Not the ones with Peter Sellers," said Nick.

"I saw *The Reasoner Case* a few days ago."

"Where?"

"It's on cable sometimes."

"I didn't know."

Billie glanced at him. "Was that Elaine the same one who visited at St. Joe's?" she said. "The chief of police?"

"Yes," Nick said.

"They were pretty hot together, Kim Delaney and Armand Assante," said Billie. "Kind of surprised me."

"The writers made a lot of changes," Nick said. Although that heat part wasn't one of them. "The Elaine thing was over long ago. Also my marriage." Cut from the movie, Nick realized, the way he cut it from his life; Hollywood quick to carve the story down to its essentials.

Billie nodded, said nothing.

The way he cut it from his life: that was probably Kathleen's view, but Nick himself had never thought of it like that until now. Kathleen and Hollywood were right. He was surprised. This new kind of connection, plus the feeling-tone sense: two indications that this mind he had now might be superior to the old in some ways.

They came to Billie's car.

"Nightcap?" Nick said.

"Better not," Billie said. "I'm on at seven."

You could tell a lot about people from their cars: that had always been part of Nick's technique. Billie drove a bright red Camaro with a bumper sticker that read: IF YOU CAN READ THIS YOU'RE TOO DAMN CLOSE.

"But you haven't seen the jacket yet," Nick said.

Billie gave him a look from the corner of her eye. "With the hole in it?"

Nick took her inside to look at it. Billie held the jacket in her hands, stuck her finger in the hole. "See?" Nick said. "How did that happen?"

"I know a good tailor," Billie said.

Getting it fixed: maybe that would ease his mind, let him sleep. "Okay," he said.

Billie emptied out the pockets. There was nothing in them but a business card. Billie got that amused look on her face again and handed it to him, a white card with pink writing and a female silhouette wrapped around a pole. *Candyland Escorts.*

"You don't seem like the type," she said.

"I'm not," said Nick. "I don't know anything about this."

"That's what they all say," Billie said.

"But I mean it," Nick said. "How the hell——" And then he saw that she was teasing him.

"You look about ten years old right now," she said, and gave him a quick kiss on the cheek. Nick dropped the cane—the only way to free his left hand, the one that did what he wanted—grabbed her around the waist and kissed her on the mouth. Billie kissed him back, didn't hesitate. For a moment, everything except that connection disappeared.

Billie stepped back. She didn't say how crazy this was or that they should think it over or that she wanted some space. She said, "That felt good."

He walked her to the street, had completely forgotten the cane, and didn't limp at all; he was positive of that.

"Don't forget your meds," she said, unlocking the Camaro. "Especially the anticonvulsants."

"Nice car," Nick said.

"This?" She glanced at it with disdain. "It's a loaner. Mine's in the shop." Her hair beads clicked a snappy little percussion as she got inside.

3 ack home, with the jacket gone for repair, Nick felt a little better. That lasted ten minutes or so. Then he found himself staring at the wall hook in the kitchen where *Desert H.S. Eastern Regional Champions* had hung. Robbed in his own house. He

went to the back door, reexamined the broken pane. Simple to see how the thief had smashed the glass and unlocked the door from inside. Broken shards lay scattered on the tile. It must have been noisy. Therefore the thief had thought the house empty, or hadn't cared. Who wouldn't have cared? A drug addict, desperate for something salable. Anyone else? He tried to think. His mind didn't want to think, at least not this way. It wanted to make connections about vacancies: the missing windowpane, the hook with nothing on it, the hole in the navy-blue jacket, the space inside his brain now filled with seven or eight wafers, Dr. Tully hadn't specified which.

Filling up the empty spaces: that was what he had to do. Navy-blue jacket—on its way to the tailor, check. Windowpane. He found some duct tape, taped it over. Check. Hole in the brain—wafers, check. That left the football picture. He wanted it back. Was it valuable? He had no idea, but doubted it was easily converted to cash. If not a drug addict, then . . . His mind writhed away from working this out.

"Think," he said, gazing out the back door; a gull flew down from the sky, a winged shadow, and splashed softly in the canal. "If not a drug addict, who else . . . Who else what? Who else wouldn't care about making noise? Someone who thought the house was empty. Right. You got there already. Or . . . Think." Nick must have raised his voice, scaring the bird. It rose in a quick jerky motion and flapped away.

"Or someone who knew there was an invalid inside." Zonked on medications.

There. He'd followed a logical chain to its end. Had to keep doing it over and over until all the neurons were robust, all the old pathways rebuilt: brain work.

Nick found his notebook, leafed past those maddening coded pages to a fresh one. His mind needed organizing. A list would help. What to write at the top? Nick saw he'd already written something.

1. Stop the wasting.
2. Build back up.

He added:

3. Brain work.

Nick turned to the next page. After a while, he wrote at the top: *Remember.* Under that heading, he began a list of everything he didn't understand.

Photo—Desert High School
Volleyball

He paused. Whose volleyball was it? Amanda's. He added:

Amanda

And something else about her, a subfact. It came to him.

Amanda—no connection to Dmitri.

He kept going.

Candyland card
CD

What was the name? That wouldn't come. He went into the bedroom, brought it back.

CD—Empty Box
Hole in jacket
Vulture

What else? He couldn't think of anything. Seven items on the list. Did they add up to some meaning? If so, was it a meaning his old self, the confident and brilliant Petrov, could have explained easily? Nick was sure of it. But now, the meaning of those seven listed items was gone, had fallen into the hole in his brain. That hole cried out for repairs. Was filling it up, finding those lost meanings, discovering what he'd been doing, a way of getting well?

Nick liked that idea. A specific kind of brain work, and a far better route to wellness than anything contained in these meds, lined up on the kitchen counter. All they did was confuse him. He got up and dropped them in the disposal. The furious sound it made grinding them up was great.

Nick poured himself one more glass of scotch, just a little one, and gazed at the list. *Organize.* What went together? The last two items, *vulture* and *hole in jacket,* for sure. And . . . and what? Vultures went with *desert* too, as in *Desert High School.* Nick wondered where it was.

fifteen

Desert High School, thought Nick. It had to be somewhere. On the other hand, maybe not: the picture
had looked old, raising the possibility that the high
school was now closed, demolished, a parking lot. And where?
Desert could mean California, but also Nevada, Arizona, New
Mexico. He needed to organize his mind. Nick found an envelope and listed the four states in alphabetical order. That was as
far as he got.

He went into the bedroom. The Candyland Escorts card and
the Empty Box CD lay on the bureau. He hunted around for the
volleyball, found it under the bed. Three—what would you call
them?—artifacts, like archaeological discoveries from a lost civi-
lization. Nick laid them on the bed in the form of a triangle.
Should really be a square, he thought, the fourth corner, the football
photograph, now missing. He tried to make sense of what was
left, touching the objects, changing their positions, hoping in
some random way to expose a connection.

This was all about connection, specifically the connection
between those last undamaged moments of what he now
thought of as Petrov's life and the beginning of Nick's. He'd
sworn to tell the truth, whole and nothing but. Then Dr. Tully
had loomed up and said, "You must be wondering what's happened to you." In between stood the lost time, like some dark
forest in a fairy tale. What went on in the lost time? He'd testified

in the Ty Canning trial, had memories of that, but all second-hand, from Dr. Tully's Court TV tape. And he'd accumulated these objects. Plus the football photograph, not merely gone or missing, but stolen.

Did he have any memories at all from the lost weekend? No memories that could be called complete, merely fragments, and only two, both strange. The first was the vulture, specifically those taloned red feet, and the stab of its beak piercing his arm. The second was a man sitting on a bed. The man wore a suit and tie but his feet were bare. Some details were clear—sharp crease in olive-colored suit pants, thick, yellow toenails. Others, like his face, were clouded over. Had Nick seen this man in real life? What kind of detective remembered toenails and not faces? But that wasn't fair. Nick didn't doubt that Petrov remembered the man's face. It was Nick, now in charge, who'd lost it, like a computer illiterate wiping out files by mistake.

But two memories were better than none. Two memories plus three objects equaled five clues. Six, including the photograph. He wanted that goddamn photograph. And the thief? Nick wanted to hunt him down, bring him in, hold him accountable; wanted to do his job. The motorcycle had made a throaty sound, like the roar of a departing predator.

Motorcycle. Another clue. He wrote it on the envelope. It now read:

> volleyball
> CD
> Candyland
> (Desert High pic)
> vulture
> barefoot man
> motorcycle

Plus the names of four desert states; the actual penmanship in each case a little wobbly and childish, executed with his left hand, the right, coming along nicely, still not quite capable of fine work.

And hadn't he made another list? If so, where was it? He went from room to room. He gazed at Dmitri's finger painting of the boy and the huge-tongued dog, Buster. When did he start thinking of the dog by that name? Why? And now, distracted by Buster, he'd forgotten what he was doing. Nick racked his brain. "Think," he said aloud. He was back in the kitchen, fourth or fifth time through on this limping journey. His eyes lit on the notebook, resting on the counter; how had he missed it? He flipped through the coded pages, all lost, like the language of Minoa, and found the second list at the end.

> REMEMBER
> photo—Desert High School
> volleyball
> Amanda
> Candyland card
> CD—empty box
> hole in jacket
> vulture

Nick placed the two lists side by side, felt a tension between them, almost magnetic. If only, if he could just . . . think what to do. There had to be some obvious next step and if he didn't find it soon he was going to die, not from anything exotic like glioblastoma multiforme but simply from stress, anxiety, sleeplessness. His mind needed organizing. He had to find something it could do and then do it.

Where was Desert High School?

Yes! A question, and the right one. Had it already come to him, once before? He thought so. But déjà vu was also a possibility, as were partial vu, almost vu and should-have vu.

Stop, Nick told himself. Wasting time was now a sin. He had to organize his mind. Concentrate. Think.

Where was Desert High School? In the desert. And where was the desert? His thoughts seemed to have passed that way already, for there on the envelope were the states, in his blocky left-handed script: *Arizona, California, Nevada, New Mexico.*

Were there Desert High Schools in any of those states? Some? All? How could he find out? The mental effort was exhausting him. His eyes started to close, inexorable as bank vault doors on a timer. He didn't have the strength to get up. His head sank down on the kitchen table. Would sleep erase all this mental work, forcing him to start over? Nick still had the pen in his left hand, but the envelope and notebook lay out of reach. He wrote on the varnished oak surface of the table: *Desert HS—where?* The question mark trailed away in a long blue streak.

Nick rose up from way down, a plantlike sleep, rooted in rich earth. A wooden knocking sounded in his ear. At first he thought it came from the table where he found himself half-sprawled, drool puddling against his forearm. Then he realized there was someone at the door.

He pushed himself up, got his feet steady. More knocking. Where was the cane? Nick didn't see it. He made his way into the hall, his stride more fluid with every step. Just a little stiff from sleeping, that was all. The truth was he was gaining strength every day. Nick opened the door.

A beautiful woman in a black minidress stood outside, hair up, jewels around her neck. "Elaine?" Nick said.

"Expecting someone else?" she said.

"I wasn't expecting anyone." He gazed at her, had never seen her look this good, or even close.

Elaine was looking at him too. "Your nose is bleeding," she said.

Nick touched his upper lip, held his fingers to the light: red. The sight confused him.

"Good thing I dropped by," Elaine said, taking his arm, leading him inside. "I happened to be in the neighborhood." She led him to the kitchen, tore off a strip of paper towel, started dabbing his face.

"I'll do it," Nick said, taking it from her.

"You should lie down."

"It's just a nosebleed," Nick said, although he couldn't remember having one since his boxing days.

"The treatment for nosebleeds is lying down," Elaine said.

Nick went into the living room and lay on the couch, paper towel pressed against his nose. Elaine pulled up a chair. "How're you doing?" she said.

"No complaints."

"You've got a nice place here."

"Thanks."

"You're going to need more paper towel."

She brought some from the kitchen. "What happened to your back door?"

Back door? For a moment, the question made no sense. Then he remembered, put it all together, filled in the blank: she'd seen the duct-taped window. "Just a little accident," Nick said. Intolerable for Elaine, of all people, to know he'd been robbed in his own house.

She took the bloody paper towel, handed him more. "Looks like it's stopping," she said. "What kind of accident?"

"Careless," Nick said. Elaine glanced at the top of his head, where the hair was growing in just fine, although no longer 100 percent black. "You're all dressed up," he said.

"Fund-raiser over at Loyola Marymount," Elaine said. "I've got something almost every night."

"You like it?"

"Fund-raisers?"

"Being chief."

Elaine smiled. "I love it."

Nick could see that she did, the word *love* no exaggeration in this case. The pleasure of it came surging off her. He could smell her, too; sex and power coming together in one body.

"You're going to be the best they ever had," Nick said.

Elaine didn't say *It's way too early for thoughts like that* or *I've got a lot to learn.* She said: "That won't be hard." A spaghetti strap slipped off one shoulder.

"And then what?" Nick said.

"After this gig?"

Nick laughed. "Yeah."

Elaine's nose narrowed in a cagey way he didn't remember from before. "I've got a few ideas."

"Like what?"

"Still Mr. Inquisitive," Elaine said. "You'll just have to wait and see."

The remark stunned him. Everything went pale and he understood, completely and irrevocably, that the world would go on—squirming with detail—without him. On her face and in her tone lay no sign of any double meaning, any knowledge of how someone with his prognosis might take that little commonplace sentence; and how would she know the prognosis? Therefore: an innocent remark.

"That's a deal," Nick said. He took the paper towel off his nose. The bleeding had stopped.

"All better?" Elaine said.

"Yup."

"How's the convalescence coming along?"

"Very fast."

"When'll you be getting back on the job?"

"I've already started."

"Yeah?" said Elaine. "Working on anything interesting?"

"You'll just have to wait and see."

Elaine went still. "I don't get it."

"A little joke," Nick said.

"How so?"

Nick started an explanation, all about how she'd just used the very same sentence and it seemed funny to him to be turning it right back on . . . but somewhere in the middle, sleep surrounded him like a sudden fog, and he lost control of all his conscious faculties.

"Nick? What will I have to wait and see?"

He couldn't get his eyes open.

"What are you doing?"

"Just can't open up."

"You want to sleep?"

"Uh-huh." His little joke seemed to have irritated her, but there was nothing he could do.

Long pause. "I'll get a blanket."

Elaine moved away.

"Where'd you go to high school?" Nick said. What a question, popping up out of nowhere, complete nonsense. Her footsteps stopped.

"What did you say?"

But he was falling, falling, into blissful sleep. He heard her coming closer, standing over him. "What was that about high school?"

Rude not to answer, but he couldn't open his eyes, also had no sensible response. Her footsteps faded again. He heard her wandering around the house. The sound was comforting. He could imagine that the intervening years had gone differently and they'd ended up together, everything turning out better.

One: stop the wasting. Two: build back up. Three: what was three? It wouldn't come.

The door to Nicolette Levy's house in Culver City stood ajar and Petrov hurried inside. She lay in the bathtub, eyes open, the crime scene photographer kneeling on the mat. Number six: that was clear at once. This time the killer had flayed nothing but the left breast, a careful incision starting about an inch below the collarbone, passing through the nipple and making a right angle, allowing the skin to be pulled back, exposing the underlying tissue. Petrov saw no other wounds, but with all the blood he couldn't be sure.

"Shift that light for me, Nick?" said the photographer.

Petrov shifted the light. The movement must have released some molecules into the air: he could smell Elaine's smell, on him from the night before.

"Can you believe the Lakers?" the photographer said.

Petrov backed out of the room. He walked through Nicolette Levy's apartment. Framed movie posters hung on the walls—*Breakfast at Tiffany's, Dr. Zhivago, Rear Window, The Yellow Rolls-Royce, Working Girl.* A bowl of M&M's sat on the coffee table in her living room; beside it, a photo album with "Xmas, Maui" written in purple ink on the front. Petrov put on gloves, opened the album.

Nicolette in big sunglasses; strumming a ukulele; with a parrot on her shoulder; in a tiny bikini; in a tinier one; laughing with other drinkers in a bar, a handsome young man leaning sideways to get a good look at her. After that, more pictures of the handsome young man and Nicolette—snorkeling, playing tennis, dancing close, toasting each other with foamy blue drinks. Petrov turned to the last page. A photo fell out. He picked it up. Not a photo, but a postcard, blank on the back; a postcard that had nothing to do with Maui: *The Anatomy Lesson of Dr. Tulp.*

He'd seen it before. Where? The answer came immediately: among the recipes in the kitchen drawer of Cindy Motton, victim number three. No message on the back of that one either, but there was a message, all right. The next thing Petrov knew he was running out of the house.

Elaine and a uniformed cop were coming the other way, evidence kits in hand.

"What's up?" she said.

No time to explain.

Nick awoke. Not in bed—and therefore he'd missed a whole night's carmustine treatment from his wafer in the mattress—but on the living room couch. Why? Bits and pieces of yesterday got stirred up in his mind: the Queen of England in a chugging contest, Elaine holding a wad of bloody paper towel, the feel of Billie's lips on his cheek. The immediate past knit itself into a loose, imperfect pattern in his mind. He remembered that he had work to do, exactly what still in the process of coming back to him. But it didn't matter: he had everything written down. Where? In his notebook and on an envelope. So, no problem, other than the fact that he was ready to go back to sleep.

Nick got his hands in position, raised up to his elbows, levered himself up, swung or inched his legs over the side, stood. Some backsliding there, but only because he was tired. Who could doubt that he was getting stronger every day? Just see, now that he was warmed up, the way he was practically striding into the kitchen.

He went to the table, actually had his hand out, when he noticed that the notebook and envelope weren't there. On the counter? Not there either. Funny. Must have taken them to the bedroom. Didn't remember, but what did that mean? Nick tried his bedroom. Then the bathroom. The office upstairs. The living room. Kitchen again. He opened drawers, checked under pillows, leafed through the pages of books. He started over, rummaging through the whole house again, faster and faster.

"Where did I put them?" he said aloud. He needed those lists. "What the fuck is wrong with me?"

Things got tipped over. Lamp, globe, vase, microwave oven, bookcase: lots of crashing. He felt powerful, totally cured, with more than enough strength to demolish the house, wreck everything in sight. Nick was tearing through the kitchen for the seventh or eighth time when his gaze fell on the tabletop and the writing inked on it, his left-handed writing. *Desert HS—where?*

Oh, yeah. He remembered. And even better, thought at once how to answer that question, how to find Desert High. Nick climbed the stairs to his office, hoping the computer was still intact. Sweat dripped off his chin.

ow was this done? First you pressed the button with the little triangle mark. Then came a noise, the machine equivalent of throat-clearing maybe, and the screen flickered to life. This, managing the computer, was all coming back, or had never been lost in the first place, the machine interface parts of Nick's brain undamaged or recovering fast. Had to be a good sign: wouldn't the machine interface parts of the brain be among the most important?

Search engines, Google, how to use quotation marks to focus the results, Nick had the methodology on call. He typed in "Desert High School," the left hand doing the work for now just to save time, and got one—what was the word?—hit. They called them hits, all part of that strange computer jargon designed to make clerical work seem exciting, even cool.

One hit: Desert High School in Barstow, California, *Home of the Rattlers.* Nick clicked on the link. Up came a commonplace picture of a low desert-colored building with a flagpole in front, a high school like so many others, but it had a big effect on Nick—a fact on the ground. He was making connections, back at work.

He read the bullet points about Desert High: founded 1939, enrollment 1100, upcoming reunions, SAT testing dates, congratulations to the students of the month, varsity sports schedule. Click. *Go Rattlers!!!* The Rattlers, 4–0, were scheduled to play Bakersfield South on Friday. Nick looked around for a calendar, didn't find one; turning back to the screen, he saw in the top right-hand corner, pretty much by accident, that today was Friday. A computer feature he'd forgotten, but now it was back, absolutely solid.

riday, Nick's favorite day of the week, going all the way back to first grade. His spirits, already on the upswing, rose higher. Like a kid going somewhere fun, he quickly gathered supplies: volleyball, Candyland card, Empty Box CD, and two big squares of Sara Lee coffee cake for building back up. He put everything in his car, propped the cane against the passenger seat and sat behind the wheel for the first time since coming home.

One little problem: those pedals, designed for the right foot doing all the work. Before turning the key, Nick put his right foot through an audition. Up and down on the gas pedal, good enough, but the getting-over-to-the-brake-and-back part needed work. Nick assigned the brake to his left foot for now; the right could practice on the way. He backed out of the driveway, a little jerkily, like a student driver—but out on the road, free—and headed for Barstow.

On the road. Except, as he came to the end of the block, right foot easing off the gas, left foot coming down on the brake, teamwork in sync already, he realized he didn't know which way to turn. How could that be? The roads flowed through Southern California like a system of rivers and tributaries, a system that had always been available on a mental map. Nick waited for it to take shape. It did not.

Frustration fizzed up inside him, the kind that would lead to rage, banging the steering wheel, destruction. Nick took a deep breath. These things, problems, deficits, were going to happen. He had to get used to them, put a stop to useless reactions, find a way. "Suck it up," he said out loud. Find a way. He pulled over to the side of the road, bumping the curb, and opened the glove box.

Map of California. All it took was one glance: 10, 15. Couldn't be simpler. "Oh, yeah," Nick said; and had the strange and wonderful sensation, almost prickly, just behind the forehead, of all those rivers and tributaries redrawing themselves in his brain. He was getting better, and fast. Smiling to himself, he stuck the map back in the glove box, fumbling a little on account of his right hand, and knocked some scraps of paper to the floor. Nick reached down, picked them up. Three pieces. He fitted them together. They formed a card, one of those greeting cards from Hallmark. On the front was a picture of two little kids walking through a field of flowers, a wicker basket between them. Nick's eyes filled with tears. Impossible that a Hallmark card could be beautiful, right? Weren't they clichés of the most hackneyed kind? He knew that. But this was beautiful, even more so in its damaged state. Two little kids, field of flowers, torn to pieces: what more needed to be said? Nick slipped the card carefully into his pocket, unopened.

The 10 to the 15: bumper-to-bumper, a low smoggy sky that didn't clear till Cajon Junction—the kind of driving that put people in a bad mood. But not Nick. He was on the road, excited, like a tourist going somewhere new. And what was this? Hunger, awakening inside him. He ate a whole piece of coffee cake, insouciant right hand on the wheel, zipping along at seventy, seventy-five, eighty. Had he ever tasted anything this delicious? He almost started on the second. The simple things in life were the best, as everyone said. Nick hummed a funny little tune to himself as he drove, his feet smooth on the pedals, the right one even taking over completely from time to time. He was almost in Barstow, the desert spreading out all around in a peaceful sort of way, when a snatch of the lyrics to the song he was humming came to him unbidden:

> *You don't even know*
> *what's buried in your yard.*

What song was this? Where did he know it from? What was the rest of it? His mind was silent.

Desert High School, *Home of the Rattlers.* Nick pulled into the parking lot, found a space at the far end, checked the time: just after two. The school doors banged open and the kids blew out, an explosion of shouting, laughing, jostling, and littering he couldn't take his eyes off. The superabundance of energy, like those untamed gushers in the early days of the oil business: too bad he hadn't kept some of it in storage tanks from his own high school days. The kids scrambled onto the buses, jumped in their cars, zoomed off. It got very quiet, just the sound of the wind in the desert. Nick closed his eyes for a moment.

When he awoke, the sun was setting, igniting a wild spectacle of color, as though an Impressionist god were squirting paint tubes at the sky. Nick didn't notice that the parking lot was filling up again until a kid with *Go Rattlers* in red on his bare chest went by the car yelling, "Are you ready for some football?" The kid shook a wooden rattle that sounded just like a threatened sidewinder. Nick reached for his cane, got out of the car. A strange image of a snake, not a sidewinder but some thick black snake, rising up from a swimming pool, took shape in his mind. Nick waited for more, but no more came. Football fans streamed by. Nick followed them to the field.

The Rattlers wore red, Bakersfield blue. Nick stood behind

one of the end zones, his favorite spot for watching football, the holes all opening and closing so clearly from there. Number 44 in red, a lean black kid with long slender hands, backpedaled toward him to take the opening kickoff. Just from the way he moved, Nick knew this would be the boy the team was built around, running back on offense, safety on defense, possibly the kicker and punter too, on the field for sixty minutes. High school football was like one of those rigid oriental theatrical forms, the roles and rituals unchanging. His own high school team—

—Nick played outside linebacker, wore 39, one glorious night recovering a fumble against Culver City—the ball bouncing up and into his hands as if by its own will—and running it in from forty yards, the whole episode still clearer than a *National Geographic* photo in his mind; clearer, in fact, than anything else in there. *But don't go there—*

—His own high school team had been built around Aeneas Flynn, whose burst of speed—Nick had laughed out loud the first time Aeneas blew by him in practice—had taken him all the way to Ohio State on a full ride, where he'd torn up his knee freshman year and hit a long slow skid that ended with a one-column-inch obituary a few years back. Nick's own obituary, the one with Gerald Reasoner's name in the first sentence, would probably be—

Don't go there.

Thump. The ball spun through the air, black against that wild sky, an end-over-end kick, pretty good for high school football, cleanly caught by number 44 on the ten-yard line. The Rattler fans—perhaps a thousand of them in the stands to his left, about a third that number on the Bakersfield side—all shook their rattles, making a snake-pit noise, but on a giant scale. This was going to be fun. Number 44 sidestepped the first tackler, took off—very fast, but not like Aeneas Flynn—got sandwiched at about the thirty-five and coughed up the ball. Big pileup, its surface twitching from all the gouging and punching going on inside. The last player up was a groggy boy in blue, the ball in a death grip against his chest. Over on the Bakersfield side, the fans went nuts, one guy with a cowbell nuttier than the others; that would be the groggy kid's father. Number 44 and the rest of the receiving team ran off the field, heads down. Their coaches looked right though them.

"Bunch of pussies," said a man standing beside Nick, an old man with strange red marks on his head, visible through his soft, thinning hair. For a moment, Nick wondered whether he too had something bad going on inside his skull. Then he noticed how weather-beaten the man was in general, and put those marks down to years under the desert sun. Overhead, the colors started fading, blackness flowing in from the east. The stadium lights came on.

Bakersfield ran a counter on the first play, fooling the Rattlers' middle linebacker completely. Forty-four made a touchdown-saving tackle after a twelve-yard gain. The old man spat on the ground. "Pussies," he said.

Nick turned to him. "Looks to me like they're trying pretty hard," he said.

The old man had narrow eyes to begin with. They narrowed some more. "I know you from somewheres?" His gaze moved from Nick's face to the cane and back.

"No," Nick said.

The old man reached into his shirt pocket—a faded T-shirt with a coiled rattler on the front—found a pair of glasses, over-sized with black rectangular rims, stuck them on his nose. "Hell if I don't," he said. "You're the one supposed to be writing that article."

"Article?"

"Magazine article, instead of a book," the old man said, "so's if they reject it you haven't wasted too much time."

A confused old man. Nick spoke gently. "You've got me mixed up with someone else."

The old man examined him through his glasses. "Coaching philosophy then and now, supposed to be the subject matter," he said. "We were standing right here. No sense playin' mind games with me. Others have tried." He looked Nick up and down. "You been in a wreck?"

"Look, Mr. . . ."

"Moore, like I already told you. Wally Moore."

"Mr. Moore. I've never been here in my life." But that name, Wally Moore, lingered on his lips in a strange way.

Wally Moore stared at him a little more. "Suit yourself," he said, and walked off, joining some men around his own age on the Rattlers' sideline.

The Bakersfield quarterback rolled out, tried to hit his tight end on a curl pattern down the sideline. Forty-four read it perfectly, stepped inside for the interception and went all the way for a touchdown. Pandemonium on the Rattler side, snake-pit noises rising in the night. A dog got loose and scampered onto the field. An ugly-looking thing with splotchy rust-colored markings: the dog dodged the ref and bolted through the end zone; right to Nick, where it stopped dead, tongue hanging out and tail wagging.

Nick held out his hand, his right hand. The dog sniffed, then gave it a big lick. The feel of the dog's tongue, wet and rough, sent a tingling sensation up Nick's arm and right into his brain; as least so it seemed. A fact sprouted in some dark area of his mind, like a dandelion on the piled-up earth of a cave-in: the old man with the red marks on his head, Wally Moore, was the groundskeeper at Desert High. How could he have known that without having met Wally before? And when? Had to be some-time during the lost weekend. He reached down for the dog's collar, read the name on its tag: Buster.

Buster. Nick felt a little shock. The dog looked up at him, yellow eyes trying hard to convey some message. Nick stroked Buster between the ears. "Do I know you?" Buster pressed his head against Nick's hand. *You know me.* Buster sat, scratched his neck furiously with a hind paw, the expression in his eyes now changed, totally involved in canine things and impervious to human penetration. A big woman with her face painted red came striding out of nowhere, said, "Bad boy," clapped a leash on Buster and dragged him off. Buster looked back at Nick and made a high-pitched keening sound.

Nick moved up the sideline. "Mr. Moore?" he said. "Got a moment?"

Wally turned to him. "What fer?"

"I could use your help sorting out a few things."

"Huh?"

"Maybe we could go somewhere quiet."

"There's a game goin' on."

"Only take a minute," Nick said. "Besides, it's as good as won—they can't handle forty-four."

"He's a pussy," Wally said.

"But a quick one," said Nick.

"God-given fuckin' gift," said Wally, as though 44 didn't deserve it. But he stepped into a space between two sets of bleachers. "Make it quick."

Nick followed, stood before him, leaning a little on his cane. "I was in a wreck, just like you said. The problem is it's affected my memory. I'd appreciate your help filling in the blanks."

Wally looked interested. "You got amnesia?"

"Partial."

"Course I've heard about amnesia," Wally said, "but that's not the same as standin' right next to someone who's got a case." He peered up at Nick. "What don't you remember?"

Nick started to like Wally. "You've put your finger on the problem," he said. "Let's start with exactly when I was here."

"So you're admitting it?"

Nick nodded. "It must have been between Friday, September twelfth, and Sunday the fourteenth."

"I'm not so good on dates," Wally said. "But you came over by the shed, like I told you. We did a little jawin'."

"About what?"

"Your magazine article."

"Where did you get the idea I was writing a magazine article?"

"From you, for Christ sake. Think I'm makin' this up?"

"I don't write magazine articles."

"Then why'd you say you did?"

Nick had no answer.

Wally gave him a shrewd look. "Hey! That's part of the whole scenario. I'm starting to get this."

"Then you're way ahead of me," Nick said.

Wally blinked. "You're a funny guy," he said. "Truth is, I thought you were kind of an asshole that other time. Like you were jerking me around."

"How?"

" 'Fore we get to that, which is one weird question in the first place seeing as how you were the one doing it, tell me this: being that you're not a magazine guy, what is it you do?"

"I'm a private investigator," Nick said.

"Investigatin' what?"

"You tell me," Nick said.

A roar rose from the spectators. They shook their snake rattles.

seventeen

Rollover?" said Wally Moore. "Something of that nature?"

"What are you talking about?" Nick said.

"The wreck you was in."

Nick nodded. "A kind of rollover."

Wally pursed his lips, shook his head. "Biggest change I've seen in all my years on this planet. The number of wrecks."

"It is?"

"Did you know wrecks kill more people than cancer?"

"That doesn't sound right."

"Course it's not right," said Wally. "But do the powers that be give a shit? They don't even have the balls to take step one."

"What's that?" said Nick.

"Seal the goddamn borders," Wally said. He slid a pack of gum from his wallet, offered a stick to Nick, took one for himself. "As for this investigation of yours," he said, chewing with his mouth open, "main thing I recall was you showing me a picture."

"Of a Desert High championship team?"

Wally cracked his gum in a knowing sort of way. "So you do remember."

"No," Nick said. "And stop trying to trap me, Wally."

Wally looked a little hurt.

"Did I give a reason for showing you the picture?"

"You asked was it a good team."

"Was it?"

"Real good. This was late forties, early fifties, fore they all turned pussy."

"What else?"

"Have to think back," Wally said. He thought. Nick chewed his gum, peppermint gum that tasted good, but his jaw muscles tired quickly and he spat it out. "We talked a little about my own sports career," Wally said.

"Were you on that team?"

"Only as trainer. But previous, I played 'em all. Football, basketball and baseball captain at Clovis High, up near Fresno. Led the army in doubles, 1947."

Did all that talk about his sports career mean that Wally himself was the object of the investigation? Nick rejected the idea, partly because Wally wasn't acting like the object of an investigation, but mostly because his new sense seemed totally uninterested in exploring it. *His mind was changing him.*

"And beside your career?" Nick said.

"What we talked about? Coaching philosophy then and now, like I already mentioned." Wally snapped his fingers; he was one of those expert finger-snappers who could make it sound like cracking a whip. "Oh, yeah—I told you we got a girl kicking point-afters on the freshmen this year." He frowned. "You didn't see nothin' wrong with that."

"Is she any good?" Nick said.

"Exactly what you said before! When I started thinking you were an asshole. Course she's no good. She's a girl. This is football."

Nick took a wild guess. "Is her name Amanda?"

"Nope," said Wally. "Sarabeth. Her father runs the Amoco, right where you come off the highway."

"Do you know any Amandas?"

Wally scratched the top of his head, raising a little tuft of soft white hair; Nick wanted to smooth it back down. "Nope," he said. "I don't see where you're goin' with this."

Nick wasn't sure. "The thing is, Wally, someone stole that photograph."

Wally's face wrinkled up. "You think maybe money's hidden in the back of it, something like that?"

That hadn't occurred to Nick. He realized that a whole lot of other possibilities probably hadn't occurred to him either. Petrov would have known them; a maddening thought.

"Why else would anyone purloin it?" Wally said.

Nick didn't know that either. But he liked talking to Wally. The Rattler band strode onto the field at double time, playing "Tequila." Halftime.

"How about a hot dog?" Wally said.

Nick said yes, mostly so he could sit down. They ate hot dogs, lightly charred from the grill. Just a single bite in Nick's case; delicious on his tongue, but for some reason going bad as it went down, so bad he knew any more would make him sick.

Wally did his whip-cracking finger-snap again, the sound almost frightening. "Suppose I made you a copy of the missing picture?"

"How would you do that?"

Wally shrugged. "Wall of fame," he said. "They got all the photos hanging outside the AD's office, next to the trophy cases. Take it out of the frame, run it through the copier, presto."

Nick sat up straight. "How about now?"

The Rattler marching band segued into the theme from *Saturday Night Fever.* Wally glanced at the scoreboard: Rattlers 17, Bakersfield 3. "Have to be quick," he said, relish on his chin.

Nick tried to be quick, but his right leg, which had been getting so much stronger, now relapsed back to the step-dragging stage. Wally hurried on ahead, across the parking lot, into a side door of the school. Nick stumped in after him, followed Wally down a long hall lit only by dull-orange ceiling lights placed far apart. Trophy cases appeared on the left and right, trophies gleaming in the shadows.

"Here we go," said Wally. He called down the hall. "What was the year again?"

Nick didn't know. Catching up to Wally, he saw the team photos hanging in vertical rows of ten, all in gilt frames, unlike the cheap plastic frame his had been in, and each marked with the year in the bottom left corner, 1939 to the present, switching from black and white to color in 1967. Nick had forgotten to check the date, realized now he'd also forgotten something else, so basic: to read the players' names. "But I'll recognize it," he said; from that bird, soaring out of the frame, turning the picture into art.

"Late forties or early fifties," said Wally, "unless my memory's playing tricks on me."

Nick glanced at Wally to see if he was making a conscious joke, couldn't tell. He liked Wally, liked him a lot. Scanning the rows, he found no birds in the photos from 1946, 1947, 1948, 1949, 1950. Wait. That last one was 1951, not 1950. And what was this? The space where 1950 should have hung was empty, the rectangle of wall lighter than its surroundings. He ran his eye over the early fifties. No bird.

"Where's 1950?" Nick said.

"Huh?" said Wally. He peered at the empty space on the wall, grunted. "Beats me," he said.

Nick checked the photos again for Eastern Regional champions: none between 1943 and 1957. "Must have been 1950," he said. "Where is it?"

"Whyn't you take '49 instead?" said Wally. He was itching to get back to the game. "Likely had most of the same players." He stabbed at the 1949 picture with his finger. "Fact there's Georgie Rummel, the guy you were asking about in the first place."

The name meant nothing to Nick. He studied the image of Georgie Rummel without recognition, a big kid at the end of the bottom row, glaring into the lens as though the photographer were an ancient enemy. "I was asking about him?"

"Comes back to me now," Wally said. "Not unusual, it bein' Georgie Rummel. Still the best that's ever suited up for Desert High. Went on to play with Dick Butkus."

Dick Butkus. Nick knew who Dick Butkus was, of course; the strange thing was that the name brought back that image of the faceless barefoot man in a suit, only now he had a face, red, middle-aged, angry. Was the barefoot man in the suit Georgie Rummel? "What did I ask you about him?" Nick said.

"What he's doing now, that kind of thing," Wally said. "Want me to tell you again?"

"Yes."

"Thought so," said Wally. "Georgie's retired, lives just north of town."

"Can you give me directions?"

"I'll take you there myself," said Wally, "after the game."

But Nick couldn't wait, wasn't even polite about it. What virtue was patience now?

Wally shrugged. "Lives up on Calico Way," he said, and told Nick how to get there.

"Thanks," Nick said.

"No problem," said Wally. "Did you know your ear was bleeding?"

Nick touched his ear, checked his fingers in the dim light, smudged red; but just a little. "Mosquito bite," he said.

Wally gave him a look Nick read easily: *mosquitoes in the desert?*

By the time Nick got to his car, the bleeding had stopped, pretty much. He followed Wally's directions, crossing 15, passing a weathered sign that read *Silver City Ghost Town*, almost illegible, then a Western-style bar and a 7-Eleven, before coming to Calico Way, a dirt road that led out of town. Nick almost missed the turn, his mind for some reason stuck on that ghost town sign; stuck, but offering nothing more.

Nick took Calico Way. Purple lingered in the sky, as dark as purple could be. Then the moon rose, a pure white crescent so defined the points looked sharp enough to cut, and the purple vanished, leaving only black. A lone headlight appeared in the distance ahead, grew bigger very fast. In a minute or two a motorcycle roared by, the rider hunched forward, blond hair streaming in the wind.

Nick came to the end of Calico Way, parked by a mailbox with tin numbers gleaming on the front: 2928. A double-wide trailer with lights flickering in the windows sat at the base of a dark rise. Nick got out of the car. The air, cooling fast, carried a faint smoky smell, as though someone was barbecuing nearby. He walked to the door and rapped on it with his cane.

No one answered. Nick knocked again, harder. The whole structure trembled. He looked forward to the day he'd be throwing away the cane—a day he knew was coming soon— but he'd miss its knocking capacity.

No answer. Nick walked to the side of the trailer, peered through a window into a room lit by flickering light that seemed to have no source, saw a bed with a bare mattress, bottles, paper cups and cigarette butts all over the floor, a lacquered football on a shelf. He continued around to the back, past the propane tank to the only window—a small porthole, perhaps suggesting some link between trailer park life and adventure on the high seas. Nick looked through the porthole.

The room within was on fire. A curtain of flames writhed between a TV in the corner and a couch at the back. A big old man wearing briefs rose up behind the curtain, huge hands raised high, and caught fire. Nick ran back to the side window—maybe didn't run, but got there fast—smashed it out with his cane, pulled himself inside.

Smoke came flowing from the back room, turbulent and

surging, like a river in flood. Nick knelt on the floor where it wasn't as bad, crawled through to the back room. Now the walls, ceiling, floor were all burning and crackling, the air poisoning fast with smoke and plastic chemicals, not quite masking the smell of booze. The boozy smell brought back a sharply defined memory, surely from the lost weekend, of this same man holding a paper cup of whiskey; and with the memory came the ID: George Rummel. The red-faced barefoot man was someone else.

Rummel was banging on the porthole with his fist; from deep in his throat came a low, fierce animal noise. Nick rolled across the floor, rose, grabbed Rummel's massive shoulder. The skin came away in his hand.

"Rummel. This way."

Rummel looked back, eyebrows and lashes all gone, and saw Nick. He reached out, wrapped one of his hands around Nick's wrist, like a ring of fire.

"Get down," Nick said.

But Rummel would not. Nick tried to free his arm; his strength and Rummel's belonged to different orders. He tried to tug Rummel back through the flames, into the bedroom, outside, the only escape. Rummel wouldn't do that either. He raised his fist again to pound on the porthole, too small for even a child to fit through. Then came an enormous boom. *Propane.* In a tiny unit of time, Nick felt Rummel's body absorbing its force, shielding him. The next unit of time was longer and weightless.

Nick lay naked on the ground, lovely cold ground. He was scratched and bruised, but intact. Flames shot into the night, drowning the stars, but he was out of their reach. Sirens sounded in the distance; the throaty animal noise, no longer fierce, came from much closer. Nick crawled over to its source, a supine shadow at the base of the dark rise.

The fire lit what was left of George Rummel. Their eyes met.

Nick smelled a roasted-meat smell, also the alcohol on Rummel's breath.

"I know you," Rummel said.

"Lie still," Nick said. "Help is coming."

"You're the one looking for Amanda."

Connection. So many possible questions: Nick chose the one he hoped would cover them all. "Where is she?"

"Think I'll tell you now?" said Rummel.

"Why not?"

The expression on Rummel's face began to change. First toward humor, Nick thought, then toward sarcasm, finally toward rage. But it was only his skin, sloughing off. Rummel died without saying another word, drawing his last little breath just before the fire trucks came screaming up.

eighteen

"T hat took some kind of balls," said Sergeant Gallego of the Barstow Police Department.

Nick shrugged. They sat in an examination room at Desert Regional Hospital, the sergeant on a stool, Nick, his cuts and scratches all disinfected and bandaged, on the table. Nick might have shrugged, but that wasn't how he felt inside. Inside, his blood was flowing in a way it hadn't in so long, all systems strong, returning to normal.

"Mind explaining your interest in George Rummel?" the sergeant said.

"I'm working on a case."

Sergeant Gallego waited, Nick's license still in his hand. He looked young to be a sergeant.

"A missing evidence case," Nick went on, and by putting it in words, began to understand it himself. "I believed Rummel might have information."

"Must be pretty important evidence," said Sergeant Gallego, "make you run into a fire like that."

"I didn't think," Nick said.

"I never believe when people say that," said the sergeant. "Not even mommas going back for their babies."

"In this case it's true," said Nick. He hadn't thought, not about the evidence or anything else. Did that mean it had all been about saving the man, some deep and good instinct rising in him? Or was it something new, not instinctive but just as good, that made him do it? Nick opted for that, a new development. He was surprising himself.

"Still took balls," said Sergeant Gallego. "Can you describe this evidence?"

"A framed photograph of the 1950 Desert High football team," Nick said. "With your permission, I'd like to go back and look for it in the morning."

"No problem," said Sergeant Gallego. He wrote in his notebook. "What's it evidence of?"

An hour ago Nick couldn't have said; in other words, hadn't really known what he was doing. George Rummel had given him the answer, put him back on track. "I'm looking for a girl named Amanda." Girl, not woman: he knew that from the volleyball.

"Kidnapping or runaway?"

"I'm not sure."

Sergeant Gallego nodded, accepting the answer without question, obviously familiar with the central problem of so many missing kids cases. No need to bring in glioblastoma, lost weekends, forgotten codes. "If I can help, just holler," the sergeant said.

"Any word on the cause of the fire?"

"We got cigarette burns on the couch in that back room, and an almost empty forty-ouncer of rye underneath." Another memory came back to Nick from the lost time: a cigarette in George Rummel's thick fingers, burning down to the nicotine-stained skin. "Not exactly a surprise," said Gallego. "He's been busted for DUI five or six times since I got here and had a history of barroom brawls before that. Just a matter of time."

"Did he live alone out there?"

"Wife died years ago," the sergeant said. "I think there's a daughter somewhere in the picture."

"What's her name?"

"I can find out." Sergeant Gallego rose.

"Rotary's got a hero-of-the-month club," he said. "I was thinking about nominating you—there's a nice plaque goes with it."

"I couldn't accept."

"Up to you," said Gallego. He held out his hand. Nick shook it with his left. The right was feeling good, could have done it, but not the way Nick wanted. "Arm okay?" said Gallego.

"Must have jammed it a little."

Sergeant Gallego shook his head. "Lucky to be alive," he said. Nick smiled.

The doctor came in. He was still young enough to have acne traces on his chin. "How're you feeling?" he said.

"Fine."

He checked a clipboard. "Taking any medications?"

"No."

"Allergies?"

"No."

"Medical conditions?"

"None."

"High blood pressure? Diabetes?"

"No."

"Been hospitalized recently for any reason?"

"No."

"Excellent," said the doctor. "You've got your health to thank."

"For what?" said Nick.

"Reflexes, strength, eyesight—getting out of there just about scot-free," said the doctor. "Although I'm still going to recommend an overnight stay for observation."

"Thanks anyway," Nick said. No more nights in hospitals, not a single one, under any pretext.

"Then you'll have to sign a waiver."

Nick signed, and did it with his right hand. His right hand came up big, did a first-class job, not the least bit shaky; but his signature, *Nick Petrov,* didn't look the way it used to, the letters much bigger and fatter, and the *V* ending with a new flourish, like a banner in the wind. This new him might be not so bad: a potential hero-of-the-month with calligraphic flair besides.

A little after eleven, Nick walked into .45, the Western-style bar. Didn't have his cane—lost in the fire—didn't need it. He was hungry again, really hungry. Had to be a good sign. He found a seat at the bar—the place was packed, many of the customers in Rattler red—ordered a T-bone rare, fries, Johnnie Black. The final score was written on the mirror behind the bar: *Rattlers 24, Bakersfield 10. Congratulations, boys!* Some of the boys seemed to be whooping it up across the room, uncarded.

Nick ate, not just a bite or two, but everything on his plate. *Stop the wasting. Build back up. Brain work.* He was cooking on all three burners. His reflection in the mirror didn't look too bad, hair coming in nicely now, and you couldn't really call it gray, just somewhat lighter than before. A few seats down, a woman in a tank top was looking at his reflection too. She waved; she had nice arms, a little plump, but shapely. The arms, but not her face, seemed familiar. Nick waved back. She came over, beer mug in hand.

"Nick?" she said.

"Hi," said Nick.

"Don't remember me, do you?"

"Well . . ."

"Typical male behavior—I'm used to it."

"I kind of remember," Nick said. "When was this?"

"Don't pretend," said the woman. "It was right here, last month. My name's D. J. but everyone calls me Deej."

"Buy you a drink?"

"The one after this," Deej said.

Everybody slid down one and Deej took the stool beside him. Barroom conversation with women: not something Nick had ever been good at. He said the first thing that came to mind.

"Does D. J. stand for anything?"

"No one's ever asked me that," said Deej.

A clumsy barroom conversationalist: one thing that hadn't changed, therefore probably the deepest-seated behavior in his brain, undamaged. "They haven't?" Nick said.

She shook her head. "Matter of fact it stands for Donna Jean."

"So Deej is a nickname of a nickname."

"I guess," said Deej, deflating a little. "Is that bad?"

"It's good," said Nick; and a helpful thought came to him. "Probably means people enjoy your company."

Her face screwed up. "I don't get it."

"Kind of the way a favorite object gets worn smooth."

"That's pretty cool," Deej said. Her face went a little pink. She finished her beer. Nick ordered another round. Deej raised her glass, paused. "Have you lost weight or something?"

"A little."

"Atkins?" she said. "The Zone? None of them work for me." She gave him a closer look. "And you didn't even need to lose. There's no justice."

There's no justice. The words hit Nick hard, sizzled in his head like a brand, but he didn't know why. He scribbled them on a cocktail napkin, shoved it in his pocket.

"What'd you write?" said Deej.

"Something for work."

"The detective business, right?" said Deej. "How's it going?"

"Not bad," said Nick.

"How's your partner?"

"My partner?" He'd never had one.

"Rui," said Deej. "With all the tattoos. None of my beeswax, but I got the feeling he wasn't pulling his weight."

"From what?"

"The way you had to practically drag him out of here last time." She glanced at him. "You're looking a little blank."

"The truth is," Nick said, "my memory of that evening's not too sharp."

"Funny," Deej said. "You weren't acting blitzed. In fact, I'd have said you were stone-cold sober."

"It was a combination of things," Nick said. "I'd appreciate your telling me what happened. When this was, for example."

"Total blackout, huh?" said Deej. "I'm familiar. This was last month, had to of been a Saturday night——"

"The thirteenth?"

"Sounds right. Couldn't have been a Friday because I was pulling Friday graveyards all September."

"What do you do?"

"I'm a corporal in your army."

"My army?"

"The U.S. Army, Nick. Up at China Lake—ordnance, second class."

"I feel safer now," Nick said, clinking his glass against Deej's mug. She laughed, but he meant it. He was starting to like her, liked Wally too, was working and having fun at the same time, something else totally new.

"Anyways," said Deej, "I was in here with this friend of mine—Ellyn, you met her—when Rui came in, started buying us drinks, telling us all about his cases and everything. Didn't look like a detective to me, but he said he had to change his appearance for undercover work, so that explained it. But those tattoos on his arms are permanent, right?"

"The red butterfly?" Nick said, an image that popped into his mind, no explanation.

"I don't remember a red butterfly," said Deej. "Mostly eagles and barbed wire."

"Did Rui mention his last name?"

"If he did, I don't remember. But you know his last name,

right?" Her eyes widened when she saw he didn't. "Unless he's working undercover with you too. Is that it?"

Nick nodded, grateful for her improvisational skill. "He's working undercover for somebody," he said. "Let's put it that way."

"I hear you," said Deej. "Wow. This is deep. Another round?"

Nick ordered another round, feeling better and better, brain cancer so close to being forgotten that he had to make an effort to remember it.

"How come there's Johnnie Walker Black and Johnnie Walker Red?" said Deej when the drinks came.

"Bartender?" said Nick.

The bartender gave her a taste of both. "Wow," said Deej. "No comparison. This is fun." Her gaze went to his face, took it in. "You really didn't need to lose all that weight."

"I got carried away," Nick said. "These cases Rui was talking about, do you remember any?"

Deej thought. It involved rolling her eyes up toward the ceiling and biting her lip. She looked very pretty. "There was one he's working on," she said. "All about this copycat killer."

"Go on," Nick said.

"All I remember is thinking it was like the setup for a creepy movie."

"How?"

"From the way Rui explained it: Suppose there was a serial killer on the loose and you wanted to kill somebody. All you'd have to do is find out the details of the serial killings and do yours the very same way. Who would ever suspect?"

Nick thought about it. Not foolproof, especially in cases with DNA evidence, but in others—a sniper, for example—it could work. The serial killer, once caught, would plead not guilty to all counts; after the guilty verdict came down, would he then say, "Yes to all those others, but not that third-to-last one?" Why bother? And even if he did, who would believe him? Nick, having known a few serial killers, suspected they'd even take a secret pride in the one they didn't do.

Deej took a big drink of beer. "You'd get away with murder," she said. "A perfect crime."

"Maybe," said Nick. "What else did Rui say about the case?"

"Just that it was a Barstow story." She burped. "Oops. Which seemed strange to me, since we've never had a serial killer loose around here."

"How did he explain that?"

"He didn't. That was right about when you came in and took him away."

"Any idea where we went?"

Deej laughed, spraying a little beer. "This is crazy," she said, "like Alice in Wonderland. I hope you weren't driving in that condition."

A memory, like a scene glimpsed on a drive-in movie screen from the open road: Desert. Night. In the passenger seat of his own car, someone else at the wheel, the tattoos on the pale forearms of that someone else green in the dashboard glow. And Buster, panting in the back.

"I wasn't driving," Nick said.

"Small mercies," said Deej. "But I don't remember any talk about where you were going. Maybe you can work back from where you woke up that next day. I've had success with that."

Another drive-in fragment: Buster pissing on a creosote bush.

"No go?" said Deej.

He shook his head.

"There was one other thing," Deej said. "You left fifty bucks for me and Ellyn's drinks. That was nice. I thought it meant you were coming back."

"I'm back," Nick said.

There was a silence. A pedal steel guitar made lonesome sounds on the jukebox. "I notice you're not wearing a wedding ring," Deej said.

"True."

"And there's no tan line on your finger. So you're not one of those."

"The ones who wear sunblock?" Nick said.

Deej laughed. "I can tell just from you saying that that you're not married. A married guy would get all uncomfortable. And you know what else about a married guy?" She started to say something, stopped.

"Not your type in bed?" Nick said. A wild, intuitive guess, springing from the brain-damaged sense, 100 percent the new him.

"Exactly," said Deej. "How do you know something like that?"

Nick knew that in an hour, maybe less, he could be in bed with this woman— this smart, funny, good-looking woman— lost in pure physical pleasure, and wouldn't it be good to be getting nothing but pure physical pleasure from this body of his, if only for a while? Also: Why not? Was there anything to stop him? Didn't he just about have carte blanche from now on in? And he wasn't married, didn't have a girlfriend, was accountable to no one. All he had was the possible beginning of a potential something that made no sense with Billie.

That was enough to stop him. If he was going out, he wanted to go out right, in every way. Nick handed Deej his card. "If you run into Rui, please let me know."

"You're leaving?"

"It's this case."

"But now, at this hour?" said Deej. "Is it life and death?"

"Yes," said Nick. He leaned forward, kissed her on the cheek, came close to changing his mind.

nineteen

Filling in the blanks; extending his life. Nick knew they were equated; why else, as he began to fill in those blanks, was he feeling stronger and stronger? His cane, lost in the fire, was no longer needed. Hard to argue with that.

He drove through the night, back toward George Rummel's place, too wired to wait until dawn to make his search, not the slightest little cloud of sleep lurking in his mind, for once. More stars than he had ever seen shone down, so many they made the sky white and the holes in it black, if you were looking in a certain way; and Nick was. Driving under that shining dome, the car riding so softly it seemed to be gliding on air: it was then that a voice spoke, so real, so near, that Nick turned his head sharply to check the passenger seat. The voice said:

Nikolai? Are you hearing me?

The seat, of course, was empty, Nick alone in the car. But that was his father's voice, unmistakable—cool, detached, superior. Nick swerved off the road, almost losing control on the slippery sand-blown shoulder, stopped the car. Silence. Nick listened and heard nothing but the wind, not hard but steady, rustling whatever could be rustled. He'd imagined the voice, was more tired than he thought, should probably turn around, find a place to—

Nikolai? Are you hearing me?

His father's voice, even clearer now, not a memory of how his father sounded, but the sound itself. Nick looked out into the night, saw lights from a few distant houses, but no people, and certainly not his father, long dead.

Nikolai? Now with that hard, impatient edge in his tone.

"Yes," Nick said aloud. "I hear you."

Do you want to live or die?

"Live, of course."

No of course. Many would prefer to die than live, but lack the courage. Silence. *You should have studied chemistry, as I told you. There are excellent careers in chemistry. Excellent careers in chemistry. Excellent careers in chemistry. Ex—*

"Stop."

Silence.

But now we talk of the future. Does the expression spontaneous remission *mean anything to you, Nikolai?*

"Yes," Nick said.

Please define.

That was his father: no faith in him at all. "When cancer goes away by itself," Nick said.

Is that how you were taught to phrase a definition?

Did he have to listen to this? "If you've got a point to make, make it."

Is this how you talk to me?

"Make it."

The voice went silent, and as the silence stretched on, Nick again started to doubt its existence. Not a voice after all, some sort of imagining, perhaps an auditory hallucination, which suggested that something was changing inside his brain, maybe some new area being—

Find this girl, Amanda.

The voice, rising to a clarion call now, so charged with all the components of real sound that it drowned out his own thoughts, like a fifty-thousand-watt transmitter planted in his head. Nick put his hands to his ears. It did no good.

That is the road to spontaneous remission.

"Find the girl and I'll live?" Nick said, his voice rising too.

Yes.

"Find the girl and the cancer will go away?"

What is so hard to understand?

"But that's absurd."

Is it?

"Worse than absurd. Twisted. Wrong. What kind of world would it be, with deals like that going on?"

The voice went silent. Nick stayed where he was, parked by the side of the road. The sky returned to normal as though someone were adjusting the balance, blackness dominating, the stars toning down their act. The voice did not return.

Nick sat by the roadside, hands tight on the wheel, going nowhere. The voice of his father, dead for almost sixteen years: a victim of peace, or maybe of some imaginative failure on the part of Karl Marx. The story could be reduced to a few words: fall of the Berlin Wall, termination of his father's contract with the CIA, loss of job and money, maddening realization that he'd outlived the meaning of his life. If the wall had stayed up, if Communism had been a little more appealing, his father would probably still be alive. As it was, he'd shot himself while watching Reagan's farewell address on television.

Nick's own life still had meaning, he knew, more than ever. *Find the girl and live.* Sounded crazily arbitrary, but so did glioblastoma multiforme, Grade IV, erupting out of the blue. Maybe the only response to crazy arbitrariness was to dish it right back.

Nick parked at the end of Calico Way, a few yards from the scrap heap of George Rummel's double-wide, took his flashlight out of the glove box, ducked under the yellow police tape. The ground, hard and stony, still felt damp, dry air and dry soil not quite done with sucking up the water from the fire hoses. Nick shone his light into the rubble, touched twisted bits of this and that, no longer hot. He saw a television, the screen blown out; an embroidered pillow that said *Welcome to Reno;* a charred garment bag. Nick unzipped the bag. Inside hung a tuxedo, in perfect condition, the cut of long-ago design. Nick checked the label—May Company, Chicago—and also the pockets, not because he expected to find anything, but because checking pockets was what he did.

Nothing in any of them except the last one he tried, the left-hand outside jacket pocket, least likely to contain anything. There he found a small black-and-white photograph, the kind with a frilled white border, probably taken with an old Brownie. A photograph was what he was looking for, of course, but not this one. It showed three little girls, two brunettes and a blonde, on a pinto pony with a curling white mane, the two brunettes smiling at the camera, the blonde, sitting between them, lost in thought. A little boy in full Western dress, including toy six-guns and an outsize sheriff's star, led the pony. Nick slipped the picture into his pocket. He poked through the rubble for a few more minutes. No football photo, but he did find his cane, leaning against a jumble of metallic wreckage in a way that seemed almost jaunty under the spotlight of his flash. A wooden cane: why hadn't it burned? The goddamned thing didn't even have scorch marks, was completely undamaged. He stamped on its midpoint with his left foot, snapping it in two, the sound as satisfying as any he'd heard.

Back in the car, feeling good, Nick stuck the flashlight back in the glove box, pausing at the sight of the Hallmark card with the beautiful picture—two kids in a field of flowers—on the front. The way it was torn in three pieces, poignant before, now bothered him. He rummaged around in the glove box, found tape, started taping the pieces together, taping from the inside in order to leave the picture unmarred. That was when he saw what he should have seen, should have looked for, before—the writing on the card:

Hey, Rui—we'll help each other, ok? xo Amanda.

Connection. Connection between Rui, the detective from .45, and the girl he was looking for. There were probably connections all over the place, but his mind was careless. What connections was he missing? Carelessness was unacceptable. He cared, cared with all he had left. The problem was to force his mind to care the same way. *Find the girl and live.* "Think," he said aloud, trying to activate some neural pathway that would trigger thinking in his brain. He waited. It came up with nothing.

Nick drove home, fell on his bed as creamy predawn light came through the windows. In the corner of the ceiling, a spider was spinning something complicated. Nick didn't like sleeping with it right above his head like that, but he was too tired to do anything about it. Not that he lacked the strength; on the contrary, his strength was clearly coming back. It was just a simple, ordinary, healthy case of being too . . .

From Elaine's bedroom window, Petrov could see an alley lined with garages—one of which seemed to have been turned into living space for a brown-skinned family—and hear the traffic on Ventura Boulevard, a few blocks away. It was a shabby one-bedroom apartment that Elaine had done nothing to improve, but Petrov had never been more eager to get to a place or more reluctant to leave. She came out of the shower, naked except for the towel wrapped around her head.

"You're still here?" she said.

He shrugged, and maybe smiled too, shrug and smile both helpless.

"But I thought it was Dmitri's birthday," Elaine said.

Petrov walked over, put his arms around her, the feel of her skin complex and overwhelming, choking off his speech. He drew Elaine toward the bed, still in disarray from what they'd been doing there.

"A few minutes won't matter," he said.

With one hand, Petrov was tearing off his clothes; the other was already sliding down her crotch. Elaine's legs parted at once, both of them at the mercy of an undeniable force.

"Animal," Elaine said in his ear. "That's what I like about you."

She fell back on the bed, grabbed him, stuck him inside her, not gently. He moved in her, just as rough, rougher, something in the bed frame cracking beneath them, her holster, hanging on the bedpost, swinging a foot or two above the back of Petrov's head. She'd said *like*, not *love*; he made her pay for that in a way that left them both dripping sweat, and her giving him little kisses on the face, by the dozen. On the way home, speeding, darting in and out of traffic, desperate to arrive in time for the lighting of the four little birthday candles, Petrov decided to tell Kathleen the marriage was over, and soon.

Nick awoke fully clothed down to his shoes, lying on his stomach. He opened his eyes, saw blood on the pillow, two little blobs like Rorschach tests. He felt a dreadful lurch deep inside, as though he'd fallen off a rooftop.

But touching his face, nose, ears, he came upon nothing damp or sticky. So: not to worry. Nick told himself that a few times. He rolled over, or started to roll over; for one horrible moment, his body failed to respond at all. Then it came alive, and he rose, no problem; just a little creaky from a long day and a long night. The bedside clock read 4:35 and the sun flowed into his room like molten gold.

Nick checked his face in the bathroom mirror; no blood, just a little crust of something on his jaw below the right ear. He flexed his biceps, studied the reflection. Not too bad, especially the left. Pretty good, in fact, no?

He took a shower. First, for some reason, he found himself thinking about Elaine Kostelnik, specifically how she'd been in the bedroom. Then, as sometimes happened in showers, an idea came to him unbidden. Rui, whoever he was, had claimed to be his partner. Nick had never had a partner, but that didn't mean Rui wasn't a detective. If Rui was a detective, he'd be on record at the licensing board. Did Nick know anyone on the board? He did: Juwan Barnes, now head of security at the Airport Marriot, but they'd worked together in the sheriff's department out of Huntington Park. Nick hadn't seen him in years.

"Juwan? Nick Petrov."

"Hey, Nick. How you doing?"

"Great."

"Yeah? There are all these rumors."

"Nothing worth talking about," Nick said. "Still on the board?"

"One more term."

"I'm trying to track down a PI named Rui."

"Last name?"

"Don't have it."

"Just Rui?"

"Yeah."

"Come have a drink after work, say five-thirty," Juwan said. "I'll try and have something."

They shook hands in the lobby of the Marriott, Nick using his right; he had a feeling it didn't really come through for him. Juwan gave him a quick once-over; one of his eyelids trembled slightly.

"Lost some weight," Juwan said.

"Not much," said Nick, and heard the irritation in his voice. "Been doing a lot of swimming."

Juwan led him to a corner table in the bar. They ordered drinks—JD and Coke for Juwan, Johnnie Black for Nick; Juwan adding, "And how about a plate of nachos?"

"Large or small?" said the waitress.

Juwan's eyes went to Nick, real quick, but Nick caught it.
"Large."

They clinked their glasses together, ate nachos.
"Not bad, huh?" said Juwan. "Have more."
Nick had more.
"You always liked Mexican," Juwan said.
"Still do."
"We got a new chef, trained at the Ritz in Acapulco," Juwan
said. "She's Korean."
"These are great." Still hungry, and that was good.
Juwan watched him eat. "So what happened, you don't
mind my asking?"
"Just a very minor arterial thing in the brain," Nick said.
"Easily fixed."
"Glad to hear it," said Juwan. He sipped his drink, gave Nick
a glance over the rim of his glass. "We've got one Rui on file," he
said. "Last name Santiago. Works off a P.O. box in Long Beach."
"The first name's all I know," Nick said.
"That's why I asked him to come over," said Juwan. "Should
be here any minute."
"What did you tell him?"
"Just that I wanted to meet," Juwan said.
"So he thinks you've got work for him?"
"If he makes a good impression."
A man in a leather jacket came in, slicked-back hair, about
thirty. Nick had no memory of him. The man scanned the
room, scanned it again. The bar was empty except for two tables
of businesswomen and them.
"He picked the wrong career," said Juwan, raising his hand.
"That we know already."
The man came over. He had a swaggering muscle-bound
gait although he wasn't especially muscular. "Mr. Barnes?" he

said, addressing Nick, the white man, without recognition or
any sign of hiding recognition; almost certainly the wrong Rui.

"This is Mr. Barnes," Nick said.

"Oh," said the man. "Rui Santiago. Nice meeting ya." He
held out his hand. Juwan shook it, but his eyes were narrowed in
a way Nick remembered from long ago; there'd be no work
thrown Rui Santiago's way.

"This is my associate," Juwan said, indicating Nick. "He's got
a couple questions for you."

Rui Santiago gave Nick a big confident smile. "Fire away."

"Sit down," Nick said. "Something to drink?"

"That one of the questions?" Rui Santiago said.

"Funny," said Juwan.

Maybe Rui Santiago thought he meant it. He ordered a Grey
Goose martini straight up, asked for the ice shaker on the side.
Waiting for it to arrive, he glanced around the room, said, "Nice
gig you got here."

A vein throbbed in the back of Juwan's powerful hand.

"Does the name Deej mean anything to you?" Nick said.

"Deej? How you spelling that?"

Nick spelled it.

"Nope."

"Or possibly D. J.?"

"Sure," said Rui Santiago. "Spins records."

"I meant a person named D. J."

"I get it—D. J. is this Deej person," said Rui Santiago. "Nope."

"What about Amanda? Come across any Amandas in your
work?"

He shook his head, leaned forward confidentially. "Now that
you bring it up," he said, "business has been a little slow lately.
How about you guys?"

"Glacial," said Juwan.

"Huh?" said Rui Santiago.

"Mind taking off your jacket for a moment?" Nick said.

Rui Santiago removed his jacket. He puffed out his chest, probably thinking they were assessing his physical strength. He wore a black T-shirt; no tattoos on his bare arms.

"No tattoos," Nick said, surprised. Not that he held the slightest hope this could be the right Rui, but he figured him for tattoos.

"Not my style," said Rui Santiago. "Thing is, my body is my temple."

"We'll be in touch," Juwan said.

After he'd gone, Juwan ordered another round. "We had some fun, up in Huntington Park," he said.

"Yeah," said Nick.

"You get cynical with age."

"I'm going the other way," Nick said, a remark that pretty much came out by itself, and rang true inside. Juwan was watching him, waiting for him to go on, but Nick couldn't explain, didn't have it worked out. It was something about hope—one of the three great virtues, must be a reason for that—something about hope being the fuel of life, a remark that would probably end up sounding stupid.

Juwan stuck his finger in his drink, stirred the ice cubes around. "Meant to ask you," he said. "Ever find that girl?"

Nick lowered his glass. How could Juwan know anything about Amanda? "Girl?" he said.

"The one you were looking for last time you were here," Juwan said. "The escort service girl. Candyland. I looked into them. They're big."

Candyland? Last time he was here? "Was her name Amanda?" Nick said, his voice rising.

"Don't know if you ever mentioned her name," Juwan said. He looked confused. "But you know her name, right? What's all this trouble with names?"

"When was this?" Nick said.

"When was it?"

"When I was here, goddamn it."

Juwan sat back.

Nick leaned forward, laid his hand on the back of Juwan's, something he'd never have done before. "My memory's not right yet, Juwan. Friday, September twelfth, to Sunday the fourteenth is mostly blanks."

Juwan didn't withdraw his hand; Nick felt that big vein pulsing. Juwan was going to live a long long time. "This was the night the Canning verdict came down," Juwan said, "making it the Friday. You were checking out somebody in one of the rooms."

"Her client?"

"That's what I assumed."

"Can you get me a name?"

"I can try," said Juwan, rising.

They went to his office. Juwan sat at his computer for a few minutes. "Think it's this guy," he said, "had room 219." He handed Nick a printout.

James C. McMurray, VP Chemcom, Saint Paul; with home and business phone numbers and addresses.

James McMurray. "He had bare feet," Nick said, the man suddenly springing to life whole in his mind, details sharp. A familiar taste filled his mouth. What was it? Cashews. "He was wearing a suit but his feet were bare."

"Every kink you can imagine goes on here," said Juwan, but Nick hardly heard, on his way out the door. "Where're you going?"

"The airport." He could be in Saint Paul before midnight.

"Why not try Candyland first?" Juwan said.

"What for?"

Juwan looked surprised. "See if they've got an Amanda."

A much better idea. Why hadn't he thought of it? Nick came back through the door.

"Leg okay?" Juwan said.

twenty

C andyland Escort Service. How can I help?"

Nick, as every man would tell you, although in his case it was true, had never done this before, but he knew the lingo. "I'd like to arrange a date for tonight, around nine," he said. "With Amanda if she's available."

"Amanda? I'll have to put you on hold." Nick, at his kitchen table, listened to the on-hold music—"Like a Virgin"—knew the business was in good hands. He waited, was starting to doubt Candyland had an Amanda, when the receptionist came back on line. "Amanda at nine, all set."

While he waited for her, Nick searched the house again for his notebook and the envelope with the list of things to remember, couldn't find either. When had he last seen them? He backtracked to the moment of saying good-bye to Billie on the street, followed by the cleaning up of the broken glass from the break-in. After that, he'd made a list in the notebook, had a drink, started another list on the envelope. The two lists had some items in common—volleyball and CD, for example—and some not. Such as? *Motorcycle*—appearing only on the envelope. *Motorcycle* because he thought he'd heard the sound of one after the break-in. And there was a new thought about motorcycles, something important, not far down some shaft in his mind. But he couldn't get to it.

He'd made the lists. And then? Sleep. So much goddamned

sleep, like an overture to death that wouldn't stop playing. Elaine had appeared, in black minidress and glittering necklace, on her way home from a fund-raiser at Loyola Marymount. After that came more sleep, followed by the Google search for Desert High. Somewhere in all of that he'd misplaced the notebook and envelope.

Perhaps there was another approach. Nick drew three squares on a sheet of paper, labeled them Friday, Saturday, Sunday, divided them into A.M. and P.M. Friday, at about 2:45 P.M. he'd taken the stand in the Canning trial. From the Court TV tape, he knew—

Someone knocked at the door. Nick grabbed the volleyball, went into the hall, opened up. A young woman stood on the threshold. She wore a tiny skirt, tiny top and high heels that still left her a little short of volleyball height; had a diamond in her navel, a big smile and alert eyes that were taking him in and not smiling at all.

"Hi," she said. "I'm Amanda."

No thrill of connection, but that didn't necessarily make her the wrong Amanda. "Nick," said Nick. "Come in."

He held the door for her. "Hey," she said, stepping inside, "this is pretty nice."

"Thanks," said Nick. "There's a canal out back."

"You're joking."

He led her through the house, opened the back door, showed her the canal.

"A canal. Wow. I thought that was the other Venice." She gave him another look, some kind of calculation under way behind her eyes.

"Catch," Nick said, tossing her the volleyball.

"What the hell?" she said, making a clumsy attempt, almost knocking the ball out the door.

"I'm a big volleyball fan," Nick said.

"There's volleyball fans?"

Nick gazed at her; the question was genuine, beyond doubt.

She knew nothing about volleyball. "How about something to drink?" he said.

"Sure," said Amanda. "Right after we get the money thing out of the way. Did they go over the fee schedule? Three hundred an hour, a thousand for a whole night you won't forget."

"Let's try to squeeze what we can into an hour," Nick said.

"You're the boss."

Nick handed her the money, which she stuffed in a tiny rhinestone-studded shoulder purse. "What do you do, Nick?"

"I'm a consultant."

"Cool. I hear they do real well."

"What can I get you?"

"Huh?"

"To drink."

She thought it over. "How about a zombie?"

Nick laughed.

"What's funny?"

"Nothing. Tell me the ingredients."

"For a zombie?" she said, as though he'd asked how to make a BLT. "Light rum, dark rum, triple sec and OJ."

"Mind writing it down?" Nick said, pushing the sheet with the squares across the table.

"Writing it down?"

"So I'll have it for later."

"You can't remember light rum, dark rum, triple sec and OJ?" She wrote it down. Her letters were very small and spiky, totally unlike the writing on the Hallmark card—*Hey, Rui—we'll help each other, ok? xo Amanda*—which was big, loopy, schoolgirlish.

Nick made her a zombie, substituting Grand Marnier for triple sec, poured Johnnie Walker Black for himself.

"Hey," she said. "This is as good as Big Mo's."

"Who's he?"

"Not who," said Amanda. "What. Big Mo's is a bar on Melrose. Get out much, Nick?"

"Not enough."

She laid her drink on the table, came over, ran her fingers through his hair, then down the back of his neck, sending a charge right through him. "You've been working too hard—I know all the signs," she said in a throaty voice. "Time for R and R."

"Something to eat first?" Nick said.

"Naughty boy," she said, her hand now sliding down his chest. "Bet I'm going to find myself a nice big something to eat."

"We've got a whole hour," Nick said, backing away.

"It goes by pretty fast," said Amanda. She checked her watch. "And there's only fifty-one minutes left."

Nick went to the table, picked up the zombie, handed it to her. "I asked for you personally," he said.

"I heard," said Amanda.

"Any idea why?"

"Usually it's a recommendation."

Nick nodded. "Want to know whose?"

"Sure."

"Jim McMurray."

She furrowed her brow.

"From Saint Paul. He stays at the Airport Marriott."

"Never been there," Amanda said. "I don't work the Airport Marriott."

"Who does?"

"Huh?"

"From Candyland."

"Other girls."

"Do you know their names?"

She gave him a quick look. "You'll have to call the office for that," she said. "What kind of consulting do you do, Nick?"

"General," Nick said. "Sorry. I must've got Jim mixed up with someone else. Rui, maybe."

"Rui?"

"Is he a client or a friend?"

"I don't know any Rui." She wobbled on her high heels. "What's going on here?"

"A misunderstanding," Nick said. "My fault. Thanks for coming over."

And wobbled a little more. "You want me to go?"

"No rush," Nick said. "Finish your drink."

Amanda's hand tightened on her purse. "The money's for the first hour or any portion thereof," she said.

"You earned it."

"How?"

Nick sipped his drink, didn't answer.

"Are you a cop or something?" Amanda said.

"Do I look like a cop?"

She studied him closely. "I don't know. Cops are usually kind of beefy." She downed the rest of her zombie in one gulp. Nick walked her to the door. He had his hand on the knob, the door open an inch or two, when she paused and turned to him. "You're not going to complain to the office or anything?"

"Why would I do that?"

"For getting nothing for something," Amanda said.

"Don't worry," Nick said. "Enjoy your free time."

"That's a nice thing to say."

He'd meant it.

Her face softened. "You're actually not that bad looking." She leaned forward, ran her fingers through his hair again, the effect again electric. "How about a hand job before I go?" she said. "Won't take a minute."

A strange offer, almost tempting in spite of itself, and also innocent at the same time. The doorknob turned in Nick's hand. Billie walked in, his navy-blue suit jacket on a hanger.

"Billie—Amanda," Nick said.

"I was just leaving," Amanda said.

"Not on my account," said Billie.

Amanda didn't quite get that. She waved good-bye—a tiny circular motion—and hurried across the street, getting into a car parked on the other side. The driver, a jowly man chewing on a toothpick, didn't look at her or say a word, just started the car and drove off.

Nick closed the door.

"I see you're feeling better," Billie said.

Nick turned to her. How many times in his life had his heart actually lifted at the sight of another human being? Not nearly enough, but it did now.

"Here's your jacket," Billie said.

"Whatever you heard," he said, "I was only interviewing a potential witness."

"It has many names," said Billie.

"Billie, stop." Nick put his arms around her. She resisted, but only for a moment or two. He kissed her and she kissed back. The world got very small. One thing led to another in the most normal way, except that in the bedroom Nick got the weird feeling that her vitality was somehow breathing through the skin barrier and into him.

They lay in bed, Billie's head on his chest. He felt her lips move.

"We haven't talked about race," she said.

"I'm the Imperial Grand Wizard," said Nick.

Now he felt her teeth. They bit him, just hard enough to hurt.

"It's not important to me," Nick said. "Never was and now it really isn't."

"A lot of white people say it's not important," Billie said. "No black people ever do."

"The hell with everybody," Nick said.

There was a silence. He could feel her thinking, her brain an inch or two from his heart. "Some white guys have a thing for black women," she said.

"Not me."

"So my being black isn't part of the attraction?"

She shifted her head slightly, her hair, kinky, different, brushing his chest. "I wouldn't say that. It's just not high on the list."

"What's high on the list?"

"Questions like that."

"What else?"

"I'm only going to reveal one a day," Nick said.

She took hold of him, gave a little shake. "Let's the three of us put that to a vote." They had a three-way caucus.

After, Nick could hardly keep his eyes open. Billie wanted to talk.

"Tell me about this potential witness."

Nick never discussed ongoing cases; he wanted to now. He tried to organize the facts, but he was tiring and they kept slipping away. "It's about filling in gaps," he said. "The main thing is, I think I was looking for someone named Amanda when . . ."

"When you had the seizure?"

"Yes." It was better to say it. "When I had the seizure."

"Why were you looking for her?"

"I don't know."

"Doesn't someone employ you?"

"Usually."

"The client."

"Right."

"So who's the client?"

"Good question." And one that hadn't occurred to him: who was the client in the Amanda case?

"And why hasn't the client been in touch?" Billie said.

An even better one. "You're in the wrong business."

"Is that a complaint about my nursing?"

"You're multidimensional," he said. "Let's put it that way." He patted her butt. Some kind of racial attraction thing there, he couldn't deny it.

"I know what you're thinking," Billie said, "Mr. Wizard."

When Nick woke up it was morning and she was gone. He got up—slow, creaky, the right side backsliding a little, but probably because of the exertions of the night before—and went into the kitchen. She'd left a note.

Call the office—Dr. Tully wants to see you. No arguments—you're outvoted two to one.

Out in the hall, the mail fell through the slot with a soft thump. Nick gathered it up: bills from the hospital that the HMO should have handled but had not, due to codes 23 and 37, whatever they were; a catalog from Smith & Wesson; his bank statement. Nick hadn't actually balanced his checkbook in twenty years, but he always scanned the statement. He did it now, paused, looked more closely. September 13: he'd deposited a four-hundred-and-fifty-dollar check. September 13 was the Saturday of the lost weekend. He had no memory of a four-hundred-and-fifty-dollar check.

Nick drove to the bank. The bank held his mortgage, had known him a long time. He waited in the manager's office, drinking the bank's coffee. The manager came in, handed him a photocopy of the check. "It was actually deposited at an ATM in the Airport Marriott the night of the twelfth," she said, "but they didn't pick up till Saturday. Is anything wrong?"

Nick looked at the photocopy: a check for four-hundred-and-fifty-dollars made out to him and signed by Liza Rummel. She had a Van Nuys address, printed at the top.

The phone was ringing when Nick got home.

"Gallego here, Barstow police. Got a name on that daughter of George Rummel's for you."

"Liza?" Nick said.

"If you know, why ask?" said Sergeant Gallego. He sounded a little hurt. "George's funeral's the day after tomorrow, or do you know that too?"

twenty-one

Nick pulled up in front of Liza Rummel's house in Van Nuys, coming to a jerky stop on account of some right-foot braking incompetence that took him by surprise. Everyone's trash barrels stood on the street. Liza Rummel had four, plus three bloated Hefty bags, one of which had split down the side, allowing a funny-looking green thing to hang out. Going closer, he saw it was the head of a stuffed animal. Nick pulled it out: Babar. He stood there for a moment. It felt familiar in his hands, this particular stuffed animal, as if they were old friends; he almost expected it to talk. And deep within his head came a strange physical pressure, as though some thought were straining to be born. He opened the car and tossed Babar inside.

Nick walked up to the house, a small clapboard house with the stump of a recently cut palm tree still seeping slightly in the yard, and knocked on the front door, his right hand doing a good job, nice and loud, making up for that momentary right-foot letdown. A man opened the door. He had a long beard, pointy at the end, like in a fairy tale, wore a black suit, black hat, white shirt with a blue ink blot over the heart, no tie. His eyes, tiny behind thick glasses, blinked in the bright light.

"I'm looking for Liza Rummel," Nick said. He spoke extra clearly on the assumption the man's English was poor.

Which turned out not to be the case. "The previous tenant, I believe." the man said, his English as good as Nick's, possibly better. "We moved in last week."

"Did she leave a forwarding address?"

"Not with us."

Nick glimpsed a woman crossing a corridor in the shadows; her head was bald. Orthodox Jews; he'd missed it completely, the synthesizing component of his judgment way off. Just as bad, he knew there had to be an obvious next step, and that wouldn't come either.

"Perhaps the landlord would know," the man said.

That was it, the next step—landlord.

"Mrs. Franklin," said the man, anticipating his question. "She lives down the block, number 1296."

Nick thought of inviting the man along with him: he had enough brain power for both of them.

No one answered the door at 1296. Nick gazed down at the welcome mat. *Home Sweet Home,* it read, the letters garlanded with flowers, a fat bumblebee in one corner. Again he felt the pressure of a thought or memory tugging on some mental umbilical cord. This one was about bees and pouty sensual lips, but it wouldn't come free either. He knocked one last time, was turning to leave, when he heard music, faint as background bird chatter, drifting through the air. The tune was familiar.

Nick followed the music around to the back of the house. Mrs. Franklin had a nice backyard with a pool and a brick patio. A chubby girl in a baggy sweat suit sat under an umbrella, a boom box at her feet, a joint in her hand. It was a school day and she looked to be of school-going age. The boom box played, not loud, a song he knew from somewhere:

And you don't even know
What's buried in your yard
Retard.

The girl stared into the water, deep in thought. Nick stepped onto the patio, a loose bit of brick crunching under his heel. The girl looked up.

Nick raised his hand in peace. "I'm looking for Mrs. Franklin," he said.

"That's my mom," said the girl, letting go of the joint; it fell into the pool with a tiny sizzle. "Ms. Franklin. She's not home."

"When do you expect her?" Nick said.

"Not till later." The girl tilted her head to the side, gave him a close look. "Were you the detective?" she said.

"I am a detective," Nick said.

"The one who was here before, looking for Amanda Rummel?"

The two names, fusing like that, hit Nick with a force that was almost physical. He sat down in a deck chair opposite her.

"You've changed your hair or something," the girl said. "Did you use to have a mustache?"

"No," Nick said. He was a little short of breath. "I've forgotten your name."

"Beth," she said.

"Beth." She had a nice face, not fully formed—he could see simultaneously how she had looked as a little kid and how she would look in thirty years—a nice face that was anxious about something. "How old are you?"

"Sixteen. I ditched today. My mom doesn't know."

"I won't tell," Nick said.

That did nothing to make the anxious look disappear. "I'm really not feeling too good," she said.

"Sorry to hear that," Nick said.

"Thanks," Beth said. "It's kind of weird about Amanda."

"What is?"

"Like the way she's gone again."

"Gone again?"

"But you got to talk to her, right?" Beth said. "She told me you did."

"When was this?"

"Last month or so. Whenever she came back. I mentioned about you coming over here and she said she met you. This was at school. We were starting to get real friendly—she's so nice—telling each other our problems and stuff, and then all of a sudden her and her mom took off together, not paying the rent. My mom was so pissed."

A jumble. Nick looked into her eyes: they were red. "What are Amanda's problems?"

"Besides what I told you before?" Beth said. "There's this boyfriend."

"Rui."

"Yeah. He's like thirty years old or something, with problems too. She said it was fate."

"What was fate?"

"Them meeting. Guess where they met—it's so cool."

"Tell me."

"An Empty Box concert. They're both huge fans. Amanda turned me on to them too. This is Empty Box right now."

Retard, retard.

Beth handed him the CD case: Empty Box, Retards Picnic, with that picture of a burning picnic basket on the cover, same as the one he'd found in his car. Why hadn't he listened to it? Music, sights, smells: they might all trigger memory.

"What was fateful about them meeting?"

"Fateful?" said Beth. "You know—something meant to be."

"In what way?"

"Like they were two miners, that's what Amanda said. She's real smart. Two miners digging in separate—what do you call them?"

"Tunnels?"

"Tunnels. And then one day they knock down some rocks and there they are, together."

"What were they looking for?"

"Looking for?"

"Down in this mine."

"She didn't say they were looking for anything. It's one of those metaphors."

A metaphor Nick understood very well: he was down in the mine too, working on a third tunnel. He had a client—Liza Rummel. He had an assignment—find Amanda. Now, just to be sure, he said, "I'm assuming Liza Rummel is Amanda's mother."

Beth gave him a quick sideways look. "You're trying to trick me," she said.

"What do you mean?"

"By asking the same questions over and over, like on the cop shows, till the suspect makes a mistake and says something that doesn't match and then they cuff him." Beth looked like she might start crying.

"I'm not trying to trick you."

"Then why ask when you know the answer?" Her voice got a little shrill. "I already told you her real mom got killed." Pause. "Why are you looking at me like that?"

Nick wasn't aware he was looking at her at all. *Her real mom got killed?* He felt that pressure again in his head, the pressure of some memory trying—yes, like a miner after a cave-in—to squeeze through a blocked-off passage.

"Oh, shit," Beth said. She got up quickly. "I'm not feeling good." And hurried into the house, hand over her mouth.

On her deck chair lay another joint and a box of matches, perhaps fallen from her pocket. When had Nick last smoked pot? Probably some evening walking on the beach with Kathleen, back when they began. Suddenly, he had a strong desire to smoke this one: a cliché—cancer victim plus weed—that he saw no reason to avoid. Nick lit up, inhaled deeply.

Almost at once, his body felt different—lighter, straighter, at ease with itself. He realized he'd been in constant pain, pain now radiating away. And as it did, that last memory squeezed out into the open, a memory of his own speaking voice: *It's an un-solved case.* The death of Amanda's real mother was an unsolved case. And somehow that case—

"Hey!" Beth was back. He hadn't heard her coming. "You're smoking dope."

"I have a permit," Nick said.

She gazed at him, wide-eyed. "I've never seen an adult smoke dope before."

"Planning to stop when you reach voting age?" Nick said. He patted her chair. She sat down. He had her attention. "Any idea where Liza and Amanda went?" he said. "Or why they left so suddenly?"

"No," Beth said. "And I have my own problems, in case that matters."

"Such as?"

She tried to look him in the eye, could not. And now the tears came, not in torrents, more in a hopeless overflow. "I'm pregnant," she said.

"How pregnant?"

"Like in time? I don't know. Four months maybe. I took the test."

"Do your parents know?"

"There's no parents, just my mom. She'd kill me."

"Do you mean that literally?"

"No. But she'd just . . . I don't want to think about it."

Nick understood, almost knew what it felt like to be her, faced with the scariest thing life had thrown her way, and so young; he also knew it was far from the scariest thing possible. "You've got to give her the chance," he said.

"What chance?"

"The chance to come through for you."

"What if she doesn't?" Beth said, voice rising toward a wail. "Oh, God. Time is ticking away. Look." She snatched up the hem of her sweatshirt, exposed her belly, slightly rounded, taut; *with a red butterfly tattooed above her navel.* That butterfly: why did it—Beth lowered her sweatshirt. "What if she doesn't?"

Nick handed her his card. "Then call me," he said. "I know someone who'll have good advice. This can come out all right."

"It can?"

"Yes."

"Promise?" Beth said.

Promise. She was a child. "I promise," Nick said.

"Oh, thank you." She wiped her tears on her sleeve and read the card. "I can't pay you or anything."

"That's okay," Nick said. "I'll take a joint or two if you can spare them."

I f Amanda Rummel didn't work for Candyland Escorts, who did? Had to be Liza. Wrong tunnel, right direction. From his car, Nick called Candyland to arrange a date with Liza.

"We don't have a Liza," said the receptionist. "We've got a Loretta, a Lateesha and a Lexi, all very attractive."

"Did you have a Liza?"

Pause.

"Liza Rummel," Nick said. "Back in September."

"We don't release information like that. Company policy."

"This is important," Nick said.

Click.

His phone rang immediately.

"Nick? Elaine. How are you doing?"

"Great."

"Feeling all right?"

"Better and better."

"Good. You had me a little worried last time."

"Last time?"

Pause. "You don't remember me dropping in? You had a nosebleed."

"Oh, yeah. That was nothing."

"You seemed a little tired."

"I'm wide awake now."

She laughed. "Sounds like it. Back at work?"

"Yes."

"Glad to hear it. If there's ever anything I can do, say the word."

Her voice was soft, compliant, almost sweet; hardly sounded like her at all. A thought, a sinking one, came to him: *had she somehow learned the diagnosis, and now was trying her best to be sympathetic?* He didn't want that. Plus he hated to ask for help. But who better to ask than Elaine? "There is one thing," Nick said. "Who'd be good to talk to in vice?"

"Depends on the subject."

"Escort services."

"You are feeling better," Elaine said. "What's it about?"

"I need the actual operating location of an outfit called Candyland."

"Should be a file," Elaine said. "I'll get back to you."

"Thanks," Nick said, "but you don't have—"

"My pleasure."

Elaine called back in five minutes. "A woman named Sylvia Bondini runs it out of her house." She gave him an address in Malibu. "Ten to one she offers you a freebie."

Sylvia Bondini lived on a ridge off Saddle Peak Road, two thousand feet above the smog. A steep driveway wound around a rocky outcrop, ended in a car park between the garage—bigger than Nick's house—and the house itself, a multilevel pile that went on and on in all directions. Nick came to another of those jerky stops, got out of the car. The ocean, from this height a flat steel plate, stretched all the way to Catalina and beyond. Nick took a deep breath, smelled pine and eucalyptus. This was living.

"You lost?"

Nick looked up. A woman stood on a balcony of the house, two or three stories up, garden shears in hand. She was big, with a wild head of curly black hair and heavy gold cube earrings dangling halfway to her shoulders. "Don't think so," Nick said. "I'm looking for Sylvia Bondini."

She clipped the head off some plant. "And who are you?"

"Nick Petrov." He held up his license. "I'm a private investigator."

"Really."

"You're Sylvia Bondini?"

"And if I am?"

"You can help me."

"I don't see how."

"It's about a woman who worked for you."

"One of the maids? A cook? They come and go."

"Nope," said Nick. "At Candyland."

"Candyland?" she said. "You lost me."

Thick bushes parted, a few yards from Nick's left. A gardener appeared—Nick took him for a gardener—a huge shirtless man with shaved head, popping muscles and a machete in each hand. A gardener who doubled as something else. And Nick's gun (not that he'd be needing it)? In the safe at home.

twenty-two

This was the kind of moment for thinking fast but Nick couldn't think at all. His mind was preoccupied with those huge gold cube earrings, and all the blow jobs, hand jobs, and employee penetrations that had paid for them, this house, this view. No surprise: surely he'd known all his working life that the sex business was a capitalistic enterprise, built to capitalistic design on a foundation of imbalances. It had never angered, or even bothered him much, before. Now it did. He smiled at the gardener, a brown-skinned and hostile Mr. Clean.

"Don't hurt yourself with those things," he said.

The gardener, unsure what Nick was talking about for a moment, glanced down at the machetes.

"Nolo," the woman yelled down. *"Deshagate de él."*

Nick's Spanish, learned from years on the street, wasn't bad; he was pretty sure *deshagate de él* meant "get rid of him," but even a beginner could have guessed the translation from the way Nolo was crab-walking toward him, wrists cocked, machete blades upraised.

Nick, eyes on Nolo, called back up. "This is a missing person case, Sylvia. It won't go away."

"I'll worry about that," she said.

Nolo kept coming, somewhat clumsy but huge. Nick had been in situations like this a few times, had always come out well. But how, exactly? There were tricks, moves, tactics. He couldn't remember any of them. The most important thing, of course, was not to be afraid. And he wasn't. What did he have to fear now? Not a goddamned thing. How would you say, *Whatever she's paying you is not enough?* Nick came up with a Spanish version, tried it out on Nolo.

Nolo blinked, then got more belligerent-looking, his jaw muscles bulging like walnuts. Nick backed toward the car; strategic retreat had a long military pedigree of only sporadic success, but nothing else occurred to him. One option was to obediently get in the car and drive away, but he didn't feel obedient. He could also sidle around to the trunk like this, take the keys from his pocket very slowly, show Nolo—crouched, almost in striking distance—that they were only keys, harmless, and pop open the trunk. Next would be to formulate a slightly confusing sentence: "*Momentito,* while I get the senora's subpoena. And, *con permiso,* one for you too."

"Subpoena?" Nolo said; yes, a little confused, unsure of Nick's status, unaware that he wouldn't be serving subpoenas, but responsive to the power of the word.

"They're in here somewhere," Nick said, leaning into the shadows of the trunk. He felt Nolo behind him, slightly to the left. Pure good luck, that left part: Nick couldn't trust his right hand with this. With his left he got a good grip on the tire iron, said, "I know I brought them with me." A machete point ran down his spine in an exploratory sort of way. Nick thought *Explode,* and lashed out with a backhand swing.

Had he really slowed that much? And Nolo turned out to be a little quicker, a little smoother, than Nick had assumed. He managed to get one of the machetes up in time to block the tire iron, at least partially, so that instead of hitting him just below the sternum, where Nick had been aiming, it got him square on the forehead, a wicked gash already unzippering as Nolo fell behind a large planter, out cold.

"What the hell's going on down there?" Sylvia called, peering from the deck, her view blocked by the planter and the raised lid of Nick's trunk.

"Nolo hurt himself," Nick said, taking out his cell phone. "I'm calling an ambulance. Then let's talk."

"What the fuck do you mean—he hurt himself?"

"An accident waiting to happen," Nick said. He gave the dispatcher Sylvia Bondini's address, then patched up Nolo's forehead with bandages from his first-aid kit, also in the trunk. Nolo's huge chest rose and fell in a nice, even rhythm. A siren blare rose up the mountain.

Nick and Sylvia Bondini sat on a terrace that seemed to be cantilevered right over the sea. Looking almost straight down, he could see the departing ambulance shrink away on the steep, twisting road.

"I don't know why I'm being so fucking nice," Sylvia said, lighting a cigarette and flicking the match over the side. "I have friends. The kind you don't want visits from." She blew a thick column of smoke in his direction.

"I like company," Nick said.

She gave him a hard look. "Run it by me again. Nolo smacked himself with his own machete?"

"Afraid so."

"Hard to believe. But a skinny guy like you laying him out is even harder." She sucked in smoke like she needed it to live. "Let's see that so-called license again."

He handed it to her. She put on reading glasses with big heart-shaped lenses, jabbed a sharp, red-tipped finger at his photo. "Does your name ring a bell?" He didn't answer. She stabbed out her cigarette on the wrought-iron rail. "How did you find me?"

"It's not a secret," Nick said. "There's a file on you."

"Think that scares me, some goddamned file? I've made arrangements."

"Why disturb them?" Nick said.

"Is that a threat?"

"Arrangements change."

"What's that supposed to mean?"

"Everything changes. There's a new chief, for example."

"So?"

"She's going to make you forget all the others."

"Another threat? I don't like threats."

"What do you like?"

"Huh?"

"What makes you cooperate?"

Sunlight glared off fingerprints on her glasses. "Strange fucking question. No one's ever asked me that before." She thought, her face changing shape, hardening even more than it was already. "I cooperate when it makes business sense."

"There you go," Nick said.

She glared at him. A thermal upwelling of air brought the last faint sound of the ambulance siren. "Okay," she said, taking off her glasses and flipping the license back in his direction. "What do you want to know? Make it fast."

"Liza Rummel's whereabouts."

"She doesn't work for me anymore."

"When did she stop?" Nick said.

"They don't hand in resignations," said Sylvia. "They just don't show up. Liza stopped showing up last month."

"Do you know the exact date?"

"No."

"Could you get it?"

"If I wanted."

"Any idea where she went?"

"No."

"Or why?"

"They get pregnant, OD on something, go back to Nebraska, find some other line of work, which is rare, or find a rich guy to take care of them, which is never."

"And Liza specifically?"

"Pick one."

"How long did she work for you?"

"Couple years."

"How well did you know her?"

"As well as I had to."

"What can you tell me about her?"

"She was reliable."

"Did she ever discuss any problems with you?"

"Why would she do that?"

Nick laughed. "Any idea why she left?"

"No."

"So one day in September she didn't show up and that was that."

"Right."

"Meaning she didn't show up for a date with some guy."

"That's the job."

"Who was that guy?"

She shrugged; but she didn't do much to sell that shrug, her eyes taking on an inward look.

"Jim McMurray?" Nick said. "From Saint Paul?"

That did it for the inward look; her habitual anger rose in its place. "What the hell's going on here? How do you know something like that?"

Nick didn't answer right away. He just watched her face. She didn't like being watched. All her features were big, except the nose, fixed by someone who hadn't done her any favors. To his surprise, her anger faded; she even looked a little tired. "What's the rest of it?" Nick said.

"Rest of what?"

"Whatever it is you're not telling me."

Sylvia rose, stood at the balcony railing, gazed out to sea. "You never said why you're looking for her."

Nick made something up. "Her family's worried."

"She's got a family?"

"Of course. She never mentioned her daughter Amanda?"

"No. Are the police involved in this search?"

"Not yet," Nick said. "Wouldn't it be better if I found her first?"

Sylvia faced him, made a decisive little nod. A drop of sweat rolled into her cleavage and disappeared. "This asshole McMurray called me just bullshit about something Liza did. She phoned him—at the office, the stupid cunt—and asked for money. An advance, she called it."

"Advance on what?"

"Future cocksucking, ass-fucking, whatever the dickhead likes. That's not the point. The point is, you don't call the work or home numbers and you don't ask for loans. It's not professional. Plus the guy's daughter's an intern in his office, answered the phone."

"When did he call you?"

"Last week."

"What did you tell him?"

"She didn't work for me anymore and sure as hell never would again. Period."

Nick rose, handed Sylvia his card. "If she gets in touch," he said.

Sylvia tucked it in her pocket, produced a card of her own, scribbled something, handed it to him. "Good for one freebie, exclusive of tip," she said. "Finding her before the cops get involved can't hurt."

Ten-to-one shot comes through. For a moment, Nick couldn't remember who'd offered that bet, and it had been so recent. Then it came to him: Elaine. This woman Sylvia was smart and able, but not in Elaine's class. Elaine was a rocket, unstoppable.

Not professional to phone the office, but those were call-girl rules. PIs weren't so squeamish.

"Mr. McMurray, please."

"He's not in," said a woman, a young one. "Would you like his voice mail?"

"Is there somewhere else I can reach him? I'm calling for Mr. Petrov in Los Angeles. It's important."

"My—Mr. McMurray's in L.A. right now, actually. If you leave a number, I'll—"

"Staying at the Airport Marriott as usual?"

"Yes, but if you—"

Room 936, goddamn it," said Juwan Barnes, jabbing at his screen. "I was supposed to get a heads-up the moment he checked back in." He reached for the phone.

Nick went up, knocked on the door. He had a mental image of Jim McMurray, one of the few recovered from the lost weekend: a red-faced, sagging-throated, barefoot man in a suit, toenails thick and yellow. The man who opened the door was dressed for golf and had a putter in his hand, didn't have a red face. Only the sagging throat was right. He looked at Nick without recognition for a moment. Then his face got red in a hurry, overlaying Nick's memory to perfection. McMurray backed up a step, raising the putter defensively.

Another memory filled in: McMurray lying on the floor. "No need to be alarmed, Mr. McMurray."

"I'm calling Security."

"If you like," Nick said. "But this will be quick and painless—as long as you're not involved in Liza Rummel's disappearance."

"What disappearance? I spoke to her last week."

"In person?"

"On the phone. She called me at work."

"About what?"

"None of your business. If you don't leave, I'm making that call."

"Did she want money?"

"That does it." McMurray moved toward the bedside phone, knocking over his golf bag. Nick stepped into the room and closed the door.

"Security? Send someone up immediately—there's an intruder in 936."

McMurray shot Nick a look half afraid, half triumphant and backed around the bed, his putter in the en garde position. Nick picked up the bag of clubs—very heavy for some reason—leaned it against the wall. "What's your handicap?" he said.

"That's none of your business either."

"That bad?" Nick said.

The door swung open and Juwan walked in, trailed by a waiter pushing a cart.

"Security," Juwan said. "Hi, Nick."

McMurray's gaze went from Juwan to Nick and back. "You know this guy?"

"Seems like forever," Juwan said. "Here's a little snack, Mr. McMurray, compliments of the management."

The waiter uncorked a bottle of champagne, filled a flute glass, handed it to McMurray, lifted the silver lid off a plate of lobster salad, left the room.

"What's this all about?" said McMurray, red-faced, confused, but also sipping the champagne, perhaps unconsciously.

"We appreciate your business," said Juwan, "simple as that."

"Is there a glass for me?" Nick said.

"And hope," said Juwan, talking over him, "that you give Mr. Petrov the kind of cooperation he doesn't deserve."

"What's that mean?" Nick said.

"Mr. Petrov has a reputation of sometimes leaning on people a little too hard."

"Tell me about it," said McMurray.

"I've changed," Nick said.

"But since he's changed, all the more reason to help, right, Mr. McMurray?"

The inner corners of McMurray's eyebrows pinched down in thought.

"How's the champagne?" Juwan said.

McMurray tried some more. "Good."

Juwan topped off his glass, at the same time sliding the putter out of McMurray's other hand. Nick pushed the cart closer to McMurray, handed him knife and fork. McMurray sat on the bed.

"Here's a napkin," Nick said.

McMurray looked at him with suspicion but took the napkin and spread it on his lap.

"Lobster salad sure looks tasty," Nick said.

McMurray tried a forkful in a slow, mesmerized way and said, "Mmm."

"Good?" said Nick.

McMurray nodded.

"Did Liza ask for money?" Nick said.

McMurray nodded again.

Golf balls were strewn around an overturned glass outside the bathroom. Juwan toed a few of them across the room, putted one in from about twelve feet.

"How much?" Nick said.

McMurray took another bite, washed it down with champagne. "Five hundred."

"And you said no."

Juwan knocked in another.

"Actually I said yes."

Nick was surprised. "I thought you were angry about her calling the office."

"Who wouldn't be?" said McMurray, taking another drink.

Nick poured him more. "Then why did you say yes?"

Juwan knocked in a couple more golf balls, almost filling the glass.

"Holy cow," said McMurray. "What's the rest of your game like?"

"Long and straight," said Juwan.

McMurray patted the corners of his mouth with the napkin. "I'm looking for a partner, Riverside, tomorrow at three," he said. "Best ball against a couple customers who took me for a tidy sum last time."

"I'll check my schedule," Juwan said. "Right now, I'm interested in the answer to Nick's question."

"You're in on this too?"

"Academically," Juwan said.

"Why did I say yes to Liza? I've gotten to know her a little bit. She's not a bad person. And she was in trouble."

"What kind of trouble?"

"She didn't say. Just that she'd pay me back when she could."

"There was no hint of blackmail?"

"She's not like that."

"It never crossed your mind?"

"I wouldn't go that far."

"So you sent the five hundred?"

"A little less, in the end."

"How much less?"

"Four hundred."

"Meaning you sent her one hundred."

"She didn't bitch."

"Did you wire it?"

McMurray shook his head. "U.S. mail."

"To what address?"

McMurray took his notebook off the bedside table, opened it. "Seven three seven four Ventura Boulevard, Apartment 3, Encino. Care of," he squinted at his own handwriting, "Ms. Betsy Matsu."

Betsy Matsu: the volleyball coach.

Nick and Juwan had worked together for almost two years, long ago in Huntington Park, but not as smoothly as this, not close. Juwan canned one last putt, the ball nesting softly in the glass. On the way down in the elevator, he said, "I'm sending you a bill for the champagne and lobster salad."

"I didn't touch either one."

"You were never this funny," Juwan said as the doors opened. "Did I mention the gratuity? Eighteen percent."

twenty-three

Encino: Betsy Matsu—the next step. The directions, that network of blue tributaries he'd always had on call, wouldn't come. In the parking lot of the Airport Marriott, Nick opened the glove box, searched for the Thomas Guide, knocking the Hallmark card to the floor. Again. He opened it, reread the inscription:

Hey, Rui—we'll help each other, ok? xo Amanda.

Help each other do what? Wasn't that an important question? Why hadn't he asked it before? Or maybe he had, back on that weekend, back when he was . . . whole? And maybe he'd found the answer, maybe he'd written it in his notebook. But: in code that he could no longer read, and even if he could, the notebook was gone. Therefore? He had to work with what he had. Help each other do what? Amanda and Rui were like two miners digging in separate tunnels. *And then one day they knock down some rocks, and there they are, together.*

It's one of those metaphors, Beth Franklin said. Break down the metaphor: tunneling meant digging down, digging deep, into what? Into your own history, maybe, your own life. Amanda and Rui, each digging into their own pasts, had found each other way down there somewhere. And why had they been digging? Because they each needed help. Help with what? What had gone wrong in their lives? He had one fact, one fact about Amanda, and that was all: *Her mom got killed.* Plus he had one memory fragment, left over from the initial investigation, of his own voice: *It's an unsolved case.*

Had he already solved it? Solved it and didn't even know? Did the fact that Liza and Amanda were back together, at least before they skipped out on the rent, point in that direction, that the case was solved? Maybe he'd already delivered, and there was no case. Could he argue with that? Not logically. But it felt wrong.

Find the girl and live. That felt right.

But he had a horrible thought anyway, based on something else Beth had said: *time is ticking away.* He and Beth had a lot in common, both of them pregnant—Beth with a baby, he with glioblastoma multiforme, Grade IV—and the clock ticking down. He had to get organized and fast, fill in all the gaps in the lost-weekend calendar, make some systematic arrangement of his bits of evidence. Fast, fast, fast. Nick started going fast inside, although on the outside he was still. An unfamiliar feeling. Was this panic?

Is this what you call thinking, Nikolai? Is that what you call systematic?

His father's voice, so real, not coming from inside his head, but somewhere else. That was what made it so easy to talk back.

"What's wrong with my thinking?"

You've forgotten the next step already.

The next step. It was . . .

Betsy Matsu. Of course: how could he get so twisted around? He waited for more—help? advice? meddling? sabotage?—but the voice was silent, more than silent, absent; the difference between a person not speaking and a person not there.

The next step: Coach Betsy Matsu, the volleyball connection. Maybe it would all end easily in an hour or so, he, Liza and Amanda having dinner in some ethnic restaurant on Ventura Boulevard. Nick stuck the key in the ignition, and at that moment had a crazy pregnancy thought on top of the horrible one: what if he and Billie adopted Beth's baby?

Nick paused, hand on key, key in ignition. His eyelids grew very heavy, very fast, as though the earth's gravitational power had suddenly shot up. Adopting Beth's baby—his brains were scrambled, but good. He fell asleep in the car.

I t was dark by the time Nick found 7374 Ventura Boulevard, a four-story red-trimmed building with a sushi bar on the ground floor. Around the corner was a door with four buzzers. He pressed number three. A woman's voice came over the speaker, small and scratchy.

"Sarah?"

"No," Nick said. "Are you Betsy Matsu?"

"Who's this?"

"Nick Petrov."

"I don't know you."

"I'm a private investigator working for Liza Rummel."

Long pause. Nick didn't say anything, wasn't even tempted; that was new, a patience within, despite the pressure for speed.

Buzz. He opened up, climbed a set of stairs. A tall woman waited in the doorway of number three. Doorway yes, door no: its splintered remains hung off the top hinge. The woman's glossy black hair gleamed under the hall light.

"I'm Betsy Matsu," she said.

He shook her hand, not a name on a volleyball that had come from who knows where, but a flesh-and-blood woman, and her hand, although strong, was trembling slightly. This was real, all of it. There was a case, beyond doubt, deep, tangled, unsolved.

"What happened here?" Nick said.

"Someone broke in," Betsy said.

Nick looked beyond her, into the apartment. A nice apartment, with delicate-looking furniture, a Japanese screen separating the kitchen from the dining room, all of it undisturbed.

"Did anyone get hurt?"

"I was at work."

"What about Liza?"

"They left last night."

"She and Amanda?"

"Right."

"Where did they go?"

"I don't know. They said they'd be in touch."

"So the break-in happened after they left?"

"Today," said Betsy Matsu. "Sometime between seven-thirty when I went to work and five when I got home."

"You're a volleyball coach."

"A teacher first," said Betsy. "U.S. history. At Encino Western."

"Did you call the police?"

"They just left."

"What did they say?"

"Not much. Nothing's missing and there's no damage except for the door." Her eyes shifted to its splintered remains. "I think they took some fingerprints. It's all so . . ."

"May I come in?" Nick said.

She nodded. Nick walked in. The first thing he did was straighten what was left of the door and arrange it as near to the closed position as it would go.

Betsy watched with her hands clasped in front of her. "Thank you," she said. "I could make tea."

"Sounds good."

The tea she made was the best Nick had ever tasted. And hadn't he read something on the science page about the healing power of tea? They sat at the kitchen table, drinking from perfect little porcelain bowls with misty mountain scenes on the side. Betsy grew calmer. He guessed she was a pretty good teacher. She spoke in well-structured paragraphs, her meaning clear. All you'd have to do for a good grade on her tests was pay attention.

"I didn't hear from Amanda after she changed schools, not until last week when she called to say they needed somewhere to stay for a few days. I offered my place—there's an extra bedroom and it's no trouble at all. And Amanda's a great kid. I'd do almost anything to help her."

"What do you like about her?" Nick said.

Betsy gazed into her tea. She had beautiful skin, beautiful hair, but there was something about the set of her face, something heavy and somber, that kept her from being beautiful. "Here's an example. Amanda's freshman year she played on the varsity, which is rare at Western. She's the only one since I've been coaching. We had a pretty good team, good enough to get to the league final, against Simi Valley. Do you know volleyball scoring? Best of five sets, with a set being first to fifteen, winning by two. Simi Valley went up two–love in sets, twelve–three in the third. I called a time-out, just to let them regroup a little. No one was talking, they were beaten, some already had their minds on other things. Then Amanda, who hadn't said a word all year, spoke up. 'Let's mess up how they're going to remember this game,' she said. Everyone looked at her. It was kind of strange, but so right."

"You won?"

"That would be the Hollywood ending," Betsy Matsu said. "We won that third set, nineteen–seventeen, then the fourth seventeen–fifteen, but the kids just ran out of gas in the fifth— fifteen–eleven, I think it was. But it did change how everyone thought about that game—people still talk about it. I was very unhappy to hear she'd quit."

"Why did she?"

"I don't know. She came to the volleyball camp I run last summer, plus Van Nuys has a good program and the coach was pumped she was coming. Amanda's D-one material. But she didn't try out in the fall."

"Any explanation?"

"Not the kind that helps. I called Amanda on behalf of the new coach and she told me she was tired of volleyball. It happens, of course, and I've heard it before, but it doesn't really get to the bottom of anything. Why do some kids lose interest?"

"I'd settle for just knowing why Amanda did," Nick said.

Betsy nodded, sipped her tea. Her hands were long and finely shaped, the nails cut short. "You're working for Liza?"

"She hired me to find Amanda."

"I don't understand."

"They're in trouble."

"I know. But Amanda's not missing."

"They may both be now," Nick said. Betsy's eyes widened. "Tell me more about their troubles."

"The rent went up on their house and they got kicked out," Betsy said. "Plus Liza lost her job."

"What does she do?"

"She didn't tell you? Liza works for a catering company, but with the economy so bad they had to let people go."

"Do you know the name of this catering company?"

Betsy shook her head. "I think it's in Beverly Hills."

"Any more to their troubles than that?"

"Isn't it enough?"

"Maybe," Nick said. "But why did they leave last night?"

"Family matters, Liza said."

"Like what?"

"She didn't say."

"Did you ask?"

"I'm not like that."

"How about where these family matters were taking them?"

"Nothing about that either."

"Any visitors while they were here?"

"Not that I'm aware of."

"Phone calls?"

She thought. "There was just the one."

"Last night?"

"How did you know?" Betsy said. "The phone rang around seven. I answered. It was a man asking for Amanda. And they left an hour or so later. My gosh! You know the crazy thing? I didn't associate the family matters with that call until this very second. How dumb can I be?"

"You're not dumb," Nick said. "Did the caller give his name?"

"No."

"Did you overhear any of the conversation?"

"No. Amanda took it in their bedroom."

"Can I see?"

She led him down the hall, opened a door to a small bedroom with twin beds, the bedding stripped from each and folded on the mattress. A cordless phone lay on the bedside table.

"Have you got caller ID?" Nick said.

"Oh, what a clever idea," said Betsy. "But I don't."

Nick tried star 69. The last incoming call was from Betsy's insurance agent.

"Mind if I look around?" he said.

"Not at all."

Nick searched the room. Not from top to bottom, but from bottom to top. Long ago he'd learned . . . what? He realized he had no clue why he was searching the room this way, just did it out of habit. Under the second bed, the one by the window that looked out on a grimy alley, he found something that stunned him: a dark postcard showing a seventeenth-century physician dissecting a waxy corpse for the benefit of seven fascinated students—as fascinated as Betsy Matsu was now, watching in the doorway—and rendered by an absolute master: *The Anatomy Lesson of Dr. Tulp.*

twenty-four

I've never seen it before," said Betsy Matsu, gazing at the Dr. Tulp postcard. "Is it important?"

Gerald Reasoner's calling card: it had to be important, but how? Nick had no idea. "How long have you lived here?"

"Almost four years."

Was it possible that Reasoner had also rented this apartment, years earlier? No—Reasoner had lived in the same house in Burbank all his life, with his mother until she died and then by himself. Nick could still remember the address, 313 Coursin Street, and even the house itself, yellow with red trim, unseen in almost twelve years. Therefore this Dr. Tulp postcard had belonged to some previous guest of Betsy's or been left behind by Liza and Amanda. Neither option made more sense than the other, or any sense at all.

Unless . . . unless he considered a question he should have already asked: why had Liza chosen him in the first place? He could remember nothing of how she'd come to him—it must have been after his testimony in the Canning trial and before his first visit to the Airport Marriott, the very beginning of the lost time—but he was known as a missing persons investigator, and more specifically, she wouldn't have been the first client who'd come to him because of the movie. The Dr. Tulp postcard had figured prominently in the movie—the director had shot the opening credits over it, lit by a flickering candle. Therefore had Liza and Amanda, or one of them, left the postcard behind on the assumption he'd find it? But how could they assume he'd be looking under beds? And what was the message? Did they want to be found? What was he supposed to be doing?

Find the girl and you'll live.

"What do you think?" said Betsy.

Or—and this was a completely unexpected thought, one he didn't like at all: had the intruder left the postcard?

"I think you should find somewhere else to spend the night," he said.

"My friend's coming to get me," Betsy said.

T he friend arrived as Nick was leaving.

"Sarah," Betsy said.

"Are you all right?"

"It's horrible."

They embraced. Sarah rubbed the back of Betsy's neck and kissed her on the mouth. Nick left his card on the hall table.

N ick went home. What was the step after Betsy Matsu? He didn't know. But fast: he had to be fast. What next? Going fast inside, completely still on the outside, that panicky thing again. He poured himself a big glass of Johnnie Black, sat in his office upstairs, surrounded by Dmitri's old finger paintings, calmed down. There were procedures to follow when stuck. What was one of them? Reexamine the evidence.

Nick got up, gathered all the physical evidence: volleyball; Empty Box CD; Hallmark card; Babar; Candyland card; navy-blue suit jacket, now mended; cocktail napkin with his writing—*There is no justice;* the old Brownie photograph of the young cowboy leading three little girls on a pony; the Dr. Tulp postcard. These, his archaeological artifacts, now so many, he placed on his office desk. It was all about connection. Didn't the fact that there were more and more objects mean he was getting somewhere, toward some tipping point where you could finally say—*This is Troy?* And don't forget those missing artifacts—the Desert High team photo, stolen, and his own notebook, just simply missing. Plus there was the football photo that had actually hung by the trophy cases at Desert High: it was gone too.

Nick awoke, found he was lying on the floor of his office, half under the desk. For a moment he felt safe there, like a dog. Then he got scared. Not just that he had no memory of going to sleep like that; he didn't know if he could get back up, didn't know if he could move at all. His body didn't seem to be giving him any signals of its potential. A shaft of daylight found its way under the desk, shone on his right hand. He tried flexing it. It flexed.

Nick got up. His body, in fact, was working well, better than at any time since all this had started. It just wasn't communicating its potential. Some temporary aberration, soon to—

Someone was moving downstairs. Quietly, Nick went to the safe, spun the dial, took out his gun. Not much of a gun, a Colt .380, just a little thing he'd used symbolically several times and for real only once. Although he'd been good enough to shoot for the sheriff's team when he first joined the department, he didn't like guns. A voice called up. "Dad?"

"Dmitri!" Nick said. He started to put the automatic back in the safe, stuck it in his pocket instead. "Up here."

Nick tried to straighten himself up, his wrinkled clothes, rumpled face, but Dmitri, bounding up the stairs, gave him no time.

"How're you doing, Dad?"

"Great."

"You look like you pulled an all-nighter."

"Exactly."

"What's all this stuff?"

"Evidence."

"Of what?"

"That's what I'm working on." Dmitri moved closer to the desk, drawn by the display. "Want to hear about it?" Nick said.

"Hey," said Dmitri. "Cool."

He looked pleased. Had Nick ever discussed a case with him? No—he didn't discuss ongoing cases. But Nick wanted to discuss this one now, with his son.

"Let's start with the volleyball," he said.

Dmitri gazed at it. The expression on his face, rapt, did something to Nick. He felt tears flooding up inside, a flood that once started might never stop. Nick blocked it off, shut it down.

"What about the volleyball?" Dmitri said, turning to him. His expression changed to alarm. "What is it, Dad?"

Nick took a step forward, threw his arms around Dmitri, held on tight. A few tears came squeezing out; he couldn't help it. "I'm not doing too well," he said, his voice low and stripped of all confidence, authority, fatherly standing.

Dmitri went rigid. Then, after a moment or two, he started patting Nick's back, hesitant little pats from someone much too young to be called on for patting. This was terrible, unforgivable. Nick got hold of himself, gave a few pats of his own, brisk ones. Dmitri grew less rigid. Nick backed away. He wiped his face on his sleeve and said, "Water would be nice."

Dmitri went downstairs to the kitchen. By the time he returned, Nick had his composure back.

"Here, Dad." Dmitri handed him a big glass of water, full of ice cubes and with a lemon slice at the top. That lemon slice said a lot, like the best kind of gift.

Nick drank water. Had he ever appreciated it more? The ice cubes clinked in a homey, reassuring way. "Thanks," he said, his voice now perfectly normal, maybe even more relaxed than usual. Some kind of mending had just taken place, stitches way down deep.

"Anytime," said Dmitri. He cleared his throat. "What's with the volleyball?"

Nick turned to it. "The volleyball," he said. "I don't know where it came from—" But at that moment, he realized the answer was almost certainly Liza Rummel's old house in Van Nuys, now occupied by the Orthodox Jews. He would have wanted to see Amanda's room, first thing. This—discussing the case—might have benefits he hadn't foreseen. He told Dmitri everything he knew.

"Wow," Dmitri said. He picked up the volleyball, twirled it on his finger. "Amazing. Like a puzzle in a puzzle. What are you going to do next?"

"Look for connections," Nick said. "Find an arrangement of the evidence that tells the story."

"There must be lots of connections," Dmitri said.

"Why do you say that?"

"Like you've got three generations of this one family involved—the daughter who's missing, the mother who hired you, the grandfather who died in the fire."

An interesting approach, one that pointed back in time. Nick glanced at his son; his face intent now, completely unself-conscious. Another mind, close to his own in many ways, the intellectual and emotional connections all mixed up, was in support. It felt almost like music.

Back in time: did any of the physical evidence go back in time? The missing football picture, dated 1950, of course; and this Brownie black-and-white of the three little girls, two brunettes and a blonde, the smaller brunette still a toddler. Found in the pocket of that tuxedo in the rubble of—

"Oh, God," Nick said.

"What?"

He'd forgotten the funeral.

You'll have to do better than that, Nikolai. How could the funeral implications be missed?

Another mind, also like his own in many ways, but no music here. It spoke to him on the drive, criticism mostly, probably valid.

Why did it never occur to you to relate Liza and Amanda vanishing for the second time with George Rummel's death? They are frightened. Must I spell it out?

"Frightened of what?"

Silence.

"I'm trying, Poppa." Poppa—what Nick had called his father when he was very young. Later, he'd switched to *Dad,* later still to nothing at all.

So you think.

L ike the football field at Desert High, the graveyard on the other side of town was an oasis, a green patch in all those square miles of stoniness. Nick stood beside a Bobcat front-end loader on a little rise, not far from George Rummel's open grave. Five people stood around the grave, but no mother and daughter, no women at all, just a minister with a Bible open in his hands, Wally Moore and three other old men. Nick was close enough to hear, but the wind was blowing the other way and all he caught were disembodied scraps from the service.

"Yea, though I walk through the valley of the shadow . . ."

The Twenty-third Psalm. Disembodied scraps, but beautiful, almost impossible to believe that words could be so powerful. Was it wrong to give in to them, to accept the comfort they offered? Yes. For Nick it was. Deathbed conversions—not that there was any danger of that, he was feeling great, almost back to normal—were craven.

The grave diggers stepped in, small Latino men in white coveralls. They lowered the coffin into the dark rectangle. The minister handed Wally a spade. Wally tossed in a spadeful, red and so dry it raised a dusty little cloud, and passed the spade around. The mourners all did the same, then started moving toward the parking lot, separating fast. Nick followed, intending to speak to Wally, but he happened to glance down at the nearest gravestone. Why? Because he noticed things, had always been curious. The name on the stone, a white granite slab with a floral intaglio at the top, was Lara Deems.

Lara Deems. He knew that name. It would come to him. He stood over the gravestone, the hot wind snapping the cuffs of his pants. Lara Deems, that would be— Of course! Gerald Reasoner's last victim. He'd never forget her name, never forget any of them: Janet Cody, Cindy Motton, Flora Gutierrez, Nicolette Levy, Lara Deems. Nick counted them: he was missing two.

That didn't matter now. Think. Lara Deems. Was it possible this was the same woman, buried here in Barstow? What did he remember about Lara Deems? Her lips: that was what came to him first, pouty sensual lips. Had he seen the body, or only crime scene photographs? Nick couldn't remember. What else? Like all the other victims, she was a young woman living alone, and— no. Back up. Not true. Lara Deems was a single mother with an infant. Boy or girl? He couldn't remember, might not have known in the first place. She'd also been the only victim outside the Valley. Lara Deems had lived in Santa Monica, not far, in fact, from Nick and Kathleen's place at the time.

So: could this be her, buried next to George Rummel? Was there some connection between them? Nick couldn't imagine what. Had to be a different Lara Deems. There wasn't a single bit of evidence that could possibly connect—

But then he thought of one: the Dr. Tulp postcard he'd found the night before under the bed in Betsy Matsu's spare room. What was that if not an artifact from the Reasoner case turning up in the Amanda case? An overlap he didn't under-

stand at all. And these two graves, the coffins underneath probably only a few feet apart: was this a second overlap? Another
thought came, the kind that got him a little ahead of himself:
how long before the coffin wood rotted and busy subterranean
organisms and earthquakes did their work, mingling those two
sets of bones and teeth, uniting the two cases forever? A red drop
landed on the rounded top of Lara Deems's gravestone, and then
another. His nose was bleeding. That dreadful plummeting inside, as though he'd fallen from a rooftop: Nick felt it again.

Something squeaked nearby. Nick looked around, saw an
old black man pushing a wheelbarrow of sod up the path. He
stopped by the pile of earth behind George Rummel's open
grave.

"Where those boys go?" he said in a deep, rumbling voice;
yes, sepulchral. For a crazy moment, Nick thought he was asking one of those unanswerable questions, about why golden lads
and girls all must as chimney-sweepers come to dust; but then
the old man added, "For fillin' in the hole."

The grave diggers. "They were just here," Nick said.

The old man looked disgusted. He climbed up on the Bobcat,
eased his body into the seat, dumped a scoopful of earth in the
hole, then more, filling it up quickly and smoothing it over with
a single pass of the blade. He got down, started unloading the sod.

"Want some help with that?" Nick said.

The old man paused, gazed at him; his face sweet but his
eyes those of a longtime drinker. "You want to help with the
sod?" he said.

"Sure."

"Seen mourners do all kinds of shit," said the old man.
"Never help with the sod."

Nick helped with the sod.

"Seen a lot of shit," the old man said, possibly to himself, as
they rolled out the grassy strips, leaving a small unsodded area
for the stone.

"Been here a long time?" Nick said.

"November twenty-two, 1963," said the old man. "Day they shot JFK. Makes it easy to remember." He pressed the seams down with his foot. "Hear how I made the reference, 'they,' like in 'they shot JFK'?"

Nick didn't want to get into that. He gestured over the rows of grave sites. "Do you know who most of these people were?"

"Every single solitary one," said the old man. "You want the tour?"

"How about her?" Nick said, pointing to Lara Deems's stone.

"That's not a tough one," said the old man. "Why don't we go down to the old part, near the gate, you could ask me a tough one."

"Let's do her first."

The old man shrugged. "This here area, from where I'm pointing to them flowers, is George Rummel's plot. That's his wife, the other side of him." The stone read: CYNTHIA LOUISE RUMMEL, RIP. "And this one here, Lara, that's his daughter."

"When did she die?"

"Ten, twelve years ago. She went down to L.A., got herself killed by one of them serial killers."

Connection. That metaphor of the two miners meeting deep underground: Nick began to feel its power. "Which serial killer?" he said.

"Who knows? Dime a dozen down in L.A."

"Was it Gerald Reasoner?"

"Dime a dozen," the old man said.

"Did Lara have any sisters or brothers?" Nick said.

"A sister, 'less I'm mistaken," said the old man. "Mostly I get to know them when they land up here."

"What's the sister's name?"

"Started with L too, 'less I'm mistaken one more time. Lisa, maybe? Liza? Liza be my bet if I was a bettin' man. Which I am." The old man pulled a rag from his pocket, held it out. "Aware your nose is bleedin'?"

Nick took the rag, decorated with a picture of Bob Marley but not especially clean, and dabbed his nose. Hardly any blood at all now, not worth thinking about.

"All set for the tour?" said the old man. "Cost you ten bucks but it's worth it. We got some old whores and prospectors down there, plus the genuine Lakota Sioux brave that put an arrow through Custer at Little Bighorn. Clean through his head, so the story goes." The old man made an explosive little sound effect that seemed realistic. "Clean through." The fact, if it was one, delighted him.

3

RETARDS PICNIC

twenty-five

Two cases, overlapping. What did that imply? First, that
nothing was coincidental, everything linked by meaning. Therefore the theft of the photograph of the 1950
Desert High football champions had meaning; and the fact that
the duplicate photo that had hung on the wall of fame in the
school itself was missing also had meaning. Nick wanted that
photograph, had sensed something about it from the start. And
the bird flying out of the frame—he'd been right about that too,
the golden lads all coming to dust.

Were there other copies? If so, where? Nick, resting in the
back of his car in the cemetery parking lot—not that he was tired,
more simply taking advantage of a chance to think quietly—
tried to come up with locations for other copies. No ideas, not a
one. But there should have been: he had the feeling the problem
wasn't that difficult.

Think. But nothing. Nick smacked his head in frustration. He
got a headache right away, but no big deal, just a dull penny-
sized pressure behind the left side of his forehead, barely there.
All the same, he wanted to be near his wafer. He rose, walked
around the car, got behind the wheel. Good timing, because a
cruiser was pulling into the lot. It parked beside him and
Sergeant Gallego got out.

"Was hoping you'd show up," he said. "Find that girl yet?"

"No," Nick said. "What's up?"

"Any chance she drives a motorcycle?"

"A little young for that," Nick said. "Why?"

"We got a report of a motorcycle parked outside Rummel's place the night of the fire. Or maybe just driving by slowly."

"Who's your informant?"

"A couple of French hikers. Their English is kinda strange."

"Hiking at night?"

"Europeans are jazzed on the desert, in theory," said Sergeant Gallego. "They got lost out somewhere west of Coyote Lake—didn't realize it was dry, apparently—and homed in on the town's night glow. But the point is the fire marshal went back in daylight and found an overturned kerosene lamp on the floor in George's back room."

"Overturned on purpose?"

"Can't say. But the electricity was working so why use a kerosene lamp? Which is why I'm interested in this motorcycle."

"I didn't see one," Nick said. "Not—" He paused.

"What?"

That night ride up the unpaved section of Calico Way: first the sky purpling to black, then that pure white crescent moon with the sharp points, finally a headlight coming the other way, fast. A lone headlight. He changed his story. "A motorcycle went by on my way in."

"Get a look at the driver?"

"Male," Nick said. "Light hair."

"That's it?"

A thin description, coming from a professional: he heard the disappointment in Gallego's tone. Remembering the roar of the motorcycle, Nick added, "He was moving pretty fast."

Offered up as a flimsy excuse for failing to observe more, but Gallego took it differently: "Like someone making a getaway," he said. "This girl you're looking for—what's her connection to Rummel?"

"She's his granddaughter," Nick said, although even as he spoke he knew it might not be true, at least biologically: Amanda's real mother had been murdered. And up the hill in the graveyard lay Lara Deems. Would it be unusual for a sister to bring up her orphan niece? No. People changed positions in his mind, overlaps within overlaps. Perhaps Amanda was George's biological granddaughter after all.

"I thought you said she wasn't local," Gallego said.

"She's not," said Nick.

"It's starting to feel local to me."

It was a Barstow story: someone had told him that. Who? He remembered. Deej. And Rui had told her.

Sergeant Gallego gazed at him. "Is this starting to get a little complicated?" he said. "I hate when that happens."

Nick drove home, out of the desert, taking several wrong exits, finally lay on his bed, head directly over the wafer. Carmustine, working from inside and out, annihilating cancer cells by the hundreds, thousands, millions, a fighter like nothing they'd ever seen, relentless.

The phone woke him. His room was full of daylight, but not the heavy yellow kind that had been oppressing him so much lately. This was an airy, silvery light, almost dancing. He picked up the phone.

"Dad?" said Dmitri. "Empty Box is playing at the El Rey tonight."

"Yeah?" said Nick. "You going?"

"Am I going?" said Dmitri. "The thing is, Dad, the reason I'm telling you, is these people you're looking for, Amanda and Rui, are big fans of Empty Box, so I thought there might be a chance—"

Nick got it. "Great idea," he said.

"How about if I go with you?" Dmitri said.

"Isn't tomorrow a school day?"

"Today's Saturday, Dad."

Still Saturday? Nick studied that silvery light, which began to seem unearthly. "Can't let you, Dmitri," he said, even though, to his surprise, the idea of having Dmitri along pleased him. It wasn't the kind of job where you took your kids to the office.

Nick put on his bathing suit, walked down to the beach, perhaps limping just the slightest little bit, but very far from needing a cane or anything like that. He had a nice swim, not one of those straight-out-to-sea performances, but an easy back-and-forth fifty yards from shore, his right arm chipping in, even picking up the pace from time to time. *Build back up.* The water, cold and fresh, bubbled along his skin, relaxing and revivifying at the same time. Pillars of kelp rose up from the depths, their tops billowing just out of reach. He thought of flowers to give Billie, tulips, some lively color.

Back home, Nick fried a steak in a whole stick of butter, ate it with scrambled eggs, washed down with a bottle of Guinness. *Stop the wasting.* Dressing for the concert—khakis, a T-shirt, the little Colt in his pocket—he caught sight of himself in the mirror. Not true: he looked deliberately and examined himself closely. This was the time to be objective, to not fool himself in any way. And the verdict: he looked good, not how he had before, not like Petrov, with his thick chest and heavy shoulders, but good in a new leaner way, a different physical type, and not necessarily sick. In fact, his skin was glowing, a silvery tone that matched today's silvery light. He was even starting to need a haircut. Healthy cells were growing and subdividing all over the place. Was it only the carmustine doing its work? Partly. But the driving force of his recovery, the meaning of it, was clear: he was getting closer to Amanda. His health was a sign.

Cold out. Nick had to buy from a scalper, paying forty dollars for a twenty-dollar seat. But it was a good one, at one end of the first row of the balcony. His last rock concert? Back with Kathleen, while she was pregnant with Dmitri. Kathleen had been a big Springsteen fan, maybe still was. He'd played a small club unannounced while rehearsing some album, but one of the bouncers had slipped Nick advance word, and they'd had a stage-side table, Kat's eyes wide; and she'd pressed her foot against his when Bruce sang "Hungry Heart," her favorite. This was different: one quick look around and Nick knew he was the oldest person in the building. A girl coming down the aisle said, "Think they'll piss on the cymbals tonight?" And the boy with her said, "It's so cool the way the drops go flying." Nick glanced down to make sure the balcony was out of range.

He scanned faces. Rui? Amanda? They could be any of these people, that girl down on the floor with turquoise hair, the pimply boy three rows behind him wearing a red and white Cat-in-the-Hat hat, the girl in a long white dress dancing down the aisle although the music hadn't started yet, the bony man three seats over with the tattooed forearms. How was he supposed to judge? By how psyched they were to be there? Everyone, a thousand or more, looked psyched.

The lights went down. The crowd cheered. A spot shone down on the stage and a dwarf in a business suit stepped into it. "Ladies and gentlemen," he said, "and those in between— Empty Box."

The curtains parted, revealing a six-piece band. The acoustic guitarist was already strumming softly, and the cheering, which had been rising to a roar, died almost at once. Soft, but beautifully played, and with feeling: a pretty little melody that filled the theater with innocence, a melody that reminded Nick of something, but what? "Teddy Bears' Picnic."

Two electric guitars joined in, making buzzing and droning noises that excited everyone, Nick too, like swooping birds of prey. The lead singer, a woman on keyboards, lower body in constant motion, upper body almost rigid, started singing at the top of her lungs, but hitting every note dead center.

And you don't even know
What's buried in your yard
Retard.

The acoustic guitarist sang harmony—*retard, retard, in your yard, in your yard*—in a voice that was choirboy sweet on the outside and nasty at the core. They were great. Nick leaned forward on the rail as the keyboard woman raced through a solo that made him picture rippling spikes. The guy three seats over, the bony one with the barbed-wire tattoos festooned on his forearms, was leaning forward too, almost dangerously. He and Nick glanced at each other simultaneously, two music lovers of like mind. As their eyes met, Nick had a thought, coming out of nowhere: *313 Coursin Street is important.* Or maybe not out of nowhere, maybe all that barbed wire reminded him of prison, prison of death row, death row of Reasoner.

The man, his fellow music lover, had an odd face, the lower part soft, finely formed, childlike, the rest hard and much older-looking. Nick gave him the thumbs-up sign. The man's eyes opened wide. He jumped up, pushed his way down the row of seats, scrambled up the aisle. Was Nick's nose bleeding again, a possibly repellent spectacle? He dabbed at it with his sleeve. Nope. Not a drop. He turned back to the stage. The acoustic guitarist was leaning over the keyboard now, sharing the lead singer's mike, crooning in his nasty voice. Nick looked over to the empty seat, wondered why the bony man had left so suddenly, and thought maybe a cell phone had vibrated in his pocket, or his bladder was full, and then, way too late: *he knew me: Rui.*

Nick rose, ran up the aisle toward the exit sign—not actually running but moving with what he took for speed—and into the red-carpeted hallway. He looked around, saw no one, felt the whole building vibrate from the music. Nick headed for the stairs that led down to the lobby, passing the men's room on the way. He paused. Was Rui the clever type who'd try something tricky when the right move was simple flight? All Nick knew was that Rui called himself a detective, yet looked like no cop of any kind that he had ever seen, not even the most compromised under-cover narc. He opened the door to the men's room.

Empty. No one at the urinals, the doors of the stalls ajar, all unoccupied. Nick was backing out when it occurred to him that an extra-clever type reluctant to abandon the concert during the very first number might lurk behind this very men's room door, wait for the footsteps of any pursuer to pass by on the way outside, then return to his seat, feeling pretty smooth. Was Rui like that, extra clever? Nick sniffed the air, smelled something human, pos-sibly unwashed hair.

Nick pushed against the door. It yielded for a moment, then seemed to be pushing back. He stepped out of the way. The door came swinging shut, and there was Rui, looking exposed. He slid along the wall, reached inside his jacket, whipped out a horn-handled switchblade that came snapping open.

Nick hadn't foreseen that. "Easy, Rui," he said. "I just want to talk."

"Bad things happen when we talk," Rui said. The building rumbled around them; applause came through the walls like muffled surf. "Get away from the door."

Nick didn't move. Rui came toward him, knife out in front, making little arcs with the blade. When someone pulls a knife on you, Nick knew, the best time to react is while the pulling is still going on, a chance he'd missed. After that—watch, stay calm inside, be quick. No problem with the first two. He waited to find out how he'd do on number three.

Rui kept coming, those little arcs getting bigger. Nick stood in the doorway. Rui was going to lunge forward, slash at his face. Nick saw it coming, was actually kicking up, driving the toe of his shoe hard at Rui's wrist before Rui even started his move, at least he thought he was. But Nick's right foot: so slow, and not reaching very high for some reason. The point of Rui's blade sliced through his T-shirt, nipple to nipple. Nick didn't feel any pain, or not much, just enough to sharpen his reflexes a little bit. He caught hold of Rui's wrist on the backswing—Rui didn't know much about knife fighting; this wasn't the time for a big backswing, just the quick final stab—and banged it against a sink they were falling into. They rolled on the floor, Nick bending that thin wrist of Rui's back and twisting it with both hands. But only the left was really doing anything, and all at once Nick got cut somewhere else, and Rui was free.

Free, furious, shrill: "I'm sick of you fucking hurting me." Nick under the sinks, Rui, on his knees, coming at him, slashing wildly, out of control. That was when Nick felt something digging into his hip, something he should have thought of right away: the little Colt .380. He pulled it out of his pocket, pointed it at the middle of Rui's forehead, pictured the red caste mark just waiting to be born.

Rui should have pictured it too, should have frozen. Instead he jumped up, ran across the room, kicked out a window and crawled through.

Nick got up, went after him. From the window, he saw Rui on his way down the fire escape, three stories over an unlit alley. Nick stepped out. Rui was already one flight down, rounding the turn to the next staircase. "Hold it," Nick said.

Rui glanced up, hurled the knife at Nick, ran faster. Three actions, almost simultaneous: it was too much for Rui. His foot caught in the grated flooring, spun him around into the rail. Not a very high rail and his right arm was still in its follow-through, destabilizing him even more. The rail caught the backs of his legs, thigh-high, bending his upper body backward. He hung almost motionless for an instant, way out there like a sailor heeling in a gale, then toppled over. Rui didn't spin, didn't make any windmilling motions, just fell straight down, back first, arms and legs outstretched, as though a trampoline waited below. Whatever sound his landing made was drowned out by the music of Empty Box, leaking through the theater walls.

Nick hurried down the fire escape, unhooked the last flight of stairs and lowered them to the ground, climbed down. Rui lay on his back in a wedge of light cutting through from the next street over. Nick knelt beside him, saw no blood, no limbs twisted in impossible positions, not a mark on him. Rui was glaring.

"Are you all right?" Nick said.

Rui took a shallow breath. "Wind knocked out of me," he said. "Your fault."

"Don't move," Nick said, taking out his cell phone. "I'm calling an ambulance."

"Fuck that," said Rui.

Nick made the 911 call anyway. Rui started getting his breath back.

"You know what gets me?" he said. "How dumb you are, like in person."

"What are you talking about?"

"They made you a lot smarter in the movie."

"Lie still."

"Amanda and I watched it the other day."

"Where is she?"

"Someplace safe. You're too dumb to find her, that's for sure."

"What am I missing?"

"What aren't you missing, you stupid fuck? First I figured you were in on the cover-up, but you don't have the brains for that."

"What cover-up?"

Rui laughed, a short, violent bark. "Don't worry about it," he said. "Six out of seven ain't bad."

"Six out of seven what?"

"For fuck sake," said Rui. "Just watch the movie."

"*The Reasoner Case?*"

"Duh."

Rui was looking at him with contempt. "What happened on August twenty-third?" Nick said. "When you met Amanda at the Empty Box concert."

"Destiny, man. The most important date in human history. We met our destinies."

The two miners, meeting way down deep. "She told you who her real mother was?" Nick said.

"So slow it's painful," said Rui.

"And her real mother was Lara Deems."

"Einstein," said Rui. He sat up. "Give me a hand."

"Stay still," said Nick. He thought of the Hallmark card. "I don't understand what you're helping each other with."

"Doing your job, man."

"What do you mean?"

"Justice."

"For her mother's murder?" Nick said. "Reasoner's on death row and he'll never be free, no matter what happens."

"Six out of seven."

"What are you saying?"

"Painful," said Rui. "You been to my fuckin' house and you still can't figure this out."

Rui's house? Nick had no idea.

"Don't fuckin' tell me," said Rui, "you didn't notice the house right behind it? Three thirteen Coursin Street, you mo-ron. Check out the basement."

"What's there?"

"Another stupid goddamned question. Give me a hand."

"Wait for the ambulance."

"Don't need no ambulance."

Nick held out his left hand. Rui pulled on it, raised himself with a deep grunt. "It's not what's there now—different people now, for Christ sake. Time marches on. It's what happened down there with Uncle Jerry."

"He's your uncle?"

"Maggots aren't uncles. He's nobody's goddamned uncle."

Their eyes met. The look in Rui's, even the lighting: Nick had seen this before, although he couldn't remember where or when. But that look in Rui's eyes: something had been destroyed in there. Nick's mind, so slow, just as Rui said, finally found the path. "Did he molest you in the basement?" Nick said. "Is that it?"

There was a long pause. Tears rose in Rui's eyes. "Is giving an eleven-year-old kid weed to let you suck him off molesting? Is stickin' his dick in the kid's ass molesting? Is swearing on the Bible to kill the kid if he snitches molesting?"

Nick put his hand on Rui's shoulder. Rui shrugged it off with an angry wince. "Don't feel sorry for me," he said. "I'm getting rich off this."

"How?" Nick said.

"You're the one needs feelin' sorry for," said Rui, a drop of blood appearing at the corner of his mouth. "Do I have to spell it out?"

"Yes."

"Fuckin' hopeless," said Rui. "Try to concentrate. The night Lara Deems got killed Uncle Jerry had me in the basement. Like the whole fuckin' night. Six out of seven. How come you're so—"

No next word. Instead came a little gurgle, and then blood, pouring out, a gusher, darkest possible red in the dim light. Rui went down on one knee, looked up at Nick, anger changing to confusion in his eyes; and then nothing.

He fell facedown. The ambulance took him away, siren off, no lights flashing.

twenty-six

Across Nick's chest, a cut that really was just a scratch. Petrov wouldn't have thought twice about it; Nick thought even less. An ER doc made some remark about slow coagulation and asked questions about medications, health problems and recent hospital stays that Nick answered in the negative. A few stitches—Nick didn't catch the exact number—on the side of his leg, and he was out of there.

A detective third class named Stenowski waited outside. Nick kept it simple. Rui was a possible witness in a missing persons case, had pulled a knife and fled, falling off the fire escape. Stenowski had two questions.

One: "Who's missing?"

Nick told him. Stenowski punched Amanda Rummel into the system, got no hits.

Two: "Get to meet Kim Delaney?"

"No."

"I shook hands with Sylvester Stallone once," said Stenowski. "He comes up to here on me. I coulda crushed his hand like nothin'."

"He was never the same after the second Apollo Creed fight," Nick said.

Stenowski laughed, a laugh quickly stifled when he realized the joke might have been on him. He flicked the corner of Rui's driver's license with his thumbnail. Rui, also punched into the system, had a record of half a dozen arrests—drugs, theft, assault—and two convictions that had led to a total of fifteen months' prison time, plus three outstanding traffic warrants.

"Your basic loser," said Stenowski. "Got a number where I can reach you?"

Nick handed him his card, at the same time getting a good look at Rui's address.

Rui Estrella, 1491 Rosetta Street, Glendale. Nick parked out front, his cooling engine pinging softly in the night. *You been to my fuckin' house*. A low stucco box, its outlines not quite square: did he have any memory of it? Not one. He got out of the car, shone his flash on a real estate sign in the yard: SOLD. And the house itself was dark. Nick went to the front door, pressed the buzzer. Not a buzzer, but chimes: they made a hard, clear sound, the kind you hear when all soft surfaces are gone. No one came to the door. Nick aimed his beam through a couple of windows. The house was bare, stripped of furniture, rugs, appliances, pictures, all the comforts of home: an empty box.

Nick walked around to the back, illuminated a long diagonal earthquake crack in the wall, not even crudely plastered over before the sale, even though it had probably knocked thousands off the listing price. The back door had a new window in it, though, the Andersen sticker still in place. Nick shone light through it, into more emptiness.

He turned to the backyard, right away smelled a strong odor of . . . what? Tea. Memory stirred but wouldn't speak, just out of reach like those kelp forests under the sea. Nick drove around the block, parked in front of 313 Coursin Street, and went to the door.

He'd been here once before, a quick walk-through with forensics after Reasoner's arrest. Had he seen the basement? He didn't think so. All he remembered was that the color of the house—egg-yolk yellow with blood-red trim—had been somehow disturbing by itself. The new colors—white with aquamarine—were much better, probably even cheerful by daylight. Nick checked the time: 11:48, perhaps a little late to be knocking. He knocked.

Footsteps approached from the other side, paused. Nick knocked again.

"Who's there?" a woman said.

"Nick Petrov," he said. "I'm a private investigator working on a missing person case. Sorry to call so—"

She flung the door open, a wiry woman with electric-shock hair and angry eyes, like one of the Furies. In her hand was a sheaf of papers; on her shirt a name tag from the Forty-second Annual Convention of the Southern California CPA's Association: *Hi, my name is—Stephanie DiPardo* 😊 . "I should have you arrested," she said.

"I know it's late," Nick said, "but—"

"And the nerve, coming back like this." She glanced down at his bloody T-shirt and blinked.

Coming back like this. "Whatever happened, I'm sorry," Nick said.

"Whatever happened? You scared me to death."

"That wasn't my intention," Nick said; aware he was following his own footsteps now—Petrov's big confident footsteps—but blindly. Inspiration struck and he added: "But tell me how you saw it."

"How I saw it?" Her voice rose. "First you talk a four-year-old child into letting you in, then you call me at work with parenting advice, and on top of it you've gone by the time I get here. How would anyone see it?"

"Mommy?" A voice came from the top of the stairs. A little girl stood there, trailing a pink blanket. "I woke up." She saw Nick. "Hey," she said. "Nick's here."

"Hi," Nick said. The girl's name almost surfaced in his mind.

"Are you gonna tell Mommy the secret recipe?" she said.

"Cassie," said her mother, "get right back to bed."

"Recipe for what?" Nick said.

"Grilled cheese sandwich, dumdum."

"Sure," said Nick.

"Promise?"

"Promise."

"Okay," said Cassie. " 'Night." She disappeared in the shadows.

Stephanie DiPardo turned to him, her expression changing. "How did you make that stupid sandwich?" she said. "She won't stop talking about it."

Nick had no idea. Had he ever made a grilled cheese sandwich in his life? "I can show you," he said. Improvisation was going to be important, from now on in.

She gazed up at him, eyes narrowing.

"The missing girl isn't that much older than Cassie," he said; improvisation verging on a lie.

She let him in.

T hey moved out a couple of weeks ago," Stephanie said, in the kitchen.

"Any idea where?" People were moving out on him: Rui, Liza, Amanda and George Rummel too, if getting burned out counted.

Stephanie shook her head. "I didn't really know them."

"I'll need the cheese," said Nick. "Who lived in the house?"

"Just the old grandmother and Rui, when he was around. He worked in Alaska from time to time."

"Who told you that?"

"Mrs. Estrella. I preferred when he was away, frankly."

"Why is that?"

"Sometimes he'd stare over the fence in a creepy way."

"Garlic, mustard, honey," Nick said, improvising a little spread.

"She ate that?"

"Goofy's secret recipe," said Nick. Goofy? Where did that come from? Nothing amiss on Stephanie's face. Nick asked his next question: "Did Rui ride a motorcycle?"

"Not that I saw."

"Any motorcycles around recently?"

She thought. "There was one, now that you mention it. A week or so ago. Why I remember is because I was putting Cassie in her car seat and he went by way too fast."

"Can you describe him?"

"White, I think. And he was bent over the handlebars."

Nick waited for more, but that was all. He opened the toaster oven. "How long have you been living here?"

"Two years."

"Do you know anything about the history of the house?"

"How do you mean?"

"The previous owners, for example."

"I bought it from an Armenian couple. Before that I'm not sure."

"The Estrellas never talked about it?"

"No."

"None of the other neighbors?"

"I only know a few of them, and just to say hi. Prices are going up—there's been a lot of buying and selling. Why?"

Nick didn't want to tell her, didn't want to ruin it for them. Maybe the facts were already lost to the neighborhood memory. "I'm just following up on Rui's past." He set the grilled cheese sandwich on the counter, sliced it in two.

She picked up one half, took a bite. "Hey. Not bad." She looked at him in a whole new way. Her eyes darted, very quickly, to his ring finger. Was he suddenly becoming attractive to women?

"I'd like to see the basement," Nick said.

She stopped eating. "Was Rui in my basement?"

"Long before it was yours," Nick said. "If at all."

"I don't understand."

"Nothing for you to worry about."

"But what are you looking for?"

"Confirmation," Nick said.

"Of the layout down there?"

He nodded: it was close enough.

She took him down to the basement: storage room, laundry room, washer and dryer both on, a spartan little office, immaculately tidy except for a few balled-up papers under the desk. Nick looked out the little ground-level window at the chain-link fence glinting with reflected light, and beyond it the low shadow of 1491 Rosetta Street. Stephanie stooped for the balled-up papers, dropped them in the wastebasket. "I had a presentation today," she said. The room smelled of cleansers, ink, purpose. As for confirmation of Rui's story: not possible. The house had forgotten Uncle Jerry.

What happens if when all your energy is focused on a shaky future, the past suddenly gets shaky too? Nick remembered a line of poetry from somewhere. The poet, maybe climbing a mountain, reaches the summit, looks up and sees that "Alps on Alps arise." It was like that. How would Petrov have handled it? Not by driving home—taking the wrong exit off the 5 at that—and lying on the bed. But Nick wanted to be near his wafer. He lay there, eyes closed. Exhaustion came right away, but not sleep. Nick got worried that the wafer was gone, maybe stolen by some enemy. Who were his enemies? Nick didn't know, but one rode a motorcycle. Did that ring a bell? No. Nick sat up, removed the mattress button, checked inside. The wafer: still there. He felt its perfect smooth surface. Lying back down, he noticed that his message light was blinking. He pressed it.

"Hi, Nick. Billie. I was going to drop in tonight, but you're not there. Everything all right?"

Nick pressed the button again. And again. Once more. He wished there were a repeat function. He fell toward sleep with Billie's voice coming through the phone's little speaker. At that point, he thought of actually calling her, but by then he didn't have the energy.

Nick awoke. Still dark. Not quite exhausted now, a few steps back from that, but still dark, so why was he awake? He was afraid he knew the answer: his mind had had just enough rest, wanted to get going. Meaning that sleep, an unsettling overture, yes, but also a wonderful refuge, was being taken from him too.

His mind was changing him. Whether or not the totality of Nick was ready, his mind had caught its breath, was ready to log on, wanted to get right back to work on Rui: *six out of seven.* Rui had told him to concentrate, and on what? On this: *The night Lara Deems got killed Uncle Jerry had me in the basement.* Therefore Gerald Reasoner couldn't have killed Lara Deems. But how was that possible? For one thing, the Dr. Tulp postcard had been taped to Lara's fridge. Who had known that the postcard had been somewhere in the homes of all the victims, Reasoner's signature? Only Reasoner himself, and Nick, of course, who'd figured it out the day before Lara's murder, looking through Nicolette Levy's Hawaiian photo album. Then had come Nick's visit to the Getty and the arrest of Reasoner, too late by less than twenty-four hours to save Lara Deems.

So: impossible. And was there any evidence of child molestation in Reasoner's past? Nick remembered none. Crippled inside, a fearer and hater of women, a quiet sadist: all those, but not a child molester. Had Rui told anyone? His grandmother? And his parents—where were they? What was the next step? Nick had the nagging feeling he'd been in a situation a lot like this, and recently, but what it was wouldn't come.

Which brought to mind another problem: did his not re-membering child molestation in Reasoner's past make it so? The lost weekend was gone, but were there other blanks as well? Like what? Nick went upstairs to his office, turned on lights, opened file cabinets, found his old notebooks, going all the way back to the Reasoner case and before, leafed through. In code, of course—other blanks, for sure—and now beyond him. He'd stumbled over this before, was stumbling over it again. The dif-ference was—

Nikolai! There is no time for stumbling.

—that his notebook on the Amanda case, at least as it stood that first weekend, was missing. And the football photo, stolen, as though someone, aware of his limitations, was kicking out all potential props. He gazed at the remaining artifacts, his evi-dence, laid out on the desk. Laid out on the desk, but not the way he'd left them; rearranged by someone with an artistic sensibil-ity: Dmitri.

The artifacts now took the shape of a diamond. The cocktail napkin with the words *There is no justice* stood alone at the top, like a title. Next came the Candyland card and the Empty Box CD. Middle row: navy-blue suit jacket, rolled up, Babar, volleyball. Below that: Hallmark card and Dr. Tulp. At the bottom: the old Brownie black-and-white of three little girls on a pinto pony, led by the little cowboy with the big star on his chest.

It is a story, Nikolai. Read.

Nick tried to read the story, a very short story with a title and four lines, finishing up with three little girls, like a happy ending. A brunette and a blonde, who looked about the same age, and in back a second brunette, a year or two younger. The features of the little cowboy were shaded out by his ten-gallon hat, but the two brunettes were smiling big frozen smiles at the camera and the blond girl was lost in thought. Nick could see that, also knew a lot about the Empty Box CD, Candyland card and volleyball, even the Hallmark card; but he couldn't read the

story. Pages were missing, maybe a whole chapter. He wanted
that football photo.

Nick slid *The Reasoner Case* into the VCR. Moody music,
close-up of the postcard, but shot so that Dr. Tulp and
his students might have been real, actually posing. The credits
scrolled by. *Based on a true story; starring Armand Assante, Kim Delaney,
Dennis Franz* (miscast as Reasoner—Donald Sutherland had
backed out at the last moment).

Nick fast-forwarded to the scene where the psychological
profiler tells Armand Assante and Kim Delaney what kind of
man they're looking for. The three of them sit in one of those of-
fices outfitted with half-closed venetian blinds, for interesting
lighting effects. The profiler, played as a soft-headed academic
with no street experience, runs through a long list of psychological deficits and behavioral transgressions, none related to child
molestation. Armand Assante looks skeptical, not about the lack
of child molestation, but at the whole namby-pamby approach.
Kim Delaney says, "So you're telling us he's one evil son of a
bitch." The profiler, face lined with barred shadows from the
blinds, looks annoyed. Armand Assante grins.

Nick fast-forwarded.

Everything goes jerkily by, the speeded-up form inviting
amusement, as in a Monty Python sketch. Dennis Franz
smooths his mustache, dons scrubs and surgical gloves. He zips
down a dark corridor, seizes a woman from behind. She strug-
gles, eyes wide, screaming. His eyes. Gleam with sexual excitement. His eyes. Lamp. She hits him with it. His eyes. Excitement
changes from sexual to murderous. She almost gets away. On
the floor. Roll, bounce, tumble. He stabs her through the heart
with a scalpel. Blood. He drags her to the kitchen, gets her on
the table, opens his medical kit, begins one of those strange
pseudoautopsies that actually happened. Blood. Armand As-

sante and Kim Delaney kiss in a car parked on a dark street. They go to bed. She rolls on top of him. He rolls on top of her. Cars drive fast, a lurid sunset in the background. Armand Assante picks up a photo album, leafs through. Pictures of Maui whiz by.

Nick hit play. The story slowed back down.

Music: rising notes on a synthesizer. Armand Assante turns to the last page. The Dr. Tulp postcard falls out. Music builds. Armand Assante picks up the postcard. Close-up of his eyes. Understanding dawns. Crescendo.

Armand Assante jumps in his car. Kim Delaney comes over, camera around her neck, lock of hair dangling over one eye.

"Find anything, Nick?" she says.

But Armand Assante is already driving off.

"When will I see you?" Kim Delaney calls after him; so far from Elaine, Nick had to laugh. The camera withdraws, moving up and up, the car getting tinier and tinier and finally lost in the L.A. sprawl.

Montage: Armand Assante knocking on doors, re-searching victims' closets, opening stored boxes of evidence downtown, finding more Dr. Tulp postcards; all of this intercut with Dennis Franz, in his security guard outfit at the Getty, gazing at female nude statuary and getting itchy again.

Night: Dennis Franz, in his scrubs, slices through the screen on Lara Deems's back window. The actress playing Lara Deems—had someone told Nick she'd later done a season on *Baywatch?*—rolls over in bed, but doesn't wake up. Dennis Franz's eyes wander to photos on the wall, publicity stills of Lara Deems. An aspiring actress, Nick remembered: not successful, briefly a showgirl in Las Vegas—and was there some story she'd done a little hooking here and there? A fine time for that to pop up.

Dennis Franz wants a quick peek before he gets started. He raises a corner of the blanket. The heavily made-up eyes of "Lara Deems" fly open, run through a range of emotions, none quite clear to the viewer, or at least to Nick. Dennis Franz smiles a wet smile. She screams.

"Shh," he says. "You'll like this."

Was there any record of him saying that to a victim, or saying anything? And hadn't there been signs of resistance at the real murder scene? Nick remembered being surprised when the examination of Reasoner showed no marks on him. Why would the producers prefer that the character beg for mercy and try to shrink away, as "Lara Deems" was doing now? Dennis Franz selects an instrument from his bag, jabs it, not hard, into her neck, severing the carotid artery. Blood.

Cut to: the last Dr. Tulp postcard, taped to the fridge of "Lara Deems."

Cut to: Armand Assante running into the gift shop at the Getty Museum.

Nick stopped the tape. Nothing there to support Rui's story. Was that how it had been? A movie, of course, with many little changes to make it less particular, for reasons Nick didn't understand, but they'd gotten the basics right. Or was that a circular trap? Was it possible he'd bungled some part of the Reasoner case, and he and the movie were both wrong?

What had Rui told Deej? That it was a Barstow story, but something else, very important.

Nick tried to remember. He paced around his office until his right leg dragged. He went downstairs, made coffee, drank half a pot. He filled pages with charts and diagrams. He watched his fingertips tremble. He slapped his forehead, setting off another tiny headache, penny-size or even less. He lit up one of Beth's joints and the headache and all his other pain radiated away. At last he went to bed, falling into a deep sleep almost instantly, still not remembering what Rui told Deej.

twenty-seven

Nikolai!

Nick opened his eyes. Daylight, in bed, the sheets soaked with his sweat. An important idea began taking shape in his mind, swelling up like a cartoon genie; the phone rang and his idea broke into pieces, drifted away.

"Nick? Elaine. How're you doing?"

"Great."

"That's what I hear," she said. "Back to performing your own stunts."

"Stunts?"

"Like on fire escapes."

"You know about that?"

"The overnights are on my desk every morning," Elaine said. "Your name popped out."

There was a silence. Her voice, so familiar, dug down deep in his memory. The years peeled away, at least for him. Nick heard his tone changing, as though they were close. "Ever watch the movie?" he said.

"Our movie?"

"Yeah."

"Not for ages," Elaine said. "Why?"

"I'd forgotten that scene with the psychologist," Nick said.

"Fuck the psychologist," Elaine said. "Reasoner should have been torn apart. When were you watching it?"

"Last night."

"Sounds like a busy one." Someone spoke to her in the background. She said something, partially muffled, that might have been "Two minutes."

"Elaine?"

"Yes?"

"Before you go."

"Something wrong?"

"Did anything like that happen, Elaine?"

"Meeting some shrink? Nah. Profiling reports might have kicked around, but with a monster like Reasoner who needs psychology? That's what you said."

"I did?"

"I learned a lot from you, Nick."

"Like what?"

"Is that a serious question?" Elaine said. "I wouldn't be where I am without you." Nick heard a man laughing in the background.

"That's not true," Nick said. "You had success written all over you from day one."

"What a sweet thing to say," Elaine said. "Even if you don't mean it." More silence. "Something's on your mind," she said.

"Those reports," Nick said. "Do you remember anything about them?"

"Like what?"

"Pedophilia."

"On Reasoner's part? None whatsoever. Wasn't he fucked-up enough?"

"It doesn't necessarily have to be confirmed or solid," Nick said. "Psychological speculation about possible child molestation. Even a rumor."

Someone spoke in the background again. This time Elaine didn't quite cover the mouthpiece. "Not now," she said, her voice rising in anger. She lowered it and said, "What's going on, Nick?"

"I'd like to see those reports."

"The psychological profiles from the Reasoner case?"

"Everything," Nick said. "Everything the department's got."

"On the investigation?"

"On Reasoner," Nick said. "Everything."

"What's this about?"

"I just want it," Nick said.

"Don't tell me you're working on his appeal."

"Of course not." The idea maddened him.

"Then what?" Elaine said. "Writing your memoirs?"

"Why would I be doing that?"

"Because——" She interrupted herself. "You plan to keep working?"

Nick's voice rose. "Why not?"

Pause. Nick heard Elaine expel air through her nose, a quick expressive blast, part laughter and part something he'd never been able to pin down. He remembered feeling it on his face, one of those little things that had blown Kathleen away.

"I'll see what I can do," Elaine said.

He hated asking her for help, but who better?

Nick called Billie, got her voice mail. "Sorry I missed your call," he said. "I'm fine. My old self." He went silent, comfortable there in her voice mail, as though it were some inner room in her house. "What's your schedule?" he said after a while. "I was thinking——" And at that moment, the big idea that had eluded him on waking returned, now sharply defined and impossible ever to forget. "I was thinking we could get married."

What had he said? A marriage proposal left on voice mail? And so offhandedly phrased at that. She'd think he was insane. How to erase, delete, undo? Nick didn't know. He hung up the phone.

He made breakfast—a four-egg omelet, four slices of bacon, four slices of toast with lots of butter and jam, all those fours adding up to a four-square meal. Delicious smells spread through the kitchen, but Nick turned out not to be hungry. Could happen to anyone, meant nothing. He reached across the table for a sheet of paper. What was this?

Three squares, labeled Friday, Saturday, Sunday, divided into A.M. and P.M. *Friday, 2:45 P.M.—beginning of testimony, Canning trial. Sunday. 4:48 P.M.—admitted to St. Joe's.* In between: blanks.

Good idea, filling in those lost weekend blanks, but he'd written nothing else. Why not? He knew some of them. For example:

Friday, probably late afternoon—he'd gotten Liza Rummel's check for four hundred and fifty dollars, perhaps meeting her.

Then—already looking for Amanda, he'd interviewed Beth Franklin, the landlord's daughter.

After that—the Airport Marriott, where he'd talked to James McMurray and deposited the check.

And then? Home?

Or was it possible he hadn't gone home, but instead had driven up to the lake? Wouldn't that make sense, especially since he'd been in Barstow the next day? Nick was trying to get the geography straight in his mind when someone knocked at the door.

Billie? He hurried into the hall, opened up. Not Billie, but a uniformed cop with a thick briefcase in his hand.

"Hi, Mr. Petrov," he said.

A big uniformed cop, hair blond, mustache blond, chin square, the uniform the high-booted kind from the motorcycle unit. His Harley stood in the driveway, a passing kid gawking at it.

"Yes?" said Nick.

"Tommy Whalen," said the motorcycle cop. "Met you at St. Joe's—with the flowers. The chief sent this." He raised the briefcase. "The material you wanted."

"That was quick." Nick reached for the briefcase. Tommy swung it just out of reach, like a teasing older brother.

"Thing is," Tommy said, "it's not for keeps. I gotta stay here while you go over the material, and bring it all back, no copying neither. Chief's orders. Said if it wasn't you there'd be no way period." He glanced at Nick's chest.

Nick realized he was only wearing boxers. He and Tommy Whalen stood about the same height and were built the same, at least the same as Nick used to be. Now he felt skinny. He'd never felt skinny in his goddamned life. "Come in, then," he said.

"Thanks," said Tommy, stepping into the house. "Nice crib you got here. I'm a big fan."

"Of what?" Nick said, closing the door.

"Your work," said Tommy. "That's my ambition, going out on my own one day." His eyes went to the finger painting of the neckless little boy and the furry dog. "Who's the artist?"

"My son."

"Dmitri?" said Tommy.

"How did you know that?"

"Elai— The chief mentioned it."

"You've been discussing me?" Nick said.

"Not discussing," Tommy said. "More like the chief giving me a little background. She's a big fan too." Tommy glanced at Nick's chest again, once like a drum; that comparison Elaine's, as it happened.

"There's coffee in the kitchen," Nick said; he went into the bedroom and threw on sweats.

I n the kitchen, Nick found the briefcase on the table beside his uneaten breakfast and Tommy gazing out the back door, a steaming cup in his hand. "What a setup," Tommy said. "You mind my asking what you paid, Mr. Petrov?"

"It was years ago," Nick said. "And call me Nick." He put his dishes by the sink, sat down, tried to open the briefcase. Locked. He looked up at Tommy.

"Gone up a shitload since then, huh, Nick?" Tommy said. He came over and unlocked the briefcase.

"Haven't really looked into it," Nick said. "I'm not going anywhere."

"Good attitude," Tommy said.

Nick, opening the briefcase, paused. "In what way?"

"A house is a home first, an investment second," said Tommy. "That's what Suze Orman says."

Nick opened the briefcase. On top lay the central booking photos of Reasoner, full face and profile.

"That's him, huh?" said Tommy, coming closer. "Doesn't look like Dennis Franz—more like an accountant or something."

Nick gazed at the pictures. Didn't Tommy see beyond that high-domed forehead and recessive chin to the complexity and guardedness of those eyes, all those thoughts squirming just below the surface?

"Donald Sutherland backed out," Nick said. He turned the photo spread over, laid it on the table. Next came the M.E.'s pictures of victim number one, Janet Cody.

"Fuckin' A," said Tommy. "Did he do that shit while they were still alive?"

"No."

"Then why?" said Tommy. "What's the point?"

"No one really knows," Nick said. "He never confessed."

Nick went through the briefcase, found a folder with "Dr. Philippa Myers, Department of Psychology, UCLA" stamped on the front. He opened it and started reading. Tommy moved away.

"This smells good," he said.

Nick looked up. Tommy was standing over his breakfast plate on the counter.

"You gonna trash it?" he said.

"Help yourself," Nick said.

Tommy picked up Nick's plate. "I'll have a little picnic," he said, moving toward the back door. He noticed that a corner of the duct tape over the broken pane had come loose and tamped it down. Then he stuck a strip of bacon in his mouth, said, "Mmm," and went outside.

Dr. Myers, acting for the state, had gone through everything in Gerald Reasoner's recorded history and interviewed him twice for a total of four hours. She wrote about Reasoner's mother and father, neither pleasant, both within normal human bounds; about his schooling, unremarkable; his girlfriends, nonexistent; his friends in general, also nonexistent; his interest in S&M pornography, sporadic; his faith in his own intelligence, unshakable. Words like *infantilism, repressed, narcissistic, controlling* and *decompensatory* kept coming up. Hatred of women: Nick got that. Fear of some powerful mystery locked deep inside them: he thought he got that too. Baffled frustration at his failure to rise higher in the world: and that. But did it explain what Reasoner had done? More like it went along with what he'd done, the way modern man and Neanderthal man shared some common ancestor. And of unhealthy interest in boys, child molestation, pedophilia: not a word.

Nick looked out the back window. Tommy was sitting in the sun, the plate on his lap, gleaming there, so clean he might have licked it off. Nick rummaged down to the bottom of the briefcase, took out the M.E.'s photos of Lara Deems. That face: how well he remembered it for some reason, those heavy sensual lips especially. Nick stared at the death face of Lara Deems. Had he ever seen it in person, or just the photos? That should have been easy to remember, but for the moment it was not. That other thing he'd been trying to remember—what Rui told Deej— kept getting mixed up with his first memories of Lara Deems's face, like two FM stations sharing a frequency when you drove through their staticky border.

Reasoner had left Lara Deems's face alone, confining his surgery to one forearm, and a small area of it at that. Nick stared at
Lara Deems's face. Those lips. Familiar: Because he'd been to the
crime scene? Seen the pictures? Or for some other reason?

Nick went through the briefcase, examined the corpse photos of each victim. Reasoner had done more elaborate work on
all the other women than he had on Lara Deems, completely
opening up the torsos of three of them, and cutting deep and
strange exposures below Tiffany LeVasseur's waist that Nick's
eyes shied away from. Perhaps with the Nicolette Levy murder
so recent, less than twenty-four hours before, whatever was
driving Reasoner hadn't had time to fully recharge, hadn't been
driving him quite so hard. But if the compulsion weren't as powerful, why had he killed her in the first place?

Nick read everything there was on the Lara Deems murder.
Description of the apartment in Santa Monica: a one-bedroom
on the second floor, L-shaped. Signs of forced entry: none. Signs
of struggle: plenty, including a smashed imitation Greek vase
and an overturned bamboo kitchen chair. Cause of death: a single stab wound to the heart with a thin, sharp object, possibly a
scalpel, not recovered. Time of death: between 2:30 and 4:00 A.M.
Site of death: in her bed. Discovery of the crime: 8:35 A.M., when
a babysitter brought Lara's daughter back from an overnight at
her house. Name of daughter: Amanda. What Amanda saw: not
addressed. Dr. Tulp postcard: on the fridge, bloodstain (type A,
matching Lara's) in one corner. Fingerprints, DNA, fiber evidence: none.

The back door opened and Tommy came in, plate in hand.
"How's it goin'?"

"I'm done."

"That was quick," Tommy said. "Find what you wanted?"

"Hard to say." But he'd been looking for evidence that backed
up Rui's story, and there was none. Nick closed the briefcase.

"Anything I can help you with?"

"I don't think so."

"Must be kinda weird," Tommy said. He was at the sink, rolling up his sleeves. "Going back to the days of you and the chief working together. What was that like?"

Nick looked up at Tommy. Tommy was washing the dish, his broad back turned, suds rising around his thick forearms, covered in wiry blond hair. "How do you mean?" Nick said.

"No special way," said Tommy, placing the dish in the rack. He faced Nick. "Any chance of a quick tour before I split?"

"Tour of what?"

"Your place. I'm knocked out by it, you want the truth. Exactly what I'm aiming at, one day."

Nick took Tommy on a tour: bedroom, dining room, living room. "What's this?" Tommy said, picking up a tarnished trophy with a cactus growing inside. "Hey," he said. "You did some boxing." He gave Nick a quick up-and-down. "Me too." He rubbed his thumb over the inscription, held it to the light. "Light-heavy, huh? I was a heavyweight myself. Still spar a bit? Like up until you—up until recently?"

"No."

"Me neither. But I wouldn't mind getting back into it, just for the workout, keep my weight down. Interested in climbing in the ring some time, maybe when you're done convalescing?"

"I'll let you know," Nick said, taking the trophy out of Tommy's hands and putting it back on the shelf. He moved toward the front door.

"How about the upstairs?" Tommy said.

Nick glanced at Tommy's face. His eyes were bright, maybe with enthusiasm. Nick decided he didn't like fans. He led Tommy upstairs, felt Tommy's heavy steps behind him, tried to go up quickly, powerfully; but his right leg let him down a bit.

"This your office?" Tommy said. "Cool." He went to the desk, gazed at the diamond-shaped display: *There is no justice.* His eyes roamed over the objects, one by one. Candyland card,

Empty Box CD, navy-blue suit jacket, Babar, volleyball, Hall-mark card, Dr. Tulp, three little girls on a pinto pony. "What's all this?" he said. "You don't mind my asking."

"What does it look like?" Nick said.

"You tell me," Tommy said. He pointed to the Dr. Tulp post-card, almost, but not quite, touching. "I remember this from the movie." Tommy picked up the old Brownie photo, looked at it closely, put it back. "I thought it was a pretty good movie, Nick. Know my favorite scene? The one with Armand Assante and Kim Delaney rolling around on the beach down in Cabo. You like that one too?"

"It seemed gratuitous," Nick said.

"Yeah?" said Tommy. "I thought it was kinda hot. Couldn't help asking myself if anything like that happened in real life."

Nick looked Tommy in the eye. "And what did yourself an-swer?" he said.

A little muscle jumped in the side of Tommy's face. Then he smiled. "That's a good line, Nick. I could learn a lot from you. Elaine said so."

"She's too kind," Nick said.

Tommy's eyebrows rose.

"Thank her for sending the files," Nick said, motioning Tommy to the door.

They came to the stairs.

"After you," Tommy said, stepping aside.

Nick started down, slipping just a bit on the first stair. "Easy, there," said Tommy, putting his hand on Nick's shoulder. A heavy hand. "Easy, Nicky." Tommy loomed over him, his voice in Nick's ear.

Down in the hall, the front door opened. Tommy took his hand away. Billie came into the house.

"Nick?" she called.

He went down the stairs, no slipups. She was wearing her nurse's uniform, had a big smile on her face. "I just got your message," she said.

"And?" Nick said.

She noticed Tommy, halfway down. "Billie," Nick said. "Tommy."

She smiled at him too. "We met at St. Joe's," she said. "You brought Nick flowers."

"They weren't from me," Tommy said, picking up the brief-case. His gaze went to Billie, back to Nick. "Hope that was all right, eating your lunch."

"You were hungry," Nick said. They shook hands. Nick's right didn't embarrass him, but Tommy wasn't exerting any pressure, just hung his hand there, surprisingly hot. He went out, climbed on his bike.

Nick couldn't wait for him to be gone. He turned to Billie. "And?" he said.

twenty-eight

I don't know what to say," Billie said.

"Isn't it a simple yes or no?" Nick said.

But there was nothing simple about the expression in her eyes. "Are you sure this is what you want?" she said.

Nick didn't speak, hoped she saw the answer on his face.

"How well do you know me?" she said.

Nick looked at her, was sure he saw deep inside, sure he knew her. The way her head was tilted, like a sensitive receiver waiting for an incoming transmission; the set of her chin, strong and soft at the same time; lips slightly parted, unself-conscious, alive in the moment, thinking hard: he knew her. "Whoever loved that loved not at first sight"—there was truth in that, and if not love at very first sight, then love after those first few sight-ings, different angles setting off progressive revelations in the heart; or like one of those multistage rockets, taking off.

"I could ask the same question," Nick said.

Billie shook her head. Even that, perfect: not stubborn, not aggressive, just sure. "A nurse is in a position to know," she said, "like nobody else."

That seemed right. A detective and a nurse, a good match if everything was going to have to be speeded up.

"All right, then," Nick said, "just from your point of view: yes or no?"

"You see?" she said. "Right there: you."

"Meaning?"

"Yes," Billie said.

Yes. Nick's heart lifted, light as a boy's on the first day of no school.

"On one condition," she added, as he put his arms around her. "You have to see Dr. Tully."

"But he'll want to do that radiation thing."

"He might," said Billie.

"I can't do the radiation thing," Nick said. "Not now."

"Why?"

"It causes confusion. He said so himself. I can't have confusion, not until"—he was going to say *not until I've found this girl,* but it was much more than that now— "not until I've cracked this case."

"Can't it wait?"

"No."

"Why not?"

First, he had a client and she'd paid him four hundred and fifty dollars, fifty dollars short of his retainer for some reason, but close enough: he was working for her. Second, the client was missing too, she and Amanda out there somewhere, in danger and he didn't know why. Third, the Amanda case was tied to the Reasoner case, the biggest case of his career, maybe the defining event of his life. Nick stood on it, his foundation, in a way. What else did he have, to be blunt about it? And was it solid, real, true? He had to know.

"It just can't wait," Nick said.

Billie's hands—she'd been holding his upper arms—let go, so slowly he could feel the pressure diminishing bit by bit. "Then my answer's no," she said. "I want to marry a man with a fighting chance."

"But I'm already doing way better than that," Nick said. He spread his arms, strong, vigorous. "I'm swimming every day, just about. And eating like a pig. Steak and eggs morning, noon and night, Billie." He gestured toward the kitchen with the clean plate in the dish rack, exhibit A. "My cholesterol's going through the roof."

Her eyes were implacable. "Change your mind for me," she said.

But that was the whole point: his mind was no longer his to change, was changing him, past, present, future. "I'll see Dr. Tully," Nick said, "the day I finish with this case."

"When will that be?"

"I can't say."

"Then I'm sorry," Billie said. She leaned forward, kissed him on the lips, and then was gone; out the door and gone, so fast it stunned him. She left him with her smell, a tingling on his lips and a tear, hers, that had somehow landed on his face. He threw open the door just in time to see her driving off—in her own car now, a little BMW, ten or fifteen years old, but buffed and shiny, immaculate—driving off with both hands on the wheel and head high.

Nick went into his bedroom and lay down, not from being worn out or tired or anything like that, but just to organize his thoughts. First, he had to block out everything about Billie. Second, he had to consider the implications of Rui's last words, if true. Third, he had to remember what Rui told Deej. He closed his eyes, solely for the purpose of thinking better.

Petrov was feeling pretty good; better than that, great, fantastic, out of this world. Reasoner had been taken downtown hours ago, booked and paraded in front of the media, hundreds of them. Petrov and Elaine and a bunch of other cops, almost everyone who'd worked the case, were at Dru, a bar on San Vicente they liked, getting hammered. Although not hammered in Petrov's case: he was drinking nonstop, shot after shot

washed down by bottle after bottle of beer, like water to a desert
traveler who finally stumbles into the oasis, but it was having no
effect.

Elaine sat at the other end of a long table. She wore jeans and
a little sleeveless T-shirt, no bra. Her nipples, swollen and hard,
pushed against the fabric. She gulped back a shot of something
colorless, tequila maybe, in midsentence, continued whatever she
was saying. It made the men around her laugh. She could drink
Petrov under the table, had proved it more than once. Smoke
rose faster than the ceiling fans could whirl it away; the jukebox,
all-metal, blasted Metallica, Aerosmith, Lynyrd Skynyrd, everyone yelling over it. A reporter, trying to interview Petrov, spilled
beer on his notes. All his inky quotes went blurry and faded away.
Now Elaine was laughing too, head thrown back. Petrov wanted
to be in her mouth, just that way, standing over her. They'd done
that, done every goddamned thing. He got up and went around
the table, stood behind her.

"Let's go," he said.

Still laughing, she punched some guy in a sergeant's uniform on the shoulder, not lightly, and didn't hear him.

"Let's go," Petrov said.

She turned. Sunlight, drifting through the smoke, glinted
on those golden flecks in her eyes. "Go where?"

"Doesn't matter," Petrov said. "My place." (He'd been living
in a motel in Hermosa Beach after Kathleen threw him out.) "Or
yours." (Her shabby one-bedroom in Sherman Oaks.)

"Talk about depressing," Elaine said. "We're having fun right
here. Pull up a chair."

Petrov leaned down, spoke in her ear. "It's not the place," he
said. "Just that we could be having more fun."

Elaine laughed, spewing a little beer. She licked it off her lips,
tongue pink and moist. "I get you," she said, rising, taking Petrov
by the hand. "Be right back, boys."

They went into the men's room. Elaine locked the door. She

reached down his pants. "The star attraction," she said. "Waiting in the wings." Then her jeans were off, flung on the towel dispenser, and she was sitting on the counter by the sink, legs apart, pulling him close, stuffing him in. "More fun," she said, lips moving right in his ear. "You're so fucking right." His face, over her shoulder in the mirror, was elemental: an animal, just as she said, intelligent, fierce, dangerous. Was someone rattling the doorknob? Who cared? Her legs went up over his shoulders. They were made for each other.

M an," she said, pulling on her jeans. sticking her panties in the pocket. "I needed that and didn't even know."

Petrov zipped up. She was patting her hair in the mirror. He put his arms around her from behind, kissed the top of her head. "Tomorrow," he said, "let's start looking."

"For what?" Elaine said.

"A house, a condo, an apartment, somewhere to live."

Her face changed a little, like something had been switched off and was now back on. "No rush," she said.

"No point in waiting either," said Petrov.

"Maybe," said Elaine.

"Maybe?"

"You know what they say—don't change a winning game."

"I don't understand."

"Like this, you and me right now, the way we are—this is winning. I've never felt so fucking on top in my life."

"How's that going to change when we move in together?" Petrov said. "It'll only get better."

"Maybe."

She kept saying maybe. Petrov was aware of their eyes in the mirror, his and hers, both pairs concentrating hard. His arms were still around her, her back against his chest, both of them still wet and sticky from the other, but it all felt different from seconds ago.

"What's going on?" Petrov said.

"Not now, Nick."

He spun her around. "Not now what?"

She looked up at him, eyes unblinking, set. "It's not a good time. Not today, of all days. Here, with everybody, blitzed."

Petrov hardly heard her. "What's going on?"

"I'll think about it," Elaine said. "That's the best I can do."

Someone knocked at the door. Petrov backhanded it with the side of his fist, hard. "Shut up," he yelled at whoever it was, his eyes still on Elaine. "Think about it?" he said. "Us? Like there are pros and cons? Just give me the cons. One will do."

"Not now."

"Fucking right it's going to be now." He had his hand around her wrist, maybe squeezing a bit.

"Don't *do* that," Elaine said.

He stopped, took a step back. "Talk."

"This doesn't have to happen," Elaine said.

"It's happening."

She gave him a hard look and nodded. "You and me," she said, "is not working out." She must have seen the incredulity on Petrov's face: he'd never imagined that any relationship with a woman could be this good. "It's too much and not enough, at the same time."

He felt his face flushing. "What kind of bullshit is that?"

"You heard me."

"Tell me about the not enough."

"I wish to Christ she hadn't walked in on us."

So did Petrov, but that was in the past. "What's that got to do with anything?"

"Then you could go back to her," Elaine said. "Or wouldn't have to, you'd still be there instead of that fleabag motel."

"Go back to her?" Petrov said. "Why?"

"Because, Nick," said Elaine. "We're done."

Impossible. But her eyes: no love there all of a sudden, but looking on with deep and complicated familiarity, the eyes of an ex. He'd seen a similar look in Kathleen's eyes when he'd picked up Dmitri the week before.

"You better explain," Petrov said.

Elaine's chin jutted out, as though she wasn't going to, but then she nodded. "True," she said. "You'd figure it out anyway. It was the way you handled the postcard, Nick. It started me rethinking."

"The Dr. Tulp postcard?"

"Which you kept to yourself."

"But—"

Her temper rose. "Kept to yourself, even though we'd been working together on this day and night for more than a year with the assumption—mine, anyway—of sharing credit."

"But we are sharing credit, for Christ—"

"Don't lie to me. The big break was all you, and when you had it what did you do? Walked right by me with that postcard in your fucking pocket, not a goddamned word."

"Is that what this is about?" Petrov said. "I wasn't even sure what I had—never dreamed it was going to play out so fast."

"Not good enough, Nick," Elaine said. "The biggest break that's probably ever going to happen for either of us, and you kept it secret. That changed everything."

"Do you know how stupid you sound? I wasn't keeping it secret. I didn't even know what 'it' was."

"You're fooling yourself," Elaine said. "I didn't know you had that in you too. But you can't fool me. I heard the news on the radio, got to see your big smile on TV. What do you think I am? Some little fuck pet you come home to?"

Their faces were close now, red, hot, the men's room at Dru hot too, violence pending over them. One of those moments for Petrov too: when everything changed. And Kathleen gone.

Petrov unlocked the men's room door and went out. A few smirking guys stood in the corridor. Petrov kept going, through the noise and smoke, out into daylight, got in his car. Someone on the street, a complete stranger, recognized him and gave him a thumbs-up. AC blasting but Petrov's face stayed hot and red.

Nick rose up through layers of dreams, broke the surface into consciousness. Glioblastoma multiforme, Grade IV. *No whining, Nikolai.*

He got up, staggering just a little, but only because of his thirst. He was very thirsty, as thirsty as he'd been in the desert outside Barstow. The desert outside Barstow: in the kitchen, he drank glass after glass from the cooler, and a few desert memories flowed in, lost weekend fragments. If he lived long enough he'd recover them all, but here were three: Rui laying him out almost accidentally, a red-taloned vulture tearing at his sleeve, Buster.

Buster the Barstow dog, and this was a Barstow story. Who were the Barstow people? George Rummel, Liza, Lara, Wally Moore, Deej, Sergeant Gallego. He tried to make them add up to a meaningful sum and failed. Were there other Barstow people? He couldn't think of any.

Nick took one last glass of water up to his office, gazed at the artifacts, *There is no justice* at the top, three girls on a pinto pony at the bottom. He noticed something he'd missed before, writing on the little cowboy's outsize badge. He got out a magnifying glass, read the words: *Silver City Ghost Town.*

Nick gazed at that for a while. Then he picked up the phone and called the office of the chief of police, was put right through.

"Hi, Nick," Elaine said. "Get those files all right?"

"Thanks."

"Tommy behave himself?"

"How do you mean?"

"He's a dope, didn't you notice? But easy on the eyes. Did you get what you wanted?"

"Maybe you could help me."

"Do what?"

"I could go through channels, but——" This would be so much faster. Everything was going to have to be speeded up, and who better to ask?

Her voice rose a little. "Do what?"

"Get an interview with him."

"Who are you talking about?"

What was wrong with him? He kept slipping back to the time they were on the same wavelength. "Reasoner," Nick said.

Pause. "I'll have to know what this is about."

"He might have been involved in other crimes."

"Murder?"

"No."

"Child molestation? Beyond the statute of limitations."

"I want to know."

"What's the point?"

"I'll go through channels if that's the way you want it."

"That's not the way I want it," Elaine said. "But have you ever thought of maybe relaxing a bit, taking your foot off the pedal these last——"

He hung up on her.

twenty-nine

Was that why Elaine came through, because he'd hung up on her? Or was she just being nice, sparing him the trouble of going through channels? Nick didn't know, but she had it all set up the very next day.

Nick wrote up some notes, intending to study them on the flight, but they gave him a window seat and he couldn't stop staring out, not at anything particular, just the endless blue. Despite all you learned about it—the coldness, cruelty and carelessness, culminating in the probable nonexistence of any ultimate meaning or comfort—life could still be like this, beautiful.

An hour into the flight, they ran into dark clouds massing down from the Bay Area and the pilot nosed the plane above them. The first time Nick remembered flying above clouds like that he'd gazed down in the hope, faint but still there, of spotting the towers of heaven rising from that puffy golden floor.

They landed in the rain. Nick hadn't factored that in, neglecting to bring rain gear or an umbrella, and the shoulders of his jacket were still a little damp when the guard walked him into an interview room at San Quentin.

Interview room: cement floor, cinder-block walls, steel table bolted to the floor, attached steel benches on either side, the bench facing the door occupied by Gerald Reasoner, who was reading a paperback with a picture of a spaceship on the cover.

As Nick came in, he looked up, folded over the corner of the page he was on and closed the book, placing it facedown and edges squared on the steel-topped table.

The guard said: "We strip-searched him leaving the block and coming in. Want him shackled? Up to you."

"No," Nick said.

The guard went out, leaving the door open, and sat on a stool in the corridor, arms crossed over his chest. Nick and Reasoner were alone, two men in a concrete box, no props except that paperback.

Reasoner's gaze fixed on Nick as he took his place on the opposite bench. Reasoner had had one of those moon faces before. Now it was thinner. He was thinner in general, not buff or built up, but compact and trim, as though prison had made him fit. And although his face was thinner, there wasn't a line on it, no pallor either. In fact, he looked almost good, not simply unaged, but better than he had twelve years ago.

"What are you reading?" Nick said.

"Trash."

Only his eyes, watery, as though observing from slightly beneath the surface, remained the same. Their focus went to the top of Nick's head, down his face, neck, shoulders, hands. One other thing remained the same, that little smirking tightness around Reasoner's lips, which showed up now.

"What's funny?" Nick said. But he knew: Reasoner was delighted with the change in him.

"Nothing," Reasoner said. Something registered in those watery eyes; the smirk vanished at once. Nick realized what he hadn't understood about that smirk twelve years ago: Reasoner didn't always know it was there. The smirk had a life of its own, some inner self finding expression.

"Any idea why I'm here?" Nick said.

"It's of no concern to me," said Reasoner, "other than the welcome change in routine."

"Oh?" said Nick. "Dropping your appeal?"

"Where did you hear that?"

"It's a fair assumption. Your chances, as things stand now, are zero."

Reasoner licked his lips; his tongue sharply pointed and almost colorless. "My legal team says otherwise."

Reasoner's legal team were young pro bono lawyers supplied by an anti-death-penalty organization. "Maybe I should go directly to them," Nick said.

Reasoner watched him; Nick felt the frantic activity of his thoughts. But Reasoner remained silent. Nick started to rise.

Reasoner spoke quickly. "Go directly to them about what?"

Nick sat back down. The power of the outside world was his. "Lara Deems," he said.

"Lara Deems?"

"What do you remember about her?"

"There's nothing I remember about Lara Deems," Reasoner said. "I never harmed her in any way, never knew her, never even heard of her." The pointy, colorless tongue poked out, just for a split second. "I never laid a finger on any of them. I'm an innocent man, sentenced to death—and you played your part, a happy cog in the machine."

Nick gazed at this innocent man, an innocent man with bits of female skin, tissue and bone in his backyard, and the surgical instruments still cooking in the autoclave when forensics arrived. But Nick didn't argue, just said, "No alibi evidence was ever introduced."

"My defense was a travesty," said Reasoner.

"Meaning there were alibis?" Nick said.

Reasoner paused, rubbed his chin. His hands were finely shaped but very small, out of proportion to the rest of him. "What are you doing here?" he said.

"I thought that was of no concern to you."

Reasoner took out a pair of glasses, put them on; his eyes

shrank behind the lenses. "There's nothing you can do to hurt me now," he said.

"True," said Nick. "So let's go over the alibis. Where do you want to start—Janet Cody? Cindy Motton? Tiffany LeVasseur? Nicolette Levy? Lara Deems?"

"Those are just names to me," Reasoner said.

"That's your alibi?"

"Why should I go into details with you?" Reasoner said.

"Because I might be able to help."

"Why would you want to?" Reasoner said. "Helping me means admitting you got it wrong. You'd be undermining your own integrity." He smiled, not the smirk but a real smile, pleased with the phrase, pleased with trapping Nick in a corner.

"Burying the truth is what undermines integrity," Nick said.

Reasoner's smile faded. Some subsurface excitement began to animate his face. "You're admitting you were wrong?"

"I'm prepared to," Nick said. "Depending on what I hear from you."

"Why now?" Reasoner said. "I've been rotting here for twelve years."

But he didn't look like he was rotting; Nick, in fact, was the rotting one, rotting from within. Looking at it that way made him feel faint. Reasoner was going to outlive him, probably by many years. Nick sat still, took a deep breath, fought to keep his mind clear, to not topple over.

Reasoner's eyes narrowed. "What's wrong with you?"

Nick didn't answer. He bit the inside of his mouth hard, tasting blood, hoping pain would poke through the wooziness.

"Are you sick?" Reasoner said.

Nick took another deep and humiliating breath.

"Not cancer?" Reasoner said. He took off his glasses, peered at Nick through that watery veil. "Cancer!" He clapped his hands together. "God Almighty."

A tide of anger swept through Nick. Juwan was right: *He should have got shot while resisting arrest.* Anger washed the faintness away, restored his strength, and in a voice that was healthy and vital, Petrov's voice, he said: "God let you down. I'm fine."

"Dream on," Reasoner said. "There's cancer in this prison, lots and lots of cancer. I know it when I see it." He nodded to himself. "And now I understand what's going on—this is a deathbed conversion. You want to make things right with Him."

Nick leaned forward across the table. Their faces were close. Nick mastered the temptation to rip him apart, blocked out everything except the case. "Suppose you're right," he said. "Maybe you better take advantage of this opportunity while I'm still available."

The pointed, colorless tongue emerged, licked the air, withdrew. Nick smelled Reasoner's smell, very faint, a smell like weak sugary tea. "What opportunity?" Reasoner said.

"To win an appeal," Nick said. "To stay alive."

The sugary tea smell got stronger. It sickened Nick but he kept his face where it was, a foot from Reasoner's. The tongue again, questing; and then Reasoner said, "What do you want to know?"

"Your alibi in the Lara Deems killing."

"Why that one?"

"Why not?" Nick said.

Reasoner sat silently, his eyes pulsated slightly; or at least Nick thought they did. Why this reluctance to start with Lara Deems? Nick knew. He began to see where this could go.

"Alibis are the best defense," Nick said. "You were somewhere else at the time of the murder. In the case of Lara Deems, where was that?"

A long pause. Nick smelled Reasoner's smell, sensed the tongue flicking against Reasoner's teeth, trying to get out. "I'd have to think back," he said.

"Think back."

Reasoner thought. His eyes did that pulsating thing again; this time Nick was sure. "The night before you arrested me?" Reasoner said.

"Right."

"I was at home."

Nick leaned back a little. "Doing what?"

"The things I used to do on my time off," Reasoner said.

"Such as?"

"Reading."

Nick picked up Reasoner's book, turned it over. *Return to Shan'bu: Volume Nine in the Battle of the Three Universes Saga.* Reasoner's arm twitched a little, as though fighting the urge to snatch the book away.

"I was reading art theory at the time."

"By yourself?" Nick said.

Pulsation.

"Or can someone confirm your story?"

"I was by myself," Reasoner said.

"Are you sure?" Nick said. "Because that won't help. Try to remember."

"There's nothing wrong with my memory," Reasoner said. "I can even tell you what I was reading that night."

"What?" said Nick.

A tiny pink spot appeared on Reasoner's cheek. "Berenson's abstract on Donatello's *David,*" he said.

Nick didn't know what that was. He said: "In the basement?"

"Basement?" The pink spot spread a little.

"This reading of yours."

"I did my reading in the den."

"What went on in the basement?" Nick said.

"Laundry."

"Did you do any laundry that night?"

"I might have."

"Alone?" Nick said.

The pulsation of the eyes, the pink spot, the pointed tongue: all of them present now, as though some inner Reasoner was struggling to be free.

"I lived alone," Reasoner said.

"But what about guests?" Nick said. "Was there a guest down in the basement who could confirm your story?"

"No," Reasoner said. He realized he'd spoken loudly, glanced out at the guard, lowered his voice. "No. No guest."

"Maybe *guest* is the wrong word," Nick said.

Reasoner said nothing. The inner man asserted himself a little more.

"Too distant," Nick said. "Too detached. After all, you had him call you Uncle Jerry. What did you call him? Just Rui, or did you have a pet name?"

Reasoner's whole face was pink now, and his little hands were clenched.

"A pet name like Roo," Nick said. And suddenly, arriving at an understanding of the man in a way that he never could have before—in a way barred to Petrov—he knew the nickname, knew what would appeal. "Or Rooster," he said.

Confirmation in those pulsing eyes.

"Yes," Nick said. "Rooster was the pet name you whispered in the boy's ear when you got him down in the basement."

Reasoner's mouth opened, revealing the pointy, colorless tongue. "You're a liar," he said.

"Don't talk like that, Jerry," Nick said. "I'm trying to help you. You have a rock-solid alibi for the Lara Deems murder. You were at home that night, fucking little Rui Estrella. Now all we've got to do is get the word out."

Reasoner, bright red now, glanced at the guard in the doorway again, put his finger over his lips. "Shh," he said. "Shh. It's a lie. I would never do such a thing."

"But somehow it happened anyway," Nick said. "That's the way it is with child molesters."

Reasoner reached across the table, clutched Nick's arm. "Lower your voice," he said. "It's not true."

Nick pulled his arm away, his right arm, so he didn't do it

with the ease he would have liked. He spoke in a normal conversational tone. "You know it is, Jerry."

Reasoner leaned closer, urgent, face almost touching Nick's. "No, no, no," he said, so quietly Nick could hardly hear. "I never touched him. I was with her that night. I killed Lara Deems."

"I don't believe you."

"I swear to God."

"How did you get her into the bathtub?" Nick said.

Reasoner looked surprised. "The same as I did with Nicolette," he said. "I told her if she let me watch her bathe I wouldn't hurt her."

Didn't he deserve to die, right now? Nick did the next best thing. "Lara Deems was murdered in her bed," he said. "She never went near the bathroom."

Reasoner clapped his hand over his mouth. But too late: the confession, a double one, was already out.

"So your alibi's golden," Nick said. "When they inject you it'll be for the other six." He rose. "You must have wondered over the years who did kill Lara Deems."

No answer. Reasoner gazed up at him, eyes wide, hand still over his mouth.

Nick walked away. He was almost out the door, almost in the hall, every step taking him closer to a long hot shower, when Reasoner spoke. "Was it you?" he said.

thirty

So much to deal with, but Nick just couldn't. He slept almost the whole way back, wedged between a fat man and a fat woman, both busy on their laptops. Their overflowing flesh kept him warm and cozy—he'd caught a bit of a chill from the rain up north—until the descent at LAX. The plane banked over the ocean and he awoke with a start. Something shifted in his mind, an upheaval in memory that he felt physically. What Rui told Deej: it came to him, word for word.

Suppose there was a serial killer on the loose and you wanted to kill somebody. All you'd have to do is find out the details of the serial killings and do yours the very same way. Who would ever suspect?

"Like a baby," said the fat woman, unwrapping a stick of gum. "I can't sleep on planes to save my life."

A copycat killing, designed to look like Reasoner's work. And the killer had gone as far as imitating Reasoner's sick anatomy lesson, although with Lara the flensing was confined to one small area of the forearm, and now Nick knew why: the killer could only stomach so much. What else had the killer done? Left Reasoner's calling card, the Dr. Tulp postcard, on Lara's fridge. None of the other postcards had been planted so obviously—Cindy Motton's in a recipe drawer, for example, Nicolette Levy's in the Maui photo album. That was one line of thought to follow. But there was another, impossible to ignore: the only person who'd known about the postcard was him.

So who killed Lara Deems? That strange little headache, no bigger than a penny, started up again. Not anything you could call pain, probably a common reaction to changing air pressure. Nick put his chair-back in the upright position.

He drove home, his right foot a little balky on the pedals—but wouldn't it have been a long day for anyone?—and fell on his bed. The only person who'd known about the post-card was him. But he'd had no connection with the living Lara Deems—to the best of his recollection. How good was that? The lost weekend was mostly gone, but there were other gaps as well, the forgotten key to his private notebook code for one. Were there others? Why not? And why were those lips of Lara's so clear in his mind—was it just from the crime scene photos? Fact: unlike all the other victims, who'd lived in the Valley, Lara had had a place in Santa Monica, a few blocks from the house Nick shared with Kathleen.

Nick got his head properly placed over the wafer. No matter what, he could never have done a thing like that—*diabolical* was not too strong a word. Then he thought of the Court TV tape of the Canning trial he'd watched for Dr. Tully's little experiment. Perjury: he'd never have thought himself capable of that either.

Had anyone else even noticed the Dr. Tulp postcard, never mind realizing its significance? No. There was no one else, and his affair with Elaine had ended over the very issue of his keeping the clue to himself, not sharing credit. But could he have done the following, starting the night of the discovery of Nicolette Levy's body, ending the following day with the arrest of Reasoner?

1. *Discovered the postcard connection.*
2. *Verified it by searching the boxed effects of the four remaining victims, finding the postcard in all of them.*
3. *Bought a postcard somewhere, killed Lara Deems and planted the card on her fridge.*

*4. Gone to the Getty, gotten his second big break in the case
from the gift-shop ladies and arrested Reasoner.*

One, two and four he remembered, three not at all. The
copycat, knowing that the postcard lead almost certainly meant
the quick arrest of the serial killer, simply through normal police work, would have had to move fast. Stalk, kill, mutilate: a
frenzy but cold-blooded at the same time. Nick wasn't that kind
of man. Plus he had no memory of ever knowing Lara Deems.
Only logic—matter-of-fact, unbiased, nonwishful—pointed
straight at him.

Nick felt cold, as though someone had pulled back his covers. He reached down, felt around for them, touched a
warm hand. Billie? He rolled over, opened his eyes. Not Billie,
but Elaine, lips slightly pursed as though she was examining
him. And he was naked, although he didn't remember getting
undressed. She pulled the covers back up.

"I'm worried about you," she said.

"How did you get in?"

"The door was unlocked. Wide open, in fact. You've got to be
more careful."

A ray of sunlight fell across his room. What day was it? Her
hair, blonder than ever, now matched those golden glints in her
eyes. She sat down on the side of the bed, sending a tiny seismic
wave through the mattress. Nick felt a funny little pain in his
spine.

"Don't worry about me," he said.

"I do, Nick. Your memory's been affected by all this. Just let
it go."

"Let what go?"

"Reconstructing the past, or whatever it is you're doing. You
should be taking care of yourself."

"I am." He thought of telling her about all his eating, all his swimming, but didn't have the energy for that whole spiel. "And who said anything about my memory?"

Her tone grew gentle, or very close to it. "You did," she said.

When? It was almost funny.

"My memory's coming back," Nick said.

"It is?"

"Fast," said Nick. "And reconstructing the past is what this is about."

"In what way?"

"Let's start with Reasoner's confession."

"He confessed?"

"To two of the murders—Nicolette Levy and Lara Deems."

"How did you get him to do that?"

"Doesn't matter," Nick said. "What matters is that one of the confessions is false. Reasoner didn't kill Lara Deems."

Elaine went still. Although they weren't quite touching, he felt some change in her body, like a lion waking up. "You're not making much sense," she said.

"He had an alibi he didn't use."

"You believed him?" Elaine's voice grew scornful.

"And he still won't use it," Nick said.

"Why not?"

"Because he was doing something more shameful at the time."

"More shameful than murdering and mutilating innocent women?" Elaine said.

"In his mind."

Elaine looked into his eyes. Her intelligence had physical weight, pressed into his skull. "Is this connected to the guy who fell off the fire escape at the El Rey?" she said.

"Yes."

"Rui Estrella."

"How do you know his name?"

"My job," Elaine said. "Suppose—and I'm not buying it—

but suppose it's true. What happens to the alibi now that he's dead?"

"That's not the point," Nick said. "The point is finding who killed Lara Deems."

"The jury already decided that."

"Decided it wrong on the seventh count. It was a copycat, Elaine. Don't you see?"

She put her hand on his. Hers was hot, the blood throbbing inside. "The witness, if he was a witness, is dead. There are no grounds for reopening anything. It's history, dead and buried. Let it go."

"How can you say that?" Nick said. "Don't you want to know?"

"For your own good, Nick," she said.

"What does that mean?"

Elaine withdrew her hand, rose, walked through that thick ray of sunshine, dematerializing slightly on the other side. She gazed out at the canal. "Just go to sleep," she said.

"I'm not tired," Nick said, sitting up. "What does 'for my own good' mean?"

"Sleep," Elaine said. "I'm leaving."

Without knowing quite how he'd done it, Nick was out of bed, naked but he didn't care, had a hand around her wrist.

"Don't *do* that," she said.

He didn't let go. "Answer the question."

"I don't want to," Elaine said.

"Say it," he said.

Their faces were very close. Hers was cold and angry, but he wouldn't let go.

"You'll wish I hadn't," she said.

"Say it."

Elaine jerked her wrist free—he couldn't stop her—and said it: "How did you meet Lara Deems?"

"What the hell are you saying?" The chill he'd caught up

north dug deep into Nick's body. "I never met her. I didn't know her." But the tone of both sentences rose at the end, as though inviting question marks.

"You couldn't just fucking leave it alone," Elaine said. "Oh, no. That wouldn't be you. You pick and pick and pick." She moved away from him, into the ray of light, gilding herself. "I did some picking too," she said, "after we . . . after we ended whatever it was we had. The way you handled that postcard clue—I kept having trouble with that. So I hunted around for any connection between the two of you. Remember the Four Aces Motel on Lincoln?"

Nick remembered; it was now a parking lot.

"That's where you took her. The clerk ID'd both your pictures. You dumped her around the time I came along. She wasn't happy about it—the clerk heard you fighting through the wall. Lara slid from the fringes of acting to the fringes of hooking. After that, all I've got is speculation. But it must have been like this. She threatened to tell Kathleen and you paid her off. But she wouldn't stay paid off, the way they never do. Then your chance came along. You had to move fast, and you did. Is that about right?"

"Not a word of truth," Nick said. "It doesn't even make sense—by that time Kathleen knew about you and me."

Elaine shrugged. "So Lara found another route—like threatening she'd tell the department all about the two of you, maybe charging you with assault. Got you angry, Nick. Angry men aren't too good at judging what makes sense."

Nick stepped back, sank down on the bed. "I don't remember any of it."

"Good," said Elaine. Her tone softened. "I don't want you to." She came to the bedside, a thin sheen of sweat on her upper lip. "I'm not going to remember it either. It never happened. No one will ever know."

"I couldn't have," Nick said.

"You're forgetting what you were like in those days," said Elaine. "A powerhouse. And if a blackmailer gets what's coming to her, so what?" She leaned down, kissed him on the forehead, a tiny smear of that sweat rubbing off. "Don't beat yourself up. People like you and me—we get things done."

It added up, fit the facts. Nick knew how certain of guilt he'd be if the suspect were anyone else. Murder: just maybe. But mutilation: that couldn't have been him in any circumstances, was completely unacceptable.

"I can't drop it," Nick said.

Her voice sharpened. "Why not?"

"I just can't." He had to try to clear himself, in his own mind, and if he failed to clear himself at least know the truth. The idea of dying with so much unresolved—the meaning of his life, where he stood as a man—was more terrifying than the cancer itself.

"But look at you," Elaine said, eyes on his naked body. "How much longer do—" She interrupted herself. "Your health comes first."

They gazed at each other. He felt her will, willing him to back off, roll over, be good, and didn't give in. "I'll need your help tracking down the motel clerk," Nick said.

Elaine blew a little nasal blast of air, that half snort, half laugh of hers. "Not this time, loverboy." She pulled the blanket up over his legs. "I've got your best interests at heart."

The motel clerk. Nick went upstairs to his office, dragging himself a little, sat at his desk. The artifacts, arranged by his son to tell a story called *There is no justice.* A story he didn't understand, a story where he'd begun as a kind of reader and was now a main character, a story that scared him.

"Was it me?"

He spoke out loud, hoping to hear that voice in his head, his father's voice, replying *Never, Nikolai, my good boy, never in a million years.* But there was only silence. Was cancer his punishment for the murder of Lara Deems? And what about his perjury? Wouldn't diabetes have been good enough for that? He had a sudden, self-saving thought: maybe his mind had already been going bad during the Canning trial, and the perjury had been the venial act of a sick man. Nick rejected that argument right away: in some ways his mind was better now; he was better.

But: was it him?

The answer was in the story. Why couldn't he read it? Maybe because part—a page, chapter, section—was missing. And what was missing, had in fact been stolen from his house? The football picture, the Desert High team from 1950, with that bird flying out of the frame. His oldest piece of evidence. What else here was old? The Brownie photograph with the frilled edges, three little girls on a pinto pony, led by the boy in the ten-gallon hat—that had to be old too. Nick took out the magnifying glass, studied it again: the faces of the girls, two brunettes and a blonde, and the face of the boy, a hard little face, although mostly lost in shadow, and the inscription on his badge: *Silver City Ghost Town*

Nick pocketed the photo, ran a Google search on Silver City Ghost Town, got no hits. Neither were there any for the Four Aces on Lincoln Boulevard. He remembered the Four Aces, a run-down motel next to a run-down furniture store near the Venice–Santa Monica line, demolished five or six years ago. He'd driven past many times, but had he ever been inside? Nick had no memory of that.

The motel clerk. What was the first step? Should have been obvious, but Nick couldn't come up with it. Instead a strange and sickening thought hit him: what if the tumor had been growing for years, warping his mind, root cause of murder, blackouts, an out-of-control second life? Nick put his head in his hands. Inside that head things were happening. He could almost hear them, like curtains ripping. Dr. Tully, radiation, leaving all this buried, Billie: that was one way to go. The temptation grew and grew. The brainpower to do what needed doing simply wasn't there. Nick was actually searching around for Dr. Tully's card, not necessarily to dial the number but at least to know where the card was, when the phone rang.

He picked it up.

"Mr. Petrov?" said a woman.

"Speaking."

"This is Liza Rummel."

He gripped the phone tighter. "Prove you're you," he said.

"Prove I'm me?"

"Yes."

"Betsy Matsu said you're very nice."

It was her. "Are you all right?" Nick said.

Pause. "Yes."

"Amanda?"

"She's safe. I should never have gotten you involved in this, Mr. Petrov. I'm sorry. Remember that, whatever happens."

"Why did you?" Nick said.

"Get you involved?" He heard her take a deep breath. "I guess because of how the story ended," she said.

"What story?"

"Your story, Mr. Petrov. *The Reasoner Case.*"

Nick tried to remember the ending. They'd left out Petrov's marriage and Elaine's resentment about being cut out of the arrest, that whole scene at the bar on San Vicente, which the writers had known nothing about, but the movie had still ended with Elaine dumping him—to make it bittersweet, a publicist had told him at the wrap party. Nick could see it now: Kim Delaney, tears in her eyes, says she's found someone else, a civilian who helps her forget the horrors of her job—unlike Petrov who makes her remember. Anger flashes in Armand Assante's eyes; then, as she walks away, they just go dead.

"I don't understand," Nick said.

"It doesn't matter anymore," said Liza Rummel. "It's all over. Amanda and I are together."

"Nothing's over until I see her."

"I told you she's safe."

"Is she with you?"

Silence.

"I have to see her with my own eyes."

Silence.

"I'll never stop," Nick said.

"No one ever does with me," Liza said. He heard her exhale in a resigned sort of way. "I can take you to her."

"Now," Nick said. "I'll wait for you here."

"No," she said. "Meet me somewhere."

Where? Controlling the meeting place was important; that was basic. Was she in the city? Or up in Barstow? He chose a point in between. "I've got a cabin on Big Bear Lake," Nick said.

Long pause. "All right."

He told her how to get there. The phone rang again just as he was leaving, Billie's number flashing on the caller ID. Nick realized he couldn't answer. As long as it was possible he'd killed Lara Deems, he considered himself unclean, and couldn't have anything to do with Billie.

thirty-one

Infuriating: his own cabin, the road driven so many times over the past eight or nine years, but Nick needed to check the map. Ten, 91, up the canyon. Right, he knew that; wouldn't it have come to him if he'd been a little more patient? He had to stop putting pressure on his mind, just let it do what it could.

On the highway, Nick played his Jussi Bjoerling live concert CD. A magical voice, and it carried him away, eased his mind. A man in the audience called out "Nessun Dorma," and everyone laughed. Nick had often listened to that little moment, but now for the first time heard one woman laughing very clearly, her excitement, vitality, sexiness all evident. He thought at once of Elaine, although she wasn't interested in music. His mind started getting uneasy. Then Bjoerling sang the song, a cliché now and maybe even then, but that didn't keep it from thrilling him. His mind settled back down.

The sun was setting, a tiny blazing smear in the rearview mirror, as Nick started up the canyon road. A red band of light slid up the mountain faces, dragging the night after it, higher and higher. On the switchbacks, the lights of the western towns and cities came into view, unsteady beneath the smog. Nick turned off the music, slid down the windows, smelled the mountain air, cool and piney. Could people who'd done terrible crimes still get pleasure from little things like the mountain air? Certainly, and he might be one of them.

The long lane leading to the cabin was almost invisible in the darkness, but Nick left the headlights off. He nosed the car around a rocky outcrop at the entrance, over a stony ridge, down toward the lake. The moon was up, just a sliver, but enough to shine on a distant patch of lake, on the windows of the cabin, on a car parked out front. Nick pulled up right behind it, bumpers touching, blocking it in. He set his emergency brake, took out his flashlight, locked up.

Nick ran the flashlight beam over the other car: an old Mustang, light or medium blue, top down, inside strewn with coffee cups and candy wrappers. Somehow he knew the ashtray would be holding cigarette butts, their filter tips stained with lipstick. He leaned over the passenger-side door, flipped open the ashtray and there they were. He picked one out—*pick and pick and pick*— and sniffed it, mostly stale tobacco plus a waxy smell from the lipstick. Next, the glove box: all kinds of things cascaded out— balled-up tissues, parking tickets, giveaway shampoo from Marriott Hotels, sunglasses, a Hooters visor, a crumpled pack of generic cigarettes, a box of tampons, the registration. He examined it. The car was registered to Liza Rummel, the address her old one, where the Orthodox Jews now lived. Nick had a moment, maybe crazy, of triumph. He was back to square one and it felt good.

Nick shut off the flash, walked up the path to the cabin door. No lights shone inside. He stood still, listened, heard nothing. Then, from high above, somewhere way up in the night sky, came a faint thumping sound, the beating of heavy wings: an owl, probably—lots of owls, horned and spotted, around the lake—an owl hunting in the night, creature after his own heart.

Nick tried the door. *The door was unlocked,* Elaine had said. *Wide open, in fact. You've got to be more careful.* But this one, the cabin door, was locked. Nick took out his key, opened it and stepped inside.

He smelled the air, stuffy the way it got when he hadn't been up for a while, and felt the thin Indian rug under his feet. Nick loved this place, suddenly knew that in the back of his mind he'd always intended to retire here and spend the rest of his life as part of the surroundings. He also knew there was no one else inside.

But to make sure, he turned the flashlight back on and went from room to room. There were only three: the kitchen in the back, the living room with the screened porch and the wicker rocker, overlooking the lake, and the big bedroom upstairs. Nick checked them all, not forgetting the closets or under the bed, and found no one. At the bedroom window, he looked out at the lake, all silvery from the moon. A fish jumped: he saw it clearly, a black shadow, almost certainly a smallmouth bass, that rose and fell, shattering a little circle of silver. Sparkling concentric waves started their journey to the shore.

Her car was outside. She wasn't in the cabin. Therefore she was outside too, waiting in the darkness. But why? A question like that coming up meant it was a good time to have that little Colt .380 in your pocket. Nick felt in his pocket: the pinto pony photograph was there, but not the gun. Why not? Hadn't he made a mental note to carry it at all times? If not, he'd meant to. Nick resisted the urge to hold his head in his hands, to rub some life in it, and failing that to punish it.

Like the owl, Nikolai.

He went still. His father, who'd never had much time to be there for him, was finding at least the odd moment now.

Hunt.

Nick cut the light. He went downstairs, moving quietly, the way you could in your own place, and stood by the door, listening. A breeze off the lake came curling through the treetops. Other than that, nothing. Nick transferred the flash to his left hand, in case he had to use it for something other than making light. He turned the knob, slow and silent, and went outside.

No sound but that breeze, cool from the water. Nick's cabin

stood in a little clearing surrounded on three sides by woods. At the edge of the woods he'd built a toolshed; down at the lake, he'd also added a floating dock where he pulled up his dinghy, tying it hull up to the cleats. He tried the toolshed first, moving softly across the clearing, guided only by moonlight. From about ten feet away, he saw a narrow dark vertical that meant the door was open an inch or two. Had he left it that way? That wasn't him. And the spade, leaning against the side of the shed? Not him at all. He knelt down, ran his hand over the blade, felt damp earth.

Nick stood by the door, almost touching it, listened. He heard nothing, sensed no one. He stepped inside, switched on the flash, stabbed it around in the darkness, saw only shed things: gardening tools, paint cans on shelves, the outboard motor on its wall hook, fishing rods, tackle box, a butterfly net. He cut the light.

Nick returned to the back of the cabin, put his hand on the Mustang's hood, as he should have in the first place: cool to his touch. He walked around toward the wood box near the cabin door, raised the lid. Nothing inside but split logs, oak and pine. He was closing the lid when he had a thought: wasn't that where he kept the ax, right on top of the woodpile? He checked again. Not there.

Nick took the path down to the dock, dried-out pine needles, stiff and hard, crunching under his feet. The breeze stirred up countless facets on the lake and moonlight found them all. The moon had risen higher now, its light a little brighter. The dinghy was gone.

But when he got closer, Nick saw he was wrong. The dinghy wasn't gone, just not where he'd left it, on the dock, but sitting alongside, bobbing in the water. He abandoned the path at once, circling down through what the previous owner had called the picnic area, a triangle of three oaks jutting out from the woods. From there, he could see that the oars were already in the oar locks and——

He felt a sudden rush of air from behind, was already turning, but so slow, when something immense slammed into his back. He went flying, the flashlight shooting from his hand, and sprawled facedown on the hard ground, stunned.

Then the immense thing was on him. Nick wriggled around, or tried to, but couldn't catch his breath and his whole right side had gone useless on him. Hard steel rings clicked around his wrists, locking them together in front of him, and a bag or hood flopped down over his head.

"Not this time, buddyboy."

Nick knew that voice: Tommy.

Tommy picked him up, without effort, without even the tiniest grunt, slung him over his shoulder, started walking. Nick, his head swinging upside down against Tommy's broad back, full of pain, sensed they were moving downhill, toward the water. He tried to kick Tommy in the balls, or anywhere, but no kicking happened.

Wood planking creaked, close to Nick's head. The dock. It sank an inch or two under their weight. Tommy's hands shifted around Nick's waist, seeking purchase. His fingers dug deep into Nick's flesh, and now Tommy did grunt, and Nick was in midair. He landed hard on his back in the dinghy, so hard the real world shrank down small and went far away. He breathed.

T he real world came back with gurgling sounds, soothing and serene. Nick could see nothing, but he heard the oar pins squeaking in the locks, felt the dinghy gliding through the water. After a while, the squeaking stopped and the water slowed them down, a heavy hand pressing through the floorboards. Nick felt Tommy rise, tipping the boat a little, and then with a whoosh around his ears the hood came off.

Nick lay on his back, head toward the bow, hands cuffed in front of him. The moon was right above him at the top of the sky, a reddish planet not far from its sharp bottom tip. Mars, god of war. Tommy sat back down on the rowers' bench. He had the ax in his hands.

"Nicky," he said. "Let's do this right."

Nick said nothing.

Tommy glanced around. It was quiet out on the lake, nothing but the sound of thumb-high waves tapping at the hull. The breeze swung them slowly around. Tommy's blond hair was white in the moonlight.

"How you did Lara Deems," he said, "that's a capital crime in anybody's book."

"What's it got to do with you?" Nick said. He felt that plummeting inside, no physical cause this time, just the sickening lurch of comprehension starting up.

"I like to see justice triumph," Tommy said. He swung the ax and tossed it over the side. The lake swallowed it up with a splashless sucking sound.

"What's the real answer?" Nick said.

Tommy smiled, teeth big, moon-white. "If there is one," he said, "you're never going to know."

Nick strained against the handcuffs; useless.

Tommy lifted one of the oars out of the lock. "Here's the deal," he said. "I'm going to tap you on the head with this, not hard, just enough to put you out, the kind of whack a clumsy guy might get from falling on the gunwale, like when he's out at night chucking evidence in the lake. Then your part in this is over. I'll uncuff you, drop you over the side and swim back in. The dinghy floats around, divers go in, or maybe your body just floats up. An accidental death, but . . . what's the word? Deserved. Case closed." Tommy turned the oar in his hands, got a better grip. "Any questions?"

"How come you're enjoying it so much?"

"She still kind of likes you," Tommy said. "Pisses me off."

He stood up, raised the oar high. "But what's the difference?" he said. "You're dying anyway."

Tommy struck down with the blade edge, not with all his strength, but hard. Nick twisted out of the way, not fast enough, not far enough, taking the blow on his right shoulder. It went numb, but was pretty numb already.

"Goddamn it," Tommy said. "I told you to do this right."

He raised the oar again.

"You're the one doing it wrong," Nick said. "You've missed a basic step."

"What's that?" said Tommy, pausing, the oar up high.

"You forgot to search me."

"So?"

"There's something in my pocket you won't want the divers finding." Nick realized the truth of that as he spoke. Understanding spread wider, picking up the pieces.

"What is it?" Tommy said.

"Uncuff me and I'll show you," Nick said.

"And after that I'll buy you beers," said Tommy. "Don't fuckin' move. I'll get it myself."

"Back pocket," said Nick, although it wasn't true. "I'll have to stand up."

"No, you won't."

But Nick was already turning, rising up on his knees. How was he doing this, so weak? But he was going to stand up, goddamn it. And he did. The dinghy swayed to starboard, then righted itself. A tippy sort of dinghy that a lot of people would have replaced, but Nick was used to it.

Tommy came toward him, holding the oar in one hand. The dinghy tipped a little one way, then the other. They faced each other, the boat still not quite steady under their feet.

"Turn around nice and easy," Tommy said. "This better be good."

"You'll see," Nick said, and started to turn, nice and easy at first, but as Tommy lifted his free hand, readying it to reach in Nick's back pocket, Nick threw his own cuffed hands high, right under Tommy's arm and up into his armpit, trapping that big arm between his. Tommy jerked back, trying to get away. The dinghy flipped out from under them and they fell together into the lake, Tommy's mouth and eyes opening wide.

Nick kept his own mouth closed, inhaling a big lungful of air through his nose before his head went under. Down they went, locked together, Tommy punching, kicking, thrashing, getting all twisted between Nick's arms and the cuffs, down through the cool surface layer into the cold below. They hit bottom, total darkness.

Nick's leg struck something solid, a waterlogged tree stump maybe, stuck at an angle in all the rot at the bottom. He got both legs around it and squeezed tight. Tommy punched and kicked, clawed, scratched, butted. But Nick had him between those cuffs, all tangled up, plus he had the fingers of both hands locked tight on Tommy's shirt, and would never let go. Why would he? Tommy was right. What difference did it make where he died? He had nothing to lose.

Tommy gave a huge heave, all his strength supercharged with desperation, almost lifting Nick off the stump. But not quite; Nick hung on like a limpet. Tommy screamed a bubbly underwater scream. His legs made a few last kicks and then he went still, limp arms settling at his sides. Nick brought his own hands down, slipped them out from Tommy's arm, free. Where was up? He looked around, saw a little sparkle in the distance, kicked toward it with all his might, lungs bursting.

Nick broke the surface, filled himself with the lovely air, first in gasps, then big choking breaths, finally just nice and easy, floating on his back. He loved the water, always had. Only a water lover would live by the beach and choose a lake for his other place. Overhead the moon and stars shone down, at first everything reversed, like a negative, but soon getting back to normal. He knew how he must have looked from way up there, a skinny guy floating on his back all alone in the middle of a lake at night, hands cuffed in front of him. But he was doing all right.

He waited for his father to say, *You are.*

Nothing.

But he was doing all right, just the same. First, those cuffs. Tommy would have the keys. He'd be coming up, but not soon. What were the chances of finding him down there in the dark? Not good. But then a big bubble popped on the surface right beside Nick, and another, not quite as big, air trapped in Tommy's clothes, or from his lungs, or some gas stirred up from the bottom. Nick took a few deep breaths, held the last one and dove down through the spot where the bubbles broke.

Down and down, into the cold, into blackness. Nick had nothing to fear. His cuffed hands touched bottom. He felt along through the muck, kicking slowly, until something bumped his head. What? A tree stump. He patted his hands over it, around to the far side, down behind. His index fingertip touched something with an unmistakable texture all its own, like a shelled hard-boiled egg but firmer—a human eye. Nick jumped a little, an electric reaction he couldn't help, then ran his hands quickly over the body, found pockets, a key ring. He kicked back up.

On the surface, key ring in hand, Nick didn't feel quite so good. He lay there on his back, just breathing, feeling a current taking him somewhere. After a while, he thought about the dinghy, found the strength to look around for it.

Nowhere.

But it didn't matter. With the cuffs on, he'd never have been able to right it and climb in anyway and he wasn't going to risk losing the keys by trying to decuff in the water. And the oars— they'd be gone too.

Nick gazed at the nearest shoreline, a dark topographical silhouette, studied its dips and rises. He thought he spotted the point where the road ended in an abandoned campground, about a third of a mile past his place, picked a rounded target about ten degrees to the left, a rounded target he hoped was the outcrop at the entrance to his lane, turned on his back and kicked toward it; his left hand holding tight to the key ring and wrapped in his right.

Nick's head bumped something hard-edged. He flailed around in the water, saw what it was: the floating dock. Nick swam around it, crawled on shore, lay there. The moon, the stars, the red planet, all in motion, went their separate ways. Nick watched them for a long time. He wanted to get up, but couldn't, couldn't move at all. It took a crab, scuffling through the sand and probing a claw through his hair, to get him going.

Nick sat up, went through the keys on Tommy's ring—a ring with a dangling Harley medallion—and spotted the hand-cuff key right away, short, with the pin on top for releasing the double lock. He stuck it in the keyhole, turned once to the right, once to the left, and the cuffs snapped open.

Nick moved up the path, around the cabin. The blue Mustang was still there. He went into the cabin, found another flashlight, returned to the toolshed. The garden spade still leaned against the wall. Nick held it to the light, gazed at the fresh earth clodded at the tip. He picked up the spade and started walking his land in a grid pattern, poking his light into every shadow.

He found what he didn't want, down in that oak tree triangle, the picnic area. Almost in the mathematical center of the triangle, hard to miss, was a dug-up rectangle of earth.

Nick dug it up again. Freshly turned earth, so it should have been easy, but Nick had to take a couple of rests, leaning on the handle, trying not to pant. After fifteen or twenty minutes, his blade struck something soft. He went easy after that, exposing a thick-soled pink sandal, toenails painted the same shade, a leg, a body, a face. A woman's face, unmarked and undamaged, that he didn't recognize, although the pouty lips reminded him right away of Lara Deems. But this couldn't be Lara—she'd been buried long ago up at the family plot in Barstow.

Nick knelt down, turned her head gently to one side—there was no resistance at all—and found the cause of death: a deep cavern at the back of the skull, result of a crushing blow from a heavy object, like the blunt end of an ax.

A beaded handbag lay in there with her, conveniently by her side. Nick went through it, took out the driver's license, checked the photo. Same face. A state of California license issued to Liza Rummel. On the signature line, she'd done some cute curlicue things with that big L in Liza.

The murderer of the Rummel sisters, as history would have had it if he'd stayed down at the bottom of the lake—and might have it still—filled Liza's grave back in. A retard? Possibly, compared to what he'd been. But he knew what was buried in his yard, was on the way to understanding why.

An owl hooted in the trees.

Hunt.

thirty-two

ot this time, buddyboy.

Nick drove down out of the mountains to Barstow in the blackest part of night, moon gone now and the roads deserted. Eighteen, 247—but he knew that only from the road signs. The mental image of the route, those old blue rivers he'd always relied on, wouldn't come together, but this time he also forgot to consult the map. Preoccupied with Tommy's remark, he'd simply found himself at the wheel, somehow on the right track, his mind changing him again, maybe not in a bad way.

Not this time, buddyboy implied there'd been an earlier time, a previous fight with Tommy. Nick knew when that had to have been: the night of the break-in, soon after he'd come home from the hospital. Knocked-out pane of back-door glass, quick skirmish in the kitchen, motorcycle taking off, football photograph gone. What was in that goddamned picture?

You didn't read the names, Nikolai.

And gone too from the wall of fame at Desert High. Someone who knew the way he worked, the way he thought, would always stay a step or two ahead.

He'd missed those names, instead having . . . what would you call it? An aesthetic reaction to what should have been a clue; getting caught up in that bird flying out of the frame, fleeting youth, all that. This new him might be better than the old in some ways, suited to a number of interesting lines of work, but: detection not one of them.

For example: how to find Wally Moore in the middle of the night? Nick drove into Barstow, saw a police cruiser parked outside an all-night diner. He could go in there, ask that cop drinking something from a straw at the counter to get Sergeant Gallego on the phone, have Gallego do the work. But he didn't want Gallego involved, didn't want to answer questions. How about trying information? Nick tried it. The operator had forty-eight listings for Moore in Barstow, two of them Williams and one a Wanda, but no other Ws. What else? Nick couldn't think of anything else.

He pulled into Desert High, drove past the parking lot, bumped up over the curb and parked on the grass beside the equipment shed. Was it a school day? Still football season? Nick wasn't sure of the answer to either question, but he had a feeling it didn't matter. Wally cared about the green green grass of that football field. He'd show up.

Nick waited. He kept thinking he saw a faint lifting of the darkness in the eastern sky, a transition to a neutral tone, like dark milk. But it kept not happening. No matter. Sleep was not an issue. He was much too wired to sleep.

He slept.

Tap, tap on the roof of the car. Nick opened his eyes. Sun not up yet, but a blood-red streak ran along the bottom of the eastern sky. An old man with leathery skin was peering in through the open driver's-side window: Wally Moore.

"Mr. Private Dick," he said. "Thought so. They park on the grass where you come from?"

Nick rubbed his eyes, sat up straight. His body ached all over, the good kind of ache that comes after swimming, fighting, almost getting killed. The bad kind of ache lurked beneath it, faint, patient. "I didn't want to miss you," Nick said.

"Some people's too clever by half," Wally said.

"I agree," said Nick; which was easy now that the clever half was gone. "How's the team?"

Wally turned his head and spat. "Didn't even get to the postseason."

"How'd that tailback do, forty-four?"

"Dropped out," said Wally. "You ever find a copy of that picture?"

"No."

"Funny the way it ain't on the wall of fame. I asked the AD about it. Did a little dicking of my own, you might say."

"And?"

"Get this. It disappeared the very same day you was here, the Bakersfield game, homecoming. The AD's what some call a neat freak, notices everything that's out of place."

"Any reports of a guy on a motorcycle hanging around that day?" Nick said.

"Not oo's I heard," said Wally. "Why?"

"He's probably the one who took it."

"The perp?" said Wally.

"He set fire to George Rummel's trailer as well."

Wally's face, marked red here and there from decades of sun, grew fierce, his bony nose suddenly much more prominent. "You saying it was murder?"

"Manslaughter at the very least," said Nick.

"I didn't see nothing like that in the paper."

"This is new information," Nick said.

"But you know who did it?"

"I do."

"You gonna catch the motherfucker?"

"I need your help," said Nick.

"Say the word," said Wally. "Georgie didn't deserve to die like that."

Wally opened up the equipment shed. They sat on lawn chairs inside, a folding TV-dinner table between them. A dog barked far away, the sound very clear, no competition plus that desert air.

"Best time of day," Wally said. Soft light spread around them. "Older I get, more I like it." He filled two Desert High mugs with coffee from his thermos, opened a Dunkin' Donuts box. "Fresh half an hour ago. Glazed chocolate, cinnamon, mocha, butterscotch, jelly and that there pink one with jimmies. Be my guest."

Nick took the pink one with jimmies. He'd never made a choice like that in his life. It was delicious. And he was really hungry, didn't have to force-feed himself at all. Maybe it was just a question of menu.

"How's the amnesia coming along?" Wally said, sipping from his mug with surprising delicacy, like a maiden aunt from long ago. "Still doggin' you?"

"Getting better all the time," Nick said.

"Then maybe you can explain what this is all about," Wally said. "Starting with how come that picture's so damn important."

"I only know it's important from the effort that's been made to keep me from seeing it," Nick said.

Wally thought about that, gave Nick a sidelong glance. "Wouldn't want you for an enemy," he said.

"Spare another doughnut?" Nick said.

"Help yourself."

Jelly this time. Wally took the chocolate glaze.

"You think Georgie got killed on account of he played on that team in the picture?" he said.

"No."

"Then how come?"

"I think it goes way back," Nick said, taking the pinto pony photograph from his pocket, "but not quite that far." He handed Wally the photo, wrinkled now and slightly damp from the waters of Big Bear Lake, but the images still clear.

"What's this?" said Wally. "Another picture?" He peered at it. "Where's my glasses?"

He tried his pockets, the top of the TV-dinner table, under the chairs, pockets again. He squinted at the photo. "Can't see shit."

"In your car?" Nick said.

Wally snapped his fingers, making that whip-cracking sound. "Wouldn't want you for an enemy." He went out, came back with his glasses on, huge, rectangular, black-rimmed, covering most of his face. He picked the photo off the table, gazed at it, looked up sharply. "Where'd you get this?"

For a moment, Nick couldn't remember. He felt the whole case, slipping, slipping . . . then it came to him, like a very late gift. "In the remains of the fire," he said. "Tuxedo jacket, an old one. Front left-hand pocket."

Wally nodded. "Christening, likely," he said. "Maybe a communion."

"You can identify the kids in the picture?" Nick said.

"Sure," said Wally. "Even tell you where it got took." He scraped his chair around to Nick's side of the table so they could look at it together. Their heads were very close, a little wisp of Wally's soft, uncut white hair actually brushing Nick's cheek. Wally pointed to the little brunette on the back of the pony. "This one here's Liza Rummel. Back in those days, she was still Lisa, but she fancied it up to Liza when she got older, the way some girls do. Specially when they got a fancy-name older sister, like Lara." His index finger, a little dirt caught under the nail, touched the bigger brunette, sitting in front. "Lara, right there."

"And in the middle?" Nick said.

"Why, we discussed that one before," said Wally. "The first time you come up here, with that magazine article story. Or is the amnesia gettin' the best of you again?"

"The name, Wally."

"Elaine," said Wally. "Elaine Kostelnik. Her dad Frank was the coach. Coach K. You was askin' lots of questions about him—like what kind of coach he was, all that. Course he's dead now, like I mentioned. Natural causes, if cancer's natural."

Nick flinched at that one, deep inside. "His name would be on the team picture."

"Sure thing," said Wally. "Bottom row right—where the coaches always stand. My name's there too, seein' as I was trainer. As for what kind of a coach he was, I told you—smart and tough. Now that I'm gettin' to know you, I'll add to that a little—a mean son of a bitch too. Anythin' else you want to know?"

"Mean in what way?"

"Couldn't please him—nothin' ever good enough for Coach K," said Wally. "That it?"

Nick checked the photo one more time, couldn't think of anything. His eyes, kind of by themselves, slid over to the little cowboy leading the pony, his features hidden in the shade of the ten-gallon hat. "Can you identify the boy?"

"Course," said Wally. "That's Donny Deems."

Nick put his hand on Wally's arm. "Spell it."

Wally looked surprised. "Donny," he said. "D-O-N-N-Y. Deems. D-E-E-M-S."

Donny Deems. The name rocked him. It was all going fast, threatening to speed right by him.

"You're looking a little funny," Wally said. "Did I mess it up? Spelling was never my thing. Truth is I liked shop the best, no shame attached in those days. In fact, what with China Lake and—"

Nick held up his hand. "Tell me about Donny."

"Sure. What do you wanna know?"

"Did he marry Lara?"

"You got that right."

"Is he still in town?"

"Donny's dead. Lara too, in case you're not aware. Only ones left from this picture is Liza, down in the southland, maybe not behaving herself too well, and of course Elaine who hit the big time."

"How did Donny die?"

"Got himself killed."

"How?"

Wally shifted in his chair, looked uncomfortable. "Went and got involved in a little crime spree."

"What kind of crime spree?"

"One of those crazy young guy crime sprees, not really serious, bank robbin' and such," said Wally. "Over in Nevada. Security guard shot him outside the Pahrump National Bank, or coulda been a cop. Donny was maybe twenty-one at the time." Wally's eyes went to the picture, stayed there for fifteen or twenty seconds. "Things just get a momentum of their own, huh? Keep goin' round and round."

"In what way?"

"A bad way, I guess," said Wally. He handed the photo back to Nick. "They never caught the getaway driver."

"Who was that?" Nick said.

"Got clean away," said Wally. "Meanin' no one knows."

"I think you do."

Their eyes met. The sun rose up through the open sides of the shed, blazed away, shining red on Wally's oversize reading glasses. "Better talk to Mrs. Deems," he said.

"Donny's mother?"

"Yeah. She still lives on her ranch, up by the ghost town."

"The Silver City Ghost Town?"

"Right," said Wally. "Where this picture got took, like I was going to mention. Oldest habitation in these parts, the ghost town, where it all got started. Course it's defunct now, meaning no more tours and such, a ghost town of a ghost town, if you catch my drift, but you can find Mrs. Deems out on the Double

D. Double D for big Donny, little Donny's dad. Big Donny played on the same team with Georgie Rummel. He's gone too, if you're going to ask, which I know you are. Vietnam."

Nick rose. His right leg didn't want to help, but he forced it to, almost savagely. Wally got up too, screwed down the cap on the thermos, closed the doughnut box. They shook hands.

"Whatever this is," Wally said, "you fixin' to stop it?"

"If it's the last thing I do."

Wally smiled. He had a few teeth left. "I was gonna say— feelin' up to the task? Seein' as how you're not lookin' a hundred percent. But I won't. Sense of humor goes a long way."

Nick liked Wally, liked him a lot. "Ever have any kids of your own?" he said.

"Nope."

Wally would have made someone a good dad.

thirty-three

On the way to the Double D Ranch, following Wally Moore's directions—north on Tiefort Road, a narrow blacktop out of town, east at the third crossing hardpack track, "stop when you bump up against the mountain"—Nick started feeling a little funny. He was driving east on that third dirt track, the sun in his eyes, visor down, dust cloud trailing behind him, when the glare got a bit much and all the straight lines of the landscape began to bend. The flat land on either side curled up, like wrapping paper that had come unglued, wedging him into a trough that grew deeper and narrower. Nick glanced at the speedometer. One hundred and ten. He took his foot off the gas, hit the brake. Only that didn't happen: the signal got sent but his right foot refused its duty, stayed where it was, heavy on the gas. One fifteen, one twenty; and glare like a bomb going off in slow motion. He was shifting his left foot across to kick the right one away, get the job done, when the car shot over a rise and went airborne. In the air came a strange fearless moment of perfect peace, until some layer peeled back in his mind, revealing a memory—what he took to be a memory—of the inside of the Four Aces Motel on Lincoln Boulevard. Nick's car came down surprisingly softly, spun around in that tilting, curling landscape, careened off the track, finally coming to rest on the far side of a pile of huge red boulders, two or three hundred yards away.

Nick opened the door and got out. Fell out was the truth of it, fell out with the landscape rising up on him. An earthquake, of course, maybe the Big One, ten-oh on the Richter Scale, but absolutely silent. Nick lay on his back, half in, half out of the car. The only sounds were the beating of his heart, fast and very light, like a percussion master building to the big finish, and his breathing, which was slow and heavy. His right foot, caught twitching under the steering wheel, should have been making some sort of sound, but was not. Twitching in a spastic sort of way: it brought things back to him, the parking lot at St. Joe's, and Amanda. His leg twitched. He saw her face.

G lare all around, intense: that was the inside of the Four Aces. Lara Deems rolled over on the bed. "Don't leave me," she said. "Don't you dare."

The clerk banged on the wall.

Petrov said: "It's over."

N ick opened his eyes. No glare now; the sun had crossed the sky and he was lying in the shade of his car. He got up, dusted himself off. His right side felt a little stiff, but not as bad as it sometimes got, nothing he couldn't handle.

No earthquake, Nikolai. You've had a seizure.

"Just a little one," Nick said. He got behind the wheel, drove out from behind the giant red boulders. Jussi Bjoerling was still singing, but something had happened to the CD player and he was hitting the same note, over and over.

Go to the hospital.

"Shut up," Nick said.

His father couldn't bear to be talked to that way, and this was the first time Nick had dared. The presence withdrew to the vanishing point. Wally Moore would have made someone a good dad.

Nick bumped up onto the dirt track and turned east, toward the Double D. Traces of dust hung in the air ahead of him, as though someone had gone by a while ago. He kept the needle steady at sixty-five, totally in control. Just a little seizure, not even worth thinking about. It hadn't affected him at all. If anything, he felt stronger physically, and his memory was sharp. Wally, Coach K, Donny Deems, crime spree: it was all there, real, hard memories. Then there was that other memory, inside the Four Aces with Lara Deems. It was fuzzier. Was that because it was false or only because it was old? Nick didn't know. He knew of the existence of false memories, had read an article on the science page about how they were planted, but couldn't even remember the gist of it.

That was funny. He hoped to be laughing about it in some rosy future.

The mountain appeared, a broad-shouldered mountain that quickly came closer. A wooden sign, pitted from sandstorms, went by: DD RANCH, NO TRESPASSING. After that, deep ruts pocked the track, and Nick slowed down. A corral passed by on the left, a single horse, black and white, bent over a blue salt lick. Then came a long low stable and the ranchhouse, once painted white but now mostly sanded down to bare wood by the desert. A few hundred yards beyond the house stood fifteen or twenty sagging structures lining an old Western street, all the way to the base of the mountain. High up, spray-painted on the rocks in white and probably once visible for miles around but now almost completely faded away, were the words SILVER CITY GHOST TOWN. Ghost town of a ghost town.

Nick parked, got out of the car, approached the house. The front door opened and a lean woman came onto the porch. She wore jeans and a red shirt, had her white hair tied back in a long ponytail, moved like a girl. She was carrying a shotgun, not pointed at him but not exactly down either.

"Mrs. Deems?" Nick said.

"You read?" she said, jabbing with the barrel. "No trespassing."

"Wally Moore sent me." Just about true.

"Wally still alive?"

"Very much so."

The woman grunted, gave him a careful look. Her eyes, blue bleached almost colorless, weren't friendly.

"He says hello," Nick said, this little addition completely untrue. "If you're Mrs. Deems, that is."

"Supposing I was," she said. "What's your business here?"

"My name's Nick Petrov," Nick said. "I've been looking for your granddaughter, Amanda."

The barrel swung in a short arc, lined up with the middle of his chest.

"I'm on your side," Nick said.

Her eyes looked him up and down, shifted to his car, back. "You've got thirty seconds to prove it." She didn't lower the gun, held it easily, not too tight, like someone who knew what they were doing. "At this distance," she said, as though following along in his mind, "blow you in two."

"Liza hired me to find Amanda," Nick said.

"So?"

"It's all tied together," Nick said. "Donny, Lara, Amanda."

"Tell me something I don't know," said Mrs. Deems. "That's my one and only family you're talking about, two-thirds dead and gone."

"Liza's dead too," Nick said.

The shotgun wavered a little. Mrs. Deems lost some of her force and straightness, looked older just from the change in carriage.

"I want to keep Amanda alive," Nick said.

"Liza too?" said Mrs. Deems, her voice weaker, as though she'd punctured a lung.

"Murdered by a motorcycle cop from L.A.," Nick said.

The barrel dipped directly down, too heavy to hold. "It doesn't stop," she said.

"Not by itself," said Nick.

"Never knew what they were dealing with, Lara and Liza," said Mrs. Deems. "So headstrong the both of them."

"And your son Donny," Nick said, "was he headstrong too?"

"Did Wally say that?"

"No."

"Good," said Mrs. Deems. "Because that wasn't Donny. Donny was always an obliging boy."

"Is that what got him in trouble?" A guess, uneducated, but correct—he saw it in her eyes.

"You might say so."

A horse neighed, not far away.

"Tell me about the robbery," Nick said.

Mrs. Deems's hand tightened on the stock of the gun. "Why dig that up?"

"Isn't it where everything started going wrong?" Nick said.

Mrs. Deems nodded, exposing her neck, withered and thin. The pride and defiance he read in it—this new skill of his— made him want to protect her. "Donny and Lara," she said, "they were homecoming king and queen at Desert High. Did you know that?"

"No." But it didn't surprise him.

"They got married a week after graduation, although just Lara did the graduating, and she got pregnant right off the bat. Maybe the other way around. Pregnant with Amanda, if you're following me. Lara worked here at the attraction, selling tickets, doing the tours, and Donny found himself a construction job in town. That's where she got her hooks in him."

"Elaine Kostelnik?" Nick said.

"You're a good guesser," said Mrs. Deems. "Or else you're playing me for a fool."

"You've got the gun," Nick said.

"And I know how to use it," said Mrs. Deems, flicking the barrel a little, but the fight was going out of her; he could feel it. "Coach K and George Rummel owned the company. She did the books." Mrs. Deems gazed at some remote distance, beyond the horizon. "Never understood what she was after in Donny. Was she bored, simple as that? Always too fast for a town like this. Skipped two grades, for example. Most likely to succeed. Course no one knew about this affair at first. Donny supposedly took on a weekend job for a surveying company based in Baker. Turned out every Friday night they went a little farther than that, all the way to Vegas."

"And Donny was no gambler."

"You got that right. Lost everything. But this crime spree they talked about, there was nothing like that, not tied to Donny. Just the one convenience store in Bullhead City—they caught him on the video—and then that bank in Pahrump."

"Was Elaine in on it?"

"They shot Donny on the steps of the bank. Money intact to the penny—two thousand and eleven dollars—end of story, case closed."

"But what do you think?"

"Donny's car turned up in a parking lot in Vegas," said Mrs. Deems. "Tell me how he got to Pahrump and how he was planning to get away."

"How?" Nick said.

"She drove him," said Mrs. Deems. "She was sitting in that car outside the bank, maybe around the corner or down the block. When it went bad she took off."

"What did the police think of that theory?"

"They never heard about it."

"Why not?"

"It's all in the details, like they say on TV. We didn't even know about the affair till after we buried Donny. First was the news that Donny's surveying job in Baker didn't exist, then all these people who'd seen them together in Vegas started coming out of the woodwork. By then she'd moved down to L.A. Never came back."

"Elaine?"

"You know who I'm talking about."

"Why would she get involved in something like that?" Nick said.

Mrs. Deems gave him a long look. "Some people, like the kind that think they're smarter than everybody else, make up their own rules. Haven't you noticed that by now?"

Nick thought back to his old perjuring self.

"I see that you have," said Mrs. Deems.

Elaine and Petrov: how similar had they been? How bad was the answer to that question going to be? Nick wasn't sure he wanted to find out. "Did Lara share your belief that Elaine drove the getaway car?" he said.

"More so," said Mrs. Deems. "After she had the baby she started getting restless. Young widow, couldn't blame her. She decided to try her luck in Hollywood, like homecoming queens sometimes do. Lara was a very pretty girl and still a bit young for knowing just how many pretty girls are out there."

"And down in the city she found out Elaine had joined the LAPD," Nick said.

"I don't know that firsthand."

"Liza told you."

"She might've."

And then? Elaine had already explained all this, just shifting things around a bit. At the very least the department would have investigated any stories involving Elaine and bank robberies, and Elaine was ambitious: it wasn't inconceivable that she'd set her mind on the top job from day one. "Did Lara blackmail her?" Nick said.

"I don't know anything about that either," said Mrs. Deems, "but she stole Lara's man and got him killed, didn't she? Would it be a big surprise if Lara dropped her a hint about how she'd found an eyewitness over in Pahrump?"

"Did Elaine pay her off?" Nick said.

"She might've."

But she wouldn't stay paid off, the way they never do.

"More than once?" Nick said.

"I wouldn't know about that," said Mrs. Deems.

"More than once always leads to trouble," Nick said. *If a black-mailer gets what's coming to her, so what?*

"Lara found that out, didn't she?" said Mrs. Deems. "But for the longest time I just accepted it was that monster."

"Gerald Reasoner?"

"Yes."

"Until Amanda met Rui Estrella."

"That's right," said Mrs. Deems. "The fact that this Reasoner person couldn't have done it made everything clear." The shotgun—a beautiful old Purdy side-by-side, Nick couldn't help noticing—came up a little. "Except for your role," she said.

"My role?" said Nick. He steeled himself for some remark about the Four Aces, some confirmation of a past he'd had with Lara Deems.

But she didn't go there. "Whether you helped," said Mrs. Deems. "Not with the actual killing, but arranging the evidence, the timing, such-like."

"I didn't," Nick said; but how could he be sure?

"That's what Liza thought. She must have watched that movie a hundred times, seeing what you were like. Especially the ending."

The ending: Kim Delaney walking out, Armand Assante's eyes flashing anger and then going stony dead, the kind of ending that might make a viewer think Nick Petrov would relish bringing Elaine Kostelnik down years later; but a total invention. "It's just a movie," Nick said.

"It says 'based on a true story' at the very beginning," said

Mrs. Deems. "We didn't know what else to do. If only—we almost didn't do anything. Oh, I wish to Christ."

"But Rui got the blackmailing bug too," Nick said. "Is that what happened? And then things started rolling." What had Rui said? *Don't feel sorry for me. I'm getting rich off this.*

Mrs. Deems gave a slight nod. "No stopping him, even though Liza tried—caused a blowout with Amanda. Course there were all the drugs, and Rui falling for Amanda like a lost soul, and Rui of all people her first boyfriend—an unstable mix."

"How did Rui contact Elaine?"

"Don't know that either," said Mrs. Deems. "But he did, because the danger of it hit them, too late, of course, and they took off to her granddad's, Amanda and her boyfriend. That's when Liza got the idea of bringing you in."

"To do what?"

"What you do," said Mrs. Deems. "Solve things. Blow this all sky-high. She even left clues—under beds and things where she knew you'd look. But the kids got scared of you and ran back to the city, dumbest thing they could have done."

It was all clear, start to finish, except for that one little problem: who but he could have taped the seventh postcard to Lara's fridge? Nick was wondering if there was any point in pursuing that question with Mrs. Deems when some override function took over, part of the new him, and a question popped out of his mouth.

"Amanda's here, isn't she?"

Mrs. Deems opened her mouth to answer. A horse neighed, louder this time. She turned quickly. The black-and-white horse—pinto, maybe a descendant of the one that had carried the three little girls—was prancing in a small circle on the wrong side of the corral fence.

"What the hell?" said Mrs. Deems. "Oreo's loose."

She strode down off the porch, the shotgun in one hand. Then came a little cracking sound and she toppled facedown in the dust. For a moment, Nick thought that crack was her hip bone breaking, an old-woman thing. He hurried down, knelt beside her.

"Mrs. Deems?"

Her eyes were wide open, a beautiful blue of the lightest possible shade, but sightless. Stroke? He turned her over, still couldn't see what was wrong with her. The color of her shirt fooled him, masking what was going on. It was only when he checked his hands, suddenly sticky, that he began to understand: red, red, red.

Nick looked up, real slow, like a dumb guy seeing the light. Elaine stepped out of the stable, a handgun raised. Nick went for the shotgun, but that was slow too. Another crack and a puff of dust rose right beside him.

"Don't be stupid, Nick."

Nick had seen her on the firing range. He left the shotgun alone, got to his feet. Elaine walked toward him, unhurried, the gun held casually in her hand. Behind her, Oreo had stopped prancing, stood still, sniffing the air. Nick got ready to die, but that was the work of a moment. He was already ready.

Elaine stopped about ten feet away. She was dressed for the city in a black skirt, gray silk shirt, pearls around her neck. The Colt .380—same model as his—should have looked out of place, but did not. Elaine's gaze went to Mrs. Deems, then to Nick's red hands, finally his face. He could feel a plan forming in her mind.

Same model as his. "Is that my gun?" Nick said.

"Of course," said Elaine.

thirty-four

Of course it was his gun. She'd been in his house, wandering around while he slept, more than once. Gun gone, notebook gone, plenty of time for doing other things, like bugging his phone, listening in on Liza's call, sending Tommy to the cabin.

Elaine made a prompting gesture with the gun. "What happened to Tommy?" she said.

"No idea," Nick said. "Is he the new me?" *As I was the new Donny.*

"Not in your class," said Elaine. "And he knows it. He's insanely jealous." She gazed at the house. "Where's the girl?"

"Don't know that either," Nick said; but from the corner of his eye he caught a quick movement halfway down the street of the ghost town. He willed himself not to look, not even to think about it in case she was reading his mind. Fruitless: Elaine's head snapped around. Nick looked too. A tall girl ran to the end of the ghost town main street and disappeared into a black hole at the base of the mountain.

Elaine made an irritated sound with her tongue. "I don't have a lot of time for this," she said. She pointed the gun at Mrs. Deems. "Put her in your car," she said. "Backseat."

Mrs. Deems turned out to be heavier than Nick would have thought. He wanted to pick her up, carry her in his arms, be respectful, but he didn't have the strength and ended up dragging her, his hands, the right one hardly doing a thing, under her armpits. He opened the rear door, hoisted her torso up onto the seat, crammed her in. Elaine watched without expression.

"Now drive," she said.

"Where?"

She got in the passenger seat. "You used to be a lot smarter than this," she said. "To the mine."

Nick sat behind the wheel. His right hand found the key no problem, but wasn't quite capable of turning it. He had to use his left. Elaine saw.

"If I ever get like that," she said, "just shoot me."

"How about now, just in case?"

She laughed. She'd always had a great laugh, at least to his ear, loud and unrestrained; now he heard something in it he detested. There was a difference between wild and savage; a distinction understood too late.

"I really did like you," Elaine said. "If only you'd been in some other line of work." A strange remark, lending a little long-after-the-fact truth to the movie's factitious ending.

But changing nothing. Nick idled through the ghost town, right foot limp beside the pedal; past the barbershop, HAIRCUT AND SHAVE, 5 CENTS, the assay office, GUARANTEED 100% HONEST WEIGHT, the saloon, POSITIVELY NO GUNPLAY.

"Me knowing Lara Deems," he said. "The Four Aces."

"You bought it, huh?" said Elaine. "Wow. That was just me improvising, taking off from a note or two on your chart."

"You saw my hospital chart?"

"These things aren't difficult," Elaine said. "I was trying to put this on a nonviolent track, make you see that backing off was safest for all concerned. But you just won't stop."

"I don't like loose ends," Nick said.

"That's your problem."

He braked—left foot—a few yards from the black hole in

the mountain. A big black hole with a sign—SILVER CITY MINE— and a plaque—$2 MILLION WORTH OF SILVER GOT DUG FROM THIS MOUNTAIN, 1888–1902. TWELVE MEN NEVER CAME OUT. Steel rail tracks led into the mine, a weathered ore cart in place.

"The Dr. Tulp postcard," Nick said. He realized he was falling back into the shorthand talk of their partnering days.

"Knew that would be bothering you," Elaine said. "When you ran out of Nicolette Levy's place you left the card on top of that photo album. I realized I'd seen it before too—Tiffany LeVasseur, in the desk drawer with her GED certificate."

Nick looked at her, couldn't see past those gold flecks in her eyes. Somehow he'd missed that one, must have: otherwise Nicolette Levy would still be alive, maybe Lara too, and none of this would have happened.

"You're not the only brainy one around," Elaine said. She pointed at the ore cart. "Put her in there."

Nick got out, dragged Mrs. Deems to the ore cart, lifted her in in stages. Elaine watched. He laid Mrs. Deems on her back, closed her eyes, straightened the collar of her red shirt.

"Got a flashlight?" Elaine said.

"No."

She reached through the passenger-side window, flipped open the glove box, took out a flashlight. "Of course you do." She turned it on, pointed into the mine. "After you."

Nick put his shoulder to the cart. It wouldn't budge.

"Christ," said Elaine.

That enraged him. He kept it inside, heating up, giving him a little more strength. The cart began to roll.

They went into the mine, Nick pushing the cart, Elaine a few steps behind him. In the entrance, still lit by the sun, stood a display of miners' equipment—augurs, shovels, picks.

"Don't even think about it," Elaine said.

The tunnel bent toward the right, began to narrow, grow darker. The flashlight's yellow circle swept back and forth across the rock walls, shored up here and there with old beams. Soon the light glinted on a heavy chain, hung across the passage, bearing a sign: *No Entry Beyond This Point—Danger.* Beyond the chain, the shaft was much smaller, ceiling lower, walls closer together, and it began sloping down. Elaine stepped forward, unhooked one end of the chain, heaved it across the tracks to the other side. The clang of heavy metal echoed through the mine. In the distance, something fell from the ceiling, maybe a stone, and *ping*ed off the tracks.

"Move," Elaine said.

Nick pushed the cart. It was easy now, with the slope. The air cooled, grew damper. Somewhere nearby water trickled; a support beam creaked as they went by.

"Stop," Elaine said.

Nick stopped.

She shone the light into a low gallery cut into the left-hand wall: pile of rubble on the floor, broken pick handle, rusty canteen. The light swung around, came to rest on his face.

"Move," Elaine said.

Nick pushed the cart. The ceiling closed in some more, barely leaving room to stand erect.

"Whoa," Elaine said.

Rocks lay on the track.

"Clear them."

Nick followed the light around the cart, pushed the rocks aside. Elaine stayed a few feet behind him, gun in one hand, flashlight in the other. All he had to do was get his hands on either one. She never gave him a chance.

The slope grew steeper. Now Nick didn't have to push at all, even leaned back a little to slow the cart down. From time to time the yellow circle dipped down to Mrs. Deems's face. Her long white ponytail hung over the side of the cart, swinging free.

They came to a T. The crossing shaft was much narrower, barely had room for the cart. Nick waited. Elaine shone the light right and left. The tunnel ran on in both directions, past the range of the light. Elaine's thoughts weren't hard to imagine: if she made the wrong choice, Amanda could double back and get out, unseen. Nick tried to think of some way to make her choose wrong, which involved first figuring out—

From down the right-hand shaft came a soft crunch, the kind made by a foot stepping on something brittle, like sandstone or cinders. Elaine cut the light. Total blackness, total except for a tiny flicker, maybe a burning match, far along the right-hand shaft. Then the muzzle of the .380 flashed a foot from Nick's eyes, and a shot rang out, deafening. He swiped at the gun but it wasn't there. Something rumbled, deep inside the mountain.

Elaine, behind him again, switched on the light, gave him a push. "Try that once more and you're dead," she said. "On the spot."

That didn't scare Nick at all. He put his hands on the cart. Elaine swung the flash at the back of his head, not hard, but it ignited a hot red pain just under the top of his skull.

"Forget the fucking cart," she said. "You've gone dumb on me."

They left the cart and Mrs. Deems behind, followed the right-hand shaft, Nick first, Elaine right behind, jabbing him in the back to go faster. Nick didn't go faster, in fact slowed down, giving Amanda every chance he could.

"All you're doing is making me mad," Elaine said, jabbing at him once more. "There's only one way out. She's trapped."

Nick kept going, step-dragging now, the light glancing off cracked beams, little rock falls, strange conical dirt piles here and there. Then the tunnel bent sharply to the left and the tracks stopped. Ahead lay a dark opening, like an oval on its side or a half-open mouth.

"End of the line," Elaine said, speaking in normal tones, as though they were above ground and nothing unusual was happening. Nick felt scared for the first time.

Elaine panned the light across the black oval: another

gallery, this one like a deep cave, with a few woven baskets on the floor, some half filled with ore, a couple of overturned hand-carts, piles of chipped and blasted rock, shadows everywhere. In the center of the entrance stood a wooden beam, shoring up a heavier crossbeam under the roof. A big spider dangling down from the crossbeam hurried back up its thread when the light touched it.

"Come on out," Elaine said.

Silence.

Elaine switched off the flash. No light from inside the cave, but Nick heard a sound, very faint, like fabric rubbing on the ground. The flash came back on, pointed at one of the over-turned carts, and Elaine fired again, a shot that struck metal, clanging and reclanging under the mountain. Rocks and dirt showered down from the roof.

"Goddamn it," Elaine said, giving Nick another push. "We'll have to go get her."

They entered the cave, Nick first, Elaine right behind, the shadow of the gun leading them both. A narrow cone of light wherever Elaine shone the beam; complete blackness every-where else. Nick heard a wooden creak. A pebble fell, almost soundlessly. They moved to the back of the cave around the rub-ble piles and half-loaded baskets, to the ore cart Elaine had fired at. She stepped behind it, pointed the flash.

There, in the little yellow circle, lay Amanda, wedged be-tween the wheels, making herself small. She shrank against the light.

"Get up," Elaine said.

"Please don't hurt me," Amanda said.

"Nothing's going to hurt," Elaine said.

Nick took a quick step toward Elaine, not as quick as he'd have liked. She wheeled around on him, light in his eyes, gun aimed at his head. He froze.

Elaine turned back to Amanda, gestured with the gun.

"I never did anything to you," Amanda said.

"Grow up," said Elaine.

Amanda rose. She was shaking and covered with dirt from the mine. Just a kid, but it wasn't going to save her. Elaine did what had to be done.

"Over there," she said. "Beside Nick."

Amanda stood beside Nick, the light in their faces. He felt for her hand, took it, held on, felt her trembling. But it didn't get worse; if anything, she grew calmer. Another one of those crazy waves of triumph swept through him, completely idiotic this time. But he'd found her.

"Now we walk back to the cart," Elaine said. "That'll work best."

She was right: Mrs. Deems, Amanda and he, all shot with his gun, a case solving itself, ending tidily with the suicide of the cancer-ridden, unbalanced criminal.

"Move," Elaine said.

Amanda made a whimpering sound. Nick gave her a little tug. They started back toward the mouth of the cave, around the woven baskets, past the rock pile. Elaine stayed two or three steps behind, the light always steady, the shadow of the gun out in front.

They reached the mouth of the cave. The light shone on the support beam in the middle, and the crossbeam above. The spider, dangling back down, fled up into darkness again. Nick squeezed Amanda's hand hard, amazingly hard since it was his right hand doing it. All at once his old familiar strength flowed through him: he felt, for a wonderful moment, everything he'd been. He remembered something from the Bible. The mind, his especially, was a funny thing.

"Ow," said Amanda.

Ow? His grip on her hand must have been too strong, but he didn't soften it.

"You're not moving," Elaine said. "I haven't got all day."

Nick moved, but not the way Elaine wanted. Still gripping Amanda's hand, he pivoted to build momentum, then whipped her out of the cave. She fell into the shaft, rolling away, and in the right direction.

"What the hell?" Elaine said, a few feet behind him, the light now wavering.

With all his strength, Nick hurled himself, shoulder first, right at the middle of the support beam. It gave with a loud crack. Then came a booming one from the crossbeam above. Something hit him, spun him around. The flashlight wheeled in the air. For a moment, the light shone on Elaine, exposed the first shadow of understanding as it crossed her face, the first suggestion of fear and rage. Then a boulder the size of a car came crashing straight down from the darkness and buried her. After that: a roar of thunder louder than even Samson must have heard, and the mountain fell in.

Not dead? That hadn't been his intention at all. Total blackness, arms, legs, body unable to move, but: he breathed. This life force inside him: he didn't understand.

But breathing meant air, and he could move the muscles of his face, open his mouth, turn his head. His head, that one little part of him, was safe in an air pocket. He listened, heard muffled silence. Then he felt tiny little feet crossing his face: the spider. It stepped lightly into his hair, in and out of his ear, away.

Tap, tap, tap, also muffled. Then a panicky shout: "Mr. Petrov? Are you alive?" Followed by coughing.

"Yes," Nick said.

Silence. Maybe she hadn't heard him.

He raised his voice. "I'm alive."

"Thank God," she said. More coughing. Then came scraping, and a little tumble of rocks, close by.

"Are you all right?" he said.

"Yes."

"Are you trapped?"

"No."

"Is the tunnel clear?"

"I don't know."

"Do you have your matches?"

Pause. "Yes."

"Light one."

Another pause. No light entered Nick's little hole. Amanda said, "It looks clear."

"Then get out," Nick said. "Follow the tracks. Left at the fork." But he didn't want her looking in that cart; wanted to hold back all the bad news waiting for her.

Scraping, more scraping, another tumble of rocks.

"Amanda?"

"Yeah?"

"What are you doing?"

Cough, cough. "Digging you out."

"Stop right now," he said. "It's not safe."

Scrape, scrape.

"I said stop. Get out."

Scrape, scrape. She kept digging. Nick stopped arguing, abandoned a persuasive argument he'd been developing—*Don't risk your life for me, I'm dying anyway.* Amanda didn't need to hear that and he didn't need to say it. The time to stop fighting was when you could no longer fight. He could fight.

Scrape, scrape, tumble, tumble. Only this time a little stone fell inside his hole, bounced off his nose. A few seconds later, something soft and warm touched his face: her hand. She patted around in an exploratory way.

"Is that you?" she said.

thirty-five

Dr. Tully held the film up to the light so Nick could
see. He pointed at cloudy patches. "There," he said.
"There. There." He frowned, peered a little closer.
"Maybe there too," he said. "Missed that one."

"So it's spread a little." Nick said. "No surprise. The question
is, what are we going to do about it?"

That was what Dr. Tully liked to hear, although maybe he
didn't appreciate the tone. He slid the films back in the big
folder, rubbed his hands together, kindling enthusiasm. "Stereotactic radiation, monoclonal antibodies," he said, "plus one or
two cutting-edge things that weren't even available when you
were in here before, believe it or not. But radiation first—I'd like
to get you in tomorrow."

"What are the side effects?"

"It varies, of course," said Dr. Tully. "Everything varies.
Some tissue damage is possible, although we can usually treat
that. Confusion as well, hopefully temporary."

"Then it'll have to wait till after the wedding," Nick said.
Confusion at the wedding was out of the question. He handed
Dr. Tully an invitation. Dr. Tully turned pink with pleasure.
Nick had been on TV and in all the papers. The wedding was the
toughest ticket in town.

Nick and Billie got married on a beautiful day around Thanksgiving. By then, Nick was in the wheelchair most of the time, but the wheelchair on his wedding day? Out of the question. He consented to using a cane, but only for the walking-up-to-the-altar part. To take his vows he stood up all on his own, back straight, chin up. He kissed the bride. She looked gorgeous and tasted sweet as honey.

The reception was at Nick's place, with a tent set up by the canal, and champagne, real French champagne and lots of it. There was dancing to a reggae band and Nick danced; danced with a cane, but so did Fred Astaire. Nick also sang along, at times attempting a Jamaican accent. Billie turned out to be a great dancer. Nick made a mental note to sign up somewhere for dance lessons. Then he wrote it down on his shirt cuff in case he forgot: *dance lessons!* He saw Dmitri pouring a glass of champagne for Amanda. Dmitri caught him looking and paused. Nick made a pouring gesture, meaning pour more.

Dmitri—he had a real artist in the family, why had it taken Nick so long to see that?—had built a fleet of paper boats, all brightly colored and painted with hip-hop slogans Nick didn't get, and stuck candles in them. When night fell he lit the candles and launched the boats in the canal. As it turned out, Wally did most of the launching; he'd never seen anything like those paper boats. People on the other side came to watch.

Later, when everyone had gone, Nick, just wearing shorts over his skinny body, and Billie, in her wedding gown—she didn't want to take it off—sat on the edge of the canal, watching the candles burn down. Some of the boats caught fire and flamed out in a gratifying way. Nick put his arm around Billie's shoulders; she put hers lower down, around his back, and gave him a squeeze. They gazed at the dying fleet.

"Let's make plans," Billie said.

The last candle went out with a hiss.

"Radiation in the morning," Nick said. "After that, I'm wide open."